Cold Shot

Steve Christie

Ringwood Publishing

Glasgow

First published in Great Britain in 2015

by

Ringwood Publishing

7 Kirklee Quadrant, Glasgow G12 0TS

www.ringwoodpublishing.com

e-mail   mail@ringwoodpublishing.com

ISBN 978-1-901514-24-7

British Library Cataloguing-in Publication Data

A catalogue record for this book is available from the British Library

Typeset in Times New Roman 11

Printed and bound in the UK
by
Lonsdale Direct Solutions

ACKNOWLEDGEMENTS

To all my family and friends no longer here, I miss you all.

A special mention to my sisters, widower Paul Stuart, his fiancé Debz Buchan and my nieces and nephew, Alana, Jasmin and Paul. It's been a long hard road for all of you.

I would like to thank all my family and friends for their continued support; special mentions to John Reid, Lorraine Brown, Angela Airlie and Jeannie Whitelaw.

A big thank you to the various people who helped me out on social media with their welcome advice. Two in particular: Ann Marie Hayes and Alexis Cran … you both saved me a lot of time on research.

A big hello to the regulars at the Robin's Nest, and the Friday Gang.

Last, but in no ways least, a big shout out to all my vaping friends on social media…

Keep fighting the fight!

Dedication

I dedicate this book to my wife and soul mate Audrey Christie.

Prologue

Eight a.m, Monday morning. Mary approached the snow encrusted car that had just stopped in front of her at the side of the road.

'Excuse me, miss, any idea where Westburn Road is?'

Mary leaned over the wound down passenger window and pointed to the location on the driver's map. His face was hidden way back in his hood, she couldn't tell if he was young or old.

'If you go straight on and take the second road on the left, then … '

Before she could finish her sentence she was pulled violently into the car, her muffled screams quickly stifled by the closing of the car door. She felt a sharp pain on the inside of her left wrist. Then, through her rapidly blurring vision she watched as the syringe that had appeared from nowhere fell to the floor, as if in slow motion. The fast acting sedative took over Mary's body as the hooded stranger's vehicle took off at great speed along the quiet suburban road.

*

Victor Whitelaw awoke to the buzzing of his bedside alarm clock. He peeled his tongue off the roof of his mouth and reached for the glass of water on the cabinet at the side of his bed. He had his usual breakfast of paracetamol and a cigarette and then unsteadily made his way to the bathroom, the pounding in his head beating an accompanying tattoo to his normal morning routine. 'The drink's getting too much for me', he thought to himself as the shower head sprayed water onto the back of his neck. He'd been permanently drunk since Linda had left him six months ago. People were beginning to notice, his workload was piling up and his workmates were starting to make jokes about him perpetually smelling of mints. 'Yup, Vic, you're well and truly fucked up'. He'd just turned off the shower when he heard the phone ring.

'Shit!' He rushed through to the sitting room and picked up the receiver.

'Dad?' It was Mary, the anguish clear in her voice. He heard her screams gradually disappear into the background only to be replaced by a guttural, menacing male voice.

'Mr Whitelaw, if you want your daughter back with all her limbs still attached, listen very carefully to me.'

Chapter One

Under a thin powdery snowfall on a cold December night, a well-dressed woman pushed a wonky shopping trolley through the car park of her local supermarket. She did her best to wrap herself up against the cold blustery wind as she approached her vehicle with four bags of shopping. She wished she had dressed a little better for the weather. It was her own fault really, she thought, as she packed the boot of the small yellow Japanese sports car with her purchases. It's not like she hadn't been expecting it. The local news channel had been warning people of the approaching winter storm since lunchtime but she'd paid no heed; perhaps if she had she wouldn't be teetering through the wet snow in a pair of high heeled Jimmy Choos and her thin, designer business suit.

After returning her shopping trolley to the trolley park and retrieving her pound coin deposit, her thoughts turned to tonight's dinner party. She hoped against hope that Jonathan hadn't got the party in full swing before she got home, but then again, who was she kidding? She knew him too well. Any excuse to get pissed and Jonathan couldn't wait. He'd probably do his usual: completely ignore the food and take his sustenance in liquid form, preferably neat.

As she got back to her motor and double checked the boot - her lock had been playing up lately - she failed to see the high calibre bullet silently travelling at over two thousand feet per second, cutting through the snowflakes in her direction. The deadly projectile had been fired from the high powered rifle belonging to the prone man lying almost invisible under a thick white blanket on the artificial ski slope directly across from the supermarket car park.

As she lay dead in the snow, her eyes wide open, dark blood forming an ever widening red halo around her head, the sniper mentally congratulated himself on the perfectly executed shot and whistled a Christmas carol to himself as he carefully folded up the white blanket, wiped down his rifle and packed it away along with the rest of his deadly equipment.

*

'That was close.'

DI Ronnie Buchanan was bored; he'd spent the last half hour throwing crumpled balls of paper into his waste-paper basket while Sergeant Maxwell tried to catch them on the way in.

'It's always the same in the couple of weeks leading up to Christmas, Max, apart from the occasional shop lifter, bugger all ever happens.'

'Well, it is supposed to be the season of goodwill, sir, maybe all the criminals have taken a few weeks off,' said Max, pulling off an extremely athletic save. 'Either that or they're all too busy taking their kids off to see shopping mall Santas.'

Buchanan laughed out loud. 'Know what I find strange, Max?'

'What, sir?'

'Parents, school teachers and their ilk spend hours telling kids not to go near or talk to strangers, right?'

'Right,' replied Max.

'They tell them not to accept gifts from strangers, right?'

'Right again, sir.'

'Then how come when it comes to Christmas, they pick up their cherished ones, plonk them down on the knee of a weird looking stranger with a red suit on and tell them to talk to him and take whatever gifts they get.'

Max laughed. 'I'd never thought of it like that, sir.'

'Anyway, as long as it stays quiet, it suits me,' said Buchanan as he picked up the phone which had just began to ring. 'Checking-in time', he thought to himself. 'Same time every afternoon since she'd left, as regular as bloody clockwork.'

'Hi, Michelle, how's your mother doing?'

'How did you know it was me?'

'Well let's see … It's three o'clock, who else would it be? Anyway, how's your mother doing?'

'She still can't get around much, they gave her some crutches but she can't seem to get the hang of them so I'm still running around getting all her shopping and whatever else she needs.'

'What about her broomstick?' asked Buchanan. 'She could fly around on that.'

Max stifled a laugh as he headed towards the coffee machine.

'Very funny, Ronnie.'

Buchanan smiled to himself.

'How long you planning on staying down there anyway?'

'At least another couple of weeks, Ronnie, but I'll be home by Christmas. How are you getting on? I hope you're remembering to eat properly.'

'Well sort of, I've been using the chip shop most nights but I'm getting a bit bored with their offerings …'

'I told you to do a shop; you can't eat that deep-fried shit every night, think about your cholesterol!'

'Stop being so preachy, you know the hours I work, how the hell am I supposed to go home and prepare a freshly cooked meal every night?'

'You don't need to cook from scratch nowadays; there are plenty of decent ready meals available at most supermarkets.'

'Okay, you've made your point, there's not much happening here, so I'll go and get some food in now.'

'Make sure you do then, I'll have to go, Ronnie, Mum is shouting on me.'

'Bye, love.'

He put the phone back in its cradle, rubbed the stubble on his chin and sighed.

'Let's go shopping, Max.'

*

With both the car heater and the windscreen wipers going full tilt, Buchanan and Max pulled into the supermarket car park just as it was beginning to get dark. They weren't going shopping though. The call had come in just as they were leaving: a young woman had been shot and Buchanan and Max had been given the case.

6

'So much for nothing happening at this time of year, eh, Max? What sort of callous bastard shoots a woman out shopping this close to Christmas?'

Max carefully parked the car, the tyres crunching on the frozen snow. They both turned up their collars at the same time like mirror images of each other and reluctantly left the warmth and comfort of the vehicle. They walked towards the large white tent which had been put in place to protect the crime scene from the snow fall that was getting heavier by the minute.

'They could have picked a different colour for the tent,' said Buchanan. 'The fucking thing is almost invisible in this weather.'

They said their hellos to the three uniformed police officers who were doing their best to hold back the ghoulish shoppers eager for a glimpse of the body. Buchanan noticed one of the oglers was wearing a red and white Santa hat, which added a strange surreal aspect to the whole scene playing out before him. They ducked under the yellow crime tape and approached Joe Styles, the pathologist, who was kneeling down, studiously examining the young woman's body. The high powered flood lights enveloped in steam from the snowfall cast an eerie yellow glow around the corpse, making her look as if she was playing the part of a murder victim in a macabre stage play.

'Evening, Doc,' said Buchanan, rubbing his hands in front of the warm portable gas heater. 'What can you tell us?'

'I can tell you without a doubt that these spotlights make you look rougher than normal, if that's at all possible. It seems to highlight all the lines and creases on your face.'

'Thanks for that, Doc, but I was referring to the dead body, the one you're currently hovering over.'

'Well, Ronnie, at first glance, judging by the amount of ejected tissue in not only the exit wound but also the bullets entry point, I would say this woman was shot by a high powered rifle.'

'What! You telling me she's been shot by a sniper?' said Buchanan, 'In Aberdeen?'

He lit a cigarette off the flame of the heater.

'Inconsiderate of her, too, I was all set for a quiet night in watching *A Christmas Carol;* the Alistair Sim one no less. What the Dickens is going on here?'

Joe Styles shook his head.

'That's terrible!'

Max laughed.

'Take a look over here.' Joe slowly got to his feet with a groan.

'Your back playing up again?' asked Buchanan.

'Aye, Ronnie, it's always worse in the cold.' He approached the nearby car and pointed to the broken blood stained back window.

'That fine spray you see there is classic high velocity blood splatter. Add to that the brain matter and the severe trauma to the back of the right hand side of her head and you can see that the bullet has gone straight through the poor woman, yet still had enough momentum to also go through the car's window … you wouldn't get that sort of power from a hand gun.'

'Jesus,' said Buchanan. 'What a mess.'

'One other thing, Ronnie, this is off the record mind, the entry wound indicates she was more than likely shot from an elevated position but we'll have to clarify that.'

Buchanan slowly turned through three hundred and sixty degrees taking in his surroundings and looking for the most likely place for the rifle shot to have come from.

'Would she have dropped to the ground right away, Doc?'

'Oh yes, death would have been instantaneous.'

'So,' said Buchanan, 'she's packing her shopping away in the boot and the bullet hits her here ...' he pointed to the left side of his forehead just above his eyebrow.

'Correct,' replied Joe.

'Could she have turned her body on the way down?'

'Doubtful, she'd have dropped to the ground like a sack of spuds, like this.'

Joe dropped to his knees then fell to the side, a perfect replication of the dead woman's position.

'Max, go and ask the SOCOs to check out that ski slope across the road, see if they can find any evidence that our shooter was there. And while you're at it, see if we have an ID on the victim.'

'I'll get on to it right away, sir.' said Max.

'How come you know so much about bullet wounds, Doc? It's hardly a regular occurrence round here.'

'Funnily enough, Ronnie, I attended a fire arms seminar just the other week, put on by the MOD. You ought to

9

have seen some of the photographic evidence they showed us there - this pales in comparison. There was this young soldier in Afghanistan … '

'Save me the gory details, Joe, I haven't had my tea yet.'

Joe sighed.

'How is Michelle's mum doing, by the way?'

'They gave her some crutches, she can't get used to them though.'

'Remind me how she broke her hip again …?'

'You know bloody well how it happened, that arsehole octogenarian boyfriend of hers decided to teach her how to ski. She's seventy-bloody-two years old for fuck's sake. Just because he's wearing well for his age and tries every sport imaginable doesn't mean everyone of that age can cope.'

'Especially ones with arthritis!' replied Joe, shaking his head.

'Mind you,' said Buchanan, 'it's maybe just as well, the daft old bastard had her signed up for a bungee jump next.'

They both creased themselves laughing just as Max returned, the top of his head covered in large snowflakes.

'What have we got then, Max?'

'Her names Emily Jackson, she's twenty seven years old, married and a mother of one. A young daughter, I believe.'

'You got an address?'

'Yep, 18 Rubislaw Den North.'

Buchanan whistled.

'They must have plenty of money then.'

'Aye, right enough, you couldn't afford to live there unless you were on ten times our salary!' said Max.

'I imagine her husband is loaded, plenty of money there to hire a hitman.'

'Sir! Surely you don't think the husband is behind it?'

Buchanan gave Max a wink.

'You know me by now, Max, I'm a suspicious bastard. I'll answer that after I've seen him.'

Buchanan stifled a yawn.

'Let's go see this husband then and rip the guts out of the poor sod's Christmas. Oh, and take someone from uniform to break the news, somehow I don't feel up to it.'

'Isn't that family liaison's job, sir?' asked Max.

'We'll phone them when we get there. I want to see the husband's reaction first.'

Max shook his head.

'Fair enough, sir, it's your call!'

Buchanan, Max and WPC Atkins pulled up outside the huge detached granite residence in one of the city's most prestigious west end addresses. As soon as Buchanan left the vehicle, he heard the loud music and the myriad voices coming from the open windows of the huge detached property.

'This is all we need, it looks like they're having some sort of celebration and we're about to become major party poopers.'

They approached the imposing double doors and rang the

11

ornate brass doorbell beneath the frost covered red and green Christmas wreath.

'Okay, PC Atkins, the floor is all yours,' said Buchanan stepping back behind his two colleagues. The door was opened by an inebriated middle aged man dressed in a red tartan kilt.

'One of the Stuart Tartans', thought Buchanan. He wasn't sure which one but if he had to bet on it he'd go for the Royal. Buchanan's eyes focused on the sporran. It hung from a chain around the drunk man's waist. It was one of the regimental ones, made from horsehair, unusual to see with a dress kilt.

'Can I help you, officer?'

'We're looking for Mr Jackson, it's a matter of great urgency,' said PC Atkins.

'Who's dead then?' asked the man laughing into his lead crystal whisky glass which sparkled as it caught the reflection of the light above the door.

The young PC, frowning, looked towards her two colleagues.

Buchanan stepped forward bringing his face up close to the man in the doorway. He was so close he could practically taste the whisky.

'Just go and get Mr Jackson if you don't mind, sir, before I make you eat that sporran.'

Max tried to hide his laughter by turning around and coughing into his hand as PC Atkins looked at her feet.

'Do you know who I am, officer? I could have you up on a charge for that last statement of yours,' said the man, smirking as he finished his drink.

The cold menacing look in Buchanan's eyes told him that this was not a man to make an enemy of; it was time to back down.

'Must we stand out here all night?' asked Buchanan. 'This IS a matter of great urgency.'

Beginning to realise the seriousness of the situation he stood to the side and gestured to them to enter the large opulent hallway.

'I'll just go and get Jonathan, take a seat in the snooker room, second door on your right. Help yourselves to a drink.'

The three officers, with Buchanan leading the way entered the room and awaited the arrival of the dead woman's husband.

Chapter Two

'Archie! If you don't get that fucking finger out your nose you'll get bugger all from Santa!'

The small child looked up at his mother. He was close to tears. He suddenly screamed.

The old man sitting unobtrusively on his own at the back of the bus reading his book on Scottish history had been quietly minding his own business until now. He quickly looked up and shook his head at the interruption. He wiped his glasses and then slowly took in his surroundings. The rest of his fellow passengers, of which there were quite a few, consisted of a mixture of workers on their way home from work, some in suits, some in manual labour clothes, and some Christmas shoppers weighed down by thick jackets, heavy carrier bags and large boxes. They had obviously taken advantage of the larger stores in the nearby city.

The bus was heading for Stonehaven: a small north-east coastal town fifteen miles from Aberdeen. As the snowflakes fell against the outside of the window, the old man put his book to the side next to his half-finished bottle of mineral water, closed his eyes and thought back to the time he'd spent in the small fishing village as a child; of course it was very different now compared to what he had remembered.

As he watched, the imposing silhouette of Dunotter Castle appear like a ghost through the white blanket of harsh winter weather, he remembered stepping off the train as a seven-year old boy and smelling the North Sea up close for the first time in his young life. He remembered poking sticks into rock pools looking for crabs, starfish, sea anemones or any other strange sea creatures he could find. He thought back to one particular sunny day when his uncle Ted, a man who looked every inch the fisherman, had taken him and his two pals out on his small fishing boat. The Lady Lisa, he could still remember the name. They had only gone about two miles from the harbour at most, but to a child who had never seen the sea it had seemed a thrilling adventure.

He could remember it all as if it was yesterday, the haunting cries of the seagulls from the blue sky above as the fishing boat's bow cut through the waves, showering him in sea spray which left a salty taste on his lips. He remembered his head burning from the sun high above them and his uncle tying the wet, grubby, faded, blue handkerchief around his head, providing him some protection against the rays.

Just as he was drifting back in time, once again a screaming child nearer the front of the bus stirred him from his peaceful reverie, which was just as well as he had reached his destination. He looked out the window just as the bus was pulling slowly into the bus station near the centre of town. He yawned, stretched his arms, then reached above him for his long black case, zipped up his jacket and headed slowly to the front of the bus. He whistled quietly to himself as he stood in line patiently awaiting his turn to disembark.

After struggling to pull his hood up against the elements, he began the two minute walk to the hotel, which had been his home for the last three days. He walked through the front door of the imposing Victorian building, welcoming the warmth that suddenly enveloped him from head to toe. He gave his jacket a shake to get rid of the snow resting on his shoulders, then after he'd wiped his sodden boots on the huge welcome mat he proceeded to make his way to the bar.

'Same as usual, Stan?' asked the barman, reaching for the bottle of Glenfiddich before he got an answer.

'Yeah, but make it a double, Bob, it's perishing out there.'

'Any luck finding the relatives?'

'A few leads, I spent another few hours in the registry office in Aberdeen today, just me and my list of names, dead quiet it was, quite relaxing in a strange sort of way …'

'So, when are you heading back to Canada?'

He took a large sip of his drink before answering. 'Soon as my work here is done, Bob, another few days hopefully.'

'Well, let's hope the weather calms down a bit for you.'

'Cheers, Bob.'

He raised his glass and took another drink.

'You want another one of those?' asked Bob, nodding in the direction of the almost empty whisky glass.

'Sure, why not, I'll take it through to the restaurant with me.'

The old man picked up his black case in one hand, his newly replenished whisky in the other and went off in search of something to eat.

*

Buchanan lay down on the large leather sofa with his hands behind his head and half closed his eyes. They'd been waiting over half an hour and there was still no sign of the dead woman's husband. He tried taking some deep breaths, hoping to calm himself down. It didn't work. Impatience got the better of him.

16

'Bugger this.'

He jerked up off the seat in one smooth motion.

'Max, go and find out where that inconsiderate bastard's got to,' he said loudly, not caring who heard.

'Will do, sir,' replied Max. 'PC Atkins, could you come with me, please?'

The two of them left the room as Buchanan once again lay back on the sofa, closed his eyes and tried to relax. He was getting annoyed and the last thing he needed was to let rip at the soon to be grieving husband. He'd been a bit irritable lately, which he put down to not being able to sleep properly since Michelle had gone to her mother's. That, and the fact he hadn't been eating well. 'You're right as always, Michelle,' he thought to himself.

He was unaware he had drifted off to sleep until he felt the cold drips hitting the right hand side of his head, stirring him awake. He opened his eyes to be confronted by a young, blonde-haired, blue-eyed, elven-looking child. He abruptly sat up, wiping his hand across his forehead. When he looked at his fingers his initial thoughts were that he was either bleeding or hallucinating due to lack of sleep, but when he looked more closely he realised the consistency was all wrong; the thick red liquid looked suspiciously similar to the tomato sauce in the bowl that the young girl with the small heart-shaped mark on her left cheek was dipping her chips into.

'Why you lying on my daddy's snooker seat?' asked the girl, her huge eyes staring at him hypnotically. She stood just a few inches from his face.

'I'm just resting, sweetheart, can I have a chip?'

'Not sure, I'm not s'posed to talk to strangers.'

Buchanan was reminded of his conversation with Max earlier on in his office. 'Okay, I'll tell you what, I'll tell you my name then you can tell me yours, that way we won't be strangers anymore, okay?'

The girl looked deep in thought, then with a confused look on her face, she replied. 'S'pose so.'

Buchanan stretched out to shake hands.

'Hello, I'm Mr Tomato Face, and you are?'

The girls eyes widened and she burst into a fit of giggles.

'That's not your real name, is it?' she replied, folding her arms in front of her.

'No, I'm only joking, my name's Ronnie. Ronnie Buchanan. And I'm a police officer.'

'Let me see your badge, copper.'

This time Buchanan laughed. 'I haven't got a badge, but I do have this,' said Buchanan handing over his warrant card.

The girl studied the photo for a few seconds then looked up at him and curtsied.

'Samantha Jackson.'

'What you doing through here on your own, Samantha?' asked Buchanan.

'I stay here; I'm looking for my mummy. You haven't seen her have you?'

Buchanan kept his emotions in check.

'I'm sorry sweetheart, I haven't seen her … '

Just then Max and PC Atkins entered the room.

'He's gone, sir, five minutes after we arrived he jumped in his Land Rover and took off.'

Buchanan turned to Samantha.

'Do you know where your daddy's gone, sweetheart?'

'He's gone to the White House, says he won't be long.'

The three officers looked at each other totally perplexed.

'Where is the White House?' Buchanan asked Samantha.

'It's our other house … it's in the woods.'

'Max, go check with the party guests, see if you can dig up more on this White House, it's probably a holiday home or such like, and you, PC Atkins, what's your first name, by the way?'

'Jenny,' came the softly spoken reply.

'Well, Jenny, see if you can find someone related to Samantha here, an aunt or an uncle, someone who can take care of the poor girl.'

As they left the room, Buchanan racked up the snooker balls then helped himself to a snooker cue and a large whisky from the crystal decanter next to the table.

'What's that bastard up to?' he thought to himself as he struck the ball with far too much force than was necessary.

*

'My compliments to the chef,' said the old man as the waitress removed the plate containing the remnants of his recently eaten meal.

'You always say that, you're such a gentleman,' said the

19

young woman.

'The waitress service is above excellent as well, of course. Here, this is for you,' he said slipping the woman a twenty pound note.

She smiled then looked from side to side before pocketing her tip.

'I shouldn't really take it you know, but it's getting very near Christmas and I've been trying to put a bit aside to buy our Penny a new bike so … thank you very much.'

'No problem, you earned it. Now, I think I could manage one more whisky before I retire for the evening, if it's not too much trouble.'

'Right away, sir.'

'Stan will do, just call me Stan.'

After finishing his whisky, the old man slowly got up. He carefully replaced his chair back under the table, said goodbye to his waitress and the rest of the restaurant staff, then slowly began the short walk back to his room.

'Good night, Stan,' said the receptionist.

He replied with a friendly wave as he headed towards the stairs.

Once in his room he carefully put his case at the foot of his bed and turned on the television, using the remote to flick to the local news channel. As he carefully folded up his clothes and laid them on the back of the chair, he watched as a shivering reporter, her head sheltered under a huge red and blue golf umbrella, informed him about a shooting in a supermarket car park in Aberdeen.

A large crowd of shoppers had gathered around her, their breath visible in the cold night air. One of them bizarrely was wearing a Santa hat.

'Witnesses say that the woman had just finished loading her shopping into her boot when she suddenly fell to the ground. So far no one has come forward to talk to the press or the authorities about sighting the gunman, as far as we are currently aware. Police have at this time refused to name the victim,' she told him.

But he knew her name. He gave a chilling smile as he opened the case and began to haul out the various parts of the sniper rifle, he laid them all very carefully on the bed and began to methodically clean them one by one as he whistled the first few bars of Chopin's funeral march.

Chapter Three

The snow was getting heavier by the minute as the Land Rover driver did his best to keep his wheels from sliding off the road. 'Thank fuck for four-wheel drive,' he thought to himself. The road was empty of traffic and the headlights cast an eerie glow through the large snowflakes falling from above. He used his hands-free system to phone his wife, for the third time in a row he was told to leave a message.

'Emily, for fuck's sake, pick up your phone. If you check my previous messages, you'll know where I'm heading and you'll know that the police have been to the house. Do whatever you can to stall them, I'll get rid of you know what, bye!'

He looked up just in time to avoid the fox that was sitting in the middle of the road, its yellow eyes reflecting the cars headlights as he drove past. *Not far now*, he thought as he turned off the main road.

He knew they should have gotten rid of it by now but Emily kept putting it off, she always found other things to spend their time on. In fact she wouldn't even talk about the subject, as if ignoring it could make the problem disappear. He couldn't just blame her, of course. Nothing had been stopping him from driving out before now and dealing with it on his own.

He was surprised that the police hadn't shown up before now. They had both expected them to show up the next day after the accident, but then days turned into weeks, weeks turned into a month, and now it had been two months since it happened. They both called it an accident but they both knew it was his fault; he shouldn't have been drunk behind the wheel. Still, as long as they both stuck to their story, should they need it …

*

'The White House,' declared Max as he handed the framed photo over to Buchanan. 'It's out near Banchory.'

Buchanan looked at the happy scene in front of him. Standing in front of a small whitewashed cottage were Mr and Mrs Jackson and Samantha. All were smiling, and Emily Jackson was hugging her daughter. The picture had been taken on a bright sunny day, the family looking like they didn't have a care in the world.

Buchanan sighed and looked up at Max.

'Get on to the police station located nearest to this cottage; take a photo of Mr Jackson here with your phone,' Buchanan tapped the photo just above Jonathan Jackson's head. 'Then send it on to them and ask if they can send a car to the cottage. If they find him tell them to keep him in custody until we get there. You got that, Max?'

'No problem, sir.' replied Max, but just as he was about to take the photo his mobile rang.

'… Hold on, he's standing here.' Max looked at Buchanan then handed over his mobile. 'It's for you, sir. It's Steve Kershaw, he's phoning from the crime scene … '

Buchanan tentatively took the phone.

'Ronnie! Do you never answer your fucking mobile?'

'Sorry, Steve, I forgot to charge it, what's up?'

23

'Seems like your hunch was right, the shot came from the ski slope right enough. We found a vague imprint in the snow where the guy was lying.'

'It was hardly a hunch, Steve. The shot could have only come from either there, or the flats above. Did you find anything else?'

'Yes, we did actually … a single red rose. It was just sitting there, sticking out of the snow next to the area where we reckon the shot was fired from. Apart from that just some footprints and a couple of cigarette ends. We're still searching, but I doubt we'll find much else. It's turning into a blizzard out here, not the best conditions to go searching for evidence.'

'What are you doing out there anyway? I thought you preferred lab work to getting your hands dirty at a crime scene?'

'All hands on deck for this one, Ronnie. I was told from on high to get out here and coordinate the search, make sure nothing was missed by the scene-of-crime guys.'

'Okay, Steve, I'll let you get back to your team. If you find anything else let me know.'

'No problem.'

Buchanan handed the mobile back to Max just as PC Atkins entered the room. Buchanan wasn't aware of her arrival; he was too busy thinking over what he'd just been told. Why a rose?

He closed his eyes and pictured the single red rose against the snow, his mind's eye morphing it into the crimson halo left by the victim at the crime scene.

The White House looked almost invisible in the snow as Jonathan pulled up outside the large wrought iron gate. He removed the key from the glove compartment and got out of the car completely oblivious to the police vehicle parked at the side of the house.

After opening the gate, he headed for the large weather beaten oak door, mentally preparing himself for the grisly task ahead.

The door wouldn't open. He'd unlocked it but some moisture must have gotten in between the door and the jamb and frozen solid.

'Fuck!'

He barged into it with his shoulder. It moved a touch. A couple more shoulder charges and he was in. He was sweating now, despite the temperature, and his left shoulder was aching.

He entered the eerily quiet cottage, and by torchlight, found his way to the hall cupboard and turned on the power. Next, Jonathan made his way to the kitchen, where he opened a drawer and after a quick search through the various items within he found what he was looking for: a small padlock key on an old rusty key ring.

The man left the kitchen by the back door, folding up his coat collar against the soul-crushing wind and snow. He headed towards the back of the garden where the shed suddenly appeared like a ghost in the moonlight. It was old and rickety, it had been there for years and had seen much better days.

He unlocked the padlock, opened the shed door and

after rummaging about amongst the contents for a couple of minutes, he found what he was looking for. With the spade in hand, he stood with his back against the shed door and carefully walked ten long measured paces straight ahead.

*

'What the fuck is he doing?' PC Harper asked his colleague PC Taylor.

'Fucked if I know ...' came the reply.

The two officers were bent down hidden behind the three foot high garden wall, shivering in the cold air.

'Here have some of this,' said the older PC, producing a small silver whisky flask from his pocket. 'I want to see what the bastard's up to before we grab him.'

*

Jonathan cleared some of the snow from where he'd stopped and began to dig up the frozen earth below. It was hard work, hampered somewhat by his damaged shoulder. He wasn't getting anywhere fast. He stopped digging and caught his breath as he felt the cold sweat running down his back. He looked down at the ground to see what he had accomplished so far.

'This is no good,' he thought to himself, 'I'll need something else to break up the earth.'

*

'He's digging up a body, that's what he's doing!' said Harper.

'You watch too much of that Murder Investigation shit on the TV,' came the reply. 'He could be digging up anything.

Now, give me back my flask.'

Harper handed back the half empty flask. PC Taylor gave it a shake and then gave his partner a funny look.

'You're a greedy bastard.'

'Sorry, Charlie. Jesus! Look, he's got a fucking pickaxe now.'

'Sshh! Keep your voice down lad, he'll hear us.'

*

Ten minutes into his task and he had found what he was looking for. He carefully cleared the earth around the polythene-wrapped object and bent down to haul it out of the ground. His hands were frozen however and he couldn't get much purchase on the icy-cold polythene.

Just as he turned round to head back to the shed for some rope to help him with his task, he heard a loud voice from behind.

'Hold it right there, sir,' said the burly policeman with whisky breath. He had suddenly appeared from behind the garden wall and then forcibly wrenched Jonathan's arm behind his back. The one attached to his sore shoulder.

He screamed in agony.

'Charlie! I've got the bastard; get the cuffs out.'

Charlie reached into his pocket as his partner held the man in what looked very much like a wrestling hold he'd seen on SkySports the night before. He put the restraints around their prisoner's cold clammy wrists and marched him back to their vehicle.

After forcefully shoving him into the back of the police

car and making sure he was secure, they decided to go and see what Jonathan Jackson had buried at the bottom of his garden.

'It's a body, I'm telling you,' said Harper.

'You're letting your mind play tricks on you, lad!' came the reply from the older PC. 'Like I said earlier, it could be anything, so let's not jump the gun till we have a look, eh.'

The polythene wrapped object was half in and half out the newly dug hole. It was all steamed up with what looked like frozen condensation and its shape didn't give any clues as to what was contained inside.

'Right, get your gloves,' said Charlie, 'we don't want to go buggering up the forensics now do we?'

'Good call,' replied Harper. 'Here, Charlie, you cut it open with that pen knife you carry everywhere and I'll hold the torch.'

'Way ahead of you,' replied Charlie, who had already removed the knife from his pocket ready to make the incision. As the small knife shone in the beam cast by the torch, he began to cut. There was a hiss of gas followed by a horrendous sickly sweet stench. The face before them was bloated, the skin grey and waxy, almost shining in the moonlight; it looked as if it belonged in Madam Tussauds. The sunken milky filmed eyes gazed up at the torch beam in a questioning ghostly stare.

Harper dropped the torch then violently threw up while his partner downed the rest of his whisky flask in one huge gulp.

'Looks like you were right enough, lad, it is a body.'

They'd stopped off at Buchanan's house on King's Gate when they got the call.

'They've got him, sir,' said Max, ending the phone call. 'And, get this, he was found digging up a body at the back of that white cottage.'

'Jesus! Two bodies in one day! Right, we'll finish these coffees and head out there next. Looks like my shopping will have to wait yet again.'

'We could nip in by the station and borrow a four by four. I don't know about you but I don't fancy a drive to Banchory in this weather in that thing out there.'

'Good idea, Max, get on to it, son. In fact see if they'll drop us one off, save us a journey.'

'I'm on it, sir.'

'What about me, sir?' asked the voice from the corner of the room.

'Jesus, Jenny, I'd totally forgotten about you. I'll get someone to drive you home when they drop off the car.'

Buchanan instantly picked up on the disappointed look on her face.

'That is unless you fancy a snowy trip to Banchory?'

'I'm game, sir,' said PC Atkins, her grateful smile lighting up the room.

'You can do me a favour first though, somewhere in the kitchen, god knows where, you'll find a huge stainless steel flask, fill it up with coffee, extra strong. And, if it's not too much trouble, fetch me a Guinness from the fridge.'

'The car will be twenty minutes sir,' said Max. 'They're sending us a driver as well, seems like they don't trust us with the motor.'

'Grab a beer while you're waiting then, there's plenty in the fridge, and see what Jenny wants.'

'I'll have a Guinness, sir, if it's okay with you,' said the quiet voice from the kitchen.

'Really! I haven't met many women that enjoy the black stuff; I think I'm in love.'

Max laughed as the young PC came out of the kitchen with the drinks and a bright-red face.

Chapter Four

The old man, now dressed for bed in his pyjamas and dressing gown, sat hunched over the bedside table. He fired up his laptop, clicked on the folder named "Targets" then opened up the file on Darryl Morrison.

Forty four years old, married with two kids, currently residing in Bucksburn Aberdeen, works for the council at Woodhill House.

He scrolled down to the bottom of the page. Currently drives an 09 registration, blue Vauxhall Astra.

He took out his notebook and wrote down the registration and then moved over to his makeshift workspace on the dresser in the corner of the hotel room. He turned on the table lamp, put on his glasses and painstakingly began to construct the intricate explosive device. He'd done the exact same thing many times before but that was almost a full lifetime ago. Back then, he was paid a lot for his skills, but this time it was personal. He hoped Mr Morrison would be sent screaming straight to hell where the bastard belonged.

*

Half an hour later, with the construction accomplished, he carefully moved the device to the side, wiped the beads of sweat off his glasses, breathed on them, gave them a quick clean and then looked at his alarm clock.

He sighed a heavy sigh.

'Time to check in,' he said to himself.

He turned on his webcam as he religiously did every night since he had been away at this time, to be met by his wife Clara, currently residing in the cancer ward of the Princess Margaret Hospital in Toronto.

She looked mainourished, tired and very pale.

'Harry, my love, what sort of day have you had?'

'One down four to go. Still a few people to see but I'm getting there.'

'Glad to hear it. Which one of your distant relatives did you visit first?'

'The woman, she didn't look too good, she had a pretty bad headache.'

Clara erupted into an unhealthy laugh then wiped her mouth with the stained handkerchief she held in her emaciated hand.

'What's next on the agenda?'

'I'm going to leave a present for Mr Morrison in his car as way of an introduction, so to speak.'

'Make sure it's a decent sized present then.'

'Of course, the bigger the better, I always say.'

Clara's mouth opened in a huge yawn.

'I'm very tired tonight, Harry, that latest bout of chemo has knocked me for six. Do you mind if I cut our conversation short? I really could do with a sleep.'

'I'll let you get your rest,' said Harry. 'I'll give you an update as soon as I can.'

'I'll look forward to it, see you same time tomorrow.'

Harry turned off his webcam, then carefully wiped his tears off the keyboard.

Time for some music he thought, it always seemed to drag him out of his sombre mood. He clicked on the icon for his media player looked up the artists and clicked on Johnny Cash. He lay on his bed with his eyes closed as the rich voice of the man in black filled the room.

*

The going wasn't good. If it weren't for the expertise of Edgar, their driver who had come with the borrowed motor, they could have found themselves spinning off the road into the snow covered pine trees or farmlands on numerous occasions. They were currently on North Deeside Road and had just passed Peterculter, just over halfway through their journey to Banchory. Buchanan was in the front passenger seat coffee in hand with Max and PC Atkins in the back.

'Did you hear about the bank snatch in Union Street today, sir?' asked Edgar.

'No, what happened like?'

'This guy walks into the Bank, cool as you like, joins the queue like a normal customer and then when the security guys drop off some money he makes as if to tie his shoelace, then, quick as you like he makes a sprint for the counter. He grabs one of the bags and legs it straight out the front door like his arse was on fire.'

'Surely they must have followed him out and apprehended him?' answered Buchanan.

'Well that's the thing, they couldn't.'

Edgar laughed. 'Get this. The bank has a solid wooden

door at the front and then two glass swing doors on the inside that meet in the middle with brass pull handles, right, so the guy pulls out a baseball bat he had hidden down the leg of his jeans and puts it through the two handles locking the security guys and all the bank staff inside. Then cool as you like he turns round, gives everyone watching the finger then scarpers. By the time they'd called the cops, and the two security guys had eventually made their way out the back door, the guy was well gone, lost himself in amongst the crowd of Christmas shoppers in Union Street.'

'That's bloody genius!' said Buchanan.

'They must have him on camera,' came Max's voice from behind.

'They have, won't do us much good though. He was wearing a baseball hat and had a scarf pulled up over his mouth, he came prepared, that's for sure.'

'They should check the last few weeks' footage,' said Buchanan. 'Especially if they have a camera pointed at the front door. He must have cased the joint sometime in the past, he might not have been so careful about hiding his features then.'

'How do you figure that out?' asked PC Atkins.

Buchanan turned around to face the young police officer.

'It's obvious, he must have planned it in advance, he would need to have a rough idea of what thickness the object he needed to lock the doors would have to be. I'd be looking for someone hanging around the bank entrance paying too much attention to the glass doors. I mean he'd look a real prick if he'd grabbed the money bag and then tried to lock the handles with something that would have been too thin and fallen out, or too thick to have been threaded through the handles in the first place. Who has the case, Edgar?'

'Thornton, sir.'

'Max! Remind me to go see Jack Thornton in the morning.'

'Will do, sir.'

'Now, Miss Atkins, tell me a bit about yourself.'

'Not much to tell, sir, it's all about the job with me. I don't socialise much. Well … not in the real world anyway. Most nights you'll find me on Facebook or swotting up for my next police exam.'

'Any family?'

'Not really, sir. My mum and dad are both dead and I've no brothers and sisters.'

Buchanan thought for a moment.

'A word of advice, Jenny … find yourself an interest outside the force. If you don't it'll drive you mad. Believe me.' He raised his cup. 'Nice coffee, by the way.'

They arrived at the station in Banchory under a huge bright full moon which lit up the frost hardened snow on the ground beneath. The bitter cold air hit them like a slap in the face as they left the warmth of their vehicle.

Banchory was covered by the Marr local police team. They took a community-focused approach and covered all towns and villages within the Marr area. As well as Banchory, it took in Huntly, Aboyne, Alford, Ballater and Braemar. Places where their various sized Police Stations were located.

'Jesus, it's a lot deeper here than in Aberdeen,' said Buchanan. His words left a visible cloud in the cold night air.

'It must be about minus ten out here,' said Max.

'Minus twelve actually,' said Buchanan. 'I checked the temperature in the car before we got out.'

They headed towards the police building.

'You made it then,' said the portly middle-aged man at the entrance, who extended his huge muscly arm and shook Buchanan's hand.

'We have the bastard locked up safe and sound for you. Would you like to see him now or would you and your colleagues like a hot drink first?'

'Coffees all round would be gratefully appreciated before we get down to business, if you don't mind, Mr … ?'

'Sorry I forgot to introduce myself. Where's my manners? William Forest, just call me Bill.'

'Nice to meet you, Bill, I'm Ronnie Buchanan and this is Sergeant Maxwell and WPC Atkins. Right, Bill …' said Buchanan as he stretched his fingers to recover from Sergeant Forest's strong grip on his hand. 'Now that the introductions are over, we'll just sit ourselves down on these comfy couches here while you rustle up the coffees and - if it's not too much trouble - could you send us the two officers who apprehended the suspect? I'd like a word with them, please.'

'No problem, Ronnie, I'll see to it right away. Oh! Wait a minute I forgot, the younger of the two officers, PC Harper, has gone home. Said he was in shock after seeing the body, can't blame him like, it's in a hell of a state.'

'No problem,' said Buchanan, 'Just send the other guy then, that'll be fine.'

'PC Taylor at your service, sir,' said the grey haired man. 'The young lad has gone home, but hopefully I can tell you what you need to know.'

'Have a seat,' said Buchanan, gesturing to the opposite side of the small coffee table.

Charlie ran through his account of things at the White House as Buchanan listened intently and sipped his coffee.

'So, you actually saw him pacing out the distance from the shed to the burial site?'

'Watched him with my own eyes, sir,' replied Charlie. 'It reminded me of one of those old pirate movies where some guy with a peg leg pulls out a map and measures out the distance to the treasure. Not that he had a map, mind.'

'So,' said Buchanan rubbing his chin, 'he'd obviously made a mental note of exactly where the body was. Sounds like he was always intending on moving it then, or else he would have just buried it in any old part of the garden. What do you two think?' he asked, turning to Max and Atkins.

'Sounds a fair assumption to me,' said Max.

'I concur,' said PC Atkins, nodding her head in agreement.

Buchanan drank down the last of his coffee as he looked at a noticeboard on the wall. Something had caught his eye. It was a photo of a Border Collie that had gone missing. The owner was offering a hundred-pound reward. It reminded him of his own dog, Jess, it had the same white flash on the top of its head. This, in return, reminded him of the argument

37

he and Michelle had the morning she had left to go look after her mother.

Buchanan thought back. He had unintentionally started it off. He had simply asked whether Michelle had had any word from the adoption agency. Bad move. Michelle had gone off on one.

'Don't you think I would have told you if I had? How stupid do you think I am?'

Even their normal walk in Hazlehead woods with the dog hadn't calmed her down. She had walked ten paces behind him all the way. Each time he looked around, she was staring daggers at him.

'Sir!'

Buchanan turned to face his two colleagues.

'Right, PC Taylor, could you show us to the interview room and send through our grave digging friend. Let's see what he's got to say for himself.'

Jonathan Jackson looked haggard. His long hair was a black greasy mess, his left arm was in a sling and his white designer shirt was covered in a mixture of sweat stains and dried mud.

'You look like you've been sleeping rough for a week,' said Buchanan.

Jonathan looked up furtively, his blood shot eyes taking in the three people in front of him.

'You haven't exactly caught me at my best right enough. Anyone got any cigarettes?'

'You can't normally smoke in here, sir,' said Buchanan.

'But seeing as you and I are going to try and build up some sort of rapport here, I'll join you in a cigarette.'

Buchanan took his cigarettes out of his inside pocket and pushed the packet across the table towards Mr Jackson.

'Thanks,' said Jonathan.

His hands were shaking and he had trouble freeing one from the packet.

Buchanan lit both their cigarettes then peered through the newly formed smoke cloud that had appeared between them.

'Who's the dead woman?'

'I've no idea,' replied Jonathan.

'I find that hard to believe, sir.'

He stared at Jonathan for almost a full minute before he continued.

'I hope you're not deliberately trying to be evasive, sir. The longer this takes the shorter my temper is going to get. Ask Max here, he'll tell you what sort of bastard I can be if someone fucks me about.'

Max nodded his head in confirmation.

PC Atkins looked confused. She felt like a gooseberry.

Jonathan tried to hold up both hands, forgetting one was damaged. He winced visibly.

'I'm not trying to be evasive. I intend on telling you everything. Why do you think I never asked for my solicitor? I just want this shit over with; it'll be a relief for my wife and myself.'

Buchanan took a huge draw on his cigarette and looked

grimly at his colleagues.

'We should have come clean when it happened,' said Jonathan, bursting into tears.

They gave him a couple of minutes to pull himself together.

'You'll feel better when you get it off your chest,' said Buchanan, looking at the small red light to make sure the recording was turned on. 'Now, pull yourself together and tell me what happened.'

Jonathan took a few deep breaths, looked at each of the officers in turn, then began his story.

Chapter Five

'It was October the 12th, my birthday, believe it or not. Emily and I had booked a meal at Cinnamon's at the top of Union Street. I'd only intended on having a couple of beers as I'd taken the Jag with me, but two led to three, then four, and - before I knew it - I was on the whiskies. I figured, what the hell? It's only a short drive home and - as I said - it was my birthday after all. Anyway, we ended up arguing over the amount I'd drunk, a common occurrence these days. Emily insisted we get a taxi home. I'd have none of it, of course, I insisted on taking the Jag.'

'Why didn't your wife drive?' asked Max.

'Emily had had a few drinks by then herself and she's not as big an arsehole as me basically, she knows when she's had too much. I, on the other hand … '

He shrugged his shoulders.

'I take it it's quite a regular occurrence with you? … Driving home pissed, I mean?' asked Buchanan.

Jonathan looked up with a pained look on his face

'Why not just ask me straight? Do I have a problem with alcohol?'

'Well, do you?' asked Buchanan.

He blew a cloud of smoke towards him. Jonathan sighed and put his head in his hands. After rubbing his temples, he looked up at Buchanan with his blood shot eyes.

'Do you mind?' he asked, helping himself to another

cigarette.

'Help yourself,' answered Buchanan.

'The answer is yes by the way,' said Jonathan as he blew the smoke back across the table. 'Once I have a drink I can't stop. If I open a bottle of malt, I have to finish it. I'm what you call a functioning alcoholic, at least that's what my doctor tells me.' He laughed. 'He should know, he puts back damn near a whole bottle himself of an evening.'

Buchanan lit up his own cigarette.

'Back to the restaurant,' he said, steering the conversation back on track. 'What happened when you left?'

'The argument continued in the car. "You need help; you're slowly killing yourself," blah, blah, blah.'

Jonathan suddenly paused and took an extra-long drag on his cigarette.

'Then, as we were just passing the Albyn pub heading towards Queens Road, this girl suddenly appeared from nowhere. Emily screamed as the girl flew over the bonnet - her head made a helluva noise as it banged into the windscreen. If I close my eyes sometimes I can still see it, clear as day. It replays itself over and over again in my mind, it stops me sleeping, I can't eat properly. It's been doing my fucking head in for weeks.'

'Poor you!' said the heavily sarcastic voice of WPC Atkins, shaking her head.

Buchanan quickly turned his head, staring daggers in her direction, causing her to look at the floor as Jonathan continued his story.

'I didn't think it was a big deal at first, she fell off the bonnet like a rag doll, but then she stood up as if nothing had happened. There wasn't a mark on her, she wasn't even bleeding, she was a bit unsteady on her feet granted, but I assumed she'd just come out of the pub and was a bit … well … pissed. Anyway, she said she felt fine, her head hurt a little but that was all. However, just to be on the safe side, Emily decided that we should take her to Forresterhill Hospital to get her checked out. We planned on dropping her off at accident and emergency.'

'So, what happened?' asked Buchanan.

'We put her in the back seat, Emily was talking to her, she seemed fine. Then, on the way to the hospital, she took some sort of seizure, she stopped breathing, turned a funny colour and that was it. Next thing we knew we had a dead body on our hands.'

'Why didn't you report what happened? You could have come clean, thrown yourself on the mercy of the courts,' said Max.

'What, and get charged with vehicular manslaughter and drunk driving? They would have thrown the book at me!'

'So, you and your wife now have a dead girl on your hands. Who had the idea to bury the body at the cottage?' asked Buchanan.

'Both of us. We'd worked too hard to get to where we were to throw it all away so we decided to get rid of the evidence. We never intended to leave her body there indefinitely. We were planning on moving it somewhere else. Emily had the idea of throwing the body in a ditch at the side of the road in the middle of nowhere, we could make it look like she'd been hit by a car somewhere else, we just never got round to it.'

Buchanan let his anger get the better of him and slammed his hand down on the table.

'That poor lassie probably has parents somewhere wondering what the hell has happened to their daughter and you two bastards are more concerned with protecting your status?'

Jonathan visibly shook at Buchanan's tirade and lowered his voice.

'Don't blame my wife too much, I got her into this situation. If I'd only listened to her at the time none of this would have happened. I take sole responsibility. Now if you don't mind I'd like to make a phone call. I tried phoning Emily earlier but I couldn't get through.'

Buchanan took a deep breath and once more reached for his cigarettes. He lit up two, giving one to Jonathan Jackson.

'Tell him, Max.'

*

After telling Mr Jackson about his wife's shooting and leaving him in bits, they were once again sitting in the foyer having a coffee.

'What next, sir?' asked Max.

Buchanan put down his cup.

'I'll arrange to move the body and that murdering bastard back to Aberdeen. Joe can do the autopsy and give us some idea of how she died, we'll see if Jackson's story holds up. Max, you can go and check out Mrs Jackson's place of work in the morning, see if she's received any threats recently.

This could be a revenge thing, maybe someone found out what happened to the girl and rather than come to us they've decided to dish out their own kind of justice.'

He turned towards the young woman.

'PC Atkins, how do you fancy working with us for a while?'

'I'd love to, sir.'

'I'll straighten it out with the bosses in the morning. I'd like you to look into missing persons. Once we get a rough age and description from the body, use what you can to see if we can give this poor girl a name. Now, let's hope Edgar hasn't got bored shitless and buggered off somewhere. We need to get back to Aberdeen, I'm knackered and I'd like to get started early in the morning. Oh, and Jenny, lose the uniform, you're playing with the big boys now. And one other thing for future reference: never, ever, interrupt a man when he has his confession in full flow.'

Chapter Six

Max wiped his slush sodden feet on the burgundy welcome mat and entered The Jackson Brown Design Agency. It was a small granite-terraced building situated in Bon Accord Crescent. He'd phoned ahead and made an appointment to see Garry Brown who had been Emily Jackson's business partner for the last three years. He had arrived slightly early and slightly wet - thanks to the early morning sleet - and was extremely grateful for the hot strong coffee handed to him by the petite blonde secretary sitting behind the desk in the tastefully-decorated reception area. She kept weeping and wiping her eyes with the tear-stained handkerchief she kept up the left sleeve of her red silk blouse.

He looked at the name plaque on her desk. Sue Thomas.

'Have you worked here for long, Mrs Thomas?'

She rubbed both eyes before answering.

'I've been working here for just over a year now, Sergeant.'

'So, you must have known Emily Jackson quite well, then?'

Out came the hanky again, followed by the strangest sobbing noise Max had ever heard, it sounded more animal than human.

'Just give me a minute to compose myself, please, Sergeant. I just can't believe what's happened, poor Emily.'

Max focused on his coffee.

'Emily was a good friend to me, Sergeant, she was more than just my boss.'

'Did you socialise quite a lot?'

'Now and again, a few bar lunches, an occasional drink after work, that sort of thing.'

'Did she talk about her home life much?'

'Emily was quite a private person in that respect, although she did moan quite a bit about her husband, but then again, who doesn't?'

'Moan about what exactly …?' asked Max.

'His drinking mostly. He often turned up here pissed, I felt quite embarrassed for her whenever that happened.'

'Do you think anything had been worrying her lately?'

'I know something was. Her doctor signed her off with stress a few weeks ago, for a fortnight I think it was. She seemed fine when she came back though.'

'She never told you why she was stressed then?'

'Never mentioned it.'

A door opened on the left.

'Sergeant Maxwell! I'll see you now.'

*

Wrapped up against the elements in his waterproof jacket and trousers, the old man - face hidden behind a scarf deep in his hood - prowled the slush covered car park of Woodhill House, a government building in Aberdeen. He was picking up the rubbish lying around the grass verge of the parking area with his long metal litter pick.

'Nay a great day for that sort of job,' said the man getting out of the flash sports car to his left.

'Doesn't bother me really, in fact I find it quite invigorating,' said the man in the waterproofs.

Biding his time, he waited until the driver had entered the building then, after moving further into the car park, he purposely dropped his litter picker next to the blue Vauxhall Astra. As he bent down to retrieve it from the slush, he quickly removed the small bubble wrapped package from the inside pocket of his jacket along with a foot long piece of narrow thin metal. He placed the package in the black plastic bag he was using for the litter he had just picked up, then after making sure that he wasn't being watched, he slid the metal object down the inside of the car window and un-clicked the locking mechanism.

A high pitched sound momentarily filled the air.

It took him only a matter of seconds to gain access then open the bonnet and disconnect the car alarm.

Phase one of his plan over, he went back to his litter picking for five minutes. Then after carefully making sure no one had heard the alarm he returned to the car and attached the bomb beneath the driver's seat and carefully connected it up to the ignition.

*

Buchanan had just arrived at his workplace with a strong cup of coffee in hand when he was summoned from on high.

'That's all I need!' he said to the young PC as he dutifully made his way to Detective Chief Inspector Montgomery's office.

He knocked at the door, and after being beckoned to come in, he took a seat across from the huge pock-faced man sitting across from him at the other side of the ancient looking antique desk: a desk, if the stories were to be believed, he religiously buffed up every day. The wood panelled room smelled of coffee, stale sweat and furniture polish mixed in with a strange musky smell Buchanan couldn't quite put his finger on. Maybe his aftershave, he thought to himself.

'I'd offer you a coffee, Ronnie, but I see you've brought your own. Watch where you put it though, I don't want you leaving any rings on my newly polished desk. Use the coaster.'

'Of course, sir.'

'Did I ever tell you where it came from? The desk, I mean.'

'An estate in Ballater, your grandfather was the manager, it came out his office. You've told me many times.'

The DCI gave him a strange look.

'Right, let's get down to business. The superintendent is going apeshit. He says the last thing he needs is a sniper running amok in the city at this time of year. He's scared that it stops people going Christmas shopping, says it could bugger up the local economy, so he wants this cleared up quick. What have we got so far?'

Buchanan reached into his inside pocket for his notebook, then flicked over a few pages.

'We found the victim's husband in possession of a dead body. He had it buried out the back of his holiday cottage. Both he and his wife were involved in hiding it but he's taking full responsibility for the death. He was driving under the influence, says she came out of nowhere and he hit her.'

'And rather than come to us they decided to hide the body? What a pair of bastards,' said the DCI, interrupting Buchanan. 'Do you believe him?'

'I think so but we'll soon know if his story holds up later today when the autopsy has been done.'

'So, what's your thinking on this, Ronnie? Some sort of revenge killing?'

'Looks like it. I've got Max checking out her place of work to get a bit of background on our victim and to find out if she's had any threats or whatever.'

'You're talking about Mrs Jackson, I take it. What about the other dead body? Who does that belong to?'

'No idea yet, sir. There was no ID on the body and from what I've heard it's in a helluva state. We might have to go on dental records. I do, however, have PC Atkins checking into missing persons. Hopefully once the doc has a look he can give us a rough age and some other details we can maybe use to tie up a positive identity.'

'What about the sniper? Anything on him or her, I suppose they could be a woman.'

'Bugger all, really. I've got uniform going door to door round the houses above the ski slope, to see if anyone noticed anything, but with the weather yesterday, I'm not holding out much hope.'

'Who do you want to use to set up the incident room?'

'Sergeant Wilkins, he's a bit useless in the field but when it comes to that sort of thing there's no-one better.'

'Right, let's have it then, what's he calling it? We all know how he likes to give these things witty names.'

'Operation Cold Shot,' replied Buchanan.

'Very droll, he just happened to find that on the list did he?'

'He assures me he did,' answered Buchanan.

The DCI was referring to the UK wide list of approved names the police used for their operations.

'The aim is to choose names that are completely neutral so they will hopefully be totally unrelated to the case, doubt if he'll get away with that one. I always preferred exotic bird names myself, operation parakeet that was one of mine back in the day. A big drug case. It was all over the news about five years ago. Surely you've heard of it.'

'Vaguely, sir.'

Buchanan was slowly losing the will to live and couldn't stop himself yawning. Montgomery sighed, leaned back in his chair and put his hands behind his enormous head.

'Right, Ronnie, you seem to have things in hand. Mind and keep me informed.'

'Of course, sir.'

'Oh! One last thing before you go, Ronnie. I believe you've taken PC Atkins out of her uniform.'

Buchanan laughed, 'In a manner of speaking, sir. You don't mind, do you?'

'On the contrary, I've heard nothing but good things about her work. How do you think she'll cope?'

'She should do well, she's very keen, didn't complain at all when we hauled her out to Banchory last night. She'd finished her shift too.'

'She's been accepted on to ACDP, did you know that?'

'No, I didn't,' replied Buchanan. 'I'm not surprised though.'

The DCI opened the top left hand drawer of the desk, then handed Buchanan a leaflet.

'Have a look.'

Buchanan gave it a quick scan. "The Accelerated Careers Development Programme (ACDP) consists of a phased developmental structure aimed at preparing and equipping police officers for senior posts within the Scottish Police Service. Originally it offered a direct entrance pathway to graduates and undergraduates applying to the Scottish Police Service. This has recently been changed to include amongst others, young officers who display exceptional potential."

The words exceptional and potential had been highlighted in yellow.

'I'm not being funny, sir, but I do happen to know what the ACDP consists of.'

'So, you should, detective, but my reason for showing you that is to make you aware that the force has great things in mind for Miss Atkins, so don't you go fucking that up. We all know how you like to cut corners, so don't you go teaching her any bad habits. Is that clear?'

'Perfectly, sir.'

'Glad to hear it. Now, be on your way.'

Buchanan headed towards the door.

'Besides, she could outrank you and me both in a few years,' said the DCI as Buchanan left his office.

*

'So, that's the history of the place, Sergeant Maxwell.'

Max was trying his best to keep his eyes open. The dead woman's business partner had one of those strange, hypnotic, monotonous voices that could send you to sleep. It reminded him of the Snake in Disney's *Jungle Book*. He'd been forced to watch the DVD a few days ago by his young niece. Mr Brown had been talking for a good hour now, mostly about the forming of the company by himself and Mrs Jackson. He hadn't told him anything pertinent to the case, so he made his excuses and stood up to leave.

'Oh! There was one other thing, Sergeant, I don't know if it means anything, damned strange though. Emily received a rather puzzling card the other day; I'll just go and get it.'

He returned with the card unfolded in his hand.

'This is all it says.'

Max looked at the italic writing inside.

"Oculus pro oculo".

'Sounds like gobbledegook to me,' said Max.

'It is a bit of a mouthful right enough, Sergeant, it's Latin, we googled it. It says, as far as we can tell, an eye for an eye.'

As Mr Brown closed the card, Max froze. Despite the dry stuffy heat in the room he felt the cold sweat running down the back of his neck as he gazed at the picture of a single blood-red rose on the front of the card.

'Strange, don't you think?'

Chapter Seven

Careful to avoid the slush topped puddles in the old cobbled street, Buchanan rubbed his hands together then entered the Prince of Wales public house. He'd been coming here for years; he enjoyed the peace and quiet of the place, no loud music to dull his thinking. He'd arranged to meet Max, PC Atkins and Joe Styles at 12:30. He'd arrived half an hour early which suited him; he liked to be early, it gave him time to get his thoughts together before the meeting commenced. He looked along the bar at the various guest ales on offer but couldn't decide on what one to try, so he ordered himself a pint of Guinness and a packet of salted peanuts. The barman came back with his change.

'Caught that bastard sniper yet, Ronnie?'

'Give it time, for fuck's sake, Harry. Anyway, how do you know I'm working on it? I'm not the only detective in Aberdeen.'

'The wife saw you on TV this morning. There was a rerun of a news report from last night, it showed you coming out of that big white tent thing and getting into your car with Max at Asda in Garthdee. They said the victim was a young mother too, what sort of bastard does that sort of thing so close to Christmas?'

'An evil sort of bastard,' replied Buchanan. 'Cheers, Harry.'

Buchanan raised his drink in salute then headed off to find a nearby table. His eyes wandered to the various flyers pinned to the pubs noticeboard. One in particular piqued his interest. It was advertising a play taking place at a local theatre … *No Deed goes Unpunished* … .

Buchanan knew a man in Edinburgh who would definitely agree with that. The guy had innocently stopped his car to help fix a young woman's flat tyre and ended up getting shot for his troubles, a prime example of being in the wrong place, at the wrong time, if ever there was one. He laughed quietly to himself as he took a large gulp of his ice cold drink. After taking off his jacket and hanging it over the radiator behind him he picked up his notebook and began to jot down a few of his thoughts regarding the case.

Sniper-military background?

Significance of Rose?

Motive?

Working hypothesis revenge killing?????

(Too tidy?)

Buchanan had just underlined his last entry in the notebook when he was interrupted.

'Inspector Buchanan, fancy seeing you here.'

He put away his reading glasses and looked up at petit blonde woman with the huge shoulder bag hovering above his table.

'Gemma, now what would you be wanting? As if I didn't know.'

'Yesterday's shooting, what can you tell me?'

'You know the score. I can't tell you anything this early on in the investigation.'

'Oh, come on, Ronnie, you can at least tell me the victim's name, surely.'

Buchanan sighed and finished the rest of his drink. 'How did you know I was here?'

'It's lunchtime. You're always here at lunchtime.'

Buchanan scratched his unshaven chin. 'Aye, you've got me there, right enough. Tell you what, buy me another pint and I'll think about it.'

The young journalist returned from the bar with Buchanan's pint and a gin and tonic for herself.

'You'll have to sit elsewhere pretty soon, Gemma, I'm meeting up with a few colleagues here in about ten minutes and it wouldn't look very good if they saw me cosying up to a journalist now would it.'

'Point taken, Ronnie. Give me something and I'll disappear.'

Buchanan handed over a sheet of paper from his notebook.

'There are two names on there: the victim's and the victim's husband. I've done you a favour so you can do one for me. The husband is a bit of a dodgy bastard, so I'd like you to dig up the dirt on him see what you can find out. You know the drill.'

'I'll get right on to it. By the way, what's with the specs? First time I've known you to use them.'

Buchanan took a long gulp of his drink and laughed to himself. 'It's a funny story, actually. A few weeks ago I was in Sainsbury's with Michelle. I was helping her pack the shopping at the checkout when I came over all dizzy. This went on for a few days and I began to think there was something seriously wrong with me, so I went to the doctor. They couldn't figure it out, they had an idea that it could be some sort of vertigo but just to be safe they arranged a few tests and gave me some medication to stop the dizziness.'

'Did it work?' asked Gemma as she took a sip of her drink.

'Did it fuck! And the more I dwelled on it the worse it got. Anyway, to cut a long story short. A few days later, I'm sitting at home squinting at the Evening Express and Michelle says, "Hey, Ronnie, try these!" She handed me her reading glasses, I put them on and Jesus! I couldn't believe how clear the print was. Turns out I needed glasses myself, just for reading mind. The guy at Specsavers said I'd probably needed them for ages, that's why I was having the dizzy spells, I couldn't believe it, I thought I had a brain tumour.'

Gemma laughed into her drink. As Buchanan drained the last of his, he saw the distorted image of Max entering the bar through the bottom of his pint glass.

'Time for you to make a move.'

'Before I go, is it true the gunman left a calling card? A single rose I heard.'

Buchanan stared back at her blankly.

'No comment.'

'That's a pity; I had such a good headline planned too.'

She picked up her oversized shoulder bag and headed for the exit.

'Gemma!' shouted Buchanan.

She turned round.

'What was the headline?'

She smiled back at him. 'Guns 'n' Roses, of course.'

*

The young woman jerked up suddenly when she heard the key rattling in the lock. She slowly eased her stiff body off the grubby mattress and carefully rubbed the chaffed skin on her ankle. The steel manacle on her leg was really beginning to bug her now. She wasn't sure exactly where the cellar that had become her home for the last few days was located. The man in the mask hadn't given her any clues and there was no way to see outside. She'd tried screaming for help the whole of the first day but no one had answered her pleas.

She looked around.

It was an ominous place, this new home of hers. It had a strange creeping chill about it. She kept hearing scurrying noises in the distance. Rats, she reckoned. She hadn't actually seen one but she somehow knew her guess was spot on. As for the smell … she couldn't quite place it, a rotten odour that clawed at her nostrils, similar to spoiled meat but not exactly. She shivered and let out a sob.

'Oh well, could be worse, I suppose'.

She couldn't in all honesty say she had been treated that badly for a prisoner, kidnap victim, or whatever the hell she had become. She had plenty of food, bottled water and she even had Sky TV. He'd carefully planned her makeshift prison out, that was obvious. Certain things led her to this belief. Like the way the chain on her leg just allowed her enough give to reach the fridge, the sink and the toilet but nowhere near the door. She had felt scared and threatened to begin with but her captor visited her daily, even allowing her a phone call to her father each day. She didn't have a clue as to why she had been kidnapped, it's not like her father was rich or anything.

She'd asked the man in the mask once. For information - that's what he told her. 'If your father plays ball, you'll be home in a week,' he'd said to her. Not long now then, she had already been here for three days. She took deep breaths to calm herself down as she heard the heavy footsteps coming down the stairs. Then she heard his hand on the handle.

The heavy steel door opened with a weird grating sound. It reminded her of the noise made by a crypt gate opening; from one of the old Hammer movies she enjoyed watching.

'Time for your phone call,' said the man in the devil mask.

Victor picked up the phone on the first ring, his hand visibly shaking. He'd taken a week off work just as he'd been told to by the man who'd taken his daughter captive.

'Mr Whitelaw, how are you bearing up?' asked the cold voice at the other end of the receiver.

'F-f-f-f-ine!' answered Victor, trying to keep his newly acquired stutter in check.

'Glad to hear it.'

'W-w-when can I get my daughter back? I've given you everything you asked for: the names, times, dates and places.'

'Mr Whitelaw, calm down, I've told you, she'll be safely back in your arms by the end of the week. Providing, of course, that the information you supplied me with is kosher and you don't involve the police. As I've said before, I have no intention of harming her.'

'Now I suggest you pull yourself together before I hand the phone over to your daughter.'

As Mary talked to her father from the cellar, the man in the mask stood in the room above her. He looked out of a crack in the boarded up window of the disused fish smoking house towards the cold grey North Sea. He hated involving an innocent in his plans, but it was a necessity. He had found out during his investigations that Victor Whitelaw had been paid off. Hush money was a good incentive to keep schtum. So, he needed to put some pressure on Mr Whitelaw and that pressure came in the shape of his daughter Mary. He'd been honest with the man though, he really did have no intention of harming the girl. He had his names, or should he say, intended victims. But releasing the girl now might give Victor the idea of going to the police, better to keep her hostage until he'd completed his task and the bastards were all taken care of. He owed it to Clara, he'd promised her. How could he refuse the last wish of his wife with whom he had shared his life with for the last fifty-two years?

He reached for his backpack and withdrew the card. After putting it in the self-sealing envelope, he wrote a name on the front.

Once Mary had finished her phone call to her father he'd deliver it. He wanted them to know he was coming for them. He wanted them jittery.

*

Darryl Morrison switched on his computer and rubbed

his eyes. The florescent lighting high above him in the office was giving him a migraine. 'Never mind,' he thought to himself, 'it'll soon be lunchtime.' He hoped there'd be a lull in the weather as he had an errand to run. He checked his e-mails, nothing exciting there, so he made his way to his internal mailbox. Nothing there either, apart from a few Christmas cards from his colleagues. He picked them up but decided to open them later. Darryl walked downstairs to the coffee machine to kill some time before he made the car trip to pick up his daughter from the train station. Sarah was coming home from university for the holidays and he was looking forward to seeing her. She hadn't exactly left in the best of moods thanks to a stupid argument he'd started. They'd made it up over the phone since, thankfully, so everything was set for a relaxed family Christmas. Even his youngest daughter Annie was looking forward to Sarah's return home, and they usually fought like cat and dog.

He smiled to himself as he walked past the brightly decorated Christmas tree in the office and listened intently as the radio told him how it wished it could be Christmas every day.

Life was good, he thought to himself, as he put down his coffee and picked up the phone to call his wife.

'Hi, darling, I take it Sarah caught her train all right.'

'Yeah, she just phoned, it looks like she'll be arriving early. Any chance you can take your break early to save her from standing around freezing at the station?'

'Shouldn't be a problem, I'll leave right away.'

'By the way, Annie's made some Christmas cakes, we've been baking all morning.'

'Tell her I'm looking forward to them. I'll see you when I drop off Sarah … Oh! I almost forgot, you couldn't do me a favour, could you?'

'What sort of favour?'

'I need some Christmas cards, folk keep leaving them on my desk or sticking them in my pigeon hole and I haven't any to hand back. I got another three this morning.'

'I'll get you them this afternoon but remember to write them out this year. You didn't last Christmas.'

'I'll write them out tonight. I promise.'

Humming the Christmas song he'd heard on the radio earlier, Darryl ran down the two flights of stairs to the car park. He put up his hood against the wind chill and after fumbling in his jacket pocket for his car keys he pressed the button to unlock the car, but the door was already unlocked.

'Strange!', he thought. 'I'm sure I locked it this morning. Oh well'. He jumped into the driver's seat, fastened his seat belt and put his key in the ignition.

Darryl never saw Christmas, never got his freshly baked Christmas cakes, nor did he pick up his daughter at the train station. Just as he was admiring the snow-covered pine trees that surrounded the car park the car bomb's explosion rattled windows and doors all across the building, leaving Darryl and his car a burning mess in the middle of the cold, grey, slush-covered car park.

Chapter Eight

'Right,' said Buchanan. 'Now we're all here, who wants to start us off ... Joe?'

Joe Styles took out his horn rimmed glasses from the pocket of his pinstriped waistcoat, perched them on the end of his nose and then opened his old battered leather Gladstone bag he carried everywhere with him. He took out a note book, looked at the other three people around the table in turn, making sure he had their interest, before scratching his huge walrus moustache and begining to relay his findings in his own inimitable way.

'The body was quite remarkable. The best example of Adipocere I've ever seen in all my years of medical studies.'

'Adipo what?' asked Max.

'Corpse Wax,' said the quiet female voice in the corner.

'Very good, Miss Atkins,' said Joe as he gave the young WPC an admiring look. 'You're obviously far too intelligent for these two.'

He nodded towards Buchanan and Max.

The young police officer's face turned beetroot red.

'I'll show you,' replied Joe as he reached for his inside pocket and produced his mobile phone.

'If you could just bear with me,' he said, as he flicked through the phone's photo album.

'Obviously, I couldn't take the file and photos with me

from the lab but I took a couple on my phone's camera, I couldn't resist.' He handed his phone to Max. 'Pass it around, Sergeant, don't be shy, let everyone have a look.'

After both Max and the WPC screwed up their faces at the sight before them, Buchanan took his turn and looked at the photo of the dead girl's body.

'Jesus, what happened to her? She looks like a giant candle.'

'As I said,' replied Joe. 'Adipocere. Or as Miss Atkins just reliably informed us, also known as corpse wax, Sometimes grave wax. Occasionally, the body's decomposition takes - for want of a better phrase - a strange turn, and the fat in the soft tissue transforms into the hardy soap-like substance you can see in the photos I just showed you. It typically happens when the body is contained in a moist environment. I have a working hypothesis. Based on the fact that she was found wrapped up in polythene I can only assume the body was wet when it was wrapped up. Then the moisture was obviously sealed in by the plastic sheeting.'

'How about the injuries?' asked Buchanan. 'Do they back up Mr Jackson's story?'

'They do actually, thanks to the adipocere, the body was quite well preserved, cause of death was internal bleeding to the brain. So the fact that she stood up after the accident and managed to converse with Mr and Mrs Jackson before taking a fit and dying would fit with my findings. One thing bothers me, though.'

'What's that, Doc?'

'The moisture inside the polythene, as I said earlier, it could have been down to her body being wet when it was

65

wrapped up … but it could just as easily be down to the fact that she was still breathing.'

The Doc took a sip of his whisky.

'It's impossible to tell I'm afraid. I'm having a hard enough job determining time of death.'

'Bastards!' said Buchanan.

'Max, get another round in, then you can come back and tell us what you found out at Mrs Jackson's work place.'

'Not much to tell really,' said Max getting to his feet, 'although, there is one thing I guarantee will freak you out.'

As Max left to get the drinks in, Buchanan turned to PC Atkins.

'Corpse Wax! How the hell did you know about that, Jenny? The Doc and I would love to know.'

'I saw it on a rerun of an old CSI episode the other night, sir.'

'I fucking hate that franchise,' said Joe Styles.

'Jesus, Doc,' said Buchanan. 'In all the time I've known you, that's the first time I've heard you swear.'

'Well, their forensic techniques are beyond belief, especially when it comes down to the bloody autopsies. It gives us a bad name. Thanks to that bloody programme everyone thinks we can find out the cause of death instantly, especially the press. In real life it's sometimes a long drawn out process but not on that fucking programme. Take toxicology results. They seem to get their answer in minutes. You know as well as I, Ronnie, it can take days for christ's sake, occasionally weeks. Mind you I liked the Grissom character. Never been the same since he left.'

'So, you do watch it then?' said Jenny.

'Occasionally. But only because my wife likes it.'

Buchanan laughed into his pint.

'Doc,' said Jenny, unwrapping a crumpled piece of paper from her pocket. 'Sorry, you don't mind me calling you Doc, do you?'

'Feel free. Everyone else does.'

'Did you manage to get a rough age on the girl?'

'Late teens early twenties maybe.'

'Any sign of old injuries to the body?'

'There was actually, an old fracture to her left leg, probably happened in her youth.'

'The tibia?'

'How the hell did you know that?'

She turned to Buchanan. 'Sally Adams.'

'What?'

'Her name is Sally Adams, I'm sure it is. I did what you asked, sir. Checked back on missing persons, sorted them into age groups then sourced their medical records. She fits the time frame and matches the injury. She broke her leg skiing in Austria when she was fourteen.'

Buchanan clapped his hands together as Joe Styles burst into laughter.

'I'm growing fond of you, Miss Atkins, you've just proved you deserve your reputation,' said Buchanan.

Her face went beetroot yet again as Max approached the table with the drinks.

'What's going on here, then?'

Buchanan pursed his lips and drew in a deep breath as he picked up his fresh pint.

'You have a hard act to follow, son, so put down the rest of the drinks and tell us what you found out on your travels this morning.'

After telling them about the interviews he'd had with the staff at Emily Jackson's place of work, Max produced the card he'd carefully wrapped up in the evidence bag.

'Another bloody rose,' said Buchanan, sighing to himself.

'That's not all, sir, it was hand delivered and it's got a strange message inside.'

'What sort of message?'

'It's in Latin, it says an eye for an eye.'

Joe Styles whistled.

'Looks like you've got your hands full with this case, Ronnie. It's like a plot from a Hitchcock movie.'

'Aye, and I'm playing the lead,' answered Buchanan, taking a mouthful of his pint.

'I don't suppose they kept the envelope, did they, Max?'

'No, she chucked it.'

'What's the significance of the rose? Anyone any ideas?' asked Buchanan. The table grew silent. 'Oh, come on people, it's obviously some sort of signature. A unique way of the killer to mark his work, but what's the relevance?'

They all looked blank.

'I take it you're working on it being a revenge type thing,' said Joe. 'in response to the accidental killing of the girl?'

'You're the second person that's said that to me today, Doc. I suppose, it definitely looks a possibility, but it just seems, you know, like it's too clear cut somehow.'

'Seems pretty straight forward to me,' said Joe, 'you know what they say, if you hear hooves.'

'Think horses not zebras,' interrupted Buchanan.

'There's a few things on the meaning of a single rose here,' said Jenny staring at the screen of her mobile phone. 'I googled it, it says here it usually signifies a message of love. It's been used for that sort of thing since Roman times.'

'We all know that one. Anything else?' asked Buchanan.

'It also says that early Christians at one time adopted the rose as a symbol of Christ and his suffering, the five petals representing the five wounds of Christ. It could have some sort of religious connotation, sir.'

'A bible thumping sniper? Doubtful, but then again the message in the card - an eye for an eye ... that sounds a bit biblical right enough.'

PC Atkins fingers once again sped over the keypad on her phone.

'It comes from the old testament. Seemingly the words came from God himself. The whole quote is "an eye for an eye, a tooth for a tooth". It says here it was given as a means of proper balance in punishment for crimes committed among the Israelites.'

'You're a mine of information, Miss Atkins,' said Joe Styles.

'It's not really me, I just seem to be naturally gifted at looking shit up online. Oops! Sorry, sir, pardon my foul mouth.'

Her three companions laughed.

'You'll be swearing a lot more by the time you're finished working with us,' said Max.

'I hardly ever swore before I started working with the inspector here, then one day I thought, fuck it! When in Rome …'

The table once more erupted in laughter.

Buchanan picked up PC Atkin's mobile phone.

'Fancy looking piece of kit! That makes my phone look ancient, your screen is about three times the size of the one on my relic. Could I do my food shopping on that thing?' asked Buchanan. 'It would save me having to physically go to a supermarket. I hate them fucking places.'

'Of course you can, as long as you have a credit card.'

Their conversation was interrupted by the high pitched trimming of Joe Style's mobile. He put one finger in his ear to cut out the background noise and took the call. The rest of them watched as he listened silently then stood up with an incredulous look on his face.

'You're joking! Where? How long ago?'

He put down his mobile still wearing a shocked look on his face.

'You won't believe this. There's been a car bomb

explosion in the car park at Woodhill House.'

Buchanan rubbed his chin. 'A sniper victim and a bombing victim within a day of each other, that can't be a coincidence. Who's on the case, Doc?'

'Rennie. I'm just off to confirm the death, seems a bit pointless, mind. The victim's in a pile of charred pieces from what I've heard.'

Buchanan downed the rest of his Guinness.

'Max. You're with me, let's go and see if this in anyway ties into our case. PC Atkins, you go and dig up the dental records of, what did you say her name was?'

'Sally Adams, sir.'

'Get a hold of Sally's dentist and see if you can confirm an identity.'

'I'm on it, sir.'

'Looks like my shopping's going to have to wait again.' said Buchanan.

'Well, Doc, your car or ours?'

'Mine of course, all my equipment's in the back.'

Joe Styles handed the car keys to Max.

'If anyone can get us there quickly, it's you, Sergeant.'

'I'll follow behind in our motor,' said Buchanan. 'It'll save us having to cadge a lift later.'

Chapter Nine

Various photos were being taken of the body and the surrounding area when Buchanan arrived at the crime scene, a good five minutes behind the other two. The flash of the cameras lit up the dull grey sky like flashes of lightning as he made his way towards the police cordon. The air smelt strange, a mixture of pine trees and burning. Joe Styles was suiting up as Buchanan, his breath visible in the cold air, walked over towards Max and Rennie. The overweight inspector was bent over engrossed in wiping something off his shoe with a dirty-looking handkerchief. Never known for his sartorial elegance, his rotund body was wrapped up in a ridiculously huge bright-red raincoat that matched his bright-red face. Add that to his white beard and he looked like Santa Claus without the fur. He looked up at Buchanan with his large rheumy eyes.

'All right, Bob, how's the stomach?' asked Buchanan as he bent down and ducked under the neon crime scene tape. A cold drop of water dripped down onto the back of his neck making him shiver.

'Buchanan! I never expected to see you here. I thought you'd have enough on your plate between your sniper and the two dead women.'

'I have a hunch they could be related.'

Rennie, never shy at dropping a case if he could get away with it, perked up at these words.

'Do you think so? It would suit me if it did. I'm supposed to be on holiday in a couple of days. I could do without this shit!'

Max glared at him and shook his head.

'Lazy bastard!' he said under his breath.

'So, what do we know so far?' asked Buchanan.

Buchanan watched incredulously as he used the same rag he'd used to clean his shoe to clear his nose.

'Somebody placed a car bomb under the driver's seat, must have blown up as soon as he got in, the guy is in bits. A young PC found one of his feet over fifty yards away,' Rennie pointed behind him, 'that's him over there puking his guts up.'

Buchanan spotted a camera on a pole nestled between two fir trees at the corner of the car park.

'I assume you've checked the CCTV.'

'Aye, I thought we might be lucky. Someone saw some old guy picking up litter in this part of the car park earlier when they arrived for work this morning, said he'd never seen him before, but the bloody cameras are that steamed up with the weather, you can't see fuck all.'

'I'd get a copy anyway, if it was me, then I'd see if the lab could maybe clean up the footage. Get on to Steve Kershaw - he'll sort you out.'

'Smart thinking, I'll maybe do that.'

'Did you get a description of him?'

'He says he looked like any normal old guy, well from what he could see of him.'

'What do you mean by that?'

'The witness said he had his hood up and a scarf over his face. He didn't think much of it at the time. I mean, look at the weather, he might have just been freezing, I know I am.'

Buchanan thought for a minute.

'Get someone on to the council, see if they sent one of their employees over here this morning to pick up the litter and get back to me. He might have just been doing his job, but it's a bit of a coincidence that the old guy was hanging around this particular part of the car park.'

'Will do, Ronnie.'

'Do you mind if Max and I have a look at his office?'

'Knock yourself out. I had a look already, fuck all of interest there. A few Christmas cards from workmates but bugger all else. He keeps his workspace immaculate. He must have been a neat freak.'

At the mention of the word "cards", Buchanan looked worriedly at Max.

'Let's go and have a look, son.'

They headed towards the back door of the building just as the snow started up again.

'Ronnie!' shouted Joe Styles as they passed the burnt out wreck of the car.

Buchanan and Max both stopped in their tracks.

The Doc eased his white plastic covered body out from what was left of the rear door of the motor.

'You look like you could do with a hand, in fact here's one here.'

He held up the blackened, shrivelled hand that had been blown off the bomb victim and laughed.

Buchanan shook his head.

'That's just sick, Doc.'

As they walked up the stairs towards Darryl's office, Max turned to Buchanan.

'Why do you always help out that useless bastard, sir?'

'You mean Rennie?'

'Aye.'

'Simple … he brews his own ale, Max.'

'What?'

'He brews his own ale. He makes a particularly good dark bitter, his own recipe. Every time he makes a batch, he drops me off a dozen or so bottles.'

'That's it? He gives you free beer and you help him solve most of his cases.'

'Simple as that, Max, it's what I like to call a symbiotic relationship.'

*

Darryl Morrison's office was tiny. It contained a desk, a laptop computer, a small bookcase containing half a dozen files, a small printer and not much else. Three Christmas cards lay on the windowsill next to a picture of a man, a woman and two kids. Buchanan assumed the guy was Darryl. He'd check with his workmates on the way out just to make sure. The Christmas cards were still in their envelopes.

Two simply said Darryl, the other to Mr Darryl Anderson

esquire.

'That's a bit strange, don't you think, Max? Let me see that card you found this morning.'

After removing it from his inside pocket Max handed it over to Buchanan.

'Be back in a minute, Max.'

Buchanan headed along the corridor until he found a larger office where three old women sat at their computers.

'Any of you lovely ladies have a pair of tweezers on you?'

They all reached for their handbags in unison.

'They should be sitting round a cauldron', he thought to himself.

The oldest woman of the three, she looked about ninety, got hers out first.

'Cheers, I'll give you them back in five minutes.'

He walked over to a small desk in the corner of the room to examine the card as the three witches looked on.

Five minutes later he arrived back at Darryl's office to find Max perusing the files.

'Anything interesting?'

'Extremely!' replied Max. 'The guy worked as a Children's Reporter. His remit was to investigates cases of unruly kids or kids at risk and decide whether or not compulsory measures of supervision may be required.'

'What the fuck does that mean?'

'Well basically, he referred kids to the Children's Panel.

But get this. The panel, according to this, recruits committed volunteers from all walks of life. There's a list here of the panel members. Check the second name, sir.'

Buchanan put on his reading glasses and looked at the name Max was pointing to. Emily Jackson.

'Jesus! Have you checked his laptop?'

'I tried, but it is password protected.'

'Give it another go Max, I've got a phone call to make.'

Walking back out to the corridor Buchanan took out his mobile and phoned PC Atkins.

'Jenny, you seem to be quite savvy with all this technology stuff, how are you at cracking passwords?'

'What sort, sir?'

'I'm trying to access a laptop but it's protected.'

'Not a problem, I have a few programmes on my pen-stick that'll do it.'

'I had a feeling you might. How you getting on with the dental records, by the way?'

'I've been and got a copy from her dentist, I'm just waiting on Joe Styles getting back to have a look at them.'

'Great work. Can you meet me and Max back at mine about tea time? We've discovered some stuff of our own, we can go over it, and it'll keep you in the loop.'

'Cheers, sir.'

'By the way, how are your cooking skills?'

'I do a mean curry; I'm famed for my lamb Rogan Josh.'

'Sounds good, pick up the ingredients on the way to mine, I'll square you up when I see you. I'm looking forward to a proper meal.'

'No problem, sir.'

He returned to the office to find Max still beavering away on the computer.

'Any luck?'

'Bugger all!' sighed Max.

'Right, take it with us. We'll hand it in to forensics.'

'I'll hand it to them on the way out,' said Max as he picked up the laptop.

'Not so fast, son. We'll take it in ourselves, in the morning.'

'Why the morning, sir?'

'It'll give us time to give it the once-over tonight back at mine.'

'Sir!'

'Stop panicking, Max. I'll just conveniently leave it in the car overnight. No harm done. I'll hand it in in the morning. I'll take full responsibility. Besides you know as well as me that if we put this through the proper channels, it could be days before we have access to the information it contains. Days in which our mad sniper, bomber bastard could get up to anything. We do it my way and we get a head start. Now stick it under your jacket and follow me. We have a dinner date tonight.'

'What?'

'Jenny's cooking a curry.'

They left the office and headed towards the stairs.

'Where did you get off to anyway, sir?'

Buchanan didn't hear the question. He was lost in thought.

'It's definitely the same guy, Max.'

'How do you mean?'

Buchanan pulled out the Christmas card in the envelope along with the card that Max had picked up that morning, only now, although still in the polythene evidence bag it was folded over the other way, the writing facing outwards.

'What do you see?'

Max looked from one to the other.

'The writing, sir, it's the same.'

'Exactly, Max. I bet once forensics opens this, they'll find out it's not a Christmas card.'

'No, it'll be another one of that bastard's calling cards.'

'It's a real pity we can't take a peek ourselves but I don't want to bugger up the forensics. They might find his DNA on the envelope, well if it's not a self-sealer that is.'

'What about the other card? The one I found this morning. You might have smudged a viable print on that when you opened it up, sir.'

'Impossible, Max, I used tweezers.'

'Where the fuck did he get tweezers?' Max thought as they walked back down stairs towards the car park.

After reminding the doc to check out the dental records,

Buchanan went to find Rennie. He'd sent Max straight back to the car with the computer.

'Any luck on our litter picker, Bob?'

'Fuck all! But he's not a council employee. They send a couple of guys round here twice a week. Neither one's an old guy and today's not one of their days. Do you think he was the bomber?'

'Bomber and sniper, Bob, I'm pretty sure of it. Looks like our cases are one and the same so you'd better make your way back to headquarters with me. We'll brief the team.'

'Sounds good, I'll meet you back there,' replied Bob.

'Just give me a few minutes to tie things up.'

Just as Max and Buchanan were heading back to town, an old man in a baseball hat and sun glasses approached the luxury flat complex in the west end. He pressed the services button with a gloved hand to gain entry, paused to admire the well maintained foyer and then proceeded to climb the stairway to the third floor. He found apartment 3D and posted the card through the letterbox. He knew no one was at home, he'd phoned ahead just to make sure. Then, after making his way back downstairs with the speed of a man half his age, he turned around, looked back up the stairs and in a quiet menacing voice he said to himself, 'I'll see you soon, Mr Dalrymple'.

Chapter Ten

The pale moon sat silently in the clear dark sky, looking down on the heavy blanket of snow that muffled the noise of the traffic on the main road outside Ronnie Buchanan's home. He stood in the doorway smoking a cigarette. Michelle never allowed him to smoke in the house, she complained about the smell it left behind and the way the smoke discoloured the walls and curtains. Even though she wasn't here at the moment, after much deliberation he had decided to honour their agreement.

He watched as Vince, next door's cat, looked up at him from beneath a frost covered rhododendron bush and flashed across the garden. The cat looked even blacker than usual against the clean white background.

The neighbours had only got the pet a few months ago. They'd asked him what he thought of the name Vince. He'd declined to answer. He didn't particularly like that name, he had good reason not to.

The cat ran across his path again leaving small paw prints in the snow.

'Isn't that supposed to be lucky?' he thought to himself.

He hoped so, he felt like he might need a bit of luck on this case.

As he relished the exotic smell of Jenny's cooking emanating from deeper inside the house, he thought back to the team briefing he and Rennie had given the team that afternoon. The identity of the young girl's body had been confirmed and two officers had been despatched to inform her parents. A job he'd always detested.

She was, or rather, had been, a nineteen-year old student named Sally Adams. Jonathan Jackson had been right on one point, she had just left the nearby pub but she wasn't drunk, she worked there a couple of nights a week to subsidise her grant. Ironically, she shouldn't have been working on that particular night. She had swapped shifts with another workmate.

It looked like he'd been right enough though, the Jackson's guilty secret was looking more and more like a coincidence and less and less to do with the main case. He couldn't see how Darryl Morrison could possibly be tied to the body that had been buried in the Jackson's holiday home however hard he tried. He'd had people searching for a connection all afternoon to no avail, so he'd decided to put that on the back burner for the moment and concentrate on the main case.

It had also been agreed from high up that more officers were to be provided to him and Rennie, who would work the case in tandem for the moment. At least until the end of the week, when Rennie would be off to sunnier climes on his annual leave.

They had mutually decided that Rennie would be in charge of the grunt work which involved, amongst other things, sending out a legion of officers to canvass the areas around where Emily Jackson and Darryl Morrison had been killed to see if anyone had spotted anything suspicious. The houses in the immediate vicinity of the ski slope had already been done with no success the night of Emily's death, but the target area would now be expanded. The irony of the phrase target area hadn't been lost on Buchanan.

A few officers would also be despatched to all the greeting card shops in Aberdeen to see if they stocked the rose cards, and if so, see if they could remember anyone buying a few recently. They knew it was a long shot, you could buy cards anywhere nowadays, newsagents, supermarkets, wherever. You could even design them on a computer and print them off yourself as PC Atkins had mentioned during the briefing. But they had agreed that it was worth a try.

He took a long drag on his cigarette and blew the smoke into the cold night air.

Just as a final precaution, in case they'd been bought out-with Aberdeen, he had advised Rennie that he should maybe expand the search nationwide. A few folk manning the phones in the incident room could see to that end.

That left Buchanan and his small trusted team to have free reign to work on whatever they wanted to relating to the case, which suited him just fine. It's how he liked to work. It's how he'd planned it out for himself, if the truth be known.

He smiled to himself as he took one last draw and expertly flicked what was left of his cigarette over the garden gate, out into the snow covered pavement beyond. He was supposed to be cutting down on the smoking, he'd promised Michelle, but he was always the same when he got stuck into a new case. Masses of coffee and cigarettes, he couldn't function otherwise.

'Fuck it!'

He reached down behind the door, picked up the pint glass and took a large gulp of Rennie's homemade dark ale.

Beautiful, he thought to himself as he smacked his lips and pulled another cigarette from the packet. He removed his lighter from his trouser pocket and lit it up as Vince looked on with bright yellow luminous eyes from the far corner of the garden.

*

As Buchanan was topping up on nicotine, Max and PC Atkins sat in the living room with some drinks of their own. The atmosphere was tense and awkward; they didn't know each other very well. They'd got on like a house on fire when Max was helping her prepare the curry in the kitchen. They'd both laughed as the tears ran down Max's face as he was peeling the onions but now, in the relative silence of the sitting room, the dynamic had changed.

It didn't help that they were attracted to each other. Although neither of them would dare allow themselves to let the other one know.

'So, how long have you worked with Inspector Buchanan, Max?' asked Jenny, breaking the silence.

Max sat up straight in the brown leather arm chair.

'Quite a while now actually. Maybe two years or so, he can be a bit strange at times.'

'Why the fuck did I say that,' he thought.

He rubbed his palms on his trousers, they were getting clammy.

'Unorthodox is the word I'd use,' said Jenny. 'He has some record though, his success rate, I mean.'

'Oh yeah, it's second to none. That's why so many folk put up with his strange methods. Nine times out of ten he gets the job done, that's why the higher ups turn a blind eye to him.'

'You like him, don't you, Max?'

'I admire him and I love working with him.'

Their stunted conversation was interrupted by Buchanan entering the room.

'How are you two lovebirds getting on then?'

He paused long enough to allow both their faces to turn bright red as he knew they would, he'd been watching their interaction all day.

'Your faces talk volumes,' he said as he went through to the kitchen for another beer with a wicked grin on his face.

*

Mary woke up in her makeshift bed in the cellar trembling, her body covered in a cold sweat. She'd dreamed that she was being chased by the devil down an endless corridor. She remembered the dream vividly. It was a full on devil too, not just a guy in a mask. He had a goats head, horns, the works. He must have jumped straight out of a Dennis Wheatley novel and hidden himself away in her subconscious until called upon to terrify her in her sleep. She'd seen a picture of him somewhere before, the goat of Mendes, the devil himself.

Jesus, she was creeping herself out. When she finally got out of here she was going to cut back on watching and reading all that horror stuff. She still couldn't shake off some of the images replaying in her head though.

There had been hundreds of doors on each side of the corridor in her dream, all red, all smoking as if at any minute they might burst into flames. Also, every time she had tried to open one it was locked solid. The funny shaped lamps that looked like misshapen human skulls hanging from chains above her as she ran had cast strange shadows along the chequered mosaic floor and there'd been some weird psychedelic sitar music playing in the background.

She shook her head to clear it then walked over to the small sink in the corner accompanied by the ever present jangling of the heavy chain around her leg. She ran the tap and used the small facecloth provided her to wipe her face and the back of her neck. She shivered, not on account of the cellar being cold; she'd been left a small portable gas heater that had been practically going full blast since she'd taken up her new accommodation. It was the dampness that got to her. She could feel it in her bones and she was developing a horrible hacking cough. She had noticed earlier that when she touched certain parts of the brickwork round about her; her hand would come away wet.

A thought suddenly occurred to her. She went back to the foot of her bed where her plates and utensils lay from the meal she'd had earlier on. After picking up the desert spoon she wandered over to the corner of the cellar where her chain was attached to the wall. The thick metal eyelet was screwed heavily into the wall but the mortar round about was soaking, she could practically see the dampness running down the wall. She chipped away at the surrounding area with the business end of the spoon and to her utter amazement small pieces of the wall started coming away.

'At last some hope', she thought to herself as she moved her shackles, got herself into a comfortable position and settled down to the long job ahead of her.

Chapter Eleven

'Jesus! I'm stuffed,' said Buchanan, as he picked up the last piece of freshly-baked naan bread and eagerly wiped up the last of the spicy pungent sauce from his plate.

'That was some curry, Jenny. I wish Michelle could cook like that.'

'I gathered you liked it when you started on your third helping, sir,' replied Jenny, secretly pleased she'd impressed her new boss.

Max shook his head and laughed from across the large oak dining table.

'I've always thought Michelle was a good cook. The odd meal I've had here has been nice enough.'

'Odd meal is an interesting choice of words, Max. You ought to see some of the strange dishes I come home to. Don't get me wrong, Max,' said Buchanan through a mouthful of naan, 'certain things she cooks, she makes very well, her steak pie is excellent, but when it comes to anything exotic, like curry for instance, she always has a habit of totally fucking it up. God knows what she does wrong, she does her best to follow the recipes to the letter but she always knackers something up, they always seem to come out tasting peculiar. What is it she tried the other day …? Ah, Hungarian goulash came out tasting really sweet, the recipe called for a teaspoon of sugar to be added, god knows how much she put it but it tasted like beef in Coca-Cola.'

He pointed at him.

'Don't tell her I told you that mind.'

'My lips are sealed,' replied Max, making a locking motion at the side of his mouth.

'Right, I'm off for a fag. By the way, how is that programme of yours getting on, Jenny?' asked Buchanan as he picked up the pack of cigarettes.

'I'll just check on it, sir, after I've cleared the table.'

'No problem. Max, Jenny just cooked us a delicious meal. We can't expect her to do the washing up as well. Where's your manners? Give her a hand to clear up and load the dishwasher. There's plenty beer in the fridge, help yourselves when you're finished.'

*

'So, what is this programme?' asked Max as he stared at the rectangular box on the black screen.

He watched as hundreds of green letters and numbers scrolled across the screen at a rate of knots.

'It's called Da Vinci, it's a code breaker.'

'I get it. Like the film, *The Da Vinci Code*.'

'Exactly.'

'Nice name. How does it work?'

'It's quite simple really; the programme contains a huge database of words, names and figures. It just uses them one after another, in quick succession. It tries to match them up starting with the most common first.'

'It must take ages.'

'Not as long as you would think it might, most people

are lazy when it comes to passwords, they tend to use family names, pet names, their date of birth, that type of thing. They just don't think. If you really want to be safe make sure you use a mixture of letters and numbers, and, for extra security, make the letters a mixture of upper and lower cases.'

'I'll keep that in mind,' replied Max.

Jenny had just finished her explanation when the laptop's screen came to life with a high pitched ping. The wallpaper showed a photo of a middle aged man and woman with two teenage girls.

'Mr Morrison, I presume,' said PC Atkins.

'He certainly looks a good deal healthier than the last time I saw him,' replied Max.

Jenny playfully dug her elbow into his ribs.

'Looks like we're in, Max. Now let's see what secrets we can unfold.'

*

'You bastard!' screamed Mary as she stretched her fingers.

The joints in her hands were aching with the repetitive jagging of the spoon against the wall and her knuckles were grazed all over. She was getting somewhere though, her hard work was paying off, the steel eyelet fastening the chain to the wall was finally coming loose, if she pulled hard enough on it at the right angle she could move it ever so slightly from side to side.

She stopped for a break. Sitting down with her back against the wall she drank down her bottle of mineral water in three huge gulps. Her thirst quenched, she switched her attention to the television in the corner of the room. It was tuned to the Sky news channel.

It was the second time she had seen the car bomb report, she still couldn't believe it, at her father's place of work too. She'd recognised the car park the moment she'd seen it. They had confirmed that the victim was male, but they hadn't released his name yet, so she wasn't sure if it was a workmate of his or not. She knew quite a few of his colleagues; they were often invited round for a drink at the weekend. Well, they used to be, before mum had buggered off and left her father in a right mess. He wasn't interested in socialising much nowadays. His only constant companion recently had been a bottle of malt. He just sat there each night under a great cloud of depression. It was palpable; she felt it every time she walked into the sitting room. He looked like a man who had lost his soul.

Mary let out a sigh and threw her empty water bottle across the room. It bounced of the wall and landed dead centre in the small bucket.

'Oh well, back to the grind.'

She wiped her forehead, which was dripping with sweat, with the bottom of her T-shirt, tucked her hair behind her ears, took a deep breath and continued with her task.

She looked up at the crudely drawn devil face on the wall. She'd drawn it earlier with an eye liner pencil and some lipstick and stuck it up there to give herself some incentive.

She spat in its direction.

'Fuck you and your devil mask!'

*

'How many cases?' asked Buchanan incredulously as he warmed his hands on the radiator.

'Over six hundred, sir,' replied Max. 'It's not just his stuff; it's everything that's been referred to the whole department.'

'They go back years, too,' interrupted Jenny.

Buchanan stared at the laptop screen.

'Can you filter them down a bit?'

'That's what I'm doing now; I'm looking for the ones that Mr Morrison personally referred. Here we go. Shit! There's still over a hundred and sixty cases here, we'll be here all night at this rate.'

'Maybe not,' said Buchanan.

'Look for cases that he referred, where Emily Jackson sat on the panel.'

PC Atkins' fingers were a blur as she expertly keyed in the information.

'Twenty-eight, sir.'

'Now we're getting somewhere,' said Max. 'We ought to be able to read our way through these tonight if we split them up between us.'

'I've got my netbook in my bag,' said Jenny.

'And the DI's got a laptop,' continued Max. 'We'll take a few cases each.'

'I wonder.' said Buchanan thinking aloud to himself. 'A rose by any other name. Where does that come from?'

'Shakespeare, sir,' replied Jenny. 'A rose by any other

name would still smell as sweet. It's from *Romeo and Juliet*.'

Buchanan appeared lost in thought.

'What is it, sir?' asked Max and Jenny in unison. They both took their eyes off the screen and looked expectantly at Buchanan. He was sitting at the dining table scribbling something in his notebook.

'We could be looking at this rose thing from the completely wrong angle. Like Joe Styles said earlier. When you hear hooves think ...?'

'Horses, not zebras,' replied his colleagues in unison.

'I know this probably seems far too obvious but try cross referencing. Emily Jackson, Darryl Morrison and the word rose, it could simply be a name, indulge me.'

Jenny once again typed in the information as the three of them waited with baited breath. After what seemed like an age, a single folder appeared on the desk top.

Rose Reeder.

'Unbelievable!' said Max, shaking his head as Buchanan threw him a wink and polished off the last of his ale.

'Click it open, Miss Atkins, if you'd be so kind.'

The folder contained two files: "Background & Case Evidence" and "Melissa".

'Where do you want to start, sir?' asked PC Atkins, her fingers readily poised above the keyboard.

'Take your pick,' answered Buchanan.

As she clicked on the file marked "Background", over a dozen pages of information magically filled the screen and Rose's past came to life in front of their eyes.

Chapter Twelve

Rose was born in Canada in 1988. She'd been an only child, brought up on a small family run farm in Toronto. Three generations of the Reid family stayed in the one home, her grandparents Harry and Clara, who had emigrated there from Scotland, and her parents Frank and Melissa.

Some would say it was an almost idyllic existence; granted they worked long hours, side by side tending their land, not so much Harry to whom the day to day running of the farm was more of a side-line to his government job, a job he never talked about much, but they reaped the rewards. The vegetable farm had a large annual turnover, so they lived well, very well compared to some of their nearby neighbours.

Rose was an intelligent girl and had done extremely well at school, she'd come top of the class at art and all her teachers predicted great things ahead for her. However, when she hit the age of fourteen, everything changed.

She'd gone to the local picture house, same as she did every Friday night. She and a friend were awaiting their usual lift home. Alternating weeks, the parents of one or the other would be waiting outside the cinema to pick the two girls up. However, on that particular night things, were slightly different. It was Rose's parents turn to pick them up but there was no car waiting for them at the usual place. Instead, the street outside the cinema was awash with flashing police lights, the sirens cutting through the cold night air. It was Rose's friend Jane who realised that the mangled heap of twisted metal lying in the middle of the road had originally been her friend's parent's red station wagon.

Only later on that night, after the police had phoned her grandparents to come and take her home, had she learned the full story of what had happened.

The guy had been drunk at the wheel of his truck; her parents hadn't stood a chance. The truck driver had ploughed into them as they were waiting outside the cinema to pick her up. They'd both died instantly. He'd escaped with a couple of broken ribs.

Rose took it hard, she and her parents had been very close. Her grandparents had to have her sedated for days after the tragedy. She even missed the funeral, her grandparent's decision. A decision she would hold against them for many years.

After the funeral, she really started to go off the rails. The young girl skipped school, started hanging out with a bad crowd, got involved in drugs and eventually, a couple of years after the tragedy, she cracked. She was diagnosed with extreme paranoia and spent six months in a sanatorium.

Whether the mental breakdown was caused by the heavy drug use or the tragic death of her parents, no one could really say, a mixture of both, most of the doctors seemed to think. Her mind, already fragile from the tragedy, had been tipped over the edge thanks to the prolonged heavy drug use.

However, very slowly, she managed to pull herself back from the brink of madness, got herself off the drugs and finally returned to the family farm and the loving arms of her grandparents.

She went back to school and with a lot of hard work, she

managed to catch up with all the education she had missed and passed her grades with flying colours. Her grandparents were ecstatic and so proud of the way she had turned her life around. So much so, in fact, they decided to fund her further education. They told her she could pick any university she liked. She surprised them both by choosing the King's College in Aberdeen. She decided on there as it was quite close to where her ancestors had grown up. The interview had gone well and thanks to her good grades, she was in.

So, on a warm September day, her grandparents drove her to the airport and saw her on to the plane that carried Rose off to a bright new future.

Rose loved the University from the minute she set eyes on the place. Tucked away on its own grounds in the centre of the old part of Aberdeen, the building had stood on the same place for hundreds of years. She threw herself into her studies and left little time for socialisation, preferring to spend her free time visiting various places in Scotland that her grandfather had told her so much about. She did however become quite close to another student on the same course, Eric Reeder. They got on like a house on fire, they had the same interests in music and literature, Eric even had an uncle in Canada that he visited quite regularly so she could even discuss places relating to her home with him, places that Eric had often visited himself.

During her second year of study, she took Eric home with her to visit her grandparents on the farm. Eric and her grandfather hit it off from the word go. Her grandmother, however, seemed slightly less enamoured with the situation. She thought that the relationship might interfere with Rose's studies. She did warm to him a bit more when Rose explained that they had mutually agreed to take it easy on the relationship until they had both graduated. She assured her grandmother that Eric was every bit as focused on his studies as Rose was on hers.

They were as good as their word; they continued to see each other whilst completing their degrees but didn't make it permanent until Eric proposed six months after they graduated. Everything was going to plan until Rose fell pregnant.

By that time, they had firmly settled in Aberdeen. Their business took off and they amassed all the trappings of success. They had the house, the two cars and could afford to allow themselves three or four holidays a year. Many of these holidays were taken in Canada so that she could visit her grandparents who Rose knew she owed a hell of a lot to.

The pregnancy wasn't planned, but they both saw it simply as a blip on the landscape. Once they both got used to the idea, they decided that Rose could work from home during the latter stage of the pregnancy. Then they both threw themselves into preparing the nursery for the impending arrival of the new member of their family.

*

Melissa was born in December. Named after Rose's mother, the child lit up Eric and Rose's life from the minute she came into the world. So much so in fact that Rose couldn't bear to leave her with a child minder, and so she decided stay at home to care for her child for the first few years of infacy. She continued to work from home but even that got forgotten now and again as she spent more and more time with Melissa as she grew older.

This led to the inevitable arguments with Eric. The

accounts hadn't been done; she'd failed to look important contracts over. Eric started coming home later and later and very slowly, piece by piece, their once flourishing relationship fell apart.

They sold the swanky house, split the proceeds and went their separate ways. Rose retained full custody of Melissa and they moved into a small derelict cottage on the outskirts of the city.

Melissa was a clumsy child, she always had been. She always seemed to have skinned knees, bruises on her arms or various other minor injuries. One day however, she fell down the stairs in the small cottage and broke her left leg. Rose rushed her straight to Accident and Emergency where she went through the usual X-rays and examinations. The doctor, whilst looking at the X-ray results, noticed a few other earlier breakages to her ankle and her foot. She dutifully reported this to the social services department.

This led to a home visit and a load of personal questions regarding Melissa's home life.

About a week later Rose received the letter. She was told that the explanations she had provided were inadequate or inconsistent with the child's injuries. So, Rose had to attend a Children's Hearing.

Rose attended the Hearing, pleaded her case and Melissa was put under a child supervision order. The panel agreed that the child could continue to live at home but that she would be under the supervision of a social worker for the next year. Rose found the visits very intrusive, but she knew things could have gone a lot worse. Her legal advisor had told her that such meetings could have led to the removal of the child from the home, so she decided to grin and bear it, get on with things. She never told her grandparents about her troubles. She had done some research into Osteogenesis Imperfecta (OI) online. This literally meant 'imperfectly formed bone'. Children with the condition had a genetic defect that impaired the body's ability to make strong bones. She remembered Melissa's father talking about the numerous injuries he had received as a child. She had contacted Eric and they had both agreed that he and Melissa would give blood or tissue samples for genetic testing. In many cases, these tests were able to identify the mutation.

Three days after the tests, however, Melissa tripped and fell in the garden resulting in more broken bones. She told her mother she'd been pushed by the bad man. She had mentioned him before to the social worker and her mother. It was agreed that she was just making him up. The way some kids do with imaginary friends. There were no witnesses, and just as Rose was putting her in the back seat of the old car she had recently purchased, the social worker pulled up outside the cottage in her own vehicle. After seeing Melissa safely to hospital, Rose was questioned again. Once again her explanation was found to be inadequate. This, backed up by the fist shaped mark on Melissa's arm, which Rose strenuously denied, led to an emergency order being issued and Melissa was taken away from the family home. Rose had lost the last thing left in her life that held any meaning for her.

She left the hospital alone, drove up town and hit the first bar she came across. Once more she had become a victim to her addictions. She tried to contact social services a few times to find out where they had placed Melissa, but all they would tell her was that she had been placed with temporary foster parents. She would stay there until a Hearing could be organised. Depressed, Rose progressed from alcohol to heroin, culminating in a self-induced overdose in the early hours of the morning. She sat up all night compiling an e-mail in a drunk and narcotised state detailing to her grandfather her best explanation as to how her child had been taken from her. She ended:

'By the time you read this, I will be gone. They took my baby and they'll never give her back ... Goodbye. Rose.'

*

'That's bloody tragic,' said Buchanan as he went thought to the kitchen for another beer.

'Do you reckon she did do harm to the kid, sir?' asked Max.

'I don't suppose we will ever know, Max. What do you reckon, Miss Atkins?'

'I don't think she did, sir. There's a bit on the girl's file at the end here, looks like Rose was right enough. The genetic markers came out positive for the malformed bones thing. The results came through three days after Rose's suicide.'

'Cute kid, too,' said Max. 'Pity about the birthmark on her face though.'

Buchanan froze as he looked at the screen.

'Don't the two of you recognise her?'

'She looks familiar right enough,' replied Max.

'Picture her with shorter hair,' pushed Buchanan.

They both looked blankly at him.

'C'mon you two, Jesus, you're not very observant, are

you. Who have we seen recently with a birthmark on her face?'

PC Atkins jumped out her seat.

'It's the wee girl from yesterday! Jonathan Jackson's daughter!'

'Get that girl a Guinness, Max!'

Chapter Thirteen

Mary was breathing heavily. The sound echoed eerily around the dank cellar as she looked down at what she had accomplished.

She sat down on the floor, placed both feet firmly on the wall and grabbed the chain tightly.

One … two … three …

She pulled with all her might. The bolt moved a good inch from the hole she had dug out around it.

She pulled again, this time wrapping the chain tightly around her right wrist. It hurt like hell as it dug into her skin but once again the bolt moved. She stopped to rub the sweat out from her eyes, took a deep breath and gave another mighty pull. The bolt came free and she gave out an ecstatic cry.

'YES!'

She lay on her back and laughed to herself as she dangled the end of the chain above her head.

'How about that then devil man?'

She slowly got to her feet, splashed some cold water on her face at the nearby sink and decided to explore the parts of her prison that up until now had been out of her reach.

She started off with the small wooden hatch in the far left corner of the cellar. It confused her to start with, there was no handle, no lock to be seen, and when she pushed it stayed firm. She noticed however that there was a small gap underneath, between the bottom of the hatch and the floor. She could feel the cold air coming through. The gap was just big enough to slip her fingers under, so that's what she did. She pulled upwards and the hatch slid slowly up towards her. She heard a click as it caught on a latch at the other side. She slowly squeezed herself through the space she had created and found herself in a new, smaller sized room. It was pitch black and she couldn't see a thing.

'Fuck!'

She once again squeezed herself through the small space, returned to the cellar, picked up the small table lamp and stretched the flex as far towards the hatch as she could. It threw scant amount of light into the smaller room, but it was a hundred times better than the darkness before.

'Let's see what we have here, then.'

She hadn't realised exactly when she had first started talking to herself, but it had become a habit in the last couple of days. She'd put it down to having no one to talk to but herself, either that or she'd become a complete lunatic. She laughed to herself as she surveyed her surroundings.

The small stone room had a slight smoky smell and the walls were blackened with what looked like years of burning.

'What the fuck is this place?'

Her eyes caught something glinting in the corner; it was a key, a small key, maybe for a padlock. She picked it up and clutched it in her weakened fist.

'Now, we're getting somewhere.'

She took a good three hundred and sixty degree look around the room, four walls and a small recess for what seemed to be some kind of grate for a fire.

'It must be some sort of smokehouse.''

Then she looked up.

There was another hatch on the roof, a hatch kept closed by a small padlock and chain.

'That's too much to wish for Mary ... might as well give it a try, in for a penny, in for a pound.'

She grabbed the key from the wall, slotted it into the padlock, held her breath and turned it in the lock.

*

The old man poured himself another whisky from the bottle of malt at the side of his bed, then once again for the umpteenth time cast his eyes over the crumpled sheet of paper.

Why didn't Rose just tell them what was going on? He could have flown over. No one in their right mind could entertain the thought of her purposely harming Melissa. Rose lived for that child.

And then, to add insult to injury, she had been proven right. He couldn't believe it when Eric had told him at the funeral. Melissa did have OI, as had he. He'd never been diagnosed till recently, probably never would have if Rose hadn't insisted he take the test along with Melissa. And why on earth would he refuse custody of the child now that Rose was gone. He would have to have words with him. After, of course, he had seen to the main protagonists in the tragic affair.

He downed the whisky then poured himself another. He turned on his laptop and couldn't help but notice the small red light flashing on the camera icon. 'What the hell are you doing, moving about at this time of night, Mary', he thought as he clicked on the attached survey lance programme.

He couldn't see her. He zoomed in and panned around the room coming to a stop at the small wooden hatch in the corner.

'How the fuck did she manage to reach over there?'

Then it dawned on him.

'Shit! She must have slipped her shackles.'

He jumped off the bed with the speed of a man half his age, clambered into his clothes and hurriedly left the hotel by the back fire exit preparing to walk the half mile or so to the old fish house.

After trying to turn the key for the fifth time, Mary gave up. Either the lock had seized up or she'd found the wrong key.

'Fuck! I knew it was too much to ask for.' She wasn't about to give up though, she had come too far. 'Think, Mary, use that brain of yours for once in your life.'

On closer examination, she noticed that not only was the padlock corroded but the chain itself had seen better days. Compared to the thick chain attached to her ankle it didn't look particularly strong at all.

She slipped her shackle chain through the thinner one attached to the padlock, grabbed the other side and pulled with all her weight.

It snapped immediately sending her hurtling to the floor.

Despite the shooting pain in her rear end, she stared up

at the hatch and once again laughed to herself. A laugh, that slowly turned to tears of relief.

After calming herself down, she wiped her eyes with her hands, which had become black from touching the soot encrusted walls, took a deep breath and pushed open the hatch above her.

The cold frosty air felt great compared to the stuffy atmosphere of the cellar.

Then, just as she put the hatch back in place she heard the sound of quick footsteps from off in the distance, as if someone was in a real hurry to get somewhere. 'To get here,' said a voice in her head. The footsteps got closer.

'Shit, it's him, it has to be him'. Mary panicked and looked in every direction, she needed somewhere to hide. She spotted a skip lying at the other side of the road. She ran towards it and jumped in, covering herself with the tarpaulin attached to the side. It smelled of fish and something more. She didn't have the nerve to look down to see what all the slimy stuff she felt all around her was, but judging by the smell, she had a good idea. She used to work in an office in Torry, each morning she had to walk past a few fish houses to get there. She knew well enough what fish guts smelled like.

She tried to put all that out of her mind as she ever so slightly raised the tarpaulin and peered out at the building she had just escaped from across the road, and the shadowy figure of a man stealthily creeping round the corner …

The old man wasted no time; he opened the door and ran down the stairs to the cellar. As he suspected, she was gone. He approached the small hatch, produced a metal

torch from his jacket pocket and inspected the small room. Bad planning, he thought to himself. He never imagined in a million years that she would have been able to squeeze through such a small space. He shone the light up towards the broken chain, watched it swing ever so slightly and put two and two together.

'She's just left.'

He rushed back upstairs, stood in the doorway and took in his surroundings.

'Mary! I know you're close by, come out girl, I won't harm you. In fact I just came down here to release you, take you home to your father like I promised! My car is right around the corner …'

'Good God he's old, not what I expected at all, and what sort of accent is that?'

Mary watched her captor. He stood directly across the road from her hiding place. He reminded her of someone.

'Charlton Heston, that's who he looks like.'

She watched him pace back and fore as he muttered away to himself.

'Please, God, don't let him figure out where I am.'

'Where are you, Mary? There's no need for us both to freeze to death, now is there? The car's nice and warm. Let me take you home, girl.'

Mary reached down amongst the wet fish parts to see if she could find something she could use as a makeshift weapon. She drew a blank. The ankle chain, of course. It still had the heavy bolt attached. That should do the job, if need be.

Chain in hand she once more lifted up the tarpaulin to peer out. There was no sign of the old man.

'Where the fuck has he gone?'

Then she once again heard the heavy footsteps.

'Mary! You're beginning to piss me off, girl,' said the voice from behind.

'Shit! He's on my side of the road.'

Mary tried not to move. She didn't want to give herself away.

'Are you hiding in that skip, Mary?'

Mary's heart skipped a beat.

'Are you in there?' he asked as he kicked the side.

The noise echoed around her hiding place.

'Change of plan', she frantically thought to herself.

She took three deep breaths and sank down under the fish innards to the bottom of the skip, two seconds before the old man hauled back the tarpaulin.

'Holy shit! What the hell is that stench?' He gagged, took a couple of deep breaths, then covered his nose as he shone the small torch around the inside of the skip. All he could see was glistening fish parts and what seemed like hundreds of dead eyes looking up at him.

'Fuck!'

He put the cover back in place putting an end to the assault on his senses and continued to slowly walk down the street, shining his torch in doorways and alleys as he went.

Mary slowly resurfaced and raised her head. She wiped

the slime from her hair and face and violently threw up into the corner of the skip. She watched as the beam from the man's torch disappeared into the distance, then slowly eased herself out of her stinking surroundings and ran for her life in the opposite direction. She was tired, dirty, stinking … but she was free. Now all she had to do was contact her father. She was sure that the old man would do the same, he would expect her to go home.

'What you gonna do now, Mary?'

She had to find a phone, so she knocked on the door of the first house she came to that had lights on. 'God knows what they'll make of me,' she thought as she picked a fish eye off her stained T-shirt. She rubbed her soot blackened hands on her jeans as she waited anxiously for the door to be opened.

An old woman answered, peering around the corner, the eyes behind her thick lensed glasses taking in the site before her.

'Good grief, what happened to you, lass? And what in God's name is that awful smell.'

'It's fish. Three drunk guys threw me into a skip full of rotten fish guts. Can I use your phone to call my dad?'

The old woman, who was holding a scruffy looking cat in each arm, looked her up and down.

'I suppose so, but first you need a good bath. I'll see what I can find in the way of some clothes for you. My granddaughter has some stuff she keeps in the spare room, I'm sure she's about your size.

Come, get yourself in here out of the cold. I'll stick the kettle on after I've run your bath and you can tell me the whole story of what happened.'

'Cheers,' answered Mary.

'Watch out for the cats though. I have quite a few and no doubt they'll smell the fish off you. They'll think you're a walking meal.'

The old woman cackled like a witch.

'Trust me to find the local mad cat woman,' Mary thought to herself.

She just wanted to make the phone call but she was too shattered to insist on it so she followed the old woman, and another two cats that had appeared from nowhere, to the bathroom.She thought of her father, the old man might go after him. She stopped dead.

'Mrs …?'

'Davis, just call me Betty.'

'Betty, I really have to make the phone call before everything else, it's very important that I do.'

The woman turned around, so did the cats.

'The phones on the wall there just outside the bathroom. Make it quick. I'll run your bath.'

'One other thing,' answered Mary, trying to play down the confusion of her next question. 'Where exactly am I, Betty?'

The woman gave her a puzzled look.

'Why, you're on the outskirts of Stonehaven, I'll write down the address for you.'

*

Victor was just about to leave with the hurriedly-packed suitcase full of clothes for himself and Mary when the phone rang.

'Ah, Victor, how are you? That's a clever girl you have there, very resourceful. I take it she has already phoned you?'

The voice made him tremble.

'I-I-I don't know what you're talking about.'

'Come now, do you think I'm stupid? Who else would she call? By the way look out the window, I'll give you a wave.'

Starting to panic he rushed to the window and raised the blinds. He saw nothing, but he heard manic laughter coming from the other end of the phone.

'Victor! I'm just messing with you but listen to this very carefully. Go meet your daughter; I was planning on letting her go in a couple of days anyway. If, however, I find out you have gone to the police, or talked to anyone that could get in the way of my plans, I will track you down, that's a promise. I'll kill Mary very slowly and make you watch, you got that?'

'Y-yes.'

'You will know by now, if you have been watching the news, exactly what I'm capable of. I am not a man to be messed with, have I made that clear enough?'

' Yes … you have.'

'Good, Victor, as long as we have an understanding.'

The line went dead.

The old man stuck the mobile phone back in his inside

pocket and picked up the petrol can. He threw the contents around the room leaving the last of it to pour a thin stream back out towards the entrance to the cellar.

He reached for the small box he had left just outside the door, struck the match and set light to the room.

He watched as the flames raced towards the centre of the smokehouse, lighting his cigar from the last of the match.

'Things could have gone better,' he thought to himself. He was pretty sure Victor wouldn't involve the authorities. He had never met such a spineless weasel of a man, he was scared shitless. His daughter though, she was a bit of a worry, she had some spunk that girl.

He watched as the few items of furniture in the room were engulfed in flames. Oh well, what was done was done, he would carry on with his plan regardless. He knew the likelihood of having left any evidence in the place was minimal. If by any chance he had ... the fire would soon take care of that.

He left the building and walked quickly down the street as the sound of the fire engine in the distance cut through the cold night air.

Chapter Fourteen

Buchanan yawned loudly as Max drove slowly along Wellington Road heading towards Aberdeen Prison. Craiginches Prison some people still called it or Craigee to most of the inmates. The roads were still icy and Max had to keep concentrating on the road ahead. Buchanan watched as an icy fog moved heavily along the cold grey water of the River Dee below the steep embankment to his right. They were on their way to visit Jonathan Jackson who had been charged with the young girl's murder and remanded in custody.

They drove towards the imposing building then into the complex itself as the radio DJ told them to remember to wrap-up well. The temperature was due to drop to minus six, he informed them. After parking the car in one of the visitors bays, they left the warmth of the vehicle behind them and headed across the fore court to the entrance block.

'Can I help you, gentlemen?' asked the portly guard as they walked through the door.

Buchanan hauled out his ID.

'DI Buchanan, this is Sergeant Maxwell. We're here to see Jonathan Jackson. I arranged it this morning.'

'Oh aye, he's all ready for you, sir, just follow me, I'll take you to the interview room. My names Terry, by the way, Terry Macduff.'

'Well, lead on, Macduff,' said Buchanan, swinging his arm ahead as Max, smiling to himself followed behind.

Jonathan Jackson sported several stitches in his lip and a heavily bruised left eye. He looked sedated.

Buchanan bent forward and peered at his damaged face.

'What the hell happened to you?'

'A huge fucking Polish psycho called Olaf happened to me. Seems he took offence to my pony tail. Look!'

Jonathan turned so they could see the back of his head. There was a huge bald patch, covered by a blood encrusted dressing.

'The bastard damn near scalped me. Then he stuffed it down the back of his trousers and started jumping about the place making horsey noises. Everyone seemed to think it was fucking hilarious.'

Buchanan tried not to laugh as he walked over to the other side of the room to open the window.

'Right, Jonathan, we have a few questions for you but first … tell me about Samantha.'

Jonathan yawned and rubbed his eyes.

'What do you want to know?'

'I take it she's adopted?'

'Yes, we couldn't have any of our own. We hadn't been on the register for that long; we were very surprised when we got word of Samantha. Emily fell in love with her from the get go. Took me a bit of time to bond with her, but she's a great kid.'

Buchanan leaned forward.

'Tell me about her mother. Her birth mother.'

He leaned back in his seat and lit himself a cigarette.

'Can I have one, Inspector?' asked Jonathan.

Buchanan took a long drag and blew the smoke towards the man at the other side of the table.

'That will depend on the answers you give me, Mr Jackson.'

Jonathan looked at the cigarette packet lying in front of him on the table.

'All I can tell you is that she was a victim of abuse. We don't get told who the mother is.'

'Bullshit!' screamed Buchanan. 'That's maybe how it's supposed to work but not in your case. Your wife sat on the god-damned panel that took Samantha - or should I say Melissa - away from the mother. So, try again, and remember, I don't button up the back.'

'Sir!' interrupted Max. He was looking at his mobile. 'Jenny has sent us an email.'

Buchanan peered at the small writing on the screen, and then turned back towards Jonathan Jackson.

'I'll give you ten minutes to think about it while Max and I grab a coffee. C'mon, Max.'

'The cigarette!' shouted Jonathan.

'Once we return and you give us a decent answer, you can have the packet,' answered Buchanan as he slammed the door shut.

'Right, Max, read me out that email.'

'It's quite long, sir, you'd be better off reading it yourself …'

He handed the phone to Buchanan who pulled out his reading glasses and looked at the screen.

Spoke to the expert, sir, her name is Ann Marie Taylor. This is what she had to say when I explained the situation:

All prospective adopters should be considered on their own merits, but this would be a very unusual situation. Usually, there are plenty of people waiting to adopt, and unless there was an exceptional reason to bypass people already on the waiting list, then there would be no reason to assess Mrs Jackson as a priority, just because she was on a Children's Panel. In fact, due to the fact that she sat on the panel that originally dealt with the case, it would likely be determined that if anything, she was too close to the situation ...

She thought it sounded decidedly dodgy. At the very least it should have raised a few red flags and been investigated. Off the record she told me it looked like it had been deliberately hushed up, either that or there's been a few back handers chucked about to ease it through.

Saddest thing of all though is the fact that she should never have been taken away from her mother in the first place. If the case had been investigated properly, Melissa should have been checked for any underlying disease that could have led to the injuries. You were right enough, sir, it's a tragic case, there are no other words for it.

'Human error, that's what it was put down to. Do you believe that shit? It doesn't cover it by a long shot.'

Buchanan shook his head and handed the phone back to Max.

'Right, he's stewed long enough, Max, let's get back in there.'

When they got back to the room Jonathan Jackson was half asleep.

Buchanan pushed the table towards him. Jonathan gasped as it hit him in the solar plexus.

'Wake the fuck up and tell me who you paid off to rush the adoption through.'

'I don't know what you mean.'

'Cut the crap! We're currently working on the theory that the shooting of your wife and various other incidents all tie into the case involving Melissa and her mother. Anyone remotely associated with the case is a possible victim. Of that I have no doubt. That list - as I'm sure you are aware - includes yourself. Don't think you're safe because you're in here. There's ways and means to get around that obstacle believe me.'

Jonathan sighed and looked at Buchanan … He felt complete and utterly drained, so much so he really had to concentrate on keeping his eyes opened. He decided things had gone too far to hold anything back.

'Give me that cigarette and I'll tell you everything I know …'

*

'After the initial Hearing, Emily became obsessed with the girl. We were looking to adopt but we were way down the register. Before the case came up we were going to privately adopt. I'd already started the procedure, but no … She had her mind set on that one. No matter how hard or often I tried, I just couldn't dissuade her. She knew ways to bump us up the list she kept telling me, she had a few contacts that could make things happen. I kept telling her, we can't just hope that something else will happen to the girl. She was under supervision, but she was still staying at home with her mother. How could we be sure she would be taken into care at all? "I'll figure it out," she said in that chilling voice of hers.'

Jonathan took a drag on the cigarette.

'So … She put her plan into action. She went out of her way to befriend the social worker in charge of the case, the one who visited the home. She had already done her homework on her, of course. She hired a private detective to dig into the woman's background. When he looked into her background he found out that she had a good bit of debt piled up, so, they came to an arrangement. Emily would pay off some of her debt and get her mortgage up to date and in return she would receive copies of the weekly reports that were being filed on Samantha. She had already picked out the name, as I told you, she was obsessed.'

'What did she hope to gain by seeing these reports?' asked Max.

'She was convinced the mother would harm the child again and, if so, she was going to step right in there and put her adoption plan into operation.'

'I don't like where this is heading,' said Buchanan as he

lit a cigarette for each of them. 'So, what you're basically telling me is that if another suspicious injury happened to the child it was to yours and your wife's benefit.'

'You could say that.' answered Jonathan.

Buchanan thought back to what he'd learned the night before, particularly the bit concerning the bad man.

'Listen to me very carefully,' said Buchanan. 'Did your wife have anything at all to do with the injury that led to the girl being removed?'

'I don't believe so, she was beginning to think along those lines, but then the second injury happened and the girl was taken away. As far as I'm aware, the only two folks present during that incident were the girl and her mother.'

Buchanan stayed silent for a minute and rubbed his eyes with the palms of his hands.

'So, … how did you end up with the girl?'

Jonathan sighed.

'You were right in the first place, Inspector. We used our wealth to ease the adoption through. I'm not sure exactly who Emily paid, I know that she used some lawyer friend of hers to make the pay offs look legit and to draw up certain binding contracts. I often wondered how deeply involved the crooked bastard was in the whole thing. I can't remember his name off hand but I can give you the names of three other people who were involved in one way or another. They may be able to help.'

'Go ahead.'

'Her husband Eric, he had to be persuaded not to apply for custody. That was easy enough. His business was going down the tubes so Emily paid him enough to keep it afloat. Susan Ferguson, the social worker. She still works here as far as I'm aware, and last but not least, Victor Whitelaw, he also works for social services. He expressed concerns as to why we ended up with the girl. He proved difficult. It cost us a pretty penny to persuade him to keep out of it.'

Buchanan wrote the three names down in his notebook then shook his head.

'Max, go and tell the guard we're finished with this piece of shit. I'm off to grab a coffee. I'll see you in the canteen.'

*

Mary had just finished her third shower of the day. She was convinced she could still smell fish. 'It has to be my imagination,' she thought to herself as she combed her hair in front of the huge mirror. She was staying in the Holiday Inn in Chapel Street. Her father had quickly grabbed a suitcase and stuffed it full of the first clothes from their respective wardrobes as he could find, in what little time he had. The old man could have turned up at any time so he did the best he could. He'd picked her up from the mad cat woman's house and driven straight to the hotel.

Mary, deciding she was as clean as she was ever going to be, left the bathroom to find her father sitting on the bed with a full glass of whisky in his hands. He was unshaven and visibly shaking.

'For God's sake, Dad, look at the state of you. Get a grip on yourself.'

He looked up at her through bleary eyes.

'You don't know what this guy is capable of, Mary, don't be fooled by his age. He's already killed two people.'

'… What?'

He grabbed her hand.

'Sit down and I'll tell you the whole story.' He sat her down on the bed beside him. 'After the initial phone call, when he told me you had been kidnapped, he asked me for some detailed information.'

'What sort of information?'

Victor took a large swig of his drink.

'He wanted the details, names, addresses and other personal stuff on several people involved in a particular child protection case. He told me to photocopy the files, drop them off to him and then take a few days off work and sit tight. If I went along with his demands, you wouldn't be harmed.'

'Why did he want these files?' asked Mary.

'He never said. However …' Victor dropped the glass, put his head in both hands and sighed heavily.

Mary drew one of his hands away and gave it a squeeze.

'What is it, Dad?'

He pulled himself together.

'Did you hear about the shooting and the recent car bomb?'

'Yes, I watched them on the news, on the small television in the cellar.'

'Emily Jackson and Darryl Morrison. Both of them were on the list.'

'You mean he was responsible for their deaths?'

'I'm positive. He either accomplished it by his own

120

hands, or paid someone to do it.'

'We have to go to the police, how many were on the list?'

'Six people, some of them weren't directly involved in the case, not as far as I could see. It took a lot of sneaking about at work to get a hold of the details in their case.'

He refilled his glass.

'That leaves three then, we can't just sit back while he goes after them. I can't have that on my conscience.'

He took both Mary's hands in his.

'We can't go to the police. I wasn't going to tell you this but I must. He phoned me last night, five minutes after you did. I won't go into details but he made a threat that shook me to the core. Even though he doesn't have you captive anymore, he's still holding us to the same deadline, pardon the pun. So, if we just sit tight here, it'll all be over in a few days.'

'So, what you're saying is, if we stay out of it, we survive …?'

'Exactly.'

Mary looked up at what was left of her father.

'I'm sorry, Dad. I don't think I can do that.'

He stroked her hair.

'We must, Mary, we must!'

Mary sighed. 'Tell me the names of the people on the list.'

Chapter Fifteen

Buchanan had just finished talking to Michelle on the phone in his office when Max arrived with the coffees, slowly followed by PC Atkins. She carried a pack of chocolate digestives in her hand.

'My favourite biscuits, Miss Atkins, are you trying to impress me?'

She smiled as she handed the packet over.

After helping himself to four, Buchanan took out his notebook and looked at the three names in front of him.

Eric Reeder

Susan Ferguson

Victor Whitelaw

'Right, folks, we have a few names here need checking out. I still believe that this case is tied into Rose and the kid. What do you two think?'

'Well, sir,' replied Atkins, 'I reckon we need to go back to the child protection case file, locate everyone who was in any way involved with it and give them protection, any one of them could be the next victim.'

'Exactly what I was thinking, get on to it, Jenny, make a list of all the people involved, find out their addresses then get back to me. Once you get me the information, I'll have a word with Rennie to arrange the protection.'

'We already know of one, sir,' interrupted Max, 'well

three really, but two are already dead.'

'Aye, I hadn't forgotten about the social worker, Max. That's where we're going next. Get the car heated up, I'm off for a quick catch up with Rennie.'

'Oh! By the way, Jenny, after you compile your list of names, get in touch with Rose's husband. Find out why the bastard didn't apply for custody of the kid, put some pressure on him, see if he admits to taking the cash to stay out of the affair, and check his alibis for the times of the murders. Also, I'd like you to phone the grandparents in Canada. See what they can tell you about Rose; see if she had any boyfriends since she split up from her husband. It looks like someone is out for revenge … it's our job to find out who.'

PC Atkins finished writing down her list of tasks.

'I'm on it, sir.'

'What about the other guy on the list, this Victor Whitelaw?' asked Max.

'I've already been on to him, Max. No answer at home and he called in a sickie a few days ago. I'll get Rennie to send a car round, see if they can find him and bring him in. Now off you trot, the two of you. I won't be long with Rennie. Max, give me five minutes.'

*

The old man sat on the end of his hotel room bed holding his head in both hands. He knew that he would receive the phone call he'd been dreading someday, but he didn't expect it to have been so quick. He'd expected to receive it back in Canada, not in a hotel room thousands of miles away from home.

123

Clara had died in her sleep; the fluid in her lungs had been too much to cope with. She had literally drowned in her bed. He had nothing to live for now, apart from the work. There was always the work.

'Never leave a job half done.' That had been one of her favourite sayings. God knows how many times he'd heard that down the years.

He laughed to himself, a laugh that gradually turned to sobbing. He wiped his eyes and slowly pulled himself together. He gulped as he looked at Clara's photo at the side of his bed.

'I promised you I'd avenge her, Clara. The last promise I ever gave you and I mean to hold it up.'

She had been part of his life for so long that he felt a huge part of him had been taken away. A part he knew he'd never get back. The fact that he hadn't been there at the end crushed his soul.

He kissed the photo, his tears soaked the frame.

'See you soon, my love.'

He dried his eyes with the bed's quilt cover, packed his small black holdall and threw the wrapped rose on top before leaving his hotel room and heading for Aberdeen.

*

'Fuck! That's all I need. A profiler, what fucking use is she going to be?'

Max pulled up outside the granite block of flats in Urquhart Street. The building reflected the gloom of the sky above.

'When's she going to be here?' asked Max.

'She left Edinburgh earlier on this afternoon. She's probably here by now. I thought Rennie was taking the piss when he told me. She's some psychologist woman attached to one of the universities down there.'

'They can have an impact on a case; I watched a documentary on the crime channel the other night. It was about an American profiler, Dayle somebody or other; she's helped catch loads of people.'

'Bollocks! You only ever hear of their successes, they conveniently overlook the cases they were bugger all use on.'

'What do you have against them, sir? Surely anything's worth a try, no?'

Buchanan lit a cigarette and opened the passenger window, totally ignoring the fact that the smoke blew straight back in towards Max.

'This is why I disagree with them, Max. They'll give you some bollocks like "I believe the perpetrator will be in his forties, find it hard to form relationships and probably still stays at home with his parents." '

Max laughed.

'That's what Dayle said the other night, almost word for word.'

'Aye but say they get it totally wrong, Max. They go on record with that shit and suddenly everyone goes looking for someone that fits the profile. You see what I'm saying, the murderer could be hanging about the crime scene but if he's in his mid-twenties and a bigamist, well no one's going to look at him are they? Because …'

'He doesn't fit the profile,' replied Max. 'I see what you're saying.'

'Anyway, forget the profiler for the minute; let's have a go at the social worker.'

'You got something against them as well like?'

'Don't get me started, Max.'

*

The door of the ground floor flat was opened by an old man in a baseball hat and glasses.

'Can I help you, gentlemen?'

Buchanan flashed his ID.

'We'd like a word with Susan Ferguson, if we could, please. We phoned ahead, she should be expecting us.'

'Sure, come on in.'

They followed the old man through to the lounge.

'Just grab a seat, gentlemen, I'll stick on the kettle and let Susan know you're here. She's having a bath but she shouldn't be long. Make yourselves at home. I shan't be a moment.'

The room was immaculate, not a thing was out of place.

'This looks like somewhere out of one of those ideal home exhibitions,' said Buchanan. 'If I lived here I'd be scared to bloody move in case I messed up the place.'

They heard the old man knocking on the bathroom door.

'Susan, love, that's the police here to see you. What's

that? Five minutes? I'll let them know.'

He returned to the sitting room.

'Would you two gentlemen like a coffee?'

'Milk and two sugars please,' answered Buchanan 'Max here likes his black.'

'No problem, shan't be a minute.'

Buchanan stood up.

'I didn't get your name, Mr … ?'

'Ferguson, the same as my daughter's, Inspector.'

'Ah, of course, you're her father. Would you like a hand with the coffee?'

'I may be getting on, Mr Buchanan, but I think I'm quite capable of making a coffee, just grab a seat. I'll be back in a couple of minutes.'

Just as he sat down, careful to not move the mass of perfectly placed cushions, his mobile rang.

'Inspector Buchanan?'

'Yes. Who is this?'

'Lucy Jacobs, I'm the profiler that's been assigned to your case. I just got off the phone to Jenny Atkins, she's filled me in on the details.'

'Oh, she has, has she? I thought you weren't arriving till later on today.'

'I'm on my way, I'm phoning from the train.'

'Look, Lucy, I commend you on your enthusiasm but this is not a good time for a conversation, I'm just about to interview someone. Give me your number and I'll phone you back later.'

'Oh no! That won't do at all, this is very important.'

Buchanan sighed.

'Okay, Lucy, you have five minutes. Dazzle me with your insight.'

'Listen, Detective, you're not the first person to have me thrust upon them as part of a major case. I'm used to such sarcasm. I'm not here to tell you what to do. I'm more here in an advisory role. I tell you stuff , and you use what you see fit.'

'Four minutes.'

'God, you're infuriating.'

'So they tell me.'

'Listen, Inspector, I've been looking at the case file, I take it you're looking at it as some sort of revenge for what happened to Rose.'

'I am looking at it along those lines, yes. Go on.'

'Right … statistically speaking, when we look at revenge killings, especially when there's a daughter involved, we look to the parents.'

'Aye, but the parents were wiped out in a car crash. That doesn't help me.'

'Hear me out, Inspector. What about the surrogates?'

'You've lost me.'

'When the natural parents are deceased, someone always steps in. In this case it was the grandparents. The grandparents took over the parental role.'

'Makes sense, I suppose.'

'So, using that criterion, I would be looking at them, as far as the revenge angle was concerned. Now, it would be very unusual, to say the least, that the grandmother was involved - in the actual killings I mean. She might be pushing his buttons but she wouldn't be immediately involved. So … I would be looking at the Grandfather.'

'The man's in his seventies, he's hardly your normal serial killer now is he?'

'Don't be swayed by his age, inspector, revenge is a great motivator. All I'm telling you is to be very wary of any old man that either injects themselves into the investigation or you see appearing on the outskirts. Basically, treat any old guy you come across as a suspect.'

'Shit!'

'What is it, sir?' asked Max.

'See where that old bastard's got to, Max.'

He returned to the phone call.

'I'll have to call you back, Lucy. Something's come up. Max!'

'He's gone, sir, the kitchen windows open.'

'Fuck! Get out the back; see if you can spot him and phone in his description, see if there's any cars in the area.'

'I'm on it, sir,' replied Max. He went tearing out the back door as Buchanan approached the bathroom with a great amount of trepidation.

He rapped loudly on the door.

'Mrs Ferguson!'

There was no reply, not that he was expecting one.

He tried the handle, the door was unlocked.

Its hinges made a strange eerie squeal as he slowly pushed it open.

The sharp metallic smell hit him right away, then, through the slowly-dissipating steamy haze, he saw the body.

Susan Ferguson, lay at the bottom of the bath under two feet of water. Blood-red water. Her throat had been slashed. The cut was so deep that her head lay at an unnatural angle, held on to the rest of her body by not much more than a flap of skin. Her lifeless eyes stared up at the red rose floating above her as if in question.

'Jesus! Not another one!'

He gave out a heavy sigh, sat down on the toilet seat, lit himself a cigarette then took out his mobile.

'Rennie, it's Buchanan. There's been another one.'

Chapter Sixteen

After phoning in the old man's description, Max went tearing through the back garden of the flats exiting the old rusty gate at the far end. He found himself in a narrow alley. It had half a dozen graffiti-scrawled car lock ups on the far side. To his right hand side was nothing; it led to a dead end. To his left, about a hundred yards down, it opened onto the main road. He checked the doors on the lock ups as he made his way towards the road. All of them were locked.

As he exited the alleyway, he heard the three police vehicles before they came screeching into view.

He ran out to the middle of the road, held out his ID and flagged one of them down.

He told them to check out the lock ups, just to be sure, then headed along the road to see if there was any sign of the old man.

At the corner of the street, he came across a small newsagent. It looked like it had stood there for years. The windows were grimy and some of the products advertised on the discoloured posters were obviously from years gone by.

He entered the shop, once again flashing his ID at the young woman behind the counter. He was just about to ask the woman if she had seen anything, when the old man suddenly appeared from the side of the door with a small fire extinguisher in his hand. He saw a quick flash of red and then everything quickly turned black.

*

Max felt the cold water on his face as he slowly became aware of his surroundings.

'Wake up, Mr Maxwell. Or can I call you Phil? Nice photo by the way.'

Max opened his eyes. His head was pounding and it took him a minute or so to figure out exactly where he was.

He was in what he assumed was a small storeroom in the back of the shop sitting next to the young shop assistant. They were both bound and gagged sitting on the floor with their backs against the wall. The old man stood above them, he had a bottle of water in one hand and Max's warrant card in the other. He stuck the card in his pocket and then removed the tape from Max's mouth.

'Do you have any idea who I am?'

'Not a clue, but I assume you're not Susan Ferguson's father.'

'Your assumption is correct. Tell me what the police have discovered so far.'

'About what, exactly?'

Max coughed violently.

'Here, have some of this.'

The old man held the bottle of mineral water to Max's lips.

'It is pretty dry and dusty in here. This should help.'

'Thanks.'

'You're most welcome, officer. What have they found out so far regarding the recent three murders?'

'There's only two that I know of.'

'Three, I think you'll find. Your superior is probably discovering her right now as we speak. I slit her from ear to ear, the bitch deserved no less!'

'Three down. Exactly how many to go?' asked Max.

'Nice try. I take it you know what they all have in common?'

'I'm saying nothing.'

'That's a pity, I was hoping not to have to resort to violence.'

'You can do what you want to me, I'm telling you bugger all.'

'Brave man, but who said the violence would be targeted at you, Max? It's your fellow captive I'm talking about.'

The old man carefully removed the young woman's left shoe and then, seemingly from nowhere, produced a hammer.

'I'll ask you again, tell me what you know.'

'We don't know anything, it's early days. The case is still fresh.'

'Wrong!'

The man brought the hammer down hard on the woman's big toe. It made a sickening thud.

The woman turned her head into Max's shoulder. He could feel the stifled scream through his shirt.

'One down nine to go!'

He raised the hammer again.

'No!' screamed Max. 'I'll tell you what we know.'

*

After digesting the information he had just been given, the old man sighed and once again picked up the hammer. He playfully tossed it from hand to hand.

'How do I know you're telling me everything, Max?'

'You don't, you'll just have to take me at my word.'

The old man stared at him.

'What did you make of the whole affair? The whole child protection issue I mean?'

'I think it was tragic. If it had been investigated properly the case would have gone nowhere. The girl should have been tested for any underlying medical issues. That would have put an end to it, for Rose and the child.'

'I agree, Max. How is my great-granddaughter by the way?'

'Your great-granddaughter?'

'Don't be so slow on the pickup, Max. Surely you've guessed who I am by now.'

'Good God, of course. You're Rose's grandfather!'

He bowed towards Max.

'The one and only.'

He rubbed his beard.

'Let me ask you something, Detective. Do you, in any way agree with what I'm doing?'

'Of course not. I think there should be an inquiry maybe,

but you've appointed yourself judge, jury and executioner.'

'I believe in a higher judgement, Max. An eye for an eye, these people must pay.'

'So, I believe, I saw the cards.'

The old man laughed. 'Complete theatre, I thought it was a nice touch though. That, and the roses of course. Although … '

He paused for a few seconds. Max thought he saw the beginnings of a tear forming in his eye.

'I'd like to think that when they saw them, they thought of the poor girl, even if just for a minute. Talking of the cards, everyone that is related to the case in any way either has one, or will receive one. So, that's not going to help you in figuring out which ones I have my beady eye on.'

He violently shook his head.

'Max, do you ever hear music in your head? Music that seems so real that you'd swear you had earphones in your ears?'

Max exchanged a glance with the shop assistant.

She shrugged her shoulders.

'What are you planning on doing with us?' asked Max.

'Nothing, of course. Why should I? I've nothing against you or the young girl here. I'm planning on leaving you locked in here till the morning. Then I'll phone and let someone know where you are. You'll both find your mobiles upstairs on the counter; they're turned off of course.'

He finished the last of the water and tossed the empty bottle to the side before re-gagging Max.

'No doubt I'll be seeing you again, Sergeant Maxwell, once my work is done. Try not to soil yourselves too much.'

And with that, he was gone.

Once he was sure that Mr Reid had finally left, Max fought against his restraints, but it was no good. The old man had used thick tie wraps, there was no way he was going to manage to break them with brute force and the more he tried the more painful they became. The young woman was still sobbing; he could hear her muffled cries through the duct tape that was wrapped around her mouth.

'Think, Max, think.'

He carefully surveyed his surroundings.

It was your typical small shop store room a few shelves full of various merchandise and not much else. Mind you, the corners of the shelving units looked quite sharp …

He stood up. He still felt slightly dizzy from the blow to his head so he took a few deep breaths and walked over to the shelves. He placed his back against the unit, placed his tie wrapped wrists against the edge and using his shoulders, he vigorously worked his wrists up and down. The young woman raised her head up and down in encouragement. He began to sweat profusely and his hands began to go numb but after a good few minutes he felt the tension break and he was free. His relief was soon replaced with pain as the blood returned to his hands.

He made fists until the pain eased slightly, then he ripped the tape from his face.

'Bastard!'

On the shelf to his left, he found a Stanley knife which he

used to release the young woman.

'Thanks! My name's Meg … thank you!'

Max held out his hand. 'Phil Maxwell, most folk call me Max. How's the foot doing?'

'Hurts like a bastard. I can't move it, he must have broken the thing.'

'Hold on, I think I saw some painkillers over there, they won't help that much but they might take the edge of it.'

'That would be great, cheers, Max.'

'Think nothing of it.'

He returned with the painkillers and a fresh bottle of water for each of them.

'Do you think its worth shouting out, Meg? I mean do you think anyone will hear us?'

'I doubt it very much. I mean, there are flats above us, but this cupboard we're in is down a steep flight of stairs, it's more a cellar really.'

Max took a mouthful of water.

'How the hell did the old bastard get me down here when I was unconscious then?'

'There's two great long planks, we use them to cover the stairs so we can slide down boxes and stuff. He just slid you down them.'

'What about the owner, when's he due back? Surely you don't just work here on your own?'

'Not normally no, but you're out of luck today, he's off down south, visiting relatives in London, will be till the weekend.'

'Great!'

'But hey - feel free to shout away, I'll join in if you like, anything's worth a try.'

After half an hour, they gave up.

'I think these painkillers are helping at least,' said Meg. 'Either that or my foot is just going numb.'

Max gave out a sigh. 'I'm bloody starving.'

'Look around you, food is one thing this makeshift prison of ours isn't short of.'

'Aye, right enough, you fancy some crisps?'

'Cheese and onion, they're over in the corner.'

Max returned with four bags of crisps and a couple of Mars Bars.

'Cheers, Max.'

'Oh! Look what else I found.'

He produced two miniatures from his pocket.

'Whisky or vodka? We might as well make ourselves comfy till the cavalry arrive.'

She chose the vodka, then she pointed to the left.

'There's a radio on that bench over there, might as well have some music. And, if it's not too much trouble, could you get me a can of Coke for the vodka?'

'Sure.'

When Max returned, the shop assistant took a large gulp out of the can, poured in the vodka, then they both sat in silence enjoying their makeshift picnic in the cellar.

*

'Where the fuck is he?'

Buchanan was talking to himself as he paced back and forth outside the police headquarters.

He lit up his third cigarette in a row just as Rennie came out and joined him for a smoke.

'Bloody strange right enough, Ronnie. He seems to have vanished into the ether.'

'Tell me again when he was last sighted.'

'I told you, he flagged down one of our vehicles on Urquhart Road, told them to check out the lockups behind the victims flat and then he disappeared into thin air. It's a fucking mystery.'

'No joy on the mobile phone trace?'

'Bugger all, it's either turned off or bust.'

'Sir!'

Buchanan turned round to see PC Atkins standing in the doorway.

'I have an idea; meet me in your office when you've finished your smoke.'

Buchanan threw down his half-finished cigarette and crushed it underfoot.

'If it'll help us find Max, I'll come straight away. Let's go.'

They rushed up the stairs and into the office. Atkins took Buchanan's usual seat behind the desk. She had his PC up and running.

'This is Google Maps. I have its view set on the social worker's flat on Urquhart street we can follow where Max went. Well at least up until he disappeared.'

'Show me.'

Atkins zoomed into the back of the flat.

'He must have gone through the gate at the end of the garden and then turned left in that alleyway and made his way down to Urquhart road. He wouldn't have gone right, it just leads to a dead end - that ties up with what the officer he flagged down said. Now watch.'

She clicked the mouse and set the programme into street view and started panning left to right along the road.

'What do you see, sir?'

'It looks pretty much like every other street around that area, loads of terraced flats at either side of the street.'

'Take a closer look at this corner.'

Atkins zoomed in even closer.

'It's a corner shop, not many of them left nowadays.'

'I checked with the officers that canvassed the area. It was locked up, with no lights on, yet it had one of those boards outside, the ones that advertise the day's newspapers headlines. Don't you think that's a bit suspicious, sir?'

'It certainly is, Miss Atkins. C'mon, grab your coat.'

'Shouldn't we organise some backup, sir?'

'I didn't hear that. Anyway, the quicker we get there the quicker we can check it out. Organising backup takes time. I want to check this out as soon as we can.'

Atkins gave it some thought before making her decision.

'Fair enough, sir.'

*

After banging at the shop door for a couple of minutes and getting nowhere, Buchanan turned towards the young PC.

'Anyone told you about my hidden talents, Miss Atkins?'

'What talents would those be, sir?'

'My lock picking skills, of course.'

'No, sir, first I've heard of them.'

He removed the small tools from his inside pocket and went to work on the Yale lock above the door handle. In less than a minute they were in.

'Let's see if we can find the light switch, shall we.'

With the shop illuminated they had a look around.

'Do you hear anything, sir?'

They both stopped in their tracks. Buchanan heard what sounded like muffled voices.

'I can actually. It's coming from that door in the corner if I'm not mistaken.'

'It has another lock on it, sir; you'd better get your tools out.'

Buchanan gave her a funny look.

'No need for that, Jenny, hand me that fire extinguisher by the door.'

She picked it up and handed it to Buchanan. Her hands came away sticky and wet.

'There's blood on it, sir. I'm getting a bad feeling about this.'

'Stand back, Jenny.'

Buchanan slammed the base of the extinguisher directly at the lock, the wood at the edge splintered and the door flew open. They both ran down the steep flight of stairs and entered the storeroom at the bottom. They found Max and his fellow captive laughing and joking surrounded by miniature bottles of alcohol, many of them empty.

'Max! What the hell are you up to? Half the force has been looking for you and here you are, cavorting about in a storeroom with an attractive young woman. You weren't planning on drinking all those, were you?'

Chapter Seventeen

Buchanan was standing outside the A&E in Foresterhill. He had just lit a cigarette and taken a sip of his vending machine coffee when his phone rang.

'Ronnie! It's Joe.'

'Hi, Joe, how's tricks?'

'The social worker woman, I've just had a look at the body.'

'And?'

'She was incapacitated first, before the real damage was done. He used a taser on her. It's a pretty vicious neck wound as well, one of the worst I've seen. There must have been a great degree of anger involved in this one. He damn near cut her head clean off.'

' "A great deal of anger involved"? Have you gone all profilery on me, Joe? Anyway, I thought that was Miss Jacobs's job. To be honest though, between you and me, I can't see the point of her being here. Not now that we know who we're looking for.'

He took a draw on his cigarette.

'You have a definite suspect?'

'Pretty much so - it's the grandfather. He more or less admitted it to Max.'

'How is he by the way? A pretty nasty bang on the head I heard.'

'Aye, they want to keep him in overnight, in case he shows any sign of concussion. He's having none of it. You know what he's like.'

'He always has been a bit of a tough bastard, but as long as they've done the basic tests he should be safe enough. Keep an eye on him though, if he gets sleepy or starts slurring his words get him back down there as soon as possible. Tell him I'm asking after him by the way.'

'Will do, Doc.'

'One more thing before you go. I take it you haven't met our Miss Jacobs yet, Ronnie?'

'I've not had that pleasure; I've talked to her on the phone though. She gave us a great lead. Seems very professional.'

Joe laughed loudly, 'You're in for a treat then. Remember to wear your sunglasses.'

'What the fuck is that supposed to mean?'

Joe laughed once again.

'You'll see what I mean soon enough, she's heading your way as we speak. Bye, Ronnie.'

After he'd finished his coffee and cigarette, he vigorously rubbed his cold hands together then he went off to look for Max.

He found him sitting on a bench; his head was being stitched by a pretty young nurse.

'How's he doing?'

'Well … we would prefer him to reconsider staying the night, but I don't think that's going to happen.'

Max smiled at Buchanan.

'Aye, you're wasting your time there, nurse. Just patch him up and I'll take him with me.'

The young nurse laughed as Buchanan checked out the wound.

'Looks a sore one. By the way, how's the shop assistant doing?'

'A couple of broken bones, they think they might have to pin them,' answered Max.

'Evil old bastard! Anyway, I'm off to the canteen, see if I can rustle myself up a sandwich. I'll meet you up there when you're finished being seen to.'

After settling down at the table with yet another coffee and a rather limp looking cheese sandwich, Buchanan took out his notebook and began to write.

How many people involved in the child protection case?

3 victims so far. How many more is he likely to go after?

Check into background of the grandfather.

He had just finished writing when he saw a large middle aged woman approaching his table. She had a thick blue folder under one arm and a bulging carrier bag in her left hand. She was dressed like a rainbow. Every article of clothing was a different colour, some of them bright to the extreme, none of them matched.

He watched as she piled all her stuff on the table and took off her woollen hat. It looked like it belonged in Peru, he'd watched a documentary about the place on Discovery, just the other night, and the villagers wore something very similar.

She sighed heavily as she sat down across from him.

'Mr Buchanan. I'm Lucy Jacobs.'

She held out her hand.

'Pleased to meet …'

'Good God,' interrupted Buchanan. 'Has the circus come to town?'

'Very funny, if you're referring to my dress sense save it. I've heard it all before. I've always believed that the way you dress and project yourself is a way of communicating your personality. Besides, it's a hobby of mine; I make most of them myself. I personally think people should reflect their character in their clothing.'

'What type of character are you trying to reflect? A Disney one perhaps?'

'Fuck you, detective!'

Buchanan laughed as he looked her up and down.

'Now I get the sunglasses thing.'

He laughed again.

'Sunglasses? What the hell are you talking about?'

'Never mind, it's a private joke. What is it Miss Jacobs? I thought you would have been on your way back home to Edinburgh by now.'

'What makes you think that?'

He took a sip of his coffee.

'We now know who the murderer is. What's the point in building a profile of someone we already know about?'

'You think you know, it hasn't been confirmed for definite. Just because he is an old man you can't assume it's the grandfather. I would get a hold of a recent photo, just to be sure.'

Buchanan took out his phone and showed the screen to Lucy.

'It's been confirmed, here's your recent photo. I got one of our officers straight onto it after I left the crime scene. It's definitely the grandfather.'

He tapped the screen.

'I saw this man with my own eyes.'

She suddenly looked deflated and started playing with her mass of blonde hair.

'One thing I don't get though, maybe you could help me out here.'

'Fire away,' replied the woman.

'Why was he quite happy to tell Max who he is? That one I don't understand.'

'That's simple. He has nothing to hide. As far as he is concerned, he's doing nothing wrong. He sees himself as some sort of avenging angel. These people must be punished and he's the one dishing out the punishment. In many such cases these people turn themselves in once they've accomplished what they've set out to do.'

'Makes sense, I suppose,' said Buchanan, finishing the last of his coffee.

'Even though we do now know who we're dealing with, Inspector, I can still be of help to you on this case. Every criminal, regardless of the type of crime involved, will work to a certain set of values. I can use this to get a better perspective on him. This guy is very methodical in his approach. He has already shown great expertise in firearms and explosives. Also …'

She flicked through some of the files on the table.

'The last crime scene had no indication of forced entry so he must possess great persuasive skills. He must have talked his way into the victim's flat, whether by subterfuge or the gift of the gab. I can use this information to help you catch him. Let me try to get inside his head. Any ideas I come up with, I'll run them by you first. I can't say fairer than that, now can I?'

'I'm not convinced,' replied Buchanan.

She sighed and put the heavy blue folder down between them on the table, then picked up another.

'This is the case file on his granddaughter Rose. I took the liberty of getting my own copy made up. As far as I can see, there are thirty-eight people directly attached to the case. Thirty-five if you take off the victims he's already taken care of. Now, once I study the actual degree of involvement by each individual, I'm quietly confident that I could work out the most likely ones that he will go after next. Give me a chance, Detective. I was right about the old man.'

Buchanan rapped his fingers on the table.

'Okay, get on to it. Setting up heavy protection for thirty-five people will be a logistical nightmare, thank God I left that to Rennie.'

He pointed a finger at her.

'Don't get me wrong, they all need some sort of protection but it would be handy to know which ones need it most.'

'By the way, how many victims do you reckon he has in mind?'

'It's very doubtful that he'll go for them all. He will have an agenda; these types of people always do, but until I get an insight into this guy your guess is as good as mine. In saying that, I'm pretty sure he'll go after the others that actually sat on the panel. They're the ones that made the decision. Emily Jackson was one of those members. You still have another two. I would say they're definitely in immediate danger.'

'Great. I thought it would be a simple case of figuring out which ones had received the cards, but according to Max they all either have or will have one.'

He crushed the empty plastic cup in his hand.

'The bastard's playing with us.'

Lucy took in his small display of anger.

'I can tell you one other thing, though. It's definitely getting more personal, the way he kills them, I mean.'

'Explain that to me.'

'The first two were distance kills, the first a high powered rifle, the second the car bomb. They weren't up close and personal, not like the last one.'

'So, what made him change to, pardon the pun, a hands-on approach?'

'That's something else I hope to find out. Probably some other tragedy that's affected him lately. It's upped the ante, so to speak.'

The woman covered her mouth and yawned loudly.

'Excuse me, Inspector, I always feel tired when I've been travelling.'

She reached into her bag for her purse.

'Would you like another coffee? I'm off to get myself one, I need it.'

'Thanks. Make it an espresso,' answered Buchanan.

When she returned with the coffees, Buchanan stared at her, deep in thought.

'What is it?'

'I'm working out your profile.'

She adopted a smug look.

'Go on then. Dazzle me with your insight, Inspector.'

'You're quite vain, probably the type of person who would wear contacts rather than glasses.'

'I'm wearing them as we talk. How did you know?'

Buchanan touched his nose.

'You care about the environment a great deal. I bet you're a member of Greenpeace or something of that ilk.'

'I'm not a member but I do support them, yes. Go on.'

'I'd bet money that you belong to some third-world support group as well. And you believe in fairness. You stand up for the little man and believe everyone should get a fair deal.'

'This is a set-up; you've been checking me out on that

big police computer of yours.'

Buchanan shook his head from side to side.

'Oh! One last thing, you spend a lot of your free time enjoying the great outdoors.'

'Now you're spooking me.'

'How did I do then?' asked Buchanan

'A near hundred percent hit. No one gets it a hundred percent right. What's your secret?'

Buchanan laughed.

'No secret. I just looked in your shopping bag. I based the so-called profile on simple observation. You have two packs of contacts in a Specsavers bag, recycled environmentally-friendly toilet rolls, a jar of coffee and a bunch of bananas, both Fairtrade, and last but not least, this month's copy of a Scottish walking magazine.'

For the first time since they'd met Lucy laughed.

'That's bloody brilliant. There's more to you than meets the eye, DI Buchanan.'

'Answer me something truthfully, Lucy.'

'Sure, what is it?'

'Why are you so adamant about staying on board with this case?'

Lucy sighed.

'Let's just say I have a lot of baggage back home in Edinburgh at the moment, I could do with a break to be honest.'

Buchanan shook his head.

'I thought it might have been something like that.'

He extended his hand.

'Welcome on board, Miss Jacobs. To be honest, I could do with any help I can get on this one. Come round to mine later on tonight, say eight o'clock, we can go over a few things and I'll introduce you to Max and Miss Atkins. I'll write down the address.'

'Let me guess … 221b Baker Street?'

This time it was Buchanan's turn to laugh.

Chapter Eighteen

The old man, once again, sat alone in his hotel room, his only company the newly-opened bottle of twelve year-old malt whisky. He stared at the stag on the label as he went over the day's events once more in his mind. They'd been very close to catching him, and now no doubt they would have anyone directly concerned in Rose's case under police protection.

He helped himself to another glass of whisky and lit up a cigar as he read the evening paper. They had a piece on his latest victim. They once again showed his photograph. It was an old photo, at least ten years old he guessed; he looked a good deal less scrawny. Just as well then that he'd dyed his hair and trimmed his beard before he'd settled at his new temporary lodgings situated just outside Peterculter, a suburb on the northern banks of the river Dee.

He'd found an old abandoned cottage slightly off the beaten track, the main building was a ruin but the old outhouse at the back wasn't too bad. It was wind and water tight, perfectly adequate for now. It even had an electricity supply, thanks to a small generator he'd found lying in one of the lockups at the back.

He smiled to himself as the fiery liquid warmed his belly.

The police protection side of things, although bothersome, didn't worry him too much at all, in fact, in a way they had played right into his hands. While they were using up their valuable resources protecting who they thought the next victims might be, he would go after his last three targets.

They had picked three each, him and Clara. His three were already gone; he was glad that he'd gone for the obvious ones first, now it was time to deal with hers. At first he had thought her choice of victims strange. He thought, maybe due to her illness, she wasn't thinking straight. Then the more he pondered on it, the more he came to realise that they played their part in Rose's demise every bit as much as the others had, maybe more so, depending on how you looked at it.

The police wouldn't have a clue who they were, they'd never guess in a month of Sundays.

He laughed, that was another one of Clara's favourite sayings. He could hear her saying it now, in his head. Her voice was becoming clearer, almost like she was standing in the room talking to him.

'Never in a month of Sundays, Harry.'

He took a sip of whisky.

There was one slight problem though.

Victor Whitelaw. He didn't have to guess who the victims may be. He knew. Maybe him and his daughter.

He didn't like loose ends, he never had. The more he thought about this the more he knew something had to be done.

He picked up his unregistered mobile phone, and laid out his list of hotel phone numbers. He had ripped the pages out of the phone book in his last lodgings earlier, and then took out Max's ID.

It was a long shot he knew, Victor and Mary could be hiding out anywhere, with friends, family, whatever, but he might as well give it a go. Besides, it would kill some time before it was time to kill.

He laughed at his choice of phrase then, after refilling his glass, he methodically began to work his way through the list.

*

Buchanan, as he often had a habit of doing depending on the outcome of the day, had changed the meeting place. Rather than meeting his small team at home as he had originally planned, he had changed the venue to his favourite watering hole, The Prince Of Wales. He and Max were joyously tucking into a plate of home-made steak pie and chips when PC Atkins and Lucy Jacobs entered the pub. Lucy had changed into a garish bright-green coat adorned with a luminous red scarf and matching woolly hat and gloves. The hat had ridiculously huge white snowflakes embroidered into it.

'Let me guess,' said Buchanan. 'Tonight, Matthew, I am going to be a Christmas tree! Whatever you do, don't stand against the pub decorations, you'll become invisible.'

Max tried hard not to choke on his steak pie as Lucy shook her head.

'You'll be seeing stars in your eyes if you don't cut that crap.'

She stared at him and shook her head. It reminded him of a snow storm.

'Anyway, look at you, how come you're always dressed like you're going to a funeral?'

Buchanan leaned forward and looked at her menacingly.

'It's to reflect the dark underbelly of society with which I have to deal with on a daily basis.'

'Now you're taking the piss. How the hell do you put up with him?' she asked Max as Atkins went up for a round of drinks.

'Pay no attention, he can't help himself. I'm Max by the way, I take it you're Lucy.'

They shook hands.

'Pleased to meet you, Max,' she replied as she unwrapped what seemed to Buchanan to be yards and yards of the bright red material of her scarf.

'The pleasure's all mine, grab a seat.'

He pushed the seat opposite him out towards her with his foot.

'Cheers, I will in a minute after I nip to the loo.'

'It's just round to your left there,' said Buchanan through a mouthful of food as she walked off in the totally wrong direction.

He shook his head.

'I wonder if she gets style tips from the same person as Rennie?' he asked Max as he polished off his last few chips.

'There is a similarity there, right enough.'

'What a couple they'd make, eh, Max. Rennie in his Santa jacket and her in her Christmas tree get up.'

Max creased himself laughing as Atkins returned with a tray full of drinks.

'What's so funny?' she asked as she placed the drinks on

the table.

'We were just discussing how Lucy and Rennie would make a great couple, that's all,' replied Buchanan.

'Ah! Got you, sir, the dress sense, I thought that myself when I saw her. She seems nice enough though, a bit kooky but I quite like her.'

'What's she drinking, by the way?'

Atkins tried to hold herself in check.

'Blue Bols.'

They all laughed.

'Fuck!' said Buchanan. 'Even her drink's luminous.'

'Are you lot laughing at my expense?' said the loud voice from behind.

'We're only taking the piss, Miss Jacobs, grab a seat and enjoy your drink.'

She smiled. 'Cheers, I'm in need of that.' She looked around her. 'Great pub by the way.'

'I very rarely go anywhere else; I've been coming here for years.'

He put his plate on top of Max's and handed them to the nearby waitress.

'Have you dug up any more info on old Harry yet?'

She hauled out some crumpled up sheets of paper from the confines of her oversized bag.

'I have actually. He had a high-up job in the government for years, strictly hush-hush, my guess is its military related but everywhere I turn I hit my head against a brick wall.'

'That would explain his shooting and bomb making skills right enough,' interrupted Max. 'By the way, I see the press have given him a name. It's in here.'

He showed them the evening paper.

'Good God,' cried Buchanan, once again shaking his head.

'The DCI is gonna love that. Right, Max, give us the details.'

' "The Festive Assassin". It's quite catchy really. Look, it's written here, under his picture.'

He scratched his head.

'Is it just me or does he look like Charlton Heston, with a beard?'

'Moses,' replied Buchanan.

'What?'

'He looks like Charlton Heston as Moses. He made a movie about him a good while ago.'

Buchanan looked on as Miss Jacobs shuffled her crumpled sheets of paper about.

She hadn't heard a word they'd said and continued as if the interruption had never occurred.

'This will interest you though. His wife's been suffering with cancer for the last few years. Until today. She died in the early hours of this morning in a Canadian hospital. According to the nurse I talked to they were inseparable. He used to visit her twice every day, well, until the last couple of weeks. That's probably when he came over here to exact his vengeance, even then though he contacted her every evening via the Internet. The person I talked to said that Clara would ask for the curtain to be drawn around her bed each night so that they could talk to each other privately via their webcams.'

Buchanan pointed at her.

'Clara's death that could be the stressor, if that's the right word for it … that's what made him change his methods in killing them. What made them more personal?'

'Very good, Inspector, I'm impressed. This makes him a very dangerous man though!'

Buchanan laughed to himself quietly as he took a drink.

'Aye, I got that impression after the third murder, Miss Jacobs.'

'No … What I mean is it makes him even more dangerous than he was before: he has nothing to live for now, except the all-consuming need to exact his revenge. In fact, it wouldn't surprise me if she agreed to it, maybe demanded it. People ask for some strange last requests from their loved ones when they think their time is coming to an end.'

She punctuated the end of her statement by downing the last of the luminous blue drink.

'Get Lucy here another drink, Max, and while you're at it get me and PC Atkins a Guinness.'

He handed Max a tenner as he left for the bar. Buchanan rubbed his unshaven chin.

'Nice work, Lucy.'

'I told you I was right about the stressor,' she replied with a smirk on her face.

She shook her thick mane of hair with a flourish as she turned to PC Atkins.

'Are you just drinking the same drink as him to impress, or do you really enjoy that stuff? It seems a strange drink to me for a young lady of your years.'

'Excuse me?'

She pointed to the two near empty glasses; one was a pint, one a half.

'The Guinness? When someone is trying to impress a person, or indeed is attracted to a person, they tend to mirror certain things. It could be their gestures, their actions, or a simpler thing, such as drinking the same drink.'

Jenny turned bright red.

'I've always drunk stout. My mother's side of the family are Irish. Every time there was a party or whatever going on in our house it was freely available. It's just a coincidence that the DI here drinks it.'

'If you say so.'

Atkins raised her voice.

'And anyway, if we're going to talk about weird drinks …'

'Ladies!' shouted Buchanan. 'Jenny, you keep your voice down and you, Miss Jacobs, save the psychology lecture for your students.'

Just then, Max arrived back with the drinks.

'Thank fuck for that,' thought Buchanan.

He drank the last of his pint then stood up.

'I'm afraid I'll have to go visit the little boys room. I'll let Max here give you a blow by blow account of his grand adventure today. I'll be back in a few minutes.'

*

After relieving himself, Buchanan was just about to wash his hands when the door opened and a huge mountain of a man entered the toilets. He had long red hair which matched the scruffy beard he was wearing. He looked like a Viking.

'Ronnie! How's it going, man? You caught that mad old bastard that's running around shooting people and blowing them up? What sort of shit's that for an old man to be doing?'

'Still working on it, Archie. You would think somebody of his age would be happy enough playing bingo or bowls, eh?'

Archie laughed as he zipped up his jeans.

'Make sure you catch him quick mind. The wife's refusing to do any Christmas shopping till they catch the bastard. The bairn will have no presents this year.'

'I'll make sure you're the first to know when we catch him. Take care, Archie.'

'Oh! By the way, who's the Christmas tree?'

Buchanan laughed.

'Some expert from Edinburgh, she's supposed to be here to help us catch him.'

Archie shook his head.

'If you do catch him, force him to wear that coat of hers. He'll be singing like a canary in no time.'

As he left the pub's toilet, he noticed another familiar face sitting at the bar. He quietly walked towards her then stood behind her and spoke quietly into her ear.

' "The Festive Assassin". One of yours, I take it.'

She turned round and smiled at him.

'Guilty as charged, Inspector. You want to get your handcuffs out?'

'I've told you before, I'm attached! And besides, that smile doesn't work on me. What is it with you journalists and your daft names?'

'It's quirky, people like quirky.'

She reached to the foot of her bar stool and reached for her bag.

'I have something for you by the way. I did a bit of digging into Mr Jackson's finances. There's something dodgy going on there. A few months ago, there were quite a few large cheques written out to individual people, not to businesses or anything like that. Seemed a bit strange to me. Some of them are for extremely large sums. It's almost as if he was paying people off. I'm going to look into it further; there could be a story in it.'

'There is. Try: "Well-heeled couple use their money to bypass normal adoption procedures." '

'Paying off people to adopt a kid! You're fucking joking, right?'

'Nope, dig into the background of the people who got the money, make the bastards pay for it.'

'Hold on though, the money they had available to them,

they could have privately adopted a kid, folk do it all the time.'

'Aye, but Mrs Jackson had her heart set on this particular kid. And what Mrs Jackson wanted, she had a habit of moving heaven and earth to make sure she got.'

'Fuck! This could be huge. Cheers, Ronnie, nice one.'

He winked at her.

'Let me know when you fit the story together.'

*

When he returned to the table, the two women seemed to have gotten over their differences and were ghoulishly examining Max's war wound.

He took his seat and rubbed his hands together.

'Right, where were we?'

'I believe it was my turn, sir,' replied PC Atkins.

'The floor's all yours, Jenny.'

She pulled out a small tablet PC from her inside pocket and put it on the table in front of her.

'Nice bit of kit, that,' said Max.

'It's new, just came out the other week.'

Max picked it up and inspected it. 'A hundred and twenty gig, great storage. I'm quite fan … '

'Children! Calm the fuck down, it's only a computer.' He looked straight at PC Atkins. 'As I said, the floor's all yours.'

'Sorry, sir.'

She turned on the tablet and began her report.

'Rose's ex-husband - his alibi checks out, not that it makes much difference now that we know who the killer is. He's been offshore for the last week or so. I managed to get a call through to him though. He was quite evasive when I mentioned Melissa. According to him, he never had much interest in the child from the off. He said he never wanted a kid, that's why when Rose took her own life he never applied for custody.'

'Did you mention the pay off?' asked Buchanan.

'Of course, he just laughed it off. It was free money as far as he was concerned, why shouldn't he take it. He never let them know that he had no intention of applying for custody in the first place. When he was approached with the incentive to stay out of the proceedings, he couldn't believe his luck.'

Buchanan shook his head.

'What an insensitive bastard.'

'Not necessarily,' interrupted Miss Jacobs. 'Some people simply never bond with their children; some actually grow to resent them. I've read the file on Rose, it's all there.'

She held up her hand and started counting on her fingers.

'One - Rose became obsessed with the child, leaving her no time to spend with him. Two - this lead to their business suffering, a business they both built from the ground up, I may add, and Three - it ultimately lead to the break-up of their marriage, all things that would never have happened had they never had a child.'

'But surely everyone that has a child has to adapt, is that not part of the process?' replied Buchanan.

'Yes! Of course it is, but not everybody sticks to the plan. Granted, most people suck it up and get on with it, but some don't, and as I said, in some cases it leads to a resentment of the child.'

'I reckon she's right, sir,' said Atkins. 'He really did sound like he didn't give a toss about Melissa.'

'What about this Victor guy?'

She looked back at her tablet and scrolled the screen up.

'Victor Whitelaw? Rennie has sent a couple of officers round on a few occasions, still no sign of the guy. He's been off his work for almost a week but according to his colleagues, the man's a mess. His wife left him earlier on this year; he's hit the bottle quite badly apparently. She left him with a teenage daughter called Mary. I phoned around some of his neighbours, just to see if they had any idea of where he could be.'

'Good move, Miss Atkins.'

'Thanks, sir. The strange thing is though, one of them ...' She scrolled down the screen. 'A ... Mrs Turly says that Victor and his daughter have been inseparable since his marriage breakup. Yet, for the last few days he's only ever been seen on his own. Most unusual she says, you never see one without the other most days.'

'That definitely sounds a bit fishy,' said Buchanan.

He turned towards Max.

'Get in touch with the incident room, get them to put a car outside this Victor guy's flat. I want to know the minute he appears.'

'Will do, sir,'

'And get them to put a trace on his phone, see if we can tie him down to a location.'

'I'm on it.'

As Max stepped outside to make the call, Buchanan stood up and rubbed his hands.

'Right, my round, I think. It's been a very busy day for everyone. So, Miss Jacobs, put away that big crumpled pile of papers of yours, and you, PC Atkins, get rid of the palm top, tablet, whatever the hell you call the thing. Now … the both of you try and relax for once. No more talk of work. In fact, I've decided that we're all going to have a game of darts.'

The two women gave each other a strange look.

He left for the bar and then stopped abruptly and turned round to face them.

'Oh! And, Miss Jacobs, I don't want to hear anything about phallic symbols, penetration or piquerism. It's only throwing some sharp objects at a bloody board.'

The two women laughed loudly as he continued on to the bar.

*

He had just finished paying for the drinks when Max turned up to lend a hand.

'We've had a bit of news, sir. Good or bad depending on how you look at it.'

'Don't be shy, Max, spit it out.'

'Someone recognised the photo in tonight's Express. He's been staying in a hotel in Stonehaven, at least he was until late on this afternoon. He's checked out now but Rennie has sent a few of the forensic guys round to see if he's left any clue as to where he's off to next.'

Chapter Nineteen

Mary, after a long deliberation, had finally managed to persuade her father to clean himself up. He hadn't half let himself go; she could still smell his body odour hanging about the hotel room like … well, like a bad smell. Not half as bad as the putrid stench coming of herself earlier, but the sickly sweet smell still made her feel nauseous. She fully opened both windows, despite the cold outside, to freshen up the room.

Her father was in the bathroom showering and shaving. She was still getting nowhere with their predicament, despite all her pleading he still flatly refused to go to the police. She had appealed to him on many levels: 'We can't have any future killings hanging over our heads; we would be much safer under police protection than hiding out in a busy central hotel. Just think how good you'll feel if you manage to save the lives of the other people still left on the list.' However, all her appeals fell on deaf ears. He was scared shitless. Not so much for himself, as for her. She could understand that, to a certain extent. Since her mother had walked out and left him, Mary was all he had left. Parents were supposed to take care of their children, but in her case, the roles had been reversed.

She looked at herself in the mirror. She still felt dirty, despite practically scrubbing herself raw.

'If he won't do it then you'll have to,' said the familiar voice in her head.

'I'd forgotten about you,' replied Mary. 'Bugger off!'

'You know I'm right,' the voice replied.

She heard the sound of the shower starting up. If she was going to do anything, now was the time.

'Dad!' she shouted.

There was no reply from the bathroom.

'DAD!' she shouted again, louder this time.

There was still no reply.

Now that she was absolutely sure that her father couldn't hear her above the sound of the shower, she walked over to the chair in the corner. She reached into the inside pocket of her father's jacket, removed his mobile, turned it on and quickly dialled 999.

'Hello, I'd like to talk to someone. It's concerning the recent murders. Could you put me through to someone in charge please? I have some very important information.'

She heard a keyboard clicking.

'Could you hold the line please?'

Mary listened to the silence at the other end of the line for what seemed like forever.

'Hurry up, for fuck sake,' she muttered under her breath.

Finally, she heard the receiver being picked up at the other end.

'Incident Room. How can I help?'

Chapter Twenty

'Yes, sir, can I help you?'

The old man held up the police ID.

'Sergeant Maxwell, Grampian Police. I phoned earlier regarding a Mister Whitelaw. I need to interview him. He's staying in this very hotel seemingly, him and his daughter.'

The man gave him a quizzical look and arched his eyebrows above the frames of his thick rimmed spectacles.

'You look a bit old for a copper.'

The old looking man laughed and combed splayed fingers through his newly dyed hair.

'I get that all the time, I'm not as old as I look actually, I have a very demanding wife.'

The hotel employee laughed.

'A colleague took the phone call, he left me a note. I've been expecting you. We're always happy to help out the local constabulary.'

He looked at a sheet of paper on his desk. 'They booked in early this morning. He used the name Mr Smith.'

'How original. What's the room number?'

'He's in Room 205. It's on the second floor.'

The desk clerk tapped his pen against his teeth.

'They're not dangerous, are they? I mean, I follow the news. We've had a shooting and a bombing in this town in the last couple of days. They're not going to run around the place shooting the shit out of the guests are they?'

The old man laughed.

'Doubtful, sir, this is a completely different enquiry.'

He walked up the stairs, then along the dimly lit corridor until he found the room he was looking for.

He looked right and then left, then once he was sure he was alone he removed the handgun from the shoulder holster beneath his jacket and attached the silencer.

He knocked on the door and adopted a Scottish accent.

'Police. Open up in there.'

'What do you want?' came the reply. Victor's voice was all a quiver.

'Am I talking to Victor Whitelaw?'

There was a long pause but no answer came.

'If I am talking to Mr Whitelaw, it's very important you listen to me. We believe you to be in immediate danger, sir, you and your daughter. Mary, isn't it?'

'Yes! Yes it is.'

'We're here to take you both into protective custody.'

'How do I know you are who you say you are?'

'Look, I know you're scared Mr Whitelaw. I would be too in your position. This guy that's after you is a very dangerous man, no doubt about it, but you'll be far better off with us than sitting here holed up in your hotel room.'

'I don't know,' came the reply.

'How's this sound, open the door ever so slightly and I'll hand you through my ID. I can't say fairer than that now, can I, sir?'

'I suppose you can't.'

He heard the door unlock and watched as a slight gap appeared.

The old man handed through Max's ID. Then after a few seconds, the door slowly began to open.

He shot Victor dead centre in the forehead and watched as his body crumpled to the floor.

Quick as a flash he entered the room and slammed the door shut with his back.

He quickly surveyed the room.

There was no sign of Mary.

He checked the bathroom, it was empty. He looked under the bed, no sign.

'Where the fuck has she got to?'

He had to find the girl. He didn't know how much her father might have told her. Maybe nothing, but he couldn't assume that.

The police mustn't find out who his last three targets were. It would make his job so much more difficult.

'Bugger it!'

He grunted as he hoisted the recently deceased man onto his shoulder and bundled him on to one of the beds.

He thought things over in his head.

He decided to wait it out, wherever the girl was she

would be back, that he was sure of. He sat down on a large comfortable seat by the window and watched the snowflakes falling outside as he helped himself to some of the dead man's whisky.

*

Buchanan was standing outside the pub enjoying a cigarette when his mobile rang.

'I thought I'd turned that bloody thing off,' he thought to himself. He took a couple of draws from his cigarette before deciding whether to answer it or not.

'Bugger it!' He pressed the answer button. 'DI Buchanan.'

'Ronnie, it's Clair at the incident room. We have Mary Whitelaw here. She phoned us earlier. Her and her father have been in hiding, they're both terrified for their life. Thing is, she won't tell us much, she insists she talks to someone leading the investigation. I know you're supposed to be finished for the day but we tried reaching Rennie and couldn't get an answer.'

'What a surprise. Where's the father?'

'He's still holed up in their hotel room. She won't tell us which hotel though, not until she's talked to you, that's why I phoned.'

'Stick her on.'

He lit up another cigarette while he waited for Mary to come to the phone.

'Mr Buchanan, you won't know me, my name's Mary Whitelaw.'

The girl sounded nervous.

'Hi, Mary. How can I help?

'We need protection, me and my father. It's to do with the recent murders; we know what it's all about.'

He lit another cigarette.

'How do you mean?'

'This old guy put pressure on my dad to provide him with confidential information on six people; two of them are already dead. He knows the names of the other four.'

'Three are already dead,' thought Buchanan.

'What do you mean by "put pressure on him", Mary?'

'He held me captive for days in a dingy cellar, but I managed to escape.'

The girl suddenly broke down; he could hear her sobbing at the other end of the phone.

'Mary! Listen to me. You're safe enough where you are but we can't provide protection for your father until we know where he is now, can we?'

He heard the sobs slowly subside at the other end of the call.

'I don't know … He has no idea I'm here, he'll go apeshit. The old man told him that if we stayed out of things for the next few days and *didn't* go to the police, we would be safe.'

She started to cry again.

'But I just couldn't, I just couldn't stand by while he goes after the others on the list.'

'Look, Mary, you've obviously been through a lot but you've done the right thing coming to us. This man is extremely dangerous; in fact he's a fucking maniac.'

Mary laughed through the sobs.

'But, as I said before, we can't help without you supplying us with your dad's location.'

The line went silent as Buchanan crossed his fingers and held his hand behind his back.

'He's in the Travelodge in Bridge Street. Room 205.'

'Thanks, Mary. Can you put Clair back on now, love?'

He listened as the phone was handed over.

'Yes, Ronnie?'

'Send a couple of cars round there right away, I'll be there myself soon enough, I'm just five minutes away.'

'Will do. I'll get on to it right away.'

He threw away the rest of his cigarette and dashed back into the pub.

'Max! We have a break, get your arse moving. I'll see you two ladies later.'

*

They arrived outside the hotel just as the police vehicles drew up outside. Buchanan waited for the officers to exit the car. The town was in full pre-Christmas swing, inebriated folk were everywhere, many of them in cheap Santa hats. The snow, which had started off again and the sub-zero temperature seemed not to worry them in the slightest.

A makeshift choir stood behind them singing silent night. Buchanan blocked them out.

'Evening, gents. A quick word if you don't mind. This

guy is edgy; his wife buggered off a while ago and left him in bits. Between that and his recent troubles he's likely to be really spooked, you got that?'

The all nodded their heads.

'Besides, if he ends up shitting himself one of you lot are mopping it up.'

They all laughed.

'Right, let's go.'

They squeezed themselves past the carol singers and entered the building. Buchanan approached the guy at the desk and showed his ID. 'Room 205, where is it?'

'Second floor, what is this, a police convention?'

'What the bloody hell do you mean by that?'

'You already have one guy up there. He came in not more than half an hour ago. He looks like he belongs to the geriatric division.'

He smirked to himself as he looked at the visitor's book.

'Sergeant Phil Maxwell.'

'Shit!' Max checked his pockets.

'I forgot, sir, when he grabbed me this afternoon he took my ID, I should have reported it.'

'You did Max, to me earlier on today.'

He winked.

'Can't you remember?'

Max smiled.

'Secure the area, don't let anyone upstairs and phone in

for back up. We'll need the armed response unit. We don't know what this old bastard has up his sleeve.'

He turned to the guys in uniform.

'Follow me, lads.'

'SIR!' shouted Max. 'You can't go up there, wait till the cavalry arrive.'

He turned around and held up his hands, palms forward.

'Calm down, sergeant, I'm just going to have a look. I won't do anything stupid.'

With that, he went tearing up the stairs with the other officers close behind him.

*

The corridor was deserted. One of the strip lights above was flickering on and off. It made a strange buzzing noise as it cast strange moving shadows in all directions. Buchanan told two of the officers to wait at the top of the stairs, the others he left guarding the bottom. He stood with his back against the wall and slowly edged himself along until he was standing just to the right of room 205. He leaned over and pressed his ear against the door. He could hear nothing, no conversation, no TV, no radio. There was no sound at all coming from inside the room.

He was just about to make his way back to the top of the stairs when his mobile rang. It shattered the silence with its high pitched trill.

'Shit!'

He looked at the screen. Michelle. She always had a knack for phoning at the most ill-timed moments.

He ended the call before it had begun, turned the phone's power off and stuck it back in his inside pocket. He had just begun to make his way back towards the two uniformed officers when the door of Room 205 flew open and he was hoisted off his feet and physically dragged into the room.

He landed on the hotel room floor with a thump.

'Hello again, Inspector, you have a distinct habit of turning up at the most inopportune moments.'

He waved his gun to the right.

'Grab a seat on the bed over there and try not to disturb Mr Whitelaw, he's dead tired.'

He spotted the middle aged man, who he assumed was Mary's father, lying at a strange angle on one of the twin beds.

His eyes immediately went to the small blood-encrusted bullet hole in his temple.

'Jesus! You killed him.'

'There was no joy in it, but needs must. If his daughter had stayed put there would have been no need for his death. So, you could say that Mary killed him, or, at the very least, she instigated a rather unfortunate series of events that ultimately lead to his demise.'

Buchanan turned towards the old man who had the silenced gun pointing at his head and raised his hands.

'You do realise that there's a shit load of coppers heading towards this hotel as we speak, don't you?'

'Of that I have no doubt, Inspector Buchanan, the thing is though, we aren't going to be here when they arrive, now give me your phone and open the window.'

'What?'

'I said open the window.'

Buchanan did as he was asked.

'Now, jump out.'

'Are you fucking mad?'

'It's either that or I shoot you, the choice is yours.'

Buchanan looked back and forth between the window and the gun. The old man let out a raucous laugh.

'Don't worry, Inspector, this hotel is handily located on a corner. The street below, Bridge Street I believe, is where its entrance is situated; around the corner is Union Street.'

'Thanks for the info, but I do actually know the street names around here.'

The old man ignored the remark.

'Look down from the window, Inspector, you will see that there's a metal canopy above the shops below. It goes right around the corner, it's no more than a four or five-foot drop, now …'

He waved the handgun towards the open window.

'Get on with it.'

Buchanan jumped down as the old man covered him with the gun from the window. The surface was icy with frost; he almost went careering straight over the edge.

After closing the window behind him, the old man followed suit. He landed expertly, as if jumping on to icy surfaces was an everyday event for him.

The sound of sirens could be heard cutting through the chilled night air. They were growing ever closer.

'Now, lie down, Inspector. We're going to stay here quiet as the grave until the backup arrives. No doubt they'll all go piling into the entrance below us while we ease our way around onto Union Street and make good our escape. Always have an exit plan, that's what I always say.'

'Say, I refuse to lie down,' replied Buchanan.

He heard a muffled pop then felt the bullet zipping by his right ear.

'Refusal won't be tolerated.'

'Right! Jesus, I'm doing it, okay,' replied Buchanan as he sank to his knees and eased himself on to his belly.

They both lay there in the dark listening to the makeshift choir, who were now singing *The Holly and the Ivy* below them. They watched as the police vehicles went tearing down Bridge Street towards the hotel entrance.

The silence was broken by the old man.

'So, so predictable, it's the same the world over. Right. Now, move it, crawl around the corner till you get to the end and then drop down onto the pavement below, and remember, I have you covered. The next bullet will be a lot closer than the last, believe me.'

Buchanan began to crawl.

'If you must use that gun of yours, use it on those drunken singers below us, they're doing my fucking head in.'

*

'Max!'

180

Max turned around to see one of the uniformed officers approaching him. He had a shocked look on his face.

'The bastard has Buchanan.'

'What do you mean he has Buchanan?'

The officer caught his breath.

'Ronnie was standing outside the door, the next thing we see is him getting hauled in and the door slamming shut behind him. He's in there, Max.'

'Where's PC Thompson?'

'I left him up there; if they attempt to leave the room he's going to contact us right away.'

'Good work, Barry.'

'Max! What the fuck's going on?'

He looked towards the hotel entrance.

It was DCI Montgomery flanked by two firearms officers dressed up in riot gear.

He was dressed in a dinner suit.

'I've just been told about this, I had to leave my golf club lunch. Is it true what they're saying, that we have the old bastard cornered in his hotel room?'

'So it seems, but we have a slight problem.'

'What sort of problem?'

'He has Buchanan.'

'Has Buchanan! What the fuck is he doing up there in the first place, he should have stayed down here till we had the place secured. Does that man ever stick to the rules?'

Max shrugged his shoulders.

'For Christ's sake, we already have the armed response unit and the dog handlers out there as it is. There's also a fucking helicopter on its way. Now you're telling me I'm going to have to call in a negotiator.'

'Looks like it, sir.'

'Fuck! This will take hours. I'll never get back to my golf club. I'm supposed to be doing a speech, too.'

He looked towards the door.

'Oh shit! That's all I need. It's the superintendent.'

The tall man walked over to them. He took of his gloves and rubbed his hands together.

'Montgomery! What's the plan?' asked Jake Burns.

He shook the superintendent's hand.

'Hello, sir.'

His face began to turn red.

'I thought we had it all under control. We have the back entrance covered, Bridge Street is closed off at either end and I have some of the uniformed officers evacuating the guests from the hotel. However there's a big problem, sir.'

'What kind of a problem? Spit it out, man!'

'He's taken DI Buchanan captive, sir. They're holed up in room 205.'

Chapter Twenty One

They stood in the snow on Union Bridge. They were surrounded by other onlookers watching the spectacle playing out before them.

'Nice light show!' shouted someone to the left. He had a huge bottle of cider in his hand.

'Very festive!' cried another.

'You're putting the crappy Christmas lights to shame.'

'Holly shit!' cried an old woman. She pointed to the sky. 'Look, they've brought in a fucking helicopter.'

'Brilliant! Maybe they've flown in Bruce Willis,' said cider guy. 'He'll soon get things sorted.'

'Yippee Ki-yay, motherfucker!' shouted a guy sitting on the bench at the side.

A roar of laughter came from the crowd behind. The old man stood behind his captive, his gun pressed hard against Buchanan's back.

'They'll no doubt have the front and back covered. How long do you reckon it'll take them to work out that there's another exit staring them right in the face?'

They both watched transfixed as a young police officer, the blue lights strobing behind his back as if he was in a nightclub, held his hand up to stop a bus from carrying on along its usual route.

Buchanan was dumbfounded. They'd dropped off the

canopy smack bang amongst the late night revellers in the centre of Union Street and no one batted an eyelid. Well apart from the group of young women who gave an impromptu rendition of *It's raining men*.

'Here. This will warm you up.'

The old man handed Buchanan a hip flask full of whisky. He took a large swig, enjoying the inner warmth it provided despite his situation.

'What have you got planned for me, then?' he asked as he handed back the flask.

The old man didn't hear him. He was too busy shaking his head from side to side and muttering under his breath.

'Are you okay?' asked Buchanan.

The old man's left eye started twitching. He held his hand over it for a minute. 'Don't worry about me, Inspector. As for your question, what do I have planned for you? Nothing, most probably.'

He took a drink from the flask, replaced the cap and stuck it away back inside his jacket.

'I'm not an out and out killer, Inspector; I'm working to an agenda. Unless you're on myself and Clara's list or are, in some way, attached to Rose's court Hearing you have nothing to fear from me. As I mentioned before to you, I regret having to deal with Victor, he did a lot of work for me. He paid a penance of sorts. I suppose you could put it down to collateral damage.'

Buchanan felt the gun getting pushed harder into his back.

'Time for us to move, I think. I've seen enough here.'

They continued along Union Street. There was a strange tinkling noise in the air that Buchanan couldn't place. It sounded like a million miniature bells ringing in unison. He looked up and figured it out. It was the hundreds of tiny bulbs in the Christmas lights stretched across the street being buffeted by the icy wind. He drew his coat around him.

'Answer me this,' said Buchanan to the man behind. 'What would you have done with Mary had she been in the hotel room with her father?'

'I'm not sure to be honest. It would all depend on what she knew, I suppose.'

'So, you would have got your hammer out and broken her toes like you did to the shop assistant?'

'Not necessarily: there are many ways to extract information. That was done simply to put pressure on Max. Anyway, knowing her father, it's very doubtful he would have told her much. I reckon he would have gone out of his way to keep her involvement to a minimum.'

The old man stopped in front of two huge iron gates, he looked them up and down.

'What's this place, Inspector?'

'Saint Nicholas Kirk yard, it's an old cemetery attached to a medieval church.'

'I do know what a Kirk is, Inspector, I was originally brought up with the mither tongue. I spent most of my youth in Stonehaven, as I'm sure you know.'

The old man peered through the gates at the shadowy gravestones within.

'This should do fine for what I have in mind. Get in.'

185

They walked through the ancient churchyard. The place was deserted; its only occupants were Buchanan, the old man, and the dead. They walked up the frost covered path. The old man seemed fascinated by some of the ancient gravestones. Some of the really old ones, most of them worn smooth by the millions of footsteps from the past, were incorporated into the path itself. He went to great lengths to avoid stepping on them.

Then suddenly, out the corner of his eye, Buchanan saw a ghost. The white shape with the huge staring eyes silently came flying towards him and let out an ear-piercing scream before disappearing into the snow fall behind him.

'What the fuck was that?'

The old man laughed.

'Nothing more than a barn owl, Inspector, now keep moving.'

They continued up the flagstone path until they reached the imposing church at the end.

'Such magnificent architecture, don't you think?' asked the old man.

Buchanan looked skywards towards the tall gothic spire above him.

'I suppose it is.'

The old man's eyes looked back and forth, as if in search of something.

'Right, detective, this is where we part company; it doesn't look like we have anyone on our tail so you've outgrown your usefulness as a bargaining tool.'

He motioned with the hand gun, 'Walk over to that rather ornate looking Victorian street lamp tucked away by the door there.'

Buchanan did as he was asked.

'Now turn around and back up against it.' The old man stood at the other side of the lamp. 'Arms out behind you.'

He used a tie wrap to secure Buchanan's wrists together, effectively tying him to the base of the street lamp.

'I'll fucking freeze standing here, I won't be able to move.'

'It does impede your movement somewhat, but you can stamp your feet up and down, whatever. I'm sure an enterprising fellow like you can come up with something. Anyway, there's no need to panic you won't be here that long.'

He reached into his pocket and brought out Buchanan's phone. He pressed the button to turn it on and then scrolled through the address list till he found Max, then pressed the key to make the call.

'Sir!'

'Very polite of you, Max, not enough young people nowadays respect their elders.'

'It's you! What have you done with Buchanan?'

'He's safe enough, don't worry, he's just a bit tied up at the moment, he can't come to the phone.'

'Why aren't you answering the hotel room phone, we've been ringing for ages. We want to discuss terms.'

'That won't be necessary, Max; there are no terms to

discuss.'

'You do know you're surrounded don't you? There's no way you're getting out of here.'

'The only people I'm surrounded by here Max are the dead.'

'What! You don't mean …'

The old man produced a wicked laugh.

'Calm down, young Philip. I'm not even in the room you and your colleagues are staking out anymore, neither is Buchanan. You'll find your beloved inspector in Saint Nicholas churchyard. Bye for now.'

He stuck the phone back in Buchanan's pocket.

'See you later, Detective. I have a barbecue to prepare for.'

He walked towards the steps in the far corner of the graveyard and slowly, like the owl before, he disappeared into the blanket of snow.

*

Max went in search of DCI Montgomery.

He had to push his way through the mass of people attempting to leave the hotel. There was a rumour going around the residents that the sniper was in the hotel. Someone had started it on Twitter, oblivious as to how close they were to the truth.

He found the DCI standing in front of the reception area trying to direct the panic and utter chaos the all around him. He was fighting a losing battle. Standing in his dinner jacket with his arms waving around manically, he looked like some demented orchestra conductor.

Max approached him and raised his voice to be heard above the din.

'I've just had a phone call, sir, from the old guy that snatched DI Buchanan. According to him, they're not even in the room anymore. They're in the old church yard down the road.'

He shook his head.

'Impossible! We have all the exits covered and we've had surveillance on the hotel room door since Buchanan went into the room. He's yanking your chain, Max, there's no way they could have possibly left that room without someone seeing them.'

'There's always the windows,' said the clerk behind the desk.

Montgomery bullishly turned to face him.

'What?'

'The windows. We had a couple of Polish guys working the night shift a couple of months ago. We had to get rid of them. They were clocking in, changing into their best gear up in one of the rooms and then sneaking out the window to hit the night clubs. They'd been doing it for a while seemingly.'

'And you're just telling me this now. Well, that's fucking great!'

The desk clerk shrugged his shoulders.

'Nobody asked. There's a canopy below the windows, it's easily accomplished.' He hit the palm of his hand with his fist. 'Biff, bash, bosh. Out the window, onto the canopy, then drop down onto Union Street.'

Montgomery's face went beetroot. Max was convinced he could see steam coming out of his ears.

'I ought to fucking charge you with withholding information.'

He got on the radio to one of the firearms officers.

'Derek, where are you?'

'I'm right at the top of Bridge Street, on the corner with Union Street.'

'Look up at the building and describe it to me.'

'What?'

'Just humour me, tell me what you see.'

'I'm looking up at the hotel now, it's a granite building with heaps of windows, not much to tell really.'

'Is there some sort of canopy there?'

'Aye, just above the shops, directly below the hotel.'

'Fuck!'

He turned back to the clerk.

'Room 205, looking from outside, could you show us where the window to that room is?'

'Of course.'

'Right, come with me, you too, Max.'

They went outside and found Derek.

'I want a man up there, on that canopy; I want him to very carefully take a peak in the window of room 205. You got that?'

'Sure, we were planning on doing that anyway, once the cherry picker gets here.'

'Fuck the cherry picker; I want someone up there now.'

Derek shook his head.

'Health and safety won't like that.'

'I couldn't give a fuck; just get someone up there pronto.'

Derek looked up.

'I'll do it myself, but first thing in the morning I'm getting on to my union rep about this.'

'Aye, you do that.'

He stared at Montgomery.

'What window is it exactly?'

'It's the eighth one along, above the entrance in the first row,' interrupted the desk clerk.

'I thought it was on the second floor,' replied Montgomery.

'That is the second floor. The first floor is tucked behind the shops, it just contains offices.'

'Can I make a suggestion, sir?' asked Max.

'Fire away,' replied the DCI.

'Look across the road, sir, there's an Indian restaurant; it has a window directly across from the room. Why not get someone up there with a pair of binoculars, see what we can see from there before we risk putting anyone up on the canopy.'

'Great idea, Max,' said Derek 'You ought to have his

job.' He nodded towards Montgomery. 'He's obviously no use at it, he's a fucking lunatic.'

Montgomery's face went bright red once again as he lunged at Derek. He wrapped his fingers around the officer's throat.

'What the fuck did you say?'

'SIR!' shouted Max. 'The press are watching, calm down eh.'

He pulled them apart. Derek adjusted his clothing, and rubbed his Adam's apple.

'I'll get you for that, you fat bastard.'

He shouted to a younger fire arms officer, 'Sam, lad, grab the binoculars from the van and nip across the road to that restaurant. See if you can get a good look into that window up there.'

He pointed up, 'First row, eight along from the entrance. Call me when you're in position.'

'Yes, sir.'

He ran across the road.

DCI Montgomery glared at the firearms officer as they awaited the call.

'I have a visual, sir.'

'What do you see?'

'Not a lot really. There's one guy lying on the bed. Hold on I'll zoom in a bit. Fuck! Pardon my language, sir.'

'You're pardoned. What is it?'

'The guy on the bed, sir! He has a bullet wound to the

head. Dead centre shot.'

'Describe the guy.'

'Early forties, blonde hair, quite skinny.'

'That must be Victor,' said Max.

'Any sign of anyone else in the room, alive or dead?' asked Derek.

'Negative, sir, it's a big window, I can see the whole room. Even the bathroom door's open. There's bugger all sign of anyone else.'

Montgomery, who had finally calmed down, turned to Max.

'Get down to the churchyard; take a couple of officers with you and one of the armed guys just in case it's a set up. I'll get on to the superintendent; see if I can get the go ahead to enter the hotel room.'

He sighed heavily.

'What a fucking cockup.'

'Maybe you should have had someone up there to begin with,' said Derek smirking at him.

Max left them to their argument which had suddenly kicked off again.

After searching the outer perimeter of the graveyard they found Buchanan tied up to the old lamp post tucked away in the far corner next to the church.

'You on your stag night, sir?' asked Max

'Very funny. Someone cut this bloody cable tie, would they, I'm fucking freezing here.'

Chapter Twenty Two

The scruffy youth watched the swan swimming around in the small hole in the ice far below him. He was standing on Victoria Bridge in Torry. He took a huge draw on the last of the joint he was smoking, seemingly oblivious to the icy wind blowing the powdery snow all around him. Once satisfied it was well and truly roached, he threw the end of the joint towards the swan and laughed to himself as it was eagerly gobbled up by the bird.

'Stupid fucking arsehole!' he shouted as he rubbed his hands on the front of his oversized grubby green army jacket. The swan paid no attention to his rant. It climbed out of the water and shook itself dry as the young man bent down and picked up his cheap bottle of cider. He polished off the half empty bottle of gut rot in one huge gulp and then threw the empty vessel towards the swan. He missed by a mile.

'Fuck it!'

He wrapped his filthy jacket tightly around him and continued on his way along Victoria Road. He was heading towards the Victoria Bar, or the Rat's Cellar as it was still known to most of its local clientele.

He wiped his ever-running nose on his sleeve and then after pushing his long strands of greasy hair behind his ears he pushed himself through the swing doors.

The smell of stale beer and furniture polish hit him immediately. He paid it no heed. His eyes scanned the clientele of the small bar. Big Tam was sitting in the corner waiting for him, dressed as ever in one of his many track suits. He often wondered why he always wore such things; he'd certainly never seen him play any sports. He watched him fold away his paper and look towards him.

'Billy! Where the fuck've you been, you got my gear?'

He gave him a wave and sauntered over.

'Aye, I could only get ye a gram though, there's not much on the go. I only got six grams all together; four of them are for other people. He's getting more this afternoon though, at about two o clock, he said.'

'Give us it then. That'll have to do.'

'Get me a pint first, I'm gasping.'

'Fuck's sake! Do you ever buy yer 'ain?'

Tam made for the bar as Billy, once he was sure that he was out of sight, took a huge swig from Tam's pint.

'Is that Billy I saw you with there, Tam?' asked the barman as he poured a pint of cider.

'Aye, I'm surprised you canna smell the bastard from here!'

The barman laughed.

'I'm not sure what smells the worst around here, the fish hooses or Billy.'

'What is that weird smell that hangs about him anyway?'

'That's a question that bugged the shit out me for ages, but now I think I've got it sussed. It's a mixture of real bad body odour and patchouli oil. He douses everything he wears in the stuff, it's fucking rank!'

'What does he do that for?'

Tam laughed and leaned closer.

'Get this; he reckons that if he's carrying and he comes across a cop with a sniffer dog in tow, the dog won't smell the drugs because of the patchouli.'

'Who the fuck told him that?' asked the barman.

'According to him it was an ex-cop from the drug squad.'

The barman shook his head.

'What a plonker.'

'Aye, he's a dick.'

'Are you having another pint yourself, Tam?'

'Aye you better gimme one, that greasy bastard's probably tanned the rest of mine already. That's his fucking usual trick.'

The barman finished pouring Tam's drink.

'A pint of cider and a pint of Best. That'll be four pounds eighty, please.'

The minute Tam left with the two pints the barman picked up the phone. Once he was sure Tam was out of earshot, he looked at the post it pad on the wall and made the call.

'Hello, is that you. That toe rag you were looking for, he's here now. Aye, I'll let you know when he leaves. By the way, when do I get my money?'

*

'Here you go, Bill. Now gimme the gear.'

He furtively looked around the bar and then handed Tam a small polythene bag containing a white powder.

'It looks short,' said Tam. 'Have you had a line out of this?'

Billy rubbed his nose.'Have I fuck!'

Tam shook his head, 'This is a well named pub for you, ye rat bastard!'

'Honest, Tam, I never touched the stuff.'

He reached into his pocket, 'Look I've got my own gear, it's the exact same stuff.'

'That means fuck all.'

Tam reached under the table for his holdall.

'Only one way to tell.'

He reached into the side pocket and produced a set of micro scales.

'A gram you say.' He threw the packet onto the small metal plate. 'It's just over three quarters, ye robbin' bastard.'

'They sold me short then, its fuck all to do wi' me.'

'Is that right? Chuck yours on then.'

Billy did as he was asked.

'A gram exactly,' said Tam.

He held his left hand palm up and wiggled his fingers

'Hand the fucker over, you can have this one.'

Billy shook his head and sighed.

They swapped packets and settled down to have their drinks.

*

After five pints, a couple of joints shared outside with big Tam and a quick line in the pub's toilet, Billy was buzzing. He tripped on the step on the way out and landed face down on the pavement. He had tried to raise his arms to protect himself but his reactions were far too slow.

'Bastard!' he cried.

'You okay, lad?'

He looked up at the old man and rubbed his bleeding nose on his jacket. The blood seeped into his sleeve mixing with the plethora of older stains.

'Aye, I'm just a bit pissed, that's all.'

The man reached into his pocket and took out a handkerchief. 'Here, use this.'

Billy gratefully accepted it.

'Do you know this area well?'

'We'll enough,' said Billy, 'Why?'

The man moved closer.

'I'm looking for something. Something I'm thinking you might be able to help me with.'

'Woh! Wait a minute, pal, I don't take it up the arse, I'm no fucking pervert. Get that shit right oot yer heid!'

The old man laughed. 'I think you have the wrong idea, I'm looking to score.'

This time it was Billy's turn to laugh. 'Score! Aren't you a bit old for that sort of shit?'

'It's not for me, it's for my employer, you wouldn't believe the stuff he asks me to do for him.'

'What's he after like?'

'Anything he can get. Coke, speed, smack, anything. He's organised a big party for tonight. He's out to impress.'

Billy rubbed his chin.

'I don't know, I'd like to help you out but I'm pretty smashed. I just want to get home and crash.'

The old man hauled out a huge wad of bank notes.

'I could take my custom elsewhere.'

Billy's eyes lit up at the huge pile of money and even more so at the prospect of ripping the old man off.

'Have you got transport?'

'Aye, my car's parked in a small street around the corner.'

'Let's go then.'

Billy stopped half way there.

'I've seen your face somewhere, have you been on TV or maybe in the papers?'

'I get that a lot, my boss is quite recognisable in the media, you've probably seen a piece on him, I was probably floating about in the background somewhere. I often am.'

'Aye, that could be it. Who is your boss by the way?'

'That's one question I can't answer, Billy.'

The young man suddenly stopped.

'Hold on, how do you know my name?'

The old man looked shocked. 'You told me, don't you remember?'

'No!'

The old man laughed. 'You really are shitfaced, lad.'

Billy laughed along with him. 'Aye, you're right enough. Where's this motor then?'

*

'Nice fucking vehicle, what is it?'

'An Audi A7. It's not mine, I borrowed it.'

'From your boss?'

The old man nodded his head up and down in reply.

'One thing though, don't sit in the passenger seat, he goes fucking mad if people sit in the passenger seat. That's strictly reserved for the many women in his life.'

'No problem, I'll just get in the back, you can be my chauffeur.'

As he leaned down to get in the car, he felt a quick jolt then a slight tingling sensation as the Taser made contact with the back of his neck. He watched, unable to react, as the old man hauled out a syringe and stuck it deep into his thigh.

'Sleep tight, Billy!'

*

When he woke up, he was in agony. His head was pounding, but that was the least of his worries. He stood on an old rickety wooden chair. He was balanced on his toes. His hands had been tied behind his back and then his arms had been raised up behind him by a rope that was attached to a hook on the roof. The pressure on his upper arms was intense and he could feel a burning in his shoulder blades.

He tried to lower his feet on to the chair but he couldn't, it only added to the pressure, the pain was unbearable, he felt like he was about to pass out. He breathed heavily till the swirling dots and the tingling disappeared. Once he felt slightly better, he blinked the sweat out of his eyes, blew his fringe out of his face and looked at his surroundings.

He seemed to be in some sort of an old barn, it was hard to make out though as the only light in the area came from a small oil lamp propped on top of what looked like an old barrel of some sort.

He heard a rustling from the corner and saw a small pair of bright yellow eyes glinting in the glow of the lamp. He watched as the rat scurried under the chair and ran off into the distance.

'Hello!' he cried.

There was no answer.

'HELLO!' he cried again, louder this time.

His breath filled the cold air like a frozen cloud.

'Billy Redmond, how are the old arms doing?'

The voice was alien to him; he couldn't remember ever hearing such an accent before.

He looked around the immediate area but he couldn't see anyone. As his eyes grew used to the dark surroundings, he became aware of a shadow moving in the distance. It slowly took human form. He watched, fascinated, as the figure approached him through the dim light cast by the flickering lamp.

It was the old man with the Audi.

Billy put on a false show of bravado.

'Cut me fucking loose, you've had your fun. My arms are breaking here.'

The old man was carrying a bucket of water in one hand and what looked like a can of petrol in the other.

'They're not breaking. They are, however, very close to dislocating.'

The old man seemed to stare right through him.

'What you are experiencing is a form of torture called the strappado, it was very popular in medieval inquisitions.'

The old man kicked the chair away.

Billy screamed as his full weight was suddenly supported by his shoulder sockets alone. They gave way with a sickening pop. He passed out with the pain, but not for long. The old man had brought him round seconds later with the bucket of ice cold water.

'Do you ever pause to think about the misery you cause selling that shit of yours to people, Billy?'

The suspended youth tried to gain composure. He breathed heavily, trying to gain control of his sobbing.

'Do you remember a girl called Rose? She was an extremely pretty little thing.'

'Rose?' Billy cast his mind back.'Aye, I remember her, she OD'd didn't she?'

'You remember her then. Yes, she did take an overdose. An overdose on the drugs you provided.'

He pulled roughly on Billy's legs. The young man's

screams filled the cold air once again. They were stopped abruptly by the last of the water from the bucket.

'I'm a great believer, Billy, in an eye for an eye. I think the punishment should befit the crime. You get my drift?'

Billy mumbled incoherently as the old man unscrewed the cap off the container of petrol.

'You filled my beautiful granddaughter's veins with fire, so ...'

He splashed the petrol all over Billy and took a box of matches out of his pocket.

'Fuck, man, don't do it, how was I supposed to know she would take it all at once?'

'Burn the fucker,' he heard Clara's voice say inside his head.

'Of course, dear, it's only fitting after all.'

'Who the fuck are you talking to, you crazy old bastard?' asked Billy.

Totally ignoring his captive, he flung the match and watched as the body did a flame covered macabre dance directly in front of him.

He was sure he could see Clara standing in the corner of the barn smiling at him. She looked well.

He gave her a wave as the flames reached the rope and the young mans burned remains came tumbling to the floor in front of him with a dull thud.

'Another one down, dear, only two to go and then we can be reunited once more.'

He lit a cigar off of Billy's glowing remains and watched transfixed as the flames slowly burned away.

He must have fallen asleep. When he woke up, Billy was nothing more than a vaguely human-shaped, charred lump of flesh. He yawned and then laid the red rose between the fire blackened hands and, whistling to himself, left the burning sweet smell behind him and went merrily on his way.

Chapter Twenty Three

'So, how did it go with Montgomery this morning?' asked Max, as he handed Buchanan the steaming mug of black coffee.

'Could have been worse, I suppose,' he replied. 'He told me he would have thrown the book at me if it wasn't for the fact that Rennie's off on holiday tomorrow. He'd have no one left to run the case if he suspended me.'

'You should have waited for the backup though. You got off lucky.'

'Aye, I know, Max, but you know what I'm like.'

Max shook his head, 'Only too well, sir. I'll give you a laugh though. His little fracas with Derek from the firearms unit has found its way onto YouTube. Someone filmed it on their mobile, I'll show you it later, it's hilarious. He looks like an overweight penguin in that dinner jacket of his.'

Buchanan laughed.

'He had a real go at him too, Derek's put in a grievance against him, he's got all the proof he needs thanks to the video evidence.'

'I look forward to seeing that.'

He rubbed his eyes.

'This case is really beginning to bug the shit out of me, Max. I can't believe that, despite flooding the area with patrol cars and targeting all the premises in the area last night, there's still no sign of the old bastard.'

'It would've helped if Montgomery had agreed to the search for him earlier,' replied Max.

'He's an obstinate bastard, in fact, I had to go and have a word with the superintendent or he wouldn't have performed the search at all. He thought it was a complete waste of time. Mind you … turns out he was right on that one.'

Buchanan put down the mug of coffee.

'What have you two got for me?' he asked, looking at the two women sitting in the corner.

Miss Jacobs answered first.

'Remember how I told you that I thought I knew why the killings were getting more personal?'

'Aye, you said his wife's death had tipped him over the edge didn't you?'

She nodded, 'That could be one reason but I may have been a little presumptuous there.'

'How do you mean?'

'Well, it turns out that the old man isn't exactly in the best of health himself.'

She shuffled about some sheets of paper.

'He has a brain tumour, quite a nasty one. It's deep in his right temporal lobe.'

'What exactly does that mean?'

'In a great deal of these cases these types of tumours, often as not, are likely to cause some kind of psychotic symptoms. In his case it's been certified. I have his records here.'

'He was acting pretty weird, right enough, when I met him,' interrupted Max. 'He said something about hearing music in his head.'

'That ties in with this report, Max. He's had it for a while. They initially thought they had gotten rid of it. It says here on his medical details, and I quote: "Mr Reid had undergone resection of an astrocytoma of the left basal temporal lobe which had initially presented with grand mal seizures." '

'What's a grand mal seizure when it's at home?' asked Atkins, as she helped herself to a biscuit.

'They have two phases,' She made a peace sign with her fingers. 'Tonic and Clonic. During the Tonic phase, loss of consciousness occurs, and the muscles suddenly contract and cause the person to fall down. This phase tends to last about ten seconds. As for the Clonic phase, the muscles go into rhythmic contractions, alternately flexing and relaxing. The whole convulsion, from start to finish, on average, lasts for less than two minutes. Anyway, they treated him for that; however, just over a couple of years later, it came back with a vengeance. It says here he returned to the hospital with acute onset of extreme paranoid psychosis including, amongst other things, delusions and various degrees of hallucinations, so they gave him another scan and he was found to have a relapse of the tumour.' She put the sheet of paper back on the desk. 'That was only a few weeks ago, he never went back for any treatment. He just asked for some strong painkillers for the headaches. That was the last time they saw him.'

'So, basically, he's a basket case, that's what you're telling me?'

'No, Inspector, the symptoms tend to come in waves.

207

Sometimes he'll be totally *compus mentus* but other times … ' She shrugged her shoulders. 'He could be completely delusional. The longer he goes without treatment though, the more often he'll have these episodes.'

Buchanan drank the last of his coffee, and then turned to face PC Atkins.

'How's the girl getting on, Jenny?'

'Not so good, they had to give her a sedative last night. When she found out her father was dead she went into hysterics.'

'Poor kid. I sent Rennie round to their flat this morning. I thought we might find the list Mary was talking about on his computer, the place has been trashed though and the laptop's hard drive was gone so I'm not holding much hope on that front. It looks like old Mr Reid is one step ahead of us yet again. He's really beginning to piss me off now!'

'I'd like to have a word with Mary when she's feeling up to it if you don't mind,' said Lucy. 'She might know more than she thinks.'

'What do you mean more than she thinks?' asked Max.

'I was talking to … ' She once again looked at her sheet of paper, ' … PC Clair Tarrant, she had a long conversation with her last night. According to Clair, Mary said her father had mentioned the names of the people who the old man had asked for the details on. Her father made a point of telling her how he couldn't fathom how three of the people were involved in the kid's Hearing at all. He had no idea why the old man wanted information on them, but, for the sake of Mary, he used everything available to him to gather the information and to create the dossier.'

'I take it she can't remember their names.'

'No, but that's why I want to talk to her. She could have the information floating about in her subconscious somewhere. Using relaxation techniques, or maybe hypnotism, I could possibly manage to get her to remember.'

'I don't know, the girl has been through a lot. She's been held captive for days, made good her escape and then lost her father.' He sighed out loud. 'I don't deny it's worth a shot, mind.'

'Inspector, I don't intend to force her into such a thing, but, if she's agreeable, I don't see the harm in it. It would certainly help your case if it works.'

Buchanan looked deep in thought.

'Fair enough.' He pointed at her, 'But only if she agrees to it, mind.'

'Any word on the abandoned fish house, sir?'

'Bugger all to find there, Max. The old bastard torched the place the night Mary escaped.'

'What about the hotel he was staying at in Stonehaven?'

'Once again, bugger all. He left us nothing. Everyone he came across in the place thought he was the perfect gentleman.'

Buchanan appeared deep in thought.

'Believe it or not, that's the only confirmed sighting that's been reported. How can that be Max? Anyone?'

'He must be holed up somewhere, in the back of beyond. He's purposely keeping himself off our radar,' replied Atkins.

'Plus he's changed his appearance,' said Miss Jacobs.

'Max!' said Buchanan. 'Go check with the incident room about that, we need his photo updated.'

'Will do, sir.'

They suddenly heard a commotion in the hallway outside the office and then Rennie barged through the door.

'We have another murder; it's almost certainly our man's work. A real nasty one too.'

*

Buchanan, Max and Atkins arrived at the disused barn. It was attached to a working farm stuck in the middle of nowhere. The temperature was dropping again so Buchanan grabbed his thick Helly Hansen jacket out of the boot before heading towards the crime scene. He couldn't help thinking what a cold desolate place this was to die.

The whole area was a hive of activity. The scene of crime officers were beavering about the place, collecting any viable evidence inside and out. As always, they were dressed in their white plastic suits. Every time he saw them, it made him think of a nuclear accident or some type of terrorist chemical attack on the nation - all that was missing was the oxygen masks.

He had worn them himself on occasion. He hated everything about them, especially the way they made him sweat.

The police photographers had finished documenting the scene; he could see them carefully putting their cameras and other equipment into their cases in the back of their van.

He watched as the victim, wrapped up in a body-bag, was

unceremoniously carried away from the crime scene. He was closely followed by the ever present bulk of Joe Styles.

Even from this distance, he could see the frost forming in his thick walrus moustache.

Joe gave a wave and headed towards them.

'He looks tired', thought Buchanan. He watched as Joe gave out a huge yawn, confirming his suspicions.

'Late night, Joe?'

His question went unanswered, so he tried another.

'What can you tell me, Doc?'

Buchanan expected one of his usual quips. It didn't appear. No gallows humour on the agenda today.

'This one's real nasty, Ronnie, REAL nasty! The victim appears to have been suspended by his arms from the roof of the building. Both arms are dislocated at the shoulder. He must have been in absolute agony. Then, after he had endured all that, the poor fellow was set on fire, you can still smell the petrol off him.'

'Jesus, was he alive? During the burning I mean?'

'Certainly looks that way, I'll have to confirm it of course.'

'Poor bastard, I wonder who he was.'

'It'll take time to figure that out, Ronnie. All I can give you is a rough age, it's not based on any medical evidence, it's just an observation really.'

'I'll take anything I can get on this case, Doc.'

'Well … although the body is badly charred, I did notice

211

a couple of things.'

'Like what?'

'He has a few piercings, in his ears and his nose. So I can't see him being that old, anything from late teens, to maybe, late thirties, early forties.'

'Him?'

'Oh yeah, it's definitely a male. Badly burned or otherwise I can still tell the difference between male and female genetalia.'

'Thanks, Doc.'

'I'm not finished. One of his ear rings is very unusual. It's quite a large cross, the sort of thing most people would wear around their neck on a chain. Not hang from their ear lobe.'

'Cheers again,' said Buchanan. 'Oh! One other thing. Can you do me a favour, Doc?'

'Sure. What is it?'

'Could you give PC Atkins a lift back to the station?'

'No problem.'

'Cheers, Joe.'

'Buchanan!'

He turned around and found himself facing Steve Kershaw. The crime scene manager was visibly shaking from the freezing wind that blew all around them.

'Looks like it's definitely him.'

He held up a large sealable bag with a single red rose inside.

'Did you find any ID on the remains, Steve?'

'Nope, he either didn't have any or it's burnt up. We might find something when we process the body back at the lab I suppose. To tell you the truth, we haven't found much of anything really, a few petrified animal turds inside the barn that's about it. We did manage to get a couple of casts from outside though. One from a boot, size ten I'd say, and another from a tyre tread.'

'That's it?'

Steve gave out a sigh and shrugged his shoulders.

'So, we have nothing at all to tie him to a location, no clues as to where he might be staying?'

'Sorry, Ronnie, it doesn't look like it. I'll personally look at all the stuff that's been collected, just in case but it doesn't look too good. What were you hoping for, a room key to the nearest Holiday Inn?'

Buchanan laughed.

'That, Steve, would have made my day.'

'Aye, mine too. I'm getting a bit pissed off with this case.'

'Tell me about it,' replied Buchanan. 'We know who the guy is, we have his face in the press and on the TV but we've had practically no sightings of him. It makes no fucking sense.'

He rubbed his hands together to get some heat in them.

'Anyway, Steve, make sure you keep me up to date once you work your way through what's been collected. I'd like to take a good look at his earrings.'

Steve gave him a funny look.

'A strange request, I know, but according to the doc one of them is a large cross, see if there's maybe some sort of inscription on it.'

'Will do.'

Buchanan turned his back to the wind and lit a cigarette then turned towards Max.

'I forgot to ask with all this excitement going on. When's the updated photo going in the press?'

'Should be later on today, sir. His hair has been darkened and they photo shopped out the beard, just like you asked.'

He stamped out his cigarette in the frost hardened ground, he'd only smoked half of it, he'd given up on the idea, it was too windy, it wasn't worth the effort.

He pulled out his notebook and quickly jotted down the information he had received from Joe Styles.

'Miss Atkins.'

'Sir?'

'I want you back at HQ. See if anyone's been reported missing in the last day or so. Here.'

He ripped the sheet of paper out the book. She gave him a funny look.

'That's all I've got to go on, I'm afraid. See Joe, he'll give you a lift back.'

'Okay, sir.' She turned to leave.

'One more thing.'

'Yes, sir?'

'I'm sorry for being so abrupt, can't help it.' He pointed to her. 'I really appreciate the help you're giving us on this case … it won't go unrecognised.'

She smiled at him. He winked back.

'Right, c'mon, Max. We're finally going shopping. There's fuck all food in the house.'

*

The old man sat in his cottage, he had two portable gas heaters going full tilt but he could still feel the cold creeping into his bones. His headaches were getting worse. Even taking a double dose of the strong painkillers the hospital had provided him with wouldn't take the edge off it. He needed something else; just to keep him going till his work was complete.

He picked up the four packets of white powder he'd taken from his latest victim. He didn't have a clue what it was but hopefully it would help with the pain. He'd never really tried much in the way of drugs in his long life, apart from some marijuana way back in the sixties. He'd never seen what the big deal was. He hadn't enjoyed it.

He took a small amount out of one of the packets and laid it out on the back cover of a paperback. He took out his pen knife, and then proceeded to cut the small grains up till they turned into a fine powder. He never understood the idea behind this but he'd seen it in enough movies in his time.

He withdrew a bank note from his wallet, rolled it into a tight tube and proceeded to inhale it.

'Snorting! Isn't that what this is called?'

He laughed at the irony involved.

He'd just killed a junkie for supplying drugs to his granddaughter. And now he was using the damned stuff himself.

At first he felt nothing, then the effects of the white powder slowly snuck up on him. He started to feel amazing. His whole body felt better than it had felt in years. His headache disappeared and he had an overwhelming feeling of relaxation, everything just seemed to be at peace.

He laid down on the camp bed and laughed uncontrollably.

Chapter Twenty Four

They hadn't even started shopping yet, but already Buchanan was off on one.

'Why the fuck do you need a pound coin to use the trolleys, they used to be free!'

Max sighed.

'You're not buying the thing, sir, it's a deposit, it's to make sure you take the thing back.'

'But say you haven't got a quid coin, then you have to go inside, queue up buy something to get the change, make sure there is a pound coin in the change and then come all the way back out here for your trolley before you can start shopping. It's bloody ridiculous, Max.'

'I'll give you the coin, sir, I have one here.'

Buchanan accepted it without a word of thanks and they both headed off towards the supermarket.

'I need some cigarettes, Max; I'll get them from the kiosk before I start the shopping.'

He wheeled the trolley through the supermarket entrance.

'For fuck's sake, look at the queue, I bet you half of them aren't even after fags, they'll be sticking it on the lottery no doubt. Who came up with that bright idea, putting the fags and lottery together eh? He ought to be shot!'

'You're not even going to see them on show soon, sir, they're going to have to be kept under the counter.'

'Aye and that'll cause nothing but trouble. Imagine sitting in a huge fucking queue like this only to get to the front and find out they don't stock your brand. At least the way it stands now you can have a quick glance and see if they have them on the shelf.'

'Uhoh!' said Max.

He nodded ahead.

'Looks like they've started, they all seem to be hidden behind those wee cupboards.'

Buchanan let out a sigh and shook his head.

'I'm sick of being treated like a second-class citizen just because I smoke. You can't do it anywhere nowadays. You can't even have a fag in the pub with your pint. They'll have us all carrying bells about soon, like fucking lepers.'

'How many coffees have you had today?' asked Max.

Buchanan laughed. 'Too fucking many!'

'Yes, sir, what can I get you?' asked the assistant with the overdone sun tan.

'Two hundred Regal king size, please.'

He watched as the assistant moved back and forth straining to read the brand names of the cigarettes on the individual doors.

'Check her out, Max, she looks like some demented contestant on a game show.'

Finally she found his brand. After paying for his purchase, he threw the bag of cigarettes into the trolley.

'Did you see the colour of her, Jesus? She's definitely

been tangoed.'

He laughed. 'She is a bit orange right enough.'

Their conversation was suddenly interrupted by the sound of Buchanan's mobile. He released it from his pocket and looked at the screen.

'Fuck! It's Michelle. I forgot to phone her back last night.'

'Ronnie?'

'Stop right there, Michelle, I'm in the supermarket now.'

'About bloody time, but it's not what I'm phoning about.'

He sighed.

'What is it?

'What the hell were you thinking about last night?'

'You've lost me.'

'Taking on that guy with the gun in the hotel room.'

'It wasn't planned, believe me. In fact, if you hadn't bloody phoned me, it probably would never have happened. Anyway, how did you find out?'

'I was talking to Maggie.'

'Great! So now you have Joe's wife keeping tabs on me.'

'No one's keeping tabs on you; she phoned me earlier, she just happened to mention it that's all.'

'Fair enough, I'll be more careful in future.'

Michelle laughed, 'As if!'

'Look, I'll phone you back later, you know how shopping

stresses me out, luv.'

'Do you have a list?'

'Eh … '

'You don't do you? You're unbelievable.'

'I thought I'd just pick stuff up as I go along.'

'Well make sure you get yourself some decent food.'

'I plan to, if I can ever get started. By the way, how's Sam doing?'

'He's getting a long walk every day, there's a couple of acres of woodland behind mum's new house, he's getting plenty exercise, don't worry.'

Beep-beep!

'That's my battery running out, I'll have to go.'

'Bye, Ronnie, make sure you take care of yourself. I worry about you sometimes.'

'See ya.'

He turned his phone off and stuck it back in his pocket. 'Right, Max, let's get started.'

'Fruit and veg, sir, you needing anything there?'

'I never eat fruit, it gives me indigestion. I could do with some veg, I suppose, I promised Michelle I'd make some home cooked stuff, trouble is I can't cook worth a shit!'

Max laughed.

'How about some chilli? I'll show you how to make it. It's a piece of piss.'

'Sounds good, what do we need?'

'Onions, chillies obviously, a can of kidney beans, a can of tomato sauce and a couple of jars of spices. Oh! And, of course, some minced beef.'

'You can forget the spices, Max. Michelle has every spice known to man in a cupboard at home. I can't even pronounce the name of some of them.'

Max picked up a couple of onions and they headed off to find the chillies.

'Jesus, there's loads of different ones.' said Buchanan.

He looked at one of the labels.

'Scotch Bonnet! I thought that was a hat.'

'They're a bit too hot those ones, sir, just pick up some of those green ones, half a dozen should do. Now, where's the meat aisle?'

'We'll get the mince from the butcher at the back,' said Buchanan. 'I don't trust that pre-packaged stuff.'

The sound of REM's *Losing my Religion* filled the air. Max answered his phone.

'It's for you, sir. It's Lucy. She couldn't reach you on your phone, so she phoned me.'

'Hello, Lucy, what have you got for me?'

'Mary's agreed to the hypnotism thing. She says anything that helps catch her father's killer is fine with her.'

'Well, that's some good news,' answered Buchanan.

'Let me know how you get on. By the way, come round to mine tonight. Max is cooking chilli; I'll ask PC Atkins round as well, we can go over a few things.'

'You said that last night but we all ended up in the pub, then you went off and got yourself kidnapped.'

'It'll be different tonight, make it about seven o'clock.'

'Cool. I'll see you there.'

As they approached the butchery department, a young man in a white coat and a red and white striped apron came running out the door. The front of his apron was covered in blood and he was holding a towel around a nasty gash on his arm.

'What the fuck's going on here, Max?'

The swing door barged open again. Another man in white overalls appeared. This one was older, taller and he was a good few stones heavier than the younger one. He had a blood stained meat cleaver in his hand.

'Get back here you little bastard, I'm not finished with you.'

The first man hid himself behind Buchanan and Max. He was visibly shaking.

Buchanan looked round at him.

'Don't get so close, son. If any of the blood off that apron of yours gets on my suit, I'll kill you; you won't have to worry about him.'

He looked back at the man with the cleaver and flashed his ID.

'DI Buchanan. What the hell's going on here?'

The old man pointed to the younger one.

'That little bastard has been shagging my missus. I had

my suspicions so I took a look at his phone, they've been texting each other for weeks. Now step aside till I finish the wee bastard off.'

'Are you fucking stupid? I just showed you my police ID, now drop the meat cleaver.'

'Copper or no copper, I don't give a fuck - step aside or you'll get some of this.'

He shook the meat cleaver menacingly.

Buchanan shook his head and looked around. There was a small crowd gathering and the butchery and fish department staff were all gaping over the counter. Even the fish on the crushed ice display seemed to be looking at him.

He whispered to the young guy cowering behind him.

'Stay behind me, son.'

He held up his hands, palms forward.

'Look, I don't want no trouble, just calm down.'

He edged himself back towards the fish counter.

'I've no beef with you. It's that sneaky bastard I want.'

'Good choice of word for a butcher,' thought Buchanan.

Quick as a flash, he picked up the two-foot salmon lying in the crushed ice and swung it full force towards the man with the meat cleaver's head. It made a wet slapping sound as it connected. The portly butcher went down like a sack of spuds, but he wasn't out.

As he tried to raise himself off the floor Buchanan put his size ten boot on the wrist of the hand holding the cleaver. He applied some pressure until the butcher let the lethal-looking weapon drop and then kicked it well out of harm's way. Then he hauled the guy off the floor, and expertly put him in an arm lock before shouting to the staff behind the counter.

'The show's over. Call the security guards; tell them to hold this mad bastard till the police arrive.'

The small crowd, which had now become a big crowd, broke out in applause.

Max had to lean close to Buchanan's ear to be heard.

'I've phoned them, sir, there's a car on its way,' said Max, as two burly guards appeared from the crisps aisle and relieved Buchanan of his captive.

'He's all yours, lads.'

As the crowd slowly dispersed, he walked back over to his trolley.

'Right, Max, let's get on with our shopping.'

He looked over at the young butcher who was getting his arm bandaged up.

'Maybe I will go for the pre-packaged mince. Fuck knows what this guy's been bleeding on through the back there.'

They both walked away from the scene, then Buchanan suddenly stopped.

'Wait a minute, Max. I saw something out of the corner of my eye during that little fracas; it might be nothing but …'

He walked straight towards a young teenager who was trying to hide himself behind the paramedics that were patching up the butcher.

'Gimme your phone, son.'

The young man looked worried but he did as he was asked.

Buchanan handed it to Max.

'Check his videos, Max, I'm sure he just recorded our little incident.'

Max checked the phone.

'You're right, sir, in fact he's tried to upload it to YouTube, it's not up yet, I can cancel it.'

'Do it then, I'm not being made a mockery of like Montgomery.'

Max deftly worked his thumb over the key pad.

'All done, sir, that was close mind. What should I do with the phone?'

'Just give it back to him.'

He looked up at the signs hanging from the roof.

'Now, where the bloody hell is the Ale section in here again?'

'Aisle twenty seven,' said one of the women behind the counter.

He smiled back at her and quickly glanced at the name on her uniform.

'Cheers, Emma.'

Chapter Twenty Five

'Right, Mary, close your eyes and relax. I know you've been through a lot in the last few days, try and put that out of your mind. I know it's hard but the guy who killed your father deserves to be punished and there's a good chance that some of the information that may help us do that is locked away in there.'

She tapped Mary's brow.

'Listen to your breathing. I want you to take deep breaths to a count of eight, hold them in for a count of four and then exhale, again, to eight. Do you think you can manage that for me, Mary?'

She nodded her head.

'Become aware of your breathing, don't concentrate on anything else. Any stress or tension you feel, don't hold on to it, just breathe it away when you exhale. In to eight, hold for four, out to eight. I'd like you to do that for a few minutes, if you don't mind.'

After a couple of minutes she looked at her watch.

'Now, Mary, I'd like you to concentrate on my voice. I'm going to slowly count backwards from the number ten, as the numbers get lower, the more relaxed you're going to feel.'

'Ten … your eyes are getting heavier. Nine … listen carefully to my voice, nothing else but my voice. Eight … seven … you can feel your whole body relaxing. Six … five … you can feel yourself drifting off. Four … Three …

You're now feeling completely at peace. Two … One. Can you hear me, Mary?'

'Yes, I can hear you.'

'Think back to the day your father mentioned the list but rather than trying to remember from your point of view, look at it as if it was a movie. You're standing in the background watching the conversation between you and your father. The same way you would sit in a cinema watching a film. Can you do that, Mary?'

'I think so.'

'Describe the room for me.'

'It's just your normal hotel room. It has a thin brown carpet, there are two single beds, they both have the same plain cream quilt covers. There's a chest of drawers between the beds with a small table lamp sitting on top. To the left, there's a large comfy chair sitting in front of the window. The wall directly in front of the beds has a small TV stand holding up a small flat screened television.'

'What's playing on the TV?'

'It's tuned to the Sky News channel. They're showing a piece on the bombing at Dad's work.'

'Where are you and your father located?'

'Dad is sitting on the side of his bed, he has a whisky glass in his hand, it's quite full. He looks really rough.'

'And where are you, Mary?'

'I'm kneeling down in front of him; I'm holding his hand, the one not holding the glass.'

'You're doing great. What's he saying?'

' "I did it for you, Mary. He told me if I got him the information he required you would be safe." '

'And you, Mary, what are you saying?'

' "We have to go to the police, how many were on the list?" "Six people. Some of them weren't directly involved in the case. It took a lot of work, and sneaking about to get a hold of the details in their case." He's refilling his glass.'

'Keep telling me what you hear,' said Lucy. 'Remember you're on the outside looking in. Whatever you hear from your dad and yourself just relay it to me. You understand?'

'I think so.'

'Good, go back to the conversation. There were six people on the list remember, two of them are dead.'

Lucy continued where she left off.

' "That still leaves four people then; we can't just sit back while he goes after them. I can't have that on my conscience."... He's taking my hands in his ... "We can't go to the police. I wasn't going to tell you this but I must. He phoned me last night, five minutes after you did. I won't go into details but he made a threat that shook me to the core. Basically, even though he doesn't have you captive anymore, he's still holding us to the same deadline, so, if we just sit tight here, it'll all be over in a few days."... "So, what you're saying is, if we stay out of it, we survive?"... "Exactly." I'm looking up at him ... "I'm sorry, Dad. I don't think I can do that." He's stroking my hair ... "We must Mary, we must!" ...I'm still looking up at him, now I'm crying ... "Tell me the names of the people on the list, Dad!" '

Lucy Jacobs picked up her notepad and pen.

Chapter Twenty Six

Buchanan was in a good mood for once. Lucy had informed him of her success with Mary. He had Rennie put unmarked surveillance vehicles outside the intended targets homes. They were still trying to pinpoint one of the three, some unemployed junky from Torry but they'd sent patrol cars into the area to find him.

Buchanan knew that wasn't going to happen, more than likely he was lying in the morgue, a burnt out husk of a man with a cross hanging from his ear.

PC Atkins had some news for him as well. She told him that she would rather let him know in person when she arrived. He went to the fridge for a couple of bottles of beer. A Hobgoblin for him and a lager for Max.

Gimme Shelter was playing on the digital radio in the kitchen. The music mixed with the sizzling of the onions frying on the gas hob.

'Not a bad radio station that, sir. What did you say it's called again?'

'Planet Rock, you can only get it on digital though.'

'Pity, I like a bit of classic rock now and again, I haven't got a digital radio though.'

'You've got Sky, you can get it through there'

He stopped cutting the chillies to take a mouthful of his beer.

'Careful with those chillies, sir, and whatever you do

don't go to the bog till you've thoroughly washed your hands.'

'I've learned my lesson, Max. I was helping Michelle cook something with chillies in it a while ago. She wondered where I'd disappeared to; she found me standing with my dick under the shower head. I was there for half an hour.'

Max laughed. 'Cold shower, I bet.'

'Too right. I won't be doing that again anytime soon.'

He laid his bottle of ale to the side and looked down proudly at the chillies that he'd managed to de-seed and quarter lying on the marble chopping board.

'What do you want done with these, then?'

'Just chuck them in here with the onions. Here, you can stir this while I brown the mince.'

He handed Buchanan the wooden spoon. He bent over and took in the aroma of the fried onions.

'This smells great already, Max. Where did you learn to cook like this?'

'It's only a pan full of onions and a few spices, sir. But, as for the cooking, I taught myself, I had to. It was either that or those bloody microwave ready meals every night. You don't have much choice when you live on your own.'

He unwrapped the mince and threw it in a pot.

'This is a great cooker though. Must have cost a bit.'

'It cost fuck all actually. Michelle won it in a competition. She's always entering the bloody things. She won one of them fancy hoovers the other week, the ones with the ball on the end.'

'A Dyson?'

'Aye … well, I think that's what it's called.'

The doorbell rang interrupting their conversation.

'That'll be either Lucy or PC Atkins. Get the door, Max. I'd do it myself but I'm enjoying frying these onions and chillies too much. It has a strange Zen like quality.'

Max took the browned mince off the hot plate, finished his bottle of lager and headed out to the hall.

They had both arrived together. Atkins wandered over to the settee while Lucy, bottle of wine in hand, went wandering into the kitchen.

'You got room in the fridge for this?'

Buchanan turned around.

'Should have; put it in one of the side shelves.'

Lucy did as she was asked.

'Something smells nice.'

'I told you earlier, we're making chilli.'

Lucy sighed. 'You could do with working on your people skills, detective.'

'Och, it's just my manner, you'll get used to it.'

He took the pan off the hob and wiped his hands on his trousers.

'Thanks again, by the way, for the hypnotism thing. That was a good move, I feel like we're actually getting somewhere on this case, not before time.'

'Hopefully it should just be a case of the surveillance

guys sitting tight till the old guy makes his move,' said Lucy.

'That's what I'm hoping for,' answered Buchanan, taking a mouthful of beer.

'I take it you've worked out that this William Meickle is more than likely the dead guy they found in the barn this afternoon.'

He held up his hand.

'We still have to confirm it though. I mean the delusional state this guy's going about in, I wouldn't put it past him to add more victims to his original list just for the hell of it.'

'I'm a hundred percent sure it is William,' said the voice from behind.

He turned round to see Atkins standing by the door.

'What makes you so sure Jenny?' he asked.

She hauled out her tablet.

'I did what you asked this afternoon, I looked into any recent reports of missing persons within the target parameters that you wrote down for me. There weren't any reports matching that age group in the last few days. So, then I wandered over to the incident room, again bugger all, however one of the officers managing the phone lines told me about two calls he'd had today, both times when he answered, the call was cut off from the other end. They were both from the same mobile number. First I checked out the number, it was unlisted, So, just on the off chance, I phoned it back.'

Max had now joined them in the kitchen; he started putting the chilli ingredients together as he listened to Jenny's account of her day.

'Did you get anywhere?' asked Buchanan.

'I did, actually. The first couple of times I phoned and explained who I was, the guy cut me off, but I persisted, turns out the guy at the other end, who referred to himself as Big Tam, is a mate of this William Meickle. He was drinking with him this morning. When he left the pub he saw him talking to an old guy, an old guy whose picture he saw in this morning's paper.'

'Well done, Miss Atkins, that was very intuitive of you.'

He rubbed his chin, it made a grating noise.

'Mind you, I'm surprised he recognised him, he's changed his appearance since then.'

'He says he never forgets a face, sir, with or without a beard, it's all in the eyes seemingly.'

She shrugged her shoulders.

'One other thing, sir. I asked if William, or Billy, as he calls him, had anything distinctive about him. Guess what his answer was?'

'He has a big cross hanging from his left ear?'

'Exactly, sir. He says he has more information for us but he'll only tell it to someone face to face. He won't come in to any station or tell us over the phone, he doesn't want to be seen with anyone in uniform and he wants paying for it. He seems to see himself as some sort of informant.'

'He's been watching too many movies,' answered Buchanan, once again rubbing his chin.

'Max and I will meet him; see if you can arrange it.'

She smiled at him.

'I thought you might say that, sir, in fact, I pre-empted it. I've already arranged the meeting for lunchtime tomorrow.'

Buchanan laughed.

'Where about?'

'He insisted you meet him in his local.'

She looked at her tablet.

'It's the Victoria Bar in Torry.'

'The Rat's Cellar! Now there's a blast from the past. I haven't been there in years.'

He looked into space for a few seconds then turned towards Max.

'How long will that chilli be, I'm starving.'

'About half an hour, sir, it's simmering away and the rice is in the pot ready to go.'

'Good, that gives us time to look into this list we got from Mary a bit deeper. Everybody grab a drink and we'll go through to the sitting room.'

*

Buchanan looked at the handwritten list:

Emily Jackson

Darryl Morrison

Susan Ferguson

William Meickle

Adrian Dalrymple

Scott Hastings

'The first three killings involved people that were directly involved in the Rose Reeder case,' said Lucy. 'The other three must have a somewhat more tenuous link.'

He looked at the folder containing the original list of people, the ones directly involved in the Children's Panel case, the ones they were wasting a vast amount of resources protecting.

He tapped it hard.

'They don't even appear on here. So, how do they tie in to his master plan? The latest victim for instance, how does he fit in?'

'I checked out his record, sir,' answered Atkins.

'He's not just a user; he's been done a few times for possession, small amounts of various drugs, everything from marijuana to heroin. Maybe he sold some stuff to Rose, who knows?'

'That's it!' shouted Lucy. 'Remember, Rose died of a self-induced overdose, she must have got the stuff from this Meickle guy, so, in her grandfather's' mind, it's no different than him having given her a loaded gun to shoot herself with.'

'My thoughts exactly,' smirked Buchanan. 'You just beat me to it by a second or so.'

Lucy laughed, licked her finger and marked the air.

'Okay, smart arse, what about the other two then?'

She looked at the list and scratched her head.

'Adrian Dalrymple is a lawyer and Scott Hastings is a taxi driver.'

She sighed.

'Sorry, I haven't got a clue.'

'Anyone else any idea?'

Max and Jenny shook their shoulders as he looked at the list and sighed.

'I'm as lost as the rest of you, not that it really matters how they tie into it. We now know that these are the people he'll be going for next. We have them under protection and that's the main thing. How the three of them fit in is just a loose end, but I hate loose ends.'

'What sort of protection have we given them, sir?' asked PC Atkins.

'We have unmarked surveillance vehicles outside their homes and a couple of officers inside.'

'Say he just decides on a gung-ho, all guns blazing attempt on them? Our guys don't have any weapons.'

'Our guys don't, but the Firearms Division does; we got permission to stick one of them in each vehicle, highly unusual but we got the go ahead from on high. Something tells me that they just want an end to the whole sorry affair.'

Chapter Twenty Seven

He looked at the clock. 4.17 a.m. He'd been tossing and turning all night. He couldn't sleep, the case kept playing over and over in his mind, the inevitable hamster on the wheel syndrome, that's what Michelle called it. It happened every time he got himself heavily involved in a case. He reached for the glass of water at the side of his bed and drank it down in one huge gulp.

'Bugger it!'

He got up and jumped into the en-suite shower, got himself dressed and then quietly walked to the kitchen to make himself a strong flask of coffee.

Once that was accomplished, he left Max, who had decided to stay the night, a note telling him that he'd be back in a couple of hours.

He had decided, since he couldn't sleep, to visit the surveillance vehicles to see how they were getting on. He looked at the addresses in his notebook; one was in Mastrick, the other nearer the town centre in Union Grove. He decided to make the one in Mastrick his first port of call, it was just a quick trip up Anderson Drive, it would take him ten minutes, tops.

He started the car, turned the heating up full and poured himself a coffee from the flask.

He relished the hot drink as he watched the ice clearing from his windscreen. He could have used the scraper but he couldn't be bothered. He turned on the radio. *Clowns to the left of me, jokers to the right,* sang Gerry Rafferty. He looked at the temperature gauge. Minus five degrees.

'Jesus!'

The word left a visible cloud in the air.

Once the windows were clear and the interior of the car was suitably warmed up, he eased the car out of the driveway, turned right at the roundabout and headed up Anderson drive.

The roads were deserted, he felt like the only man on earth.

Gerry Rafferty was replaced by Slade's *Merry Christmas*, it must have been about the hundredth time he'd heard it that week. The song seemed to follow him around. It was on the radio, in shops, on television adverts. He'd even heard it at work, playing in the background in the reception area. It was the same every year, of course. It marked the coming of an end to another year just as much as the December page on a calendar.

He lit up a cigarette and stuck on a CD. Five minutes later he turned off the main road and pulled into the quiet side street where the taxi driver resided. One side of the street contained rows of council tenements. Most looked identical, the odd one or two had slightly fancier windows and stone facings attached to the front of them. The other side of the street contained some small terraced houses. The majority were covered in gaudy Christmas decorations. One had gone totally overboard. The whole garden looked like Santa's grotto.

'Wouldn't fancy their next electricity bill', he thought.

He looked up at number twenty-seven, the taxi driver's

flat, which was on the second floor.

He crossed to the other side of the street.

He had no problem spotting the surveillance vehicle. The plain white van stuck out like a sore thumb. He tapped his nails quietly on the back door which was quickly opened by the firearms officer. He looked jittery and he had a gun in his hand.

'Buchanan, what the fuck are you doing here?'

'I couldn't sleep, Bill.' He held up the flask. 'I brought you coffee.'

He grabbed three plastic disposable cups, filled them up and introduced himself to the two officers manning the surveillance equipment. The screens in front of them showed a complete three hundred and sixty degree view of the street.

'Anything exciting, lads?'

'Depends what you mean by exciting, sir,' replied one of the officers, as he eagerly helped himself to one of the coffees. 'We've seen a couple of foxes raking through the buckets and an old pissed guy that tried to relieve himself behind someone's shed, he ended up running back out with a Rottweiler chasing his arse. It was hilarious, I'm seriously thinking of sticking it up on YouTube.'

Buchanan laughed and patted them on the back.

'Keep me informed if anything kicks off, eh?'

After checking on the officers who were stationed inside the taxi driver's house, he decided to have a few words with the man himself.

*

'Mr Hastings, have you ever heard of Rose Reeder?'

'Have I fuck, people have been asking me that all day, one of your officers even showed me her photo, she's a pretty girl, I'm sure I would have remembered her.'

'What about Jonathan or Emily Jackson? Either of their names ring a bell?'

'Never heard of them but remember I drive a taxi for a living, I have up to a hundred people in my cab every week.' He shook his head. 'I suppose they could have flagged down my cab at some time or another. I can't be expected to remember the names of every customer I've ever had now can I?'

'Very true, sir.'

Buchanan looked at the two dozen Christmas cards displayed on the mantelpiece, he spotted the one with the rose on it, it sat fourth from the left. The significance of the card was obviously lost on Mr Hastings; it was just another card to him.

'By the way, when can I get back to work? I'm losing a bloody fortune over this. I should have been working tonight, I was woken up at four o'clock this afternoon by your lot telling me I couldn't leave the house because this mad sniper bastard had me on some list or other. What the fuck would he want with me?'

'That's what we're trying to find out, sir, the sooner we do, the sooner we're likely to catch him, so, if you don't mind, give some thought to the people I just mentioned. Try and remember if you ever came across them, whether it was anything to do with the taxi driving or not. If you can think of anything just let one of the officers here know.'

Buchanan left the flat, got back in his motor and headed towards Union Grove.

*

The old man, now fuelled by the mysterious white powder, parked his car in a small side street. It was still dark and the roads were deserted. He picked up the long black case and his small backpack from the back seat, and nimbly climbed over the five foot high wall. He landed in a crouched position, ankle deep in snow, behind a dishevelled looking holly bush.

He looked up at the block of granite flats in front of him. There were no lights on in any of the windows.

He slowly stood up and silently walked towards the back door. He tried the handle, it was unlocked. No need for the lock-pick gun in his back pack. He walked up the stairs until he reached the third floor. The door in the flat opposite the one he was looking for had a spy hole, he reached into his pocket, pulled out the roll of duct tape and tore a small piece off the corner. He placed it over the spy hole before he quietly knocked on the door to his left.

After a minute or so, he put his ear to the door and heard the old couple muttering within. Mr and Mrs Davies, they were called, he knew quite a bit about them. A simple phone call posing as a market researcher earlier and the old woman had practically told him their life story.

They'd lived there for eight years, they were both retired and they had a son that lived in Spain. They were both big football fans, they had season tickets for Pittodrie and never missed a match.

He heard someone approaching the other side of the door.

The man of the house answered, just as he expected. The old woman stood in the dimly lit hallway behind him. She had rollers in her hair and she clasped the edges of her dressing gown tightly below her neck. He pushed his weight against the door knocking the man off his feet and pointed the hand gun at his wife.

He made eye contact with them both.

'Anyone makes a sound and you're both dead. You got that?'

The woman nodded her head. He helped her husband to his feet.

'Are you agreeable to that?'

He nodded his head also.

After tie-wrapping their hands behind their backs and gagging them with the duct tape, he locked them in a cupboard in the hallway and then went to work in the living room. He quickly cleared the scrappy looking Christmas tree from in front of the window and removed the Santa and reindeer figures from the glass.

He couldn't believe how energised he felt, but one thing was still bugging him. He had originally planned to deal with Mr Dalrymple face to face. However … when he'd driven towards the flat the evening before he'd seen the two police officers getting dropped off at the flat, then he'd spotted the white van.

He'd parked across the road to get a good look, that's when he seen the two guys getting out the front and going into the back. He watched for over half an hour - they never came back out. He knew there and then that the place was under surveillance inside and out. Hence the sniper rifle, it was the only way to go. A quick shot, then a quick getaway out the back. They wouldn't know what hit them.

He didn't hear Clara so much now since he'd started using the white powder, but he was sure she would be impressed with the alternative plan he'd come up with.

One thing he was now sure of though, the police must have the names, they could have only gotten them from Mary. Her father must have mentioned them to her after all.

He looked out the front window; the white van was still there. He could see Dalrymple's flat directly across from him. A mirror image of the one he was in now. The expensive looking curtains were wide open and the living room light was still on. He watched as the overweight lawyer paced about the room, occasionally he would stop by the large bay window and stare vacantly ahead, making himself an extremely easy target.

He laughed to himself. 'This is going to be far easier than I thought.'

He dragged the settee over towards the window and upended it to create a rest for his rifle.

It was the perfect height. Providence was on his side.

He unpacked the weapon and slid the telescopic sight into place. It made a satisfying click as it housed itself into position. He crouched down behind the settee, made himself comfortable and looked through the scope.

A cross hair appeared across the window at the other side of the street. He zoomed in slightly, focusing on a porcelain vase on the windowsill. It looked oriental. It had a painting of a dragon on it.

'C'mon, Mr Lawyer Man, show yourself.'

He watched him pace back and forth. He held a large glass of whisky in his hand and he was chain smoking. He looked worried, which was good: he wanted them to be worried.

'Look over here, there's a good man.'

He watched as another man approached the window with a coffee mug in his hand. It was a man he knew well.

'BUCHANAN! Don't you ever fucking sleep?'

Perhaps I should just take the shot anyway.

His hand hovered over the trigger of the high powered rifle as he decided on what to do next.

Chapter Twenty Eight

Max helped himself to his second cup from the coffee maker, picked up the newly delivered *Press and Journal* from the hallway and sat himself down in the lounge. He'd knocked on Buchanan's bedroom door earlier with a coffee but there was no reply. It wasn't till he sauntered back through to the kitchen that he found the note stuck to the fridge.

He was used to his boss taking off on a whim; it didn't bother him in the slightest. He put his feet up on the coffee table and unfolded the newspaper.

The front of the paper had a small interview with the farmer on whose land the burned body had been found. They hadn't connected it to the recent spate of killings which was something, but no doubt they soon would. He was just about to get torn into some of last night's chilli for his breakfast when he heard the front door open and then slam shut.

The Border Collie ornaments in the display cabinet rattled as an angry Buchanan entered the room.

'Remind me again, Max, how our man killed the first victim.'

'Sniper rifle.'

'Do you believe that the two uniformed plonkers in charge of this Dalrymple guy let him pace about the room with the lights on and the curtains fully open in full view of the flats opposite?'

'Un-fuckin-believable!'

Max shook his head as he watched him pace about the room.

'I did find out one thing though, Mr Dalrymple admitted knowing Emily Jackson, just socially of course, or so he says, but what are the chances that he's the crooked bastard lawyer that Jonathan Jackson mentioned? It makes you wonder, if he was quite happy to bung their money around to smooth through the adoption, what other part did he play in the whole sorry affair? Obviously the old guy knows, that's why he found his way onto his list.'

He paced the room.

'Fuck it, maybe we should have just let him get Dalrymple, you ought to see him, Max, he's a real odious bastard.'

'I'll get you a coffee, sir. Do you want some chilli?'

'For breakfast?'

'It tastes even better the next day, sir. I've mixed the rice that was left through it.'

He thought about it for a minute.

'Why not? I'm starving right enough. In fact, I'll have that bowl on the table there, you can get yourself another. Be quick about it mind, I have to brief the team this morning. Rennie's on holiday. I'll make it quick, the sooner we get it over with the sooner we can get out to Torry and meet this big Tam guy.'

Max wandered through to the kitchen as Buchanan stole his bowl of chilli and the morning paper and then sat down and stole his seat.

*

They drove down Market Street, passed the harbour on the left and headed straight on towards Torry.

They got caught in traffic as they crossed over the Victoria Bridge. Buchanan read the plaque attached to the stone. *"Built in 1887, following a ferry disaster in 1876, which claimed the lives of thirty two people returning from a day trip to the Bay of Nigg."*

'My dad used to take us to the Bay of Nigg, Max. The beach was a bastard to walk on though; it was full of sharp stones. We used to go looking for Buckies.'

'Buckies?'

'They're a small mussel-type shellfish, part of the whelk or cockle family, I think. You find them on the rocks when the tide goes out. Horrible slimy things. I hated them but my father loved them. He used to take bags of the bloody things home with him and boil them in the kitchen. My mother used to go mad at the smell they left behind, it hung around for days.'

Once they finally made it across to the other side, Buchanan pointed straight ahead.

'Just park around the corner here, next on the left, we'll walk back to the pub.'

Max did as he was asked and they both left the vehicle.

'Wonder why the guy's called Big Tam?' asked Max.

'Probably because he's a big fat bastard called Tam, simple as that. I doubt very much it's because he bears an uncanny resemblance to Sean Connery.'

Max laughed. 'How did he get that nickname, anyway? Sean Connery, I mean.'

Buchanan stopped to light a cigarette.

'He got it when he was a teenager; even then he was about six foot two.'

They reached the corner. Buchanan looked up at the burgundy and gold sign above the pub. The Victoria Bar, it declared.

'Welcome to the Rat's Cellar, Max. After you.'

They walked in and headed straight for the bar, where the barman, who sported an Elvis Presley hair cut, greeted them with an over-done smile.

'Yes, gentlemen, what can I get you?'

'A pint of Guinness and a fresh orange for my driver here please,' answered Buchanan.

'Right away, sirs, nothing's too much trouble for a pair of fine gentlemen like yourselves.'

Buchanan gave Max a strange look. He poured their drinks and placed them on the counter.

'Thank you very much,' said Buchanan.

Max stifled a laugh. They took their drinks over to a table in the corner.

'It's certainly a very polite place,' said Max.

The bar was quiet, there were three young men standing around the flat screen TV watching the horse racing and an older guy reading a book in the corner. No-one matching Big Tam's description seemed to be in the premises. According to PC Atkins he'd be wearing a track suit.

Buchanan's phone rang.

'Miss Atkins, how's it going? ... You're fucking joking ... What time did you say? ... Jesus! Well, keep me informed, eh!'

Buchanan put his mobile away and proceeded to drink over half his pint in one huge gulp.

'What is it, sir?'

'Mr Reid has added home invasions to his repertoire. He locked an old couple in a cupboard and took over their flat. A neighbour found them this morning. Guess where the flat was situated?'

'No idea, sir.'

'Union Grove, the flat right across from the lawyer's, and get this. It happened early on this morning, while I was there. The SOCOs are there now, according to Atkins he turned their settee over directly in front of the window. Steve Kershaw reckons it was a makeshift stand for his rifle. The fucker could have had me in his sights!' He took another drink. 'Literally!'

The barman approached their table with another Guinness.

'On the house.'

He smiled and returned to the bar missing the bemused look on the detective's face.

'He must know we have them under protection then, sir.'

'What makes you say that, Max?'

'Well, sir, if, as Lucy says, he's making the method of execution more personal now, then why go back to the sniper rifle? Why not cut his throat or set him on fire like the last two? What did Lucy call the shooting and the bombing?

249

Distance kills, wasn't it? Less hands on, she said.'

Buchanan nodded his head.

'Very good, Max. I wonder what stopped him this morning though?'

'He maybe couldn't get a decent shot in.'

The door of the bar opened and a tiny, skinny guy walked in, he couldn't have weighed more than seven stone nor stood any taller than five foot high. Buchanan and Max looked at each other and burst out laughing.

'The nickname must be a joke then,' said Max.

. 'Looks that way,' said Buchanan, wiping the tears from his eyes.

He ordered himself a pint and then walked straight towards them.

'You the coppers?' he asked quietly.

'Aye, we are,' answered Buchanan.

The tracksuited man held out his hand and shook each of theirs in turn.'Big Tam, nice to meet you.'

He sat across from them, leaned in close and whispered.

'I've told the barman and everyone in the pub that you're TV producers, you're scouting out the area for a reality show, okay?'

He winked at them.

'I do a bit of amateur dramatics, so it's quite believable.'

Buchanan now realised why the barman had been so friendly.

He nodded towards the bar.

'That stupid bastard thinks you might use his pub for a location.'

Tam laughed into his pint.

'So, Tam, what's this information you have for us?' asked Buchanan.

'Not so quick, how much will I get for it?'

'Doesn't work like that, Tam, you tell me what you know and then we'll decide what its worth. You get the idea.'

Tam rubbed his chin.

'Fair enough, I suppose. I'll begin at the start then. I met Billy in here yesterday.' He quickly glanced at the clock. 'Around about now actually. Anyway, he'd managed to score me a gram of … '

His eyes bulged as he suddenly realised what he'd just said.

'Listen, Tam,' said Buchanan. 'I'm not bothered what you scored, snorted, smoked or ingested in any way. Carry on, son.'

'Anyway, we had a few pints, a quick line in the bogs and then Billy decided to leave. He was pretty fucked up by this time and when he left he took a tumble right out the door. I jumped up, ready to help him like but when I got to the door, I saw him talking to this old guy. It was the guy your lot are looking for, I saw him in the papers. The thing is, it's almost like the guy was waiting for him, know what I mean?'

'What makes you think that?'

'I don't know really, just a feeling. I thought nothing of

it until later on. I was talking to old Bob and he told me something that throws a whole different angle on it.'

'What exactly did he tell you?'

Big Tam held up his near empty glass and put on a grin.

'That will cost you a pint I'm afraid.'

'Max, get a round in.'

'I'm on my way, sir.'

When Max returned with the drinks, another freebie from the barman, he asked Tam to continue with his tale.

'As I said, I was talking to Bob. He's a weird guy this Bob. He just sits there, on the same chair every day with his nose stuck in a book, very rarely speaks. He's like part of the furniture, so much so that people seem to forget he's there, he's almost invisible. Anyway, according to Bob, after I went up and bought me and Billy a pint yesterday, the barman picked up the phone and phoned somebody. He told the guy at the other end of the phone that Billy had just came in, then he asked when he would get his money. That ties in with my theory, don't it? I mean if it was this old guy he phoned well … '

He shrugged his shoulders.

'He would be waiting outside for him to leave,' finished Buchanan.

'Exactly.'

'Right, I'll have a word with him.' He stood up.

'Woh! Not so fast. Like I said to that bird on the phone earlier … I can't be seen associating with the police. My name will be mud around here.'

Buchanan pondered for a minute.

'Here's what we do. I get Max here to cuff you and lead you outside. You act shocked and then the next time you're here, you just tell them your version of events. How does that sound? We'll even drop you off where ever you want to go next.'

'Cool, I'm meeting a bird up the town in half an hour, at Ma Cameron's.'

'We'll take you there.'

Buchanan winked at him.

'You ready, son?'

'Go for it.'

Max, quick as a flash ran around to the other side of the table, threw Tam face first on to a soggy beer mat and cuffed his hands behind his back.

'Fucking pigs! Get the fuck off me!' cried Tam.

'Take him away, Max, I just want a quick word with the barman.'

Max led him out the door.

'You're a natural, Tam; don't give up on the acting thing.'

As Max took off with Tam, Buchanan walked towards the bar. The barman looked edgy; he seemed to be polishing the glass in his hand just a little too much.

'What's your name, son?'

'Brian … Brian Spence.'

'We'll Brian, do you remember Tam's pal Billy being in here yesterday?'

'Aye, I remember.'

'Would you like to tell me why you picked up that phone behind you there and let a certain someone know he was here?'

'Who says?'

'Don't give me that crap. You were heard by a few different people, so don't deny it. Besides we can just as easily have this conversation at my place, if you get my drift. It's up to you. Think of the hassle involved, you'd have to close the pub, lose the day's takings but, as I said, that's entirely up to you, son.'

The barman stopped his polishing, turned around to the mirror on the back wall and peeled off a post it with a phone number written on it. He handed it to Buchanan.

'He called himself Harry. He said he was looking for Billy. He told me that if I phoned him when he next came in he'd make it worth my while, said he'd bung me a few quid.'

'Did you actually see this guy?'

'No, it was all done over the phone. I never did get the money.'

As soon as he was outside, Buchanan phoned the number. When his call was answered he adopted a posh accent.

'Mr Turnbull, that's your Mercedes all ready to pick up, sir.'

'You've phoned the wrong number I think,' said the voice with the Canadian accent at the other end.

The old man cut off the call as Buchanan gave himself a wry smile.

'Bingo!'

He called PC Atkins.

'Jenny, I want you to get on to the tech guys. I want to set up a phone trace. I'll give you the number.'

Chapter Twenty Nine

Buchanan walked along the corridor with Max, PC Atkins and Frank Boyle from the tech team. They were heading towards the Major Incident Room; the control centre of the investigation. One wall was covered in maps, pictures of the various crime scenes and photos of the dead victims themselves. Another, banks of computer screens.

He shook hands with Sergeant Wilkins, who was in charge of coordinating all the various pieces of information as and when they came in, and then made his way to the front of the room with Frank for his team briefing.

Montgomery, as usual, sat at the front doing his best to make Buchanan feel uncomfortable.

Buchanan often thought that was the man's sole purpose in life.

As Frank hooked up his laptop to the smart board behind him, he put down his steaming mug of coffee on the desk took a deep breath, then after surveying the room, he began to speak.

'I know how quickly rumours travel around here, so I'm sure you've all heard that we've finally had a break in this case.'

He paused and looked at the sheet of paper in front of him.

'About bloody time, many of you are probably thinking.'

There were a few laughs in the background.

'We have Mr Reid's mobile number, thanks to some very diligent work from WPC Atkins.'

A few folk clapped and looked towards Jenny.

'He doesn't know this, so his phone is still active, which means it can be traced.'

He paused and nodded behind him.

'The guy you see beavering around in the background, for those who don't already know him, is Frank Boyle from the tech team.'

He turned towards Frank.

'Let them know what you found, and make it brief, eh, we all know how you guys like to bore us shitless with technical stuff that no bugger can understand.'

Everyone in the room erupted into laughter, all except Montgomery who just sat there with a scowl on his red bull-like face. Buchanan stepped to the side as Frank took his place. The technician put on his glasses and fiddled with his gaudy tie before looking up and addressing the assembly.

'Newer mobile phones, as I'm sure most of you are aware, use GPS. We can use the software we have available to us to pinpoint these phones to within a few feet. Unfortunately for us the phone we're targeting doesn't have this, the chances are it's probably disposable, the cheapest of the cheap. He probably bought it for cash at a garage or supermarket. It's unregistered, so basically untraceable through the normal paper-trail channels.'

He adjusted his glasses.

'However, we can still get an idea of the basic area that it's currently sitting in.'

He clicked a key on the laptop and a picture appeared of what looked like three electricity pylons arranged in a triangle. One of them was highlighted in red.

'The mobile telephone network is divided into cells with a base station at the centre of each cell. The base station …' He pointed to the highlighted pylon, '… which processes the call provides the first clue to location, giving us a basic idea of the general area in which to look.'

He pointed to the other two.

'But other base stations can also make contact with the phone and once information from another couple of these stations has been gathered, the location of the phone can be narrowed down using triangulation. The problem we have though is this: in built up areas where the base stations are close together, this can be to within a few hundred metres; in rural areas, the system is far less accurate. We picked up this particular phone's signal in an area containing mainly farms and woodland just outside Peterculter. So, all we can tell is that the phone is situated around here somewhere.'

The smart board now showed an aerial photo of farmland with a big red circle around the centre.

'We're talking about an area of roughly eight miles square in size. Of course, miles square should never be confused with square miles which … '

Buchanan stepped in.

'Thanks, Frank, I think we all get the idea.' He took a sip of his coffee. 'Right, you heard the man, we basically have a rough idea where he is and that's it. I want this search done on foot; we don't know where the old guy is holed up. He could have taken over a farmhouse and have the owners locked in a cupboard, as he did earlier today, he could be hiding in some ramshackle derelict building, he could even be staying in a tent for all we know. One thing we can be assured of though, don't underestimate this guy, he's an old man but he's extremely fit. I can testify to this, I watched the old bastard leap from a six foot high canopy and land like a cat on the pavement below. He's also dangerous to the extreme. That's why when we split ourselves into groups, each group will be backed up by an armed officer, I'm taking no chances.'

Another sip of coffee. 'I want this done right, people. I don't want it to turn out like last night's debacle.'

Montgomery squirmed in his seat.

'I wasn't there to see that personally, I was otherwise engaged.'

'Aye, engaged to a lamp post!' shouted someone from the back.

Buchanan looked up.

'Cheers, Stuart, I'll mind that one.'

More laughter.

'Sergeant Maxwell and Jenny Atkins will assign you to a group. Grab yourselves a pair of police wellies, and make sure you have a working torch; it'll be getting dark soon. You have twenty minutes to get yourselves organised, then we'll meet outside in the car park ... '

He paused to emphasise his next point.

'We all know it's getting near Christmas, no one wants to pull a double shift at this time of year,' he banged the palm of his hand on the desk, 'so let's go catch this bastard tonight, eh?'

The room erupted in applause as Buchanan left the room and headed for his office. He'd just sat down and reached for his cigarettes when Lucy Jacobs entered the room.

'Great motivational speech, you been watching Braveheart?'

He laughed.

'Och, it's what they needed to hear.'

She looked at him.

'I don't think I can do much more for you here, I think I'll head back to Edinburgh in the morning.'

'I'll be sorry to see you go.'

'Do you really mean that?'

'I do actually; you've changed my viewpoint on all this psychological mumbo jumbo.'

She smiled at him.

'I'll leave you my card; just give me a phone if you need any insight into anything, whether on this case or you're next.'

'Thanks, I will.'

She turned to leave. He felt awkward but he knew he should say something.

'Lucy! It's been great working with you, I'm honoured to know you as a colleague and a friend.'

She ran over and hugged him.

'I'm sorry about the clothes thing. I'm a weird bastard

sometimes, I get stressed and use humour as a safety valve.'

'I know.'

She let him go.

'Catch you later, Buchanan.'

'Oh! Make sure you don't dazzle any drivers with that bright yellow jacket of yours, we have enough road accidents around this time of year.'

She flicked him the V-sign on the way out the door.

Chapter Thirty

'Where the hell is that CD?'

Buchanan rummaged through the glove compartment.

'Ah here we go.'

He inserted it into the car's music player.

The track ID on the car stereo showed *I'm on the Hunt - Lynyrd Skynyrd.*

'Let's go, Max.'

It was already beginning to get dull when they arrived at the meet up point. The scene was punctuated by the sound of car engines running in the background keeping the occupants of the vehicles warm, before they had to get out into the cold air outside to begin their search. Buchanan had chosen a layby, often used by picnickers in the warmer months of the year, to give them some last minute details before they began their search. He waited until they'd all left their vehicles. There were six cars plus a borrowed surveillance vehicle in all.

'Right, you all have your maps and torches, I hope. If not, speak up now.'

No one spoke.

'Good.'

He looked at his watch.

'Hopefully we should have a wee bit of light left yet. PC Atkins and Frank from tech will be monitoring the search and relaying any information to the incident room. They'll be situated here in the surveillance vehicle, which were using as a makeshift base during the search. Now, listen very carefully. I want every team to radio in at twenty minute intervals, whether you've discovered anything or not. Everybody got that?'

There were a few murmurs and nods.

'It might seem a bit daft, but look at it this way, should you come across this guy and he captures you, he has a habit of that, we'll know from your last check in point where that's likely to have happened, so it's for your benefit as much as ours.'

He rubbed his hands to get some heat in them. He wished he'd brought his gloves out of the car.

'And remember, be tactful, don't go scaring the shit out of the local farm workers. Simply show them the photo, ask if they've seen the guy and tell them to keep their doors locked. Traffic has the main roads covered, so if we spook the guy and he takes off in a vehicle, he's not going anywhere. Any questions?'

One officer raised his hand.

'Yes, son.'

'Our search area seems to just be a few fields. Are we expected to search every inch of them, seems a bit pointless?'

Buchanan went over to have a look.

'Aye, you're right enough, but ... ' he tapped a few different areas on the map, 'if you look closely, you have what looks like a barn there and a few small tree covered areas. Focus on them.'

He looked around at everyone.

'All I'm asking you to do is use your common sense, as I said earlier, the guy could be anywhere, he could be kipping in his car under these trees here.'

He held up the young officer's map and pointed.

'That's why we reckon he hasn't been sighted, despite his face being all over the press; he's probably holed up in the back of beyond somewhere, somewhere exactly like the area we're just about to search. As for fields … obviously if you come across a field, and it's as flat as a bloody billiard table and contains nowhere to hole up, just give it a quick once over. Now, have I made myself clear?'

Every one nodded.

'One more thing, should you make an identification of this guy, radio it in straight away. Atkins here will immediately send back up. Don't engage this guy yourself unless you have to. If you're suspicious of anything in the slightest, send in your armed group member first. I purposely picked this spot as it's situated more or less dead centre of our search zone. We have an armed response vehicle heading here as I speak, once it gets here it'll only be minutes away should you need it. So now, if we're all ready, I'd like each team to drive to their allocated spot and then search their given area on foot. The best of luck to you all and be careful.'

The cars all left one by one leaving Buchanan, Max and Derek, their allocated armed officer, alone with Atkins and Boyle.

'You two, make sure you let us know if the signal changes location. There's no point in having all these officers tramping about in the freezing cold for fuck all.'

'We'll let you know if and when that happens, sir,' answered Atkins. Frank just nodded and gave a thumbs up as they both headed off into the warmth of their van.

Buchanan couldn't help feeling envious. He turned to the other two.

'I'm not very good with reading these things.'

'This is an easy one,' said Derek as he pointed at the map. 'Just search a few fields here, a wee bit of woodland and we end up at that hill, it's not that big an area. There are a couple of farms and a few cottages, that's it. It's a piece of piss.'

Buchanan checked that his torch and his radio were working.

'Let's get started, then.'

They walked up the narrow path heading towards the first cottage on the map. The ground beneath them had a thin covering of snow and contained small frozen puddles that, every so often, crunched beneath their feet.

'I heard about your set-to with Montgomery the other night,' said Buchanan.

'That prick!' said Derek

'I don't know how the fuck you can work with him.'

Buchanan laughed.

'It's easy; you just avoid him as much as possible.'

'I should have shot the bastard. I would have if I thought I would have gotten away with it. How did an arsehole like him make DCI anyhow?'

Buchanan winked.

'A few funny handshakes, I heard.'

Max pointed to a large wooden structure tucked in amongst a small copse of frost topped fir trees.

'What do you reckon that is, sir?'

'Looks like a barn or a workshop of some sort, how come it's not on the map?'

'The trees are,' answered Derek.

'Look!'

He showed them the map.

'That's the trouble with these maps they've given us, it's all Aerial views, we'll probably come across a few things like this, as will everybody else no doubt. C'mon, we better check it out.'

They stepped off the path and headed towards the dilapidated wooden shack.

The structure had a huge set of warped double doors, they were quite old and weather worn and were held fast by a simple metal bar between two hooks.

'It doesn't look locked, sir,' said Max as he pried the bar out and pulled open the door at the left hand side.

A scurry of rats, their eyes reflecting the beam of Max's torch, turned and made their escape in to the cold out of a large hole in the wall at the back.

He scanned the area with the beam.

It was empty, apart from an old tractor which was covered in cobwebs and a couple of oil cans. The other two turned on their torches and gave it a quick once over just to be thorough. They found nothing of interest, so they continued on their way.

The path got steeper as they approached the old white washed cottage. There was smoke coming out of the chimney and a warm glow coming from one of the front windows.

The old iron gate at the front gave a squeal as they opened it.

Derek rushed ahead to the side of the window, withdrew his hand gun and had a quick peak in. He whispered back at them and held up two fingers.

'There's two folk, a man and a woman; they're just sitting watching the television.'

'Get the door, Max,' said Buchanan.

Max rang the ancient looking bell; it was shaped like the head of a lion and had turned green with age. It made a strange noise, not so much a ring as a gurgle. It seemed to echo somewhere deeper inside the house.

After a few seconds, the door was opened by a tall middle aged man dressed in dungarees. His eyes grew wide when he saw the gun in Derek's hands.

Buchanan instantly picked up on this and held up his hands, palms outwards.

'Don't be alarmed, sir, we're simply searching the area.' He reached into his pocket and pulled out the photo and his ID card.

'DI Buchanan.'

He flashed his card and then showed the man the photo.

'We're looking for this guy; we believe he may be in the area somewhere.'

The farm worker put on his glasses and took a good look.

'That's the guy out the papers isn't it? "The Christmas Psycho".'

Buchanan corrected him. ' "The Festive Assassin", I believe they're calling him. Aye, you're right though, it is him. Have you seen him going about?'

'Nope, but if I did, I'd take the bastard out myself.'

He drew his left hand from behind the door; it contained an antique-looking shotgun.

'I wouldn't advise it, sir.'

'He comes near me; he's getting the business end of Bess here.' He shook the shotgun. 'I've got a wife and kid in there.'

He nodded behind him.

Buchanan was losing patience.

'Keep your doors and windows locked, you should be safe enough.' He once again reached into a pocket. 'Here.'

He handed over a card containing the incident room number. Each officer had been equipped with a stack of them to hand out to people as they went along.

'If you see him, phone this number right away.'

'Cheers. How about I round up a few of the estate workers to give you a hand?' the man suggested excitedly.

'That won't be necessary, sir, we have plenty bodies to be going on with.'

He was suddenly aware of the double meaning of his answer.

'I was only trying to help,' replied the man in the dungarees, as he slammed the door in his face.

'Charming,' said Derek as Buchanan pulled out his phone.

'I'd better check in with PC Atkins.'

He made the call.

'Jenny, how's it going your end?'

He could hear the tech guy on the radio in the background.

'Nothing much of interest has come in so far, sir. One officer got chased by a Highland cow but that's about it.'

Buchanan laughed.

'Nothing else?'

'I've had a few complaints about the locals not being too friendly, they seem to think they should have been warned way before now that the guy was in the area.'

'We just found out ourselves, for Christ's sake!'

He coughed; the cold air was catching in his throat.

'Talking of the locals, I just met a man who calls his shotgun Bess.'

This time it was Atkins turn to laugh.

'He wanted to join in the hunt.'

'That's the trouble, sir, a few of them might and you can bet your life that they'll be phoning about the place telling their workmates what's going on.'

'I'm okay with that actually, it makes our job far easier; they'll be expecting us to call.'

He heard PC Atkins shuffling something about in the background.

'I've got your map here, sir, have you got to the big farm yet?'

'Give us time, eh! We've already checked out a derelict barn and the first cottage.'

'I can't see any barn on here, except for the two behind the main farm house.'

'That's because they were hidden amongst some fir trees, the trees are on the map, just down the road from the first cottage.'

'I see them, sir.'

'God knows how many buildings are hidden amongst the vegetation around here, that's why I want you to contact all the parties and tell them again to make sure they thoroughly search these areas.'

'Will do, sir.'

'I'll be back in touch in twenty minutes.'

He put away the mobile and took out his cigarettes. He handed one to Derek who gratefully accepted it.

'Anything exciting going down?' he asked.

'Bugger all,' replied Buchanan giving him a light.

Nightfall was slowly coming upon them, the flame from his lighter lit up the area around them.

'Max, you don't smoke do you?' asked Derek.

'Nope.'

'Thank fuck for that then! You'll have been on the third light.'

'You don't strike me as a superstitious person,' said Buchanan.

'I am when there's a fucking sniper going about,' he replied before taking a draw of his cigarette.

Max looked puzzled.

'What's this third light thing all about then?'

'It was a supposed superstition among soldiers during World War I. It's basically this,' said Derek. 'If three soldiers lit their cigarettes from the same match, one of the three would be killed, usually the third.'

'Why was that?'

'The belief was that when the first guy lit his cigarette, the enemy would see the light; when the second soldier lit his cigarette from the same match, the enemy would take aim and then of course when the third soldier lit his … '

'The enemy would fire,' interrupted Buchanan.

'I'll just stand over here then, till you two have finished smoking,' said Max.

Buchanan laughed. 'Of course he could just as easily set his sights on that torch in your hand, Max.'

Cigarettes smoked, they continued up the path.

'I think I can see the entrance to the farm coming up,' said Max.

He shone his torch through the gloom to the plaque on the wall ahead of him. *Mistmore Farm*, it declared.

They walked through the huge gates where the dirt path turned into something more resembling a road. They watched as full beam headlights approached from the huge imposing house in the distance.

The black Range Rover stopped directly in front of them and a blonde haired woman stepped out of the passenger side with two flasks in her hand. She wore a green quilted jacket and a pair of jodhpurs. She and her vehicle looked like they'd came straight off the cover of *Country Life,* all she was missing was the shotgun.

A black Labrador suddenly appeared; it wandered towards them, its breath visible in the cold air. Buchanan bent down and stroked its ears. He produced a dog biscuit from his pocket; he kept them there for his own dog. The Labrador eagerly gobbled it up and sniffed at his pocket looking for more.

'You must be the police,' said the woman. 'I thought you might enjoy a hot coffee.'

Buchanan removed his gloves and rubbed his hands together.

'I wouldn't say no.'

He shook the woman's hand. 'DI Buchanan. And you are?'

'Kate Fielder. I own the farm. Well, my husband Ted does.' She smiled at him. 'I have family in the force. I'm always willing to help the police.'

'Glad to hear it,' said Buchanan, as he fed the dog another

biscuit.

'I hear we have a fugitive on our land,' she said pouring the hot coffee into a huge green mug that she magically produced from the car. It had the farm name on the side written in gold. She proceeded to fill another two for Max and Derek.

Buchanan savoured the warmth and aroma of the coffee.

'News certainly travels fast around here.'

He gave her a smile through the steam coming off the hot drink.

'It always does, all the workers around here see themselves as living in their own small community, and they all look out for each other.'

'I met a guy in the cottage down the road there; he was all for getting involved in the hunt himself.'

'Charley Wood, he did, he phoned a few of his co-workers.'

She nodded towards the distance.

'They're up beyond the hill over there searching for the guy as we speak. They know this land far better than your lot.'

'Fuck!'

'Don't worry, Inspector, if they see anything suspicious, he's going to phone me.' She held up her mobile. 'Give me your number and I'll relay anything he comes across.'

Buchanan pointed to her phone.

'Phone him now, tell him to make sure he doesn't go

shooting any of our lot.'

She shook her head.

'You must think we're all stupid around here. They know exactly who they're looking for.'

She showed him a picture on her phone.

'Harry Reid. I downloaded the picture off the *Press and Journal* website and sent it to all their phones.'

Buchanan sighed.

'We'll, that's something I suppose.'

'Now, where would you like to start?' asked the woman.

Chapter Thirty One

The old man drew back the makeshift curtain from the window on the cottage, scraped off the ice that had formed a thick frozen lair inside the glass and peered into the darkness outside.

There it was again, he could see them beyond the old ruined iron gate, small moving lights in the distance. The first time he'd seen them he was in the outhouse, he'd moved to the cottage to get a better look. At first he'd thought he was imagining them, either that or he was hallucinating, perhaps as a side effect from the white powder. He'd upped the dose; he had to, to stop the headaches coming back.

He rubbed his nose and sniffed. His nostrils felt like they were being clawed by a thousand tigers. He half shut his eyes and watched the lights getting closer. He knew now that they were real, no doubt about it.

He reached under the old oak table for the black case. Opening it, he took out the night vision scope and returned to the window. Closing one eye he stared through the black metal cylinder. He zoomed into the lights, hit the button and watched as everything became green. There were three of them, police officers, no doubt. One was armed; he could see the outline of the rifle strapped to his back.

He scanned the distance, and panned from left to right, there were more lights further away, they must be searching for him, but how had they found out where he was?

He paced back and fore in front of the old oil lamp, his thin frame casting a ghost like shadow on the bare stone walls of his temporary abode.

'Think, Harry, think!'

He'd been so careful, he'd left his vehicle hidden a good distance away, parked amongst some branches he'd made into a shelter. He only left the place in the early hours of the morning and never returned till the evening was drawing in. Any time he saw any other vehicles in the immediate vicinity he'd stop until he made sure they were well out of sight.

He glanced to his right.

He looked at the mobile lying on the windowsill, and then it dawned on him.

Of course, the phone call earlier. He was slipping; he should have ditched the mobile there and then, used a new one.

It was a bit late now, a bit like locking the stable door after the horse had bolted but there was no point in helping them any further. He reached for a brick that was lying at his feet.

'Not so fast, Harry,' said Clara's voice inside his head. 'Aren't you waiting for an important phone call?'

'Of course, thanks for the reminder, dear.'

He used the mobile one last time.

'Everything still on for the handover tomorrow?'

'It's all set up.'

There was a pause.

'The place has been scouted, there shouldn't be a

problem, in fact they should be there any time now. I'll give you a call when it's done.'

'I'll give you a new number, this one is unsafe,' said Harry.

He reached into his bag and withdrew a new mobile, a replica of the one in his other hand. He looked at the label on the box, gave out the number to the guy on the other end of the call before ending the call then proceeded to smash the original phone. The pieces flew across the dimly lit room, one almost hitting him in the eye.

'Try getting a signal out of that, you bastards.'

He walked over to the table and laughed to himself as he prepared another line of the powder.

'Just a quick one and then I can see to my guests.'

*

'Shit!'

'What is it?' asked PC Atkins.

'The signal's gone, he must have turned his phone off,' said Frank.

'The thing is, is it just a coincidence or has he sussed out that we're tracking him.'

Atkins looked at the lap top screen; the red blip on the map was no more.

'Fuck!'

'I'll have to inform the DI.'

'Buchanan.'

'Sir, the signal has gone dead.'

'What do you mean by "gone dead"?'

'His phones not emitting a signal anymore, sir.'

He sighed loudly. 'Could he have moved out of the area?'

'Possibly, but there's no way to tell now that the phone is off.'

'Shit! I take it there's been no sighting of him yet.'

'Not a thing, sir. The next check in will be in about five minutes, if I hear anything I'll let you know.'

'Cheers, Jenny.'

He put away his mobile.

'What is it, sir?' asked Max.

'The bastard has turned off his phone, so there's no way to tell if he's still in the area or not.'

He sighed heavily.

'We'll have to continue with the search though, he could still be here, he's maybe just turned his phone off to conserve the battery. I mean, let's face it if he is hiding out around here he's not exactly going to have easy access to a charger now, is he? Now let's get on with the search.'

Just as they were about to check out the second barn, the Range Rover once again appeared in front of them. It screeched to a halt, the tyres throwing up snow and gravel from the path below. The woman jumped out and came running towards them.

'Detective!'

'What the fuck now?' thought Buchanan.

'Some of the estate workers have found a Land Rover

stashed in the woods, it's been carefully hidden with a screen of pine branches, and it's definitely not one of ours. They shone a torch inside and the ignition wires are hanging out, it's obviously been hot wired.'

'Where exactly is it located?' asked Buchanan, showing her his map.

She looked at it.

'It's not on here.' She pointed to a spot a foot or so off the end.

'It would be over here somewhere, just past Rowan Cottage.'

'Rowan Cottage?'

'It's an old derelict place, just over the hill there. Hop in; we'll get you there in ten minutes. Charlie and another couple of guys are watching it till your lot get there.'

Buchanan, Max and Derek jumped in the Range Rover.

After travelling a few hundred yards up the gravel track the woman took off across the field to their right.

'It'll be quicker this way. Hold on to your hats!'

They all held on tightly to their seat belts, they had no hats. The going was tough; the car jerked them about from side to side. Buchanan reached for his phone, the motion of the car not making it easy. On his second attempt he managed to phone Atkins.

'Who has a place called Rowan Cottage on their map?'

'Gimme a minute, sir.'

He heard a frantic rustling of paper in the background.

'I can't see it anywhere, sir.'

'Look for Whinny Hill,' said the driver in a loud voice. 'That should show up on the map.'

She pointed straight ahead.

'You can see the Whinny in the distance, at the other side of the field there. Rowan Cottage is at the other side, next to a small graveyard, it has a huge dilapidated iron gate, very ornate, you can't miss it.'

'Did you hear that, Jenny?'

'Yes, sir.'

More rustling paper.

'Its team three. Logan's lot.'

'Tell them not to get too close, we're on our way. Oh! And Jenny, send the armed response vehicle out there while you're at it.'

'Will do, sir.'

Chapter Thirty Two

The three officers warily approached the derelict cottage.

'Turn off the torches, lads,' said the man in front. 'If the old bastard is here, we don't want to give him any warning.'

They had decided to cut through the old graveyard to give themselves some cover, just in case their quarry was hiding out inside one of the dilapidated structures ahead of them.

According to their map, the grounds contained the cottage itself and a couple of outer buildings around the back next to a big field.

The graveyard, which, according to the old rusty nameplate on the gate, was called The Rowans, was completely overgrown. It looked like it had been neglected for well over a century, going by the dates on the headstones. It also seemed to have a strange eerie presence attached to it. Each one of the three seemed to sense it; though neither of them let the others know.

Most of the well worn granite gravestones either lay at an obscure angle or had completely fallen over. Some lay in bits. One in particular, which had an ornate stone statue shaped like an angel carved into it, had been decapitated. The ghostly figure just sat there, headless in the moonlight, its moss covered hands clasped in silent prayer.

They had been told by the woman at the other end of the radio not to get too close as back up was on its way, but Sergeant Logan, in his infinite wisdom, had decided to scout out the place, just to see if there was any sign of habitation.

He crouched down behind the ruined dyke that bordered the strange place and gestured for the other two to do the same. They duly obliged.

'Do you have a pair of binoculars on you, Eric?' he asked the armed officer to his left.

'Of course, I never leave home without them.'

He reached into a zipped pocket on the utility belt around his waist and handed them over.

They felt cold in Logan's hands as he scanned the cottage in the distance. He couldn't make out that much detail, there was a freezing fog coming down and the only light available to him was the brightness from the full moon shining above him, and its reflection off the thin white blanket of snow below.

The old cottage looked deserted, more than deserted; it looked like no one had set foot near the place in years. The whole area was overgrown, covered in a mixture of hellebores, thick brambles and sharp looking spiny bushes. There was no obvious route of approach through the thick vegetation. The cottage just sat there like an island amidst a sea of thorns.

'Can't see how any one could be hiding in there, how the fuck could they even get near the place?' asked PC Leonard, the third member of their party.

'It's maybe easier accessed from the back,' said Logan. 'I'll see if I can get a better look.'

'Don't get too close mind,' said Eric 'We know how this guy likes to take hostages.'

'I've no intention of getting that near to the place, I just want to get a look at the back, see if there's any sign of life.'

'There's certainly bugger all signs of life here,' said the young PC, looking at a particularly macabre gravestone with a carving of the grim reaper on it. 'Plenty of signs of death though.'

He wrapped himself up tightly against the wind, it made a strange howling noise as it blew through the myriad holes in the ruined dyke.

'You hear that sound? This place is freaking me out. Can we not just wait outside the gate, till the back up arrives?'

'Just give me five minutes, and calm down for fuck's sake, it's only a graveyard. The dead can't harm you.'

He hung the binoculars around his neck, and then crouched down behind the old wall.

'Keep me covered, Eric, and if either of you see me flash my torch, move up to my location, you got that?'

They both nodded as he crawled away into the distance.

When he reached the end of the wall, he once again looked through the binoculars, all he could see was yet more of the sharp overgrown bushes.

However, on closer inspection, he noticed a small gap between the thick vegetation and the outside wall of the cottage. It seemed to lead directly to the back of the complex.

'Should I or shouldn't I?' he whispered to himself.

His thoughts went back to that morning. As usual, the day began with him having breakfast with Dianne; she'd been giving him grief, yet again.

'Why are you still a sergeant? You told me you'd be

going places, six years I've been listening to that shit! It's time you grabbed the bull by the horns.'

He knew himself that she was right, this was a big case, the biggest he'd ever been involved in. If there was ever a time to get noticed and make a name for himself, this was it.

He could see himself now, leading the old guy out in cuffs, just as the backup arrived. He could practically hear the adulation of his fellow officers. To hell with it.

He climbed up a gravestone that had conveniently fallen against the dyke and ran straight for the gap in the bushes. As soon as he arrived at the side of the cottage, he put his back hard against the wall and slowly edged his way to the far end. He turned on the torch, said a quick prayer, took a deep breath and stepped out into the yard at the back. All was silent, all was dark. The snowflakes, which seemed to be growing larger by the minute, fell quietly on the rooftops of the two small buildings that sat amidst yet more vicious looking plant life.

He slowly made his way through them the best he could and finally came to a clearing next to the first of the two buildings. Once again, he edged himself along the wall till he reached the remnants of an old window frame. He slowly stuck his head out ready to have a look when he heard a twig snap behind him.

'Shit!'

Before he had time to look round he felt the cold steel of the shotgun barrel at the back of his neck.

'Turn towards me, slowly.'

He did as he was asked and turned around to face the man at the other end of the gun.

'Who the fuck are you?' asked the tall man in the dungarees and the flat cap.

Logan held up his arms.

'I'm with the police, Sergeant Brian Logan'

'Prove it!'

He carefully put his hand into his inside pocket and produced his ID.

After a quick glance the man lowered the weapon and held out his hand.

'Charlie Wood.'

He nodded towards the back of the two buildings.

'We found a Land Rover just up the hill there, hidden in the bushes. Since this is the only place within walking distance, I thought I'd take a look. I left a couple of workers with the car, just in case. They're both armed.'

Brian laughed.

'The exact same thing occurred to me. When I heard on the radio that a vehicle had been found near here, it just seemed to make sense.'

'You on your own?' asked Charlie.

'No. I have a couple of officers with me; they're back at the graveyard. There's more on the way, they should only be a few minutes from here.'

'Good! Let's go then, we can start with the old grain store.'

'Woh! Charlie, wait for the backup to arrive. Besides, I can't allow you to put your self in harm's way ... It's more than my job's worth.'

'Bugger that!'

He looked menacingly at Logan.

'I'm here now, I might as well check it out, get it over with.'

Logan thought for a minute. He could still take charge, if he played it right.

'At least let us back you up, one of my colleagues is armed, let me get them round here.'

Charlie scratched his chin.

'I suppose, two guns are better than one, nip on then, I'll wait here.'

'I'd rather you came back with me.'

'Fuck that!' said Charlie. 'I've already squeezed through those brambles once; I've got the scratches to prove it, anyway … '

He shook the shotgun.

'I have Bess here to protect me.'

Logan shook his head and then took off back the way he had come.

Once he got to the front of the cottage, he flashed his torch towards the grave yard. After a few minutes, the other two officers appeared.

'What is it, Sarge?' asked PC Leonard.

Still dreaming of accolades and a possible promotion, Logan pondered things for a moment.

'Time for a white lie,' he thought.

'Some bloody farmer with a shotgun, he's insistent that we search the cottage and the outbuildings.'

He nodded behind him.

'He's around the back there.'

'We'll have to stop him then,' said Eric, unhooking his rifle. 'I'm just off the radio, the armed response vehicle is only a couple of minutes away; the DCI is on his way here as well. They gave me specific orders not to move beyond the graveyard. They told me to make sure that I relayed the information to your good self.'

'We've no choice then,' said the young PC. 'We'll have to stall the guy.'

Sergeant Logan was in a quandary. Go for glory or play it safe.

He bottled it and went with the second option.

'Bugger it! You're right, we'll stall him until the back up gets here, follow me you two.'

He slowly retraced his steps through the thick thorn covered vegetation. Eric found it difficult with the rifle in his hands but eventually they all stood in the clearing in the back.

The place was deserted; there was no sign of Charlie or anyone else.

'Where the fuck has he got to?' Logan asked no one in particular.

He heard a high pitched whistle, then, after shining his torch in the direction of the sound, he saw Charlie. He was standing in the shadow cast in the moonlight by the tall overhanging roof of the first building.

He gave them a wave. Logan reciprocated.

'C'mon, guys, I'll introduce you to Charlie.'

As he got nearer, he got the strangest feeling that something wasn't quite right. He couldn't put his finger on anything in particular.

'Look what I've found,' said Charlie as he turned his back to them and pointed towards the other building.

The three men quickened their pace so they could see what the man with the shotgun was pointing to.

When they were about a couple of feet behind him, Charlie quickly swung around and took out the armed officer with a hard blow across the nose with the stock of the shotgun.

Eric's nose exploded across his face as he hit the dirt. He left a fine red spray in the surrounding snow.

Logan stared open mouthed. The guy wasn't Charlie, he wore Charlie's dungarees and flat cap but this guy looked a good deal older. And then it dawned on him.

'Fuck!'

The old man winked as he bent down and picked up Eric's rifle.

He looked at it intently as its owner tried to hold what was left of his nose together with his left hand.

'Nice weapon. Heckler and Koch, I believe.'

He turned it over in his hands as if he was gauging the weight then slung the strap over his shoulder. He looked up and smiled.

'You gentlemen are looking for me?'

*

After gathering up their radios and mobile phones and then cuffing the three officers with their own handcuffs, the old man made them walk ahead of him into a small group of trees behind the farm buildings.

He'd attached one of their torches to the shotgun with duct tape and used it to shine the way ahead of them when he wanted them to take a particular route.

'Take the path to your left, it leads to an old wooden gate, move it.'

Logan turned around.

'You won't get away with this you know, there's … '

The bullet that landed an inch from his foot stopped Logan mid-speech.

'No talking, that goes for you all.'

He watched the old man inhale something off the back of his hand before turning back to the path.

'A seventy year old junkie,' he thought to himself. He shook his head. Now, he'd seen it all.

When they reached the end of the path, he asked Logan to open the gate.

They found themselves in an overgrown field. The old man shone the light towards a small hill. It had what appeared to be a metal door in it.

The young PC whispered to Logan.

'Who the fuck would put a door in a hill?'

'A hobbit maybe?' replied Eric from the front in a nasal whine.

'I said no talking,' said the old man.

When they reached the door, he told them to stop then he uncuffed Logan.

'Here,' he threw a small key attached to a chain at him. 'Unlock the padlock and open the door.'

Logan did as he was asked.

'Right, the three of you, get in there.'

Once they went through the door, he re-cuffed him and told him to lead the way.

He was surprised to find that the place was circular in shape, it reminded Logan of the turret of a medieval castle, what little light there was came from an oil lamp hanging from the wall.

'Get down the stairs, the three of you.'

The stone stairs went down in a spiral, a good twenty feet underground. There was no banister, and with their hands secured behind their backs, they found the going difficult so they leaned into the wall to give themselves some sense of balance.

'What the hell is this place?' he asked.

His voice echoed in the distance.

'It's your new temporary accommodation, now keep moving.'

When they reached the bottom, they came across Charlie.

He was sitting in his underwear, visibly shaking with the cold. He had his back against the wall and he sported a rather nasty cut above his left eye. His wrists, legs and mouth were taped up.

'The three of you, sit next to him.'

The old man proceeded to tape them up exactly as he had done with Charlie, he didn't bother with their wrists as they were already in handcuffs. He saw to Logan first, then PC Leonard, but, as he bent down to tape up Eric, the officer gave out a vicious boot with his right leg. The old man moved his chin just in time; the side of Eric's boot skimmed against his cheek leaving a nasty scrape.

'Naughty, naughty,' he said as he brought the butt of the rifle down full force between Eric's legs.

He let out a high pitched scream which was quickly stifled by the duct tape being wrapped around his mouth.

The other three captives winced at the thought of the pain their comrade had just endured.

'Well, gentlemen, I'll have to leave you for a while, I have things to see to. Bye for now, then.'

Chapter Thirty Three

The passengers inside the Range Rover were being buffeted around from pillar to post as Kate Fielder, who appeared to have no respect for life or limb, once again went tearing up yet another steep slippery hill.

'She's as mad as you are behind the wheel!' whispered Buchanan to Max.

Max just grinned.

'I'm enjoying this, sir. I've always fancied a bit of off roading.'

Derek looked like he was about to be sick, he'd turned very pale.

'Another jump,' shouted the driver, as the vehicle seemed to take off for a few seconds.

The vehicle landed with a thump, the wheels spinning to gain purchase in the snow-covered hill side. The woman laughed.

'Hang on, boys, we're almost there.'

Buchanan's phone rang. He held onto the door tightly as he removed his mobile from his pocket with his free hand. He looked at the screen, it was Atkins.

'This had better be important, Jenny.'

'It is sir; we can't reach Logan's team. The ARV guys contacted their guy a couple of minutes ago. He told them that they were at the graveyard in front of the cottage, but they haven't been able to reach him since. I've tried phoning Logan, I can't get a hold of him either.' She sighed, 'I have a bad feeling about this, sir.'

'Shit! How close are the armed response guys?'

'Just a minute or so away, sir.'

'So are we, let me know if you hear anything.'

'Will do.'

He ended the call and turned towards Max and Derek.

'Logan's group have disappeared. They were last spotted at the graveyard, it's just in front of the cottage we're heading for.'

'That doesn't look good,' said Max.

'No shit, Sherlock!' said Derek, who was looking sicker by the second. He looked towards the woman. 'How far do we still have to go?'

'We're just about there,' said Kate.

'It's just at the foot of this hill, it's a bit rough this bit mind, so once again, hold on to your hats, guys.'

'If I had a hat, I'd be puking into it, believe me!'

Max shook his head and laughed.

'I know I'm going to regret asking this,' said Buchanan, turning towards their driver.'Is there anyway you can speed things up?'

The woman laughed. 'I thought you'd never ask.'

She pressed a button, raising the suspension on the vehicle.

'Now, we're cooking with gas.'

'What model is this, anyway?' asked Max.

'It's the newest of the new, the latest Ranger Rover Sport. Believe it or not, it's made totally out of aluminium, it gives it a huge weight loss compared to the older model.'

'Impressive, what sort of engine power does she have?'

'510 horses, supercharged V8.'

'Wow!'

'Yup. Listen to her purr.'

The engine roared as she floored the accelerator and the vehicle took off down the other side of the hill. Buchanan could feel his back getting pressed into the seat as Derek took deep breaths and tried his best to keep the contents of his stomach in place.

*

After screaming down the steep incline like a bat out of hell, Kate executed a perfectly controlled forty-five degree skid and expertly stopped the Range Rover directly in front of the rusty graveyard gate.

Max applauded as Buchanan and Derek both reached for their doors, desperate to get out of the mad country-woman's car.

Buchanan looked towards the graveyard; he shivered as he remembered the old man tying him to the lamppost in just such a place the night before.

He lit up two cigarettes, handing one to Derek.

'Well, that was an experience, I thought Max was crazy

behind the wheel, but this woman's off the chart.'

'I'm just pleased to have my feet back on *terra firma*,' said Derek, gratefully accepting the smoke.

Buchanan pointed into the distance.

'For fuck's sake, check that out.'

Derek turned round to see what looked like a UFO flying across the snow in the distance. White and blue lights seemed to be cascading in all directions.

'It's the Armed Response Vehicle,' said Derek. 'And I have a good idea who is driving.'

'They could have kept the bloody lights off. If the old guy is hiding out around here, he sure as fuck knows we've arrived now.'

'Blame Justin Jarrett, or double J, as he likes to be called. He does that all the time, in fact, I'm surprised he hasn't got the siren on, that's his usual. He's an arsehole. He seems to think he's flying a chopper in Vietnam, not driving a bloody police vehicle. The other guys all hate the bastard; no-one wants to be on his team.'

'I think I've met him before, is he the guy with the sunglasses?' asked Buchanan.

'That's him. Once met, never forgotten. He transferred from somewhere down south about six months ago. Don't get me wrong, he's good at his job but, like I say, he's an arsehole and a real stickler for the rules.'

As if on cue, as the car - another Land Rover - got closer, the siren came on.

'Fucking great!' said Buchanan as he threw the last of his

cigarette into the snow.

The ARV slowed down in front of them. The driver jumped out and stood ramrod straight in front of the vehicle. He sported a buzz cut and was wearing a pair of tinted glasses despite the fact it was dark. He looked more like a US marine than a police officer.

Buchanan tried not to laugh as he shook the guy's hand.

'DI Buchanan.'

'Justin Jarrett - most folk call me double J.'

The other two officers also introduced themselves. Davie Lawson and Bruce Allan. They wandered over to join Derek and Max beside Kate's Range Rover, leaving Buchanan alone with Justin.

'Well, Buchanan, fine name by the way, have you made an assessment of the situation? Do we need armed containment?'

'Calm down, Justin, we just got here a minute before you, all we know for certain is that the three officers who were searching this area can't be contacted, either by radio or phone. The last time we heard from them they had just arrived at this graveyard here. By the way, it's DI Buchanan.'

Justin looked sheepish.

'Sorry, sir.'

'And you can put that bloody lights out, they're giving me a migraine.'

He lit another cigarette as Justin went back to the vehicle.

'Oh! And Justin …'

He stopped and looked back.

'Once you've seen to that, meet me over there beside the others.'

*

Seven of them, he counted from his makeshift platform hidden amongst the branches in the huge Scots Pine. He'd cleared a small area deep in the tree and built a shelter to keep himself dry, it was similar to a bird hide, but it wasn't birds he was watching.

He had another look through the binoculars. This time it wouldn't be so easy! Too many of this second wave were armed. Two of them he knew, Max and Buchanan, four were obviously from the armed response unit and the last one, the woman, shouldn't pose him any problems. He knew himself that with his expertise he could take them all down with a few well aimed shots but hopefully it wouldn't come to that … not unless it had to. He still felt bad about Victor though, he'd made a promise to himself that he wouldn't harm anyone that didn't deserve it, he'd killed enough innocent people in the past, for his own government too.

'You're getting maudlin, Harry, you know what you need.'

He lay the binoculars down at his side next to his ever increasing arsenal and once again took a line of the white powder. He looked upon the stuff now as some sort of magic elixir. It seemed to cure all his ills. In fact, it did more than that; it didn't just cure his headaches, it gave him a new lease of life. Without it, a man of his years couldn't possibly climb twenty five feet up a tree. The stuff seemed to make him superhuman, he didn't have to sleep, and he never felt hungry. If he managed to get out of his current situation, he'd have to hunt down the junky's supplier, find more of the stuff. He supposed that long term use might eventually harm him, but he didn't gave a shit, he didn't have a long term allocated to him. He was surprised he was still alive now, he never expected to be. They'd only given him a month at his last check up, maybe the powder was keeping him alive for a specific reason, he believed he knew what that was. He realised now that killing the last two was an impossible task, but he still believed that the last part of his plan was still attainable. It was just a pity that Clara hadn't held on longer to see the fruits of his labour.

He felt his heart rate increasing as he once again picked up the binoculars he'd taken off the police officer earlier and continued to watch the scene playing out before him.

*

They decided to split them selves into two groups, the three new arrivals in one, and Buchanan, Max and Derek in the other. Buchanan insisted that Kate stayed in her car. He told her to use the vehicle's horn if she saw anything suspicious while they were checking out the cottage and its surrounding buildings. She didn't take too kindly to this but after Buchanan threatened to phone for another car and have her physically driven back to her house, she reluctantly agreed.

Each group approached the cottage from a different side in a sort of makeshift pincer movement. Since the newest members to arrive had more firepower available to them, and due to the fact that they were far more likely to be used as a makeshift hide out, they decided to check out the buildings at the back while Buchanan's group checked out the cottage itself.

They knew that Logan, or rather his mobile, was still somewhere in the area, but as they couldn't get an answer from anyone in his group either by phone or radio, the general consensus was that the old man had taken them prisoner, or worse, was hoping to use them as some sort of bargaining tool. Either way, if their suppositions were correct, he must be keeping them somewhere, more than likely in one of the structures ahead of them. Kate had told them that one of the farmers had also disappeared, the guy with the shotgun they'd seen earlier back in his cottage. According to his colleagues back at the stolen Land Rover, he'd also last been seen heading to the disused cottage.

Derek reached into his vest and gave Buchanan his hand gun. They both knew it was strictly against the rules, but as Buchanan had said, this wasn't your normal man hunt, they needed all the protection they could get.

'Jesus! Look at the size of those thorns,' said Buchanan as he deftly turned sideways and squeezed himself towards the cottages rusty gate. Max and Derek followed suit.

The gate opened with a squeal, setting his teeth on edge. He walked around an old stone birdbath that lay on the cracked path, it's heavy pedestal was broken in two pieces and the upturned bowl was full of snow.

'Not much use for any bird in that state,' he said to his two companions who followed behind.

'Not unless it's a fucking penguin,' replied Derek.

Max laughed. The short discussion between them did little to belay their anxiety as they walked towards the entrance of the cottage.

The door lay off its hinges at an awkward angle. It was misshapen by the elements and extremely heavy. It took the strength of both Derek and Max to move it to the side.

'Max, you stay behind me,' said Derek as Buchanan drew out his hand gun.

'Take this,' he handed Max his telescopic baton. 'There's no point in being completely unarmed.' He pointed the beam of his torch towards Buchanan. 'Dirty Harry here can look after himself.'

Buchanan expertly spun the gun around his finger and gave a huge smile.

'I'm not a complete novice, Derek, me and Michelle go shooting now and again up at the black dog range. She's been a member of the full bore gun club for years, I just got into it recently.'

He turned to Max.

'You should give it a try sometime; it's a great stress-reliever.'

'I might take you up on that, sir.'

'Joking aside,' said Derek, 'if you do come across this Mr Reid and end up shooting the old bastard, the higher-ups will have a field day.'

'Don't worry about it, Derek, I'll just say you shot him. Now, come on, let's check out this cottage.'

The three men stepped into the gloomy interior completely unaware of the old man in the snow capped tree watching their every move.

Chapter Thirty Four

Kate Fielder felt totally left out of things. The adrenaline high of the fast drive across the snow-topped hillside was all but gone. She gave out a sigh. It was her land they were on, why shouldn't she take part in the manhunt? She had her shotgun with her and she knew she was a good shot, probably better than most of them, marksmen or not.

As for Buchanan, who the hell did he think he was? He'd made her feel like a naughty school girl being admonished by the headmaster. She wasn't used to getting ordered about, in the day to day running of the estate she was usually the one giving out orders.

She sighed once more to herself, blew her long fringe out of her eyes and leaned back on the bonnet of her Range Rover as she watched the beams of the officers' torches disappear into the entrance of the old cottage. She yawned and wrapped her thick coat tightly around herself.

'There's surely something you can do to help, Kate, think!'

Her eyes scanned the area ahead but she couldn't see much. The only light available was cast by the cloud covered moon. She turned on her torch but that didn't help much either.

Then she had an epiphany. She jumped into the car and turned on her headlights, the area directly in front of the cottage glowed as the snow reflected the powerful beams. She grabbed her shotgun from under the back seat walked towards the wall surrounding the old graveyard and stood guard. Now she felt part of things. If the old guy showed his face, she would be ready for him. She'd love to capture the fugitive herself, that would show Buchanan what she was made of.

Her thoughts were interrupted by the sound of footsteps. Then she heard what sounded like thin ice cracking on a puddle behind her.

She spun around quickly. Her eyes took their time to adjust from the light projected by the vehicle to the almost complete darkness behind her. She saw a shadowy figure approaching with a torch, the person was big and bulky and in their left hand they carried what looked very much like a shotgun.

She aimed her own firearm towards him or her, she wasn't sure if it was a male or a female. They were wrapped up heavily against the elements. The shapeless bulk gave her no clue to their sex.

She took a deep breath and did her best to hide her nervousness.

'Halt! Who goes there?'

She felt ridiculous saying such a thing but it was the first phrase that came to her mind.

The figure dropped the weapon and raised both glove covered hands above their head.

'Don't shoot, Mrs Fielder, its Jed.'

She lowered her shotgun.

'For God's sake, Jed, haven't you got anything better to do than sneak up on people in the dark?'

'Sorry, Kate.'

She shook her head.

'Anyway, I thought you were keeping an eye on that old Land Rover you found up the hill there.'

Jed bent down to retrieve his weapon.

'We were, but after Charlie left to have a look at the cottage Darren buggered off, he said he was sick of freezing his arse off for nothing. Anyway, before I left the whinny I disabled the vehicle.'

'How do you mean?'

'I disconnected the battery and hid it under a rock in the woods. Rest assured, Kate, that car's going nowhere.'

Kate smiled at him.

'Very clever, Jed, I'm impressed. I take it you came down here looking for your brother?'

'Aye. I'm worried about Charlie, he's still never appeared and he isn't answering his phone. You guessed right, I thought I'd come and look for him.'

'Do you fancy a coffee; I think there's still some left in one of the flasks.'

'That'd be great, cheers.'

She went to the back of the vehicle and reappeared with two steaming mugs of coffee. The aroma filled the air around them.

'Here you go, Jed. By the way, Charlie's not the only one who has gone AWOL,' said Kate.

'How do you mean?' he asked as he blew on his coffee.

'There are three police officers missing as well. This whole area seems to have turned into Culter's own version of the Bermuda Triangle.'

'Spooky! I wonder what happened to them.'

'That detective guy seems to think that this gunman they're after has captured them.'

'What! Taken them hostage you mean?'

'Seems that way.'

Jed shook his head.

'Who the fuck is this guy? I saw the photo you sent us, looked like he was an old bastard.'

'Harry Reid, he's called, and you're right enough, he is an old guy. He's from Canada seemingly; they reckon he has some sort of military background. According to that bolshy detective inspector, he's extremely dangerous, that's all I know.'

She took a sip of her coffee.

'He's that guy out the papers ain't he?' said Jed.

She nodded.

'He's killed three people so far, according to tonight's edition, blew one of the victims up with a car bomb.'

Jed looked off into the distance towards the old cottage as he drank the last of his coffee. His eyes were drawn towards the thick icicles that hung from what was left of the guttering. They sparkled as they reflected the light beam from the Range Rover.

'Good idea with the lights.'

'I thought so, too.'

She pointed straight ahead.

'Hopefully the armed cops will find the missing officers and your brother. I thought I could keep an eye on things out here, care to join me?'

Jed rubbed his chin.

'Aye, why not.'

'Great. I was getting a bit spooked out here on my own. You fancy another coffee?'

*

The inside of the cottage was not much more than a shell. It consisted of two large rooms downstairs and nothing whatsoever up stairs, the ceiling above them was destroyed and the old staircase was in ruins, just one solitary banister and two steps was all that was left of it it, a stairway that led to nowhere.

The three wary officers entered the room on the left first. It looked like it had once been the sitting room. It housed an old rocking chair, a broken table and what was left of what looked like a huge stone fireplace.

Buchanan wrinkled his nose and shivered. The whole building had a damp rotten wood smell about it and seemed, if anything, even colder than the frosty night air outside.

'This place is fucking creepy,' said Derek. 'It reminds me of that place in that movie.'

'What movie?' asked Buchanan.

'I can't remember the name of it off-hand. It was about these three students who went off to look for a ghost in the woods or something. Anyway they came across a place similar to this. Then they disappeared.'

'*The Blair Witch Project*,' said Max.

'That's it! Have you watched it?'

'Aye, a good while ago.'

'Is that the one where they find the video of the event, it's done like a documentary?' asked Buchanan.

'You've seen it too then.'

'Watched it on Sky not long ago, I know what you mean about the similarities with this place.'

Derek cast the beam of his torch about the place.

'I'll tell you one thing. If I catch sight of any spooky hand prints on the walls, I'm out of here as if my arse was on fire.'

Buchanan and Max laughed, relieving the tension.

'Right,' said Buchanan. 'Lets give this place the once over, the sooner we're done, the sooner we can get the fuck out of here.'

He raised his torch and continued to survey the area. The walls were covered in old damp peeling wall paper. It had a horrible cream coloured background decorated with huge green ferns. The background had become mottled due to the passage of time.

'My local has that very same wallpaper,' said Derek. 'Shows you how often they fucking decorate.'

There was a grimy framed black and white photograph on the main wall above the derelict fireplace, the subject matter: an unnamed rural scene with a horse and cart pictured against a field of wheat. He could just make out a river and a stone bridge set far in the background. He wondered if it had been taken locally.

'It could be the River Dee,' he thought.

Taking his mind off the picture, he walked towards the window, his footsteps echoing off the walls. He was careful to avoid the numerous missing floorboards and chipped remnants of linoleum beneath his feet.

'Check this, guys.'

He aimed the torch beam at the scraped ice on the inside of the paint-peeled window.

'Looks like someone's been here recently.'

He pointed his torch at the floor and looked down at the footprints that stood out prominently in the thick layer of dust that had accumulated over the years.

'Someone's been standing here looking out the window. They probably watched us arrive.'

He moved the beam to the left. There was a glint as it reflected off the broken screen of the old man's mobile phone.

'No wonder we're not getting a signal any more,' said Max.

Buchanan nodded his head.

'Rescue the SIM card, Max, we'll get someone to go over it later and see what information we can get off it.'

As Max bent down to retrieve the card, Buchanan drew back the scruffy makeshift curtain.

'Where's that light coming from?' he asked of no one in particular.

'I was wondering the very same thing,' replied Derek.

They all looked outside.

'That's that mad bird's Range Rover,' said Derek. 'Is she fucking stupid or what? There's a good chance that there's a sniper in our midst and she's standing there in front of her full beams.'

'Fuck!' said Buchanan. 'She'd be as well painting a target on her chest.'

He quickly hauled out his phone and gave her a call.

'What's the score with the headlights, Kate?'

'I thought it would help, it lights up the area a bit, me and Jed can cover your backs from here.'

'Who the fuck's Jed when he's at home?'

'He's the missing farm workers brother; he came to see what had happened to him.'

Buchanan sighed.

'Look, I'm ordering the two of you to stay out of it. Both of you get into the car and keep an eye out from there, and for gods sake turn the bloody lights off, you're making yourselves prime targets. Besides … '

Kate took the huff and cut him off mid rant.

He was just about to stick his mobile back in his pocket when he got a call.

'Hello …?'

'Buchanan! … Sorry, Detective Inspector Buchanan, it's

Justin, sir, thought I'd report in.'

'Go ahead, Justin.'

'There's definitely been someone here, sir; we found a camp bed and a portable gas heater in the smaller out house.'

'Any sign of the missing officers?'

'No, but there's a shitload of footprints in the snow around here, there's a good chance they belong to them, they lead off into the woods. Do you want us to follow them?'

'No! Wait till we get there, we'll be around in a minute.'

'Fair enough, sir. We also found what looks like a blood pool, it's soaked into the snow but it looks quite a substantial amount.'

'Fuck! Tell your men to stay alert.'

'Will do.'

He once again phoned Kate.

'Kate, what's at the end of the path that leads into the woods around the back of the cottage?'

'It just leads to a field.'

'That's it?'

'Well ... apart from the old Ice House.'

'Ice House?'

'Yeah, it's basically a small subterranean chamber built into a hill, they used to use it to store ice before they had refrigeration.'

'Cheers, Kate. Now remember, stay vigilant, we're off to check this Ice House out, if you see anything get right on your mobile.'

He heard a male voice in the background.

'We can't see fuck all; you made us put the lights off.'

Buchanan sighed and weighed things up.

'Okay, you can put them back on, but for fuck's sake don't stand in front of the bloody things, take cover behind the vehicle. You got that?'

'Loud and clear,' replied Kate

He turned to Derek and Max.

'Lets go, lads, looks like Justin's lot have found something.'

*

From his makeshift treehouse the old man quietly watched as the three men passed below.

Chapter Thirty Five

As they walked into the gloominess of the thick woodland, Buchanan began to feel more than a little claustrophobic. He'd never really realised before that there were different degrees of dark. Once the scant light cast by the moon had disappeared, they'd found themselves in total pitch black darkness. If it hadn't been for his torch, he wouldn't have been able to see his hand in front of his face.

As he followed the footprints and walked further up the path, the snow topped evergreen Fir trees seemed to close in on him from above. He looked up and pointed his torch. The dark canopy seemed to eat up the light, the intertwined branches reminding him of the architecture on the roof of some medieval cathedral.

He shivered involuntary; it made him aware of the cold sweat slowly running down his back. The gloomy atmosphere was tense. There was a strange eerie silence all around him. They'd left the blustery wind that had recently started up behind them at the entrance to the woods. Even their footsteps were silent, muffled by the underlying snow. It seemed unnatural.

As he walked further in to the woods, he watched as the beams cast by the other men's torches set shadows dancing off the tightly packed trees in all directions, adding another edginess to the situation he'd found himself in.

The blood back at the outhouse had worried him also; it seemed quite a large amount. Someone must be badly injured. Or worse … He shook his head to clear his thoughts;

the depressive atmosphere of the place was obviously getting to him. He had to get his mind back to the task in hand.

He looked to the path ahead. The footprints could be seen clearly in the thin layer of snow, but they were all layered on top of each other. It was impossible to tell how many people had passed this way before them. Then he saw something that piqued his interest.

'Any one have any ideas what's going on here?' he asked to no one in particular.

There were a few murmurs and shrugs from the men around him but no answers were forthcoming. He pointed his torch at the path.

'What do we see here, gentlemen?'

'A shitload of footprints,' replied Derek.

'Look closer.'

They all stopped, gathered around Buchanan and stared at where he was aiming the torch.

'C'mon, lads. I can't be the only person to see it. Max?'

Max stared at the footprints.

'I don't see what you're getting at, sir ... wait a minute.'

Max crouched down for a closer investigation then looked back to the way they had come and pointed.

'Some of them are heading back towards the cottage.'

'Close, Max. Not some of them though, one of them. Look.' He scanned the torch beam over the multitude of prints. 'He's tried to cover his tracks by walking back over the foot prints that were already there, but some of them ...'

He moved the beam slightly to the side. 'As you can see, he's veered slightly off the path. Look!'

He moved the torch beam once again. 'All these prints have the same tread pattern.'

'Bastard!' shouted Justin. 'He's lead them up here like lambs to the slaughter.'

Buchanan shook his head from side to side then stared at him.

'Are you always so fucking optimistic?'

Justin looked down at his feet. Buchanan's sarcasm had obviously hit home.

'You're a real glass half empty type of guy, ain't you, Justin?'

'Sorry, sir.'

'Let's just follow the trail and see where it leads before we go jumping to conclusions, eh.' He pointed ahead. 'Right, carry on, I'll catch you up.'

He waited until the other officers were a few paces ahead of him then took out his mobile and phoned Atkins.

'Jenny, call in the helicopter and as much manpower as we can get, it looks like our man is still in the immediate area somewhere. Tell everyone on foot to sweep towards the old graveyard, armed men to the front, and tell them to be careful.'

'Yes, sir.'

'Also, see if we can spare any vehicles from the motorway, preferably all terrain, there's a distinct lack of roads around this god forsaken place.'

'Will do, sir. Is there any sign at all of Logan's group?'

'Yes and no. It looks like they've been here, we found footprints. I think old Mr Reid did his capture the cops routine again, but I have a good idea where he's holding them.'

'That's something I suppose. I'll call you back when I have an ETA for the chopper.'

'Cheers, Jenny,' he put his phone back in his pocket and increased his pace to catch up with his colleagues.

*

'What the hell was that?'

'What was what?' asked Kate, looking towards Jed.

'I heard a noise from over beside the graveyard gate. Listen.'

'It's probably the gate squeaking with the wind.'

'It's not that type of noise, Kate. Listen … '

They both stood silently listening to the night.

There was a rustling in the distance. They both heard it this time, it sounded like someone or something moving through the overgrown bushes that stood at either side of the old graveyard's entrance.

'Thank fuck we put the the lights back on,' said Jed.

'Och, it's probably just the wind blowing around the bushes, or an animal maybe. Stop jumping at shadows.'

'You're probably right, but let's face it, Kate, it could just as likely be that mad old bastard creeping about out there. He could be crawling towards us to get a better shot or plant a bomb or some shit.'

Kate turned once again to look at him. She gave him a piercing glance.

'Are you going out of your way to scare the shit out of me, Jed? Because it's working!'

'Sorry.'

He shrugged his shoulders.

'Lets face it, though: it could be him, couldn't it? You mentioned earlier they reckoned he had some military experience, maybe he was a commando. They're used to creeping up on folk in the dark; they probably do it every day, I'll bet.'

She looked into the distance and then headed towards the driver's side door.

'I'm going to put the head lights off again; if it is him out there and we leave them on we'll be playing right into his hands. That inspector was right enough.'

'I'm not sure that's a good idea.'

Jed rubbed his unshaven chin and appeared deep in thought. He removed his cap then turned towards Kate and the Range Rover.

'How does this sound. I'll go over to where we heard the noise from and then I'll whistle. When you hear me, turn the lights back on right away. It'll surprise him, while he's startled by the lights, I'll get him with the shotgun.'

Kate nodded her head.

'Sounds good, go for it.'

She reached for her own gun.

'I'll cover you.'

Jed tentatively made his way towards the huge overgrown holly bushes. He held the stock of his shotgun hard against his shoulder and pointed the barrel straight ahead as he went. Then he heard the rustling again, closer this time. It seemed to be coming from the bush on the left; it stopped him dead in his tracks. He could feel the cold sweat running down his back and his mouth suddenly felt as dry as a bone. It took him three attempts to make the whistle.

The strong beams of the cars headlights suddenly came to life catching the glint of the bemused fox's eyes as it ran at great speed from beneath the holly bush.

Jed let out a scream that could only be described as primal as he fired the shotgun. It was an automatic reaction; the shot missed the startled fox by less than three inches. It went scarpering over the graveyard wall and disappeared into the distance between two ruined headstones. Not much more than a couple of seconds after the echo of the gunshot had faded into the night, Kate's mobile rang. She looked at the screen, not that she had to, she had a good idea who was calling. It was Buchanan.

'Shit! That's all I bloody need.'

She clicked the keypad to accept the call.

'What the fuck is going on, Kate?'

'False alarm detective, we heard a noise but it was only a fox.'

'Did you have to shoot the fucking thing?'

'It was Jed's shotgun you heard, the beast startled him,

that's all.'

She heard a heavy sigh from the other end.

'Tell him not to go shooting anything else or he'll have me to answer to. Jesus!'

The line went dead, leaving Kate feeling admonished once more.

'Fucking foxes!' said a voice in the distance. 'I hate the bastards.'

*

Just as Kate was pocketing her phone, the old man carefully made his way down the rope from his hiding place in the tree. He had his sniper rifle slung over his shoulder so he could use both hands to help with his descent. Once he reached the ground he crouched down and stayed that way for a few minutes, just to make sure he hadn't been seen. Once he assured himself he was quite safe, he disappeared into the thick undergrowth, like a thief in the night, to pick up the large canvas bag he'd hidden earlier. The bag contained the case for the rifle that hung from his shoulder and the rest of his ever growing arsenal - which now, as well as his own handgun, included the Heckler and Koch rifle and sidearm from the armed officer, and the shotgun he'd taken off the farmhand. He had taken all of their ammunition too.

He laughed to himself.

'I'm a regular one man army.'

He had his escape almost fully planned out. Either one of the vehicles at the other side of the graveyard would do him. They were both four by fours, just what he needed; he wasn't planning on sticking to the roads. He had watched as

Buchanan and the other officers had gone off into the woods in search of their colleagues. He knew that would keep them occupied for a good while.

He laughed to himself again.

He couldn't wait till they found the present he'd left them. It had cost him a bit but he'd always known that the device would come in handy.

'Flash, Bang!'

He giggled and looked across the graveyard.

That just left the farm worker and the woman. They shouldn't be a problem. They were both armed with shotguns but they were both well spooked. He'd had to cover his mouth and stifle a laugh as he'd watched the debacle with the fox.

He slid himself along the side wall of the cottage and crouched down behind an old water butt as he waited for them to turn off the headlights once again. As he watched them, he began to work out the best way to approach a tricky situation.

Chapter Thirty Six

At the end of the path, they came to an old wooden gate that led into the field that Kate had mentioned earlier. It had seen far better days. It lay at a funny angle between the old moss covered dyke on either side.

The footprints were much clearer here as the snow beneath their feet was so much deeper now that they had left the thick cover of the woods.

Derek opened the gate; he had to lift the left hand side off the ground to get it to move.

The rusted hinges made a high pitched squeal which reverberated into the night.

Buchanan shivered; he couldn't help thinking of barn owls.

He lit a cigarette and then walked to the head of the small group. Once there he turned and held up his hand to stop them in their tracks.

'If I'm guessing right,' he said as he pointed his torch at the foot prints. 'These should lead to a small hill in the field somewhere. It should have a door in it that leads to an underground chamber.'

They all looked at him as if he was mad.

'Have you turned psychic all of a sudden?' asked Derek. 'Because if you have, you can fill in this week's lottery slip for me.'

The sound of laughter filled the air. Buchanan smiled at

him and winked.

'Trust me, Derek.' He looked at them, each in turn. 'I know what I'm talking about here, so let's just find the place, eh?'

They headed across the field as the cold December wind kicked up a gear.

Buchanan proved to them he was right. When they came to the end of the trail of footprints, they found themselves standing outside the Ice House. It reminded Buchanan of one of the Bronze Age houses up in the Shetland Isles. Michelle had made a model of one recently for some history project her primary class were involved in at school. He remembered peering over her shoulder as she looked up photos and researched the buildings on her laptop.

As he scanned the structure with the beam of his torch, Max joined him at the entrance. He was scratching his head as he followed the beam.

'You're looking a bit befuddled there, Max.'

'How did you know we would end up here, sir?' he asked.

'There no magic involved, Max. Kate told me about this place. It seemed just the sort of place that old bastard would make full use of.'

Justin left the rest of the group and prowled the perimeter of the small hill. His eyes were all over the place.

'Fantastic!' he said.

'What's got you all excited, then?' asked Derek, rolling his eyes.

Justin moved both his arms out wide. He looked like a

fisherman describing the one that got away.

'This, I've read of these places but I've never actually seen one.'

'What is it?'

'It's an Ice House,' said he and Buchanan in unison.

They looked at each other.

'What do you know of Ice Houses?' asked Buchanan.

'I'm a big war buff. I watch all the movies and documentaries I can get my hands on.'

'I'd never have guessed,' said Buchanan staring at the man who looked like he'd just stepped off the set of *Apocalypse Now*.

There was laughter in the background. Someone muttered the word arsehole under their breath.

Justin was totally oblivious to it; he was far too excited about the building in front of him.

'They used these places as bomb shelters in the Second World War you know. They're so solidly built.'

He slapped the surrounding wall. 'Some go as low as sixty or seventy feet underground. They used to store ice in these specially constructed chambers as far back as the 17th century and continued up to the early 20th century.'

'You don't say,' sighed Derek, slowly losing the will to live.

'Oh, yeah,' said Justin.

'Ice was collected from local ponds and lakes and was placed in these places where, if properly insulated, it would

last the year through. These Ice Houses were usually built
… '

'Justin! Shut the fuck up,' interrupted Buchanan.

'There's a good chance our fellow officers are in there, we could have broken in by now instead of listening to you wittering on about Ice Houses and World War fucking Two.'

'Sorry, sir.'

He looked sheepish then suddenly seemed to perk up.

'I suggest we prise open the padlock.'

'With what, exactly?'

Justin reached into the side pocket of his trousers and produced a crowbar.

'With this.'

'Do you just carry that around in there to impress the ladies?' asked Derek.

More laughter.

'Hey, don't knock it,' Justin replied. 'You never know when you'll need a crowbar.'

Buchanan smiled. Despite himself, he was slowly beginning to warm to the guy.

He gestured ahead.

'On you go, Justin, just get us in there, eh!'

'Right away, sir.'

The rest looked on as Justin spat on his hands, rubbed them together then stepped forward to prise open the padlock. That's when Buchanan noticed the thin steel wire wrapped tightly around the nail hammered into the foot of the Ice House door. It caught the beam from his torch, like a flash in the night. He followed it back to the partly-hidden black tube-shaped device secured to the wall.

He shouted as loud as he could to be heard above the wind which was slowly becoming gale force.

'Justin!'

He was too late. As Justin pushed open the heavy door, the grenade went off with an enormous bang, its extremely bright flash temporarily blinding the men gathered around the entrance.

Buchanan had gone deaf as had his colleagues. They all milled about the opening to the Ice House bumping into each other in a blind panic. Those closest to the blast were stumbling, their balance put out of whack by the inner ear disturbance created by the device.

'It's only a stun grenade,' shouted Justin. 'The effects are just temporary.'

No one could hear him, he couldn't even hear himself.

*

The old man listened as the echo of the grenade disappeared into the night.

'That's my cue!'

He reached behind the water barrel for his rifle, then carefully balanced it on the rim.

There was no sign of the Range Rover's headlights being switched off; they were really beginning to annoy him now, the man and woman with the shotguns standing in front of the cars bonnet. He'd watched as they'd grabbed hold of each other when the explosion had gone off but they still hadn't moved from the vicinity.

'Fuck it!'

It would be an easy shot, probably the easiest he'd ever made, the whole area was illuminated, he couldn't fail to hit them.

He laughed to himself. He'd take them both out in quick succession.

He waited for a calm moment between the gusts of wind and then put his eye to the sight. He took a second to line things up and then softly squeezed the trigger.

Shots split the night.

He took them both out in less than a second.

'No one's putting me in the damned spotlight!'

Chapter Thirty Seven

The two men left their car on the quiet suburban street and headed into the small area of woodland at the back of the up-market housing estate in the Bridge of Don area of Aberdeen.

They didn't talk much as they both had their minds focused on the work ahead.

It wasn't their usual type of job at all but the money being offered was a small fortune compared to the pittance they usually got paid for their services.

'Barry! Stop!'

Matt pointed ahead. There was a dog walker in the distance heading towards them. They both crouched down behind a nearby bush and turned off their torches.

They both held their breath.

'Sheba! Get your arse over here, get away from that bush.'

The Alsatian started growling. Its hackles were up.

'Come here, you daft dog, it's probably a squirrel or something. Why the hell can you never do what you're told?'

Sheba began to bark loudly as Barry reached for a thick gnarled branch lying on the ground to his left.

The owner moved closer towards them.

'I thought I told you to move!' she screamed.

She had a quick look around the area but saw nothing.

'I told you there's bugger all there.'

The two men gave a sigh of relief as they watched the owner put the lead on the dog and drag it away from them. They waited until she was a good distance down the path before they left their hiding place.

'Fuck! That was close,' said Barry as they continued on their way along the snow covered path. 'Are you sure you know the way?'

'Just shut up and follow me,' replied his accomplice. 'I know where I'm going.'

The two men walked on through the woods, keeping a keen eye out for any one else in the area. It was of the upmost importance that they weren't seen.

Eventually, the trees thinned out and they reached the back fence of a large red-bricked bungalow.

Barry blew on his hands and stamped on the ground.

'My feet are fucking freezing and my toes are going numb.'

'Stop moaning, Barry. The sooner we get this over and done with the quicker we can get to the pub. Let's go.'

They both climbed into the back yard and crouched down behind a huge garden shed.

'So far, so good,' said Matt. 'Get your equipment out, it's the far right window.'

They crept across the back garden.

Suddenly the whole area lit up.

'Shit! Security lights!' cried Matt. 'Quick, back behind

the shed!'

They both dived for cover. Matt almost became a cropper thanks to an old rake precariously placed in the garden.

For the second time that night they held their breath.

Matt looked out and watched as an overweight old woman drew back the kitchen curtains and peered out into the night. After a few minutes, satisfied that she wasn't coming out to investigate they breathed a sigh of relief.

'Maybe we should just give up on this job,' said Barry.

'Fuck that! We'd be giving up a small fortune. We'll give it ten more minutes, then walk around the perimeter. If we stick close to the edge of the garden, that fucking sensor up there shouldn't pick us up.'

'If you say so,' replied Barry.

'Here,' said Matt, producing a half bottle of vodka from his pocket. 'Get some of this down you, while we're waiting.'

Barry eagerly rubbed his hands together.

'Lovely, that ought to warm me up.'

The plan worked, they kept their backs hard against the fence and eased themselves slowly along until they reached their goal.

'Right, Barry, you're up.'

Barry got to work right away. He placed the suction device on the bottom of the window pane and carefully cut a half moon shape above it.

He carefully removed the glass then stuck his hand through to unlatch the window.

'Done and dusted,' he whispered.

'Keep watch,' said Matt, shoving him out of the way as he climbed into the small dark bedroom. He turned on the torch and looked around the room. It contained the usual kids paraphernalia, colourful mobiles, toys and Disney DVDs, amongst other things.

He crept quietly over towards the bed and stared at the young girl lying under the covers. She was sound asleep with her arms wrapped around a huge teddy bear almost as big as herself. He checked for the birthmark and then purposely shone the light in her face and moved it from side to side. She slowly began to stir then opened her eyes wide.

Matt put his right hand over her mouth then put the fore finger of his left in front of his own.

'Ssssshhhhh!'

Chapter Thirty Eight

'What the fuck was that?' shouted Buchanan. He still had a loud ringing in his ears and strange black shapes floated in his vision.

'Flash-Bang, sir,' said Justin.

'What?'

Justin raised his voice and moved closer to him.

'FLASH-BANG! The bastard set up a stun grenade. It was an old one though, thank God. The newer ones can detonate multiple times. They often contain irritants such as CS or CN tear gas. As I tried to tell you all earlier, the effects should wear off soon enough. Try rapid blinking and shake your head from side to side, it sometimes helps.'

'Are you taking the piss?'

'No, sir, give it a go.'

Buchanan tried both with little effect.

'Are you just trying to make me look fucking stupid?'

Justin blanked the question.

'Most of us got off quite lightly to be honest. Well … except for young Davie over there.' He pointed at the officer to the left of them. He was on his hands and knees throwing up into the snow.

'He's totally disorientated.'

'Anyone checked inside yet?' asked Derek as he rubbed some snow into his eyes. It had little effect.

'Not yet,' replied Max, 'but I'm sure they are down there, I heard voices … well, I thought I heard voices.'

He stuck his fingers in his ears.

'Mind you, it's hard to tell when your ears feel like they're full of soup.'

'Tell me about it,' Derek yelled. He also stuck his fingers in both ears.

'I can hardly hear a fucking thing. Last time my hearing was this bad I'd just been to a Motörhead gig.'

Buchanan felt his pocket vibrate. He took out his mobile but he couldn't read the screen. He put on his new reading glasses. It didn't help much, the message was still blurred. He half shut his eyelids, it seemed to help. The message became clearer, he had four missed calls.

'Fuck!' He'd never heard any of them, hardly surprising due to the situation they'd found themselves in. he looked closer. The messages were all from Kate Fielder. All made in the last five minutes.

'This doesn't look too good,' he thought to himself.

He still couldn't hear well enough to make the return call so he decided to text her.

What's up?

The reply was immediate.

He's here. He shot out both the head lights. I'm sure I can see him moving towards us. I think he's going for the cars.

'Shit!'

DON'T engage him, take cover till we get there.

He pressed send before shouting once again.

'Justin! Where the fuck have you got to now?'

The officer walked over towards him.

'I'm here, sir, I've just had a look inside the place.'

Buchanan shook his head and pointed to his ears.

'Speak up, man.'

'We've found them, sir,' yelled Justin. 'They're all okay, including the estate worker. One of the officers has a broken nose though, a real nasty break too, I reckon that's where the blood came from.'

'How did that happen?'

'The old man bust it, he says. He's raging about it. He says if he sets eyes on the old bastard again he's shooting him, no questions asked.'

Buchanan nodded towards the officer who'd been throwing up. He had now propped himself up against the Ice House.

'He looks a lot better.'

'He's fine now, sir.'

'Listen, Justin, something's come up. I'm leaving you in charge here, make sure the captives are okay, then make your way back to the graveyard. The backup should be arriving there soon.'

'Fair enough, sir, but where are you off to, if you don't mind me asking?'

Buchanan wondered if he should tell him the truth. He knew of his reputation, he was a strictly by the book man and what Buchanan had planned was definitely NOT by the book. He laughed to himself. When had that ever stopped him?

'Something funny, sir?' asked Justin with a bemused look on his face.

'Nothing of your concern, as I said, you rendezvous with the back up. I'm off to see Kate.'

'The woman with the Range Rover?'

'Aye, she's the Estate owner, she reckons she saw something moving by the graveyard, it's probably nothing, but I'll have to check it out.'

'You can't go on your own, sir. It could be him.'

'You're right enough, Justin, I'll take Derek and Max with me.'

He walked over towards them with a smile on his face.

'Max. Derek. Come with me.'

The two men looked at each other, confused, wondering what was going on.

'I'll explain things on the way,' said Buchanan. 'Let's go.'

He ran back towards the cottage with the two officers close behind. The wind was behind him, he felt as if he was flying. But flying towards what?

Chapter Thirty-Nine

' "Don't engage him!" ' said Jed. 'Fucking right we won't. He must think we're fucking mad out here.' He shook his head. 'That Buchanan guy is an arsehole.'

'Shut the fuck up!' said Kate as she peered into the dark night. 'He'll hear us.'

They were both crouched down behind a huge rock a good distance away from the Land Rover.

Kate was shivering, as much through fear as due to the ever lowering temperature and the freezing fog drawing in around them.

The huge bang they'd heard earlier had scared them enough but then when the headlights had been shot out, they'd both scarpered like their lives depended on it, which they probably did.

Jed peered out from their shelter.

'Are you sure you've seen someone? You're not just getting spooked?'

She jerked around. She had an annoyed look on her face. She slammed the palm of her hand against the rock.

'You really are fucking stupid at times!'

Jed looked hurt.

'It's him, I'm telling you, besides, who the fuck do you think shot out the headlights? I doubt very much it was the police.'

'Right enough, I suppose,' replied Jed.

He once again removed his well worn hat and scratched his head.

'What'll we do then?'

There was a rustling from the bushes.

'You'll both hand over those rather fetching shotguns,' said the voice from behind them.

'Shit!' they both said in unison.

They threw down their guns, raised their hands and slowly turned around.

'Hello folks, how are things going for you?'

The old man stood there. He was dressed in a ghillie suit. 'He looks like a dark green yeti,' thought Kate, 'or some strange creature from an old episode of *Doctor Who*'. He pulled down the hood, smiled, and then pointed his rifle straight at them.

'And your mobile phones, please. Chop chop!'

They both did as asked.

'The police are on their way, you know, they're just a few minutes away,' said Kate as she nervously handed over the iPhone.

'Of that, I've no doubt,' he replied. 'More than likely led by our ever intrepid Buchanan. I quite like him if truth be told. He's very tenacious.'

He shook his head.

'I've always admired that quality in a man.'

He threw a roll of duct tape to Jed. He failed to catch

it and it rolled off into the distance towards the old dyke surrounding the graveyard.

'Go get it, then,' said the old man. 'And don't get any ideas or you'll be joining the residents over the wall there.'

Once Jed had retrieved it, he walked back and stared at the man with the gun.

'What the fuck are you expecting me to do with this?' he asked.

'Tape the woman's hands behind her back.'

Jed did what was asked of him.

'Sorry, Kate.' He gave a shrug then turned around to face the old man.

'What about me?' he asked.

'Mmmm … what about you indeed.' He seemed to ponder the question for a while. 'I think one hostage will suffice.'

Jed never saw the stock of the rifle coming. All he was aware of was the dark night getting even darker and the snow covered ground coming up to meet him.

'Jed!' Kate screamed as he fell with a heavy thud.

'He'll be okay. He'll have a thumping headache when he comes to but nothing permanent. By the way, what's your name?'

'K-k-k-Kate.'

'Well, Kate, here's what I want you to do.'

Chapter Forty

As the dense heavy clouds obscured the moon, plunging everything below into almost complete darkness, Buchanan arrived at the front of the cottage. He had arrived just in time to see the rear lights of the armed response vehicle go tearing off into the distance.

'Fuck!' he shouted, stopping dead in his tracks.

The other two officers drew up behind him.

'Spread out, let's see if we can find any sign of them.'

'I doubt her or the estate worker are still breathing,' mumbled Derek.

They scanned the area by torchlight, careful not to trip over the myriad of sunken rocks beneath their feet. As they approached Kate's Range Rover, Max spotted Jed. He was on his knees. He looked over in their direction, covered his eyes from the beam of the torch and did his best to stand up. It was to no avail. He fell headlong into the snow narrowly missing a large moss covered boulder.

Max ran over towards him and helped him to his feet.

'You okay, sir?'

The man had a glazed look in his eyes.

'Of course I'm fucking not.'

He wiped his bloody forehead with a grubby piece of material that he removed from the middle pocket of his oil stained dungarees.

'I feel like the old bastard just broke my skull. He knocked me clean out for a minute or so. I still feel fucking dizzy! He just appeared from nowhere. Like a ghost. Mind you even if we'd been looking in his direction I doubt if we'd have seen him. He's camouflaged himself. He looks like a fucking tree! Oh, oh!'

He made a retching noise then threw up into the snow missing Max's feet by inches.

'Sorry about that.'

'Don't worry about it, sir,' replied Max as Jed wiped his mouth with a trembling hand.

He steadied himself against the car as Max inspected the wound.

'A bit of a nasty gash you have there, sir, the bastard got me earlier.' He lifted his hair to show Jed his own wound. 'He whacked me with a fire extinguisher. I still haven't shaken off the headache.'

Jed's eyes seemed to glaze over again for a few seconds. He blinked rapidly to gain some control.

'You feeling any better yet, sir?' asked Max.

The farm worker nodded.

'Slightly.'

'Take it easy till you get your bearings back.'

Max returned to his colleagues.

'How is he doing?' asked Buchanan, blowing huge plumes of smoke into the night, the cloud rose up into the air becoming one with the heavy fog.

'A couple of stitches maybe, I don't like the way his eyes keep glazing over though. We better get him checked out. I reckon he's got a bit of concussion.'

'I'll get Atkins to send a medic … but first I'll have to have a word with him.'

He crushed his cigarette underfoot and then looked at Jed. He was breathing heavily.

'What's happened to Kate?'

Jed looked at him blankly for a couple of seconds then finally gave a reply.

'Last I know of the matter is that he got me to tape her hands behind her back. I assume he's taken her with him. He mentioned something about only needing one hostage before he whacked me with the rifle.'

Buchanan fell silent.

'He does love his duct tape, right enough,' said Max, handing Jed a coffee from the flask in Kate's car. 'Get that down you, sir.'

Buchanan looked off in the direction the fugitive had taken off in and then, after yawning heavily, he took out his mobile and phoned Atkins.

'Any sign of that bloody chopper yet?'

'You should be seeing some sight of it any time now, sir.'

Buchanan looked skywards. He could make out the bright lights cutting through the fog in the distance.

'I can see it; tell them to look out for the ARV. The old bastard managed to get a hold of it.'

'What!'

'That's not all. He's taken Kate, the landowner, with him we reckon.'

He heard a heavy sigh at the other end of the conversation.

'How the hell did he manage that?'

'Don't ask, Jenny.'

He rubbed his chin.

'He's given one of the estate workers a pretty nasty whack as well, we could do with a medic. Not just for him, one of our armed guys is also injured. He has a broken nose. This guy's a fucking menace.'

'I'll see to it, sir.'

Buchanan surveyed his surroundings.

'You'll have to send all the vehicles in the area along here soon as you can, see if we can catch up to him from this end. See if they can spare anyone off the roadblocks as well, he seems to be heading in that direction.'

He sighed once more. The case was getting to him.

'You got all that, Jenny?'

'Got it, sir. What are you planning?'

'Not much. The landowner's Range Rover is here but the bastard shot out the headlights, so it's not much use to us. We're stuck here until the vehicles arrive.'

'Sir!' interrupted Max. 'We can still use it.'

'Hold on, Jenny.'

He moved the mobile away from his ear.

'I can't see how, Max. The bastard shot out the headlights, look!' He shone his torch towards the front of the motor. 'Unless one of us suddenly develops the ability to see in the dark, we're fucked.'

Derek laughed in the distance as he relieved himself against a huge old oak tree.

'Watch this,' replied Max opening the cars door. 'He shot out the headlights right enough but there's a little something he overlooked.'

Max leaned into the vehicle as Buchanan and Derek looked on perplexed.

The whole area was suddenly flooded with light from the roof of the car as Max looked up with a huge grin on his face.

'Spotlights!' he announced with a flourish as he eased himself into the drivers seat. 'Hop in, guys.'

'Hold on, Max … Jenny, you still there?'

'I'm here, sir.'

'Seems like we can use the Range Rover, we're heading off in pursuit. Do us a favour and contact Jarrett. Let him know what's going on.'

'Will do. Be careful, sir.'

He disconnected the call and joined the other two in the Range Rover as the police helicopter flew into the distance in front of them.

'Follow those tyre tracks, Max, and put your foot down.'

'Will do, sir.'

He had a huge grin on his face.

'I've been dying for a shot of this motor!'

*

The old man kept his concentration on the dirt track ahead. It was hard to see the actual road itself for the underlying snow but luckily for him he could gauge his direction by the old stone dykes that surrounded the fields on either side of him.

Just as he slowed and steadied the vehicle for a tight corner, he heard the unmistakable sound of the helicopter overhead. Then he saw it. It lit up the sky like a comet.

The pilot flew over him then turned a hundred and eighty degrees. The spotlights on the undercarriage beamed directly through the windscreen blinding him and making it impossible for him to drive any further.

Then he heard the booming voice from above.

'STOP THE CAR AND LEAVE THE VEHICLE.'

*

Buchanan's phone rang.

'Jenny! What's up?'

'We've got the bastard, sir!'

The excitement was clear in her voice.

'Fuck! That was quick.'

'The chopper has him hemmed in. He's on a dirt road not too far ahead of you. In fact, you should see his location from where you are. The helicopter should be hovering above him. He has walled off fields on either side of him and

341

there's no room for him to turn around. He's humped, sir, pardon my language.'

'Hold on, Jenny.'

Buchanan turned towards Max.

'Stop the car.'

Max expertly skidded the car to a halt.

Buchanan stepped out into the cold air and looked into the night sky. He could see the choppers lights not too far in the distance.

'I see him, Jenny, tell them we'll be there in ten minutes. Is there any one else in the immediate area?'

'We have another couple of vehicles coming in from the roadblock in the east side. They should get there not too far behind you most probably. We also have another Armed Response Unit in the area, quite close by as it happens.'

'Christ, where are we getting all those armed guys from?'

'It's all hands on deck, sir; some are from pretty far afield. Seems like every armed officer in the country is around here somewhere, maybe it's a dry run for this new Police Scotland thing that's coming in.'

She laughed.

'Tell them to be very wary though, Jenny. This guy's a dangerous bastard at the best of times. Fuck knows what he's capable of when he's cornered.'

'Will do, sir.'

He got back into the car.

'Forget following the tracks, Max, just veer off to your

342

right till we can get a good view of this chopper.'

'I can see it from here,' said a muffled voice from the back.

Buchanan turned round to see Derek standing on the back seat with his head stuck out the sunroof.

'I'll give you directions, Max, just put your foot down.'

Buchanan laughed loudly, 'I've always said you were a mad bastard, Derek. You must be fucking freezing.'

'I'm alright,' replied the muffled voice. 'I've put on my balaclava.'

*

Harry stared out through his windscreen at the helicopter cutting off the road in front of him. He was also acutely aware of the police vehicle approaching from behind. He could see the blue flashes lighting up the night in his rear view mirror. He watched as it got ever closer.

'GET OUT THE CAR AND LAY DOWN YOUR WEAPONS,' boomed the voice from the front.

He totally ignored the demand as he calmly laid out a line of the white powder on the back of his hand and quickly sniffed it with his left nostril.

The warmth penetrated his whole being as he felt an immediate calmness. His senses became more acute.

'YOU HAVE ONE MINUTE TO COMPLY.'

One of the officers had a rifle. He watched him approach the tail end of the helicopter and rest the barrel on part of the landing gear. The whole scene playing out before him was accompanied by the staccato sound of the rotor blades echoing into the night.

He waited until the armed response vehicle pulled up behind him.

Another two armed officers jumped behind the vehicle and covered him from the rear.

'What a pretty mess you've got yourself in now,' he heard Clara say in his head.

He looked to the seat behind him. Now was not the time to make good use of his hostage. She couldn't help him here.

'Something will come up, it always does,' he said to himself, another one of Clara's favourite sayings. He had a vivid image in his head of her quoting it at him with her hands on her hips.

He burst into a fit of giggles, only stopping when his hand made contact with the car horn.

'TEN SECONDS!'

'Oh, well.'

He shook his head and sighed as he left his vehicle, a mirror image of the one blocking him in from behind.

He threw the rifle down in the snow turned towards the two armed officers behind him and raised his hands.

'Go easy on me. I'm an old man.'

'You're a fucking psycho!' said one of the officers as they both walked towards him, covering him with their rifles.

The same man shouted to the officer behind the helicopter.

'Peter, cuff this old bastard, we'll cover him from here.'

The third officer approached from the helicopter behind

him. He could hear his footsteps in the thick layer of snow which was beginning to freeze.

'Put your hands behind your back, sir.'

The old man did as he was asked, never losing eye contact with the two men in front. Both men lowered their weapons. His heightened senses made this action appear to be in slow motion.

The old man smiled to himself.

'Big mistake', he thought.

Then just as Peter slung his rifle over his shoulder to put on the handcuffs, the old man winked at the two officers ahead of him.

In a split second, he forcefully jerked his head back, breaking Peter's nose as he simultaneously withdrew the handgun from his wasteband. He shot them both through the head before they could raise their weapons and get a shot off.

They both died with a complete look of shock on their faces.

He turned back around. Peter was frantically trying to grab for his weapon, his hands, now covered in the blood that was copiously leaking from his nose, stopped him from getting a firm grasp of the thing.

The old man winked at him.

'I don't think so.'

He shot him through both legs.

'You're going nowhere.'

As he relieved Peter of his weapons, the rifle and the hand gun hidden in his vest, something moving in front of him suddenly caught his eye. He watched as the young unarmed pilot jumped one of the walls surrounding the fields and ran off at great speed into a patch of woodland.

The old man cupped his hands, raised them to his mouth and bellowed.

'Couldn't blame you, son, I'm one mean motherfucker!'

He laughed to himself once more.

'We will get you, you know,' said Peter.

He'd managed to crawl over to the wall. The trail of blood was clearly visible in the snow.

The old man coolly stared at him then nodded towards his dead colleagues.

'Not unless you send better men than them.'

After firing a few holes into the helicopter's fuel tank to render the thing useless, he moved to the side and gauged the space left between it and the wall surrounding the field to his left.

After careful consideration, he jumped back into his vehicle and slowly eased it through to the other side. He lost his wing mirror and slightly scraped the left hand door but otherwise the vehicle remained intact. He came to a stop a few yards along the road, got out the car and walked back towards the other police vehicle.

The keys were still in the ignition, so he drove it forward to fill the space he had just driven through.

He got out, taking the keys with him and looked at his

work.

'Perfect!'

He was back on the move, with the assurance that no one would be following from behind anytime soon.

As he checked the rear view mirror he heard the muffled cries of the woman trussed up in the backseat.

'They almost had us there, Kate. But I took care of the situation.'

He took his eyes of the road ahead for a second. Looking over his shoulder and gave the wide-eyed woman a manic smile.

'Isn't this exciting?'

Chapter Forty One

The three officers left the vehicle and stepped into what could only be described as a war zone. Bodies, blood and an abandoned helicopter cluttered the immediate vicinity. The smell of gunpowder and petrol hung in the air.

Buchanan lit a cigarette for himself and Derek and looked at the map Kate kept in the glove compartment to get his bearings.

He sent the two others ahead just as his phone rang. He looked at the screen.

'Jesus! Michelle. Great fucking timing!'

He took the call.

'WHAT IS IT?'

'Christ! You're in a good mood.'

'I've got a lot on my plate … '

Before he could finish his sentence, Michelle interrupted him.

'I'm home, Ronnie. I couldn't stand being with Mum for one more second, she's driving me crazy. I phoned sis, she's taking over for a while, I need a break.'

'I agree. It'll be nice to have you home.'

She totally ignored him and talked over the top of their conversation.

'She's still planning on going ahead with this bungee jump.'

'What? With a broken fucking hip?'

'No need to swear, Ronnie. According to that old bastard boyfriend of hers …' Buchanan smiled at her hypocrisy. 'He's going to take all the strain; he's going to fucking wheel her out there in her chair and strap her to his waist when they jump.'

Buchanan burst into hysterics.

'I'd pay good money to see that. Perhaps they should form a circus act.'

'You're not helping, Ronnie.'

Suitably admonished, he stopped laughing and pulled himself together.

'Look, Michelle, we'll talk about it tonight. I have a mad old bastard of my own to deal with as it happens.'

He heard a sigh at the other end.

'Can't you come home now?'

'That's impossible … '

*

'The officers are both dead, sir!' shouted Max, as he and Derek walked back towards Buchanan, who was now shouting down his mobile and gesticulating wildly.

Max leaned against the Range Rover. He was visibly shaking.

'The bastard shot them straight through the head, no messing about,' said Derek.

Buchanan covered his mobile.

'Check out the helicopter you two, there's at least a

couple of officers unaccounted for, lets hope they fared a bit better, eh?'

He nodded them away as he went back to his phone call. Just as they were nearing the helicopter, they suddenly heard a voice.

'Watch it; he's punctured the fuel tank. It's unsafe, especially if you're smoking a fucking cigarette!'

Max shone the beam of his torch to the side where the voice had come from. Neither of them missed seeing the heavy blood trail leading to the wall. Derek quickly threw the offending article into the snow behind him.

'Jesus! Peter. What happened to you?'

'Two of that old bastard's bullets happened to me. It's sore as fuck but luckily they're both through and through. I've managed to stem the bleeding, I used the medi kit from the ARV but I won't be dancing very well at this year's Christmas do. The wife looks forward to that too!'

Max and Derek laughed out loud, easing the tension somewhat.

'You ought to have seen him, Derek. The guy's good, I'll give him that.'

He visibly winced as he tried to move position.

'I never saw the fucker move. Boom, boom, boom he took the three of us out like that!'

He snapped his fingers to emphasise his point. Just then Buchanan appeared next to them, his face was red.

'Christ! Another one.'

He looked at Peter.

'How you bearing up, son?'

'Could be worse,' replied Peter, nodding towards the two dead officers.

They all nodded solemnly.

'Keep your chin up,' said Buchanan. 'We have some cars heading this way. They have a medical team with them. They'll have you right as rain in no time.'

'I can see them,' cried Derek, pointing to the flashing lights heading towards them. 'Blues and twos heading this way.'

'You stay with him, Derek. Max, you come with me, we'll have to move that vehicle so we can get past.'

He patted Peter on the shoulder.

'Hang in there, son.'

He winked back at Buchanan.

'Oh! By the way,' he said. 'there's a spare set of keys behind the sun visor. The old bastard buggered off with the original set.'

As Buchanan and Max headed off towards the helicopter, Derek suddenly withdrew his hand gun, aiming it at the wall above Peter's head.

'Show yourself!'

A head suddenly appeared from the far side of the wall just behind Peter. It was a young man with an oversized nose. It was bookended by pale white hands either side. It reminded Derek of the pictures he used to draw on the covers of his jotters at school.

"Kilroy was here" sprung to mind.

'Don't shoot, I'm just the pilot,' said the shaking man as he stood up and raised his hands above his head.

*

'Blues and twos, where the hell does that phrase come from, Max? I've always wondered about that.'

'Simple, sir. Blue lights, two tone horn.'

Buchanan stopped in his tracks and turned to stare at his colleague.

'You're a mine of totally useless information, Max.'

He sniffed the air.

'That petrol smell is getting stronger, don't you think?'

'Must be the fuel Peter was talking about, from the helicopter, sir, the old guy shot the tank, to stop it following him again, I suppose.'

'He's a crafty old bastard.'

They walked a few more feet before Buchanan shone the torch down towards their feet. They were standing in a huge pink circle at least ten feet wide. The smell was overwhelming.

'I think it'll be safer to push the car forward a bit before we start her up.'

'Good idea, sir. We might need a hand though, these cars are reinforced, the things weigh a tonne.'

'Three of us ought to manage it, just release the hand brake and well push it forward a bit,' said Derek, who had appeared from nowhere.

'I thought I told you to stay with Peter,' said Buchanan.

'Can't do much there, Ronnie. Anyway, the medics are seeing to him now.'

'How's he doing?' asked Max.

'He's lost a good bit bit of blood but he should recover. They've shot him full of morphine and stuck him on an IV that should keep him stable till they get him to hospital.'

The three of them threw their full strength into pushing the car. It only rolled a couple of feet and then returned to its original position.

'This is no use,' said Buchanan. 'The longer this takes the further that bastard gets away from us. Fuck it, I'm starting her up.'

'Sir!' shouted Max. 'The ignition spark could set the fuel off.'

'I'll risk it. Anyway most of its soaked into the snow. Surely that lessens the danger, no?'

Max and Derek shrugged their shoulders and both stood well back as Buchanan got into the car. He looked at them, shook his head and laughed

'Your faith in me, gentlemen, is astounding,' he said as he nervously turned the key.

Chapter Forty Two

Kate had spent the last five minutes listening to the old man talking to someone who wasn't there. Someone called Clara. She had heard him laugh at something funny only he could hear, cry with remorse over the two dead officers whose lives had ended simply because they had got in his way, and heard him tell Clara how his main mission had now changed slightly. It was now impossible to take out the other two on the list. Getting Melissa back where she belonged was now his main priority.

None of it made any sense to her. She felt like she had landed flat bang in the middle of a movie and had no idea of the plot or story line.

Her wrists were growing numb thanks to the restraints and, for some reason, she had a tremendous thirst. She felt the vehicle once again slowing down, then heard the sniffing. Three times this had happened since she'd been unceremoniously thrown into the back of the car. She didn't have a clue what was going on. All she could see from her position was the back of the driver's seat and the roof of the car.

Then he suddenly turned around and spoke directly to her.

'You probably think I'm some old mad psychotic bastard, don't you?'

She shook her head from side to side.

'Now now, be honest with me, Kate. Honesty is a great

virtue you know.'

Her eyes began to tear up. She was in a waking nightmare. She wasn't sure how to respond.

Finally she nodded in agreement. It seemed to be what he was wanting.

'I want to tell you a story, Kate.'

He pointed at her.

'I want you to give me an honest answer as to what you think. If you give me an honest answer, I'll let you go free. How does that sound?'

Kate nodded her head vigorously.

'I'd like to tell you things from my point of view. In case … well, in case anything happens to me.'

He ripped off the tape from her mouth and as he continued his journey along the tree covered track he told her everything. He told her about Rose, he told her about how he'd managed to get the information on his victims from Victor Whitelaw and a few others. He explained the reasoning behind the ones he and Clara had chosen as the worst of the bunch, the ones who should pay. He told her about Clara's illness and his own and then, finally, he broke down as he told her of the deep regret he had for the innocent victims in the whole affair.

By the time he had finished his soliloquy, Kate wasn't sure what she felt the deepest. Fear for her own life or pity for the sad old man.

Chapter Forty Three

Just as they were about to resume their pursuit, their thoughts were broken by yet more flashing lights reflected in the driving mirror and the loud siren from behind.

'What the fuck now!' shouted Buchanan.

Max looked in the side mirror of the ARV.

'It's Justin, sir.'

'What the fuck does he want?'

Double J approached the vehicle on Buchanan's side. He opened the window. Justin was accompanied by another officer who had something rolled up under his arm.

'What is it now?' asked Buchanan. 'It better be important.'

He looked up at the other armed officer. A tall heavily built guy, he was sporting a thick plaster squarely across his nose. Both his eyes were blackened. He looked like he'd gone ten rounds with Mike Tyson.

'What the hell happened to him?'

'He's one of the kidnapped officers from the Ice House,' replied Justin. 'The old guy broke his nose.'

Buchanan shook his head.

'He did the same to the officer back there. You got off lightly, son, he also shot him through both legs.'

The officer nodded.

'Looks nasty though,' said Buchanan. 'Nut you, did he?'

The officer tenderly rubbed his nose.

'The old bastard whacked me with the stock of a rifle. I had to reset it myself, couldn't fucking breath otherwise,' said Eric in his nasal whine.

Buchanan winced.

'We thought you might like a hand, sir,' said Justin. 'With the pursuit of the fugitive I mean.'

'He's not going anywhere, Justin, this road leads to the motorway. He's heading straight towards the road blocks, we have it covered.'

'But you don't, sir, that's the thing!'

'What do you mean?'

He watched as Justin grabbed the map off the other officer and unrolled it. He crouched down next to the passenger door and shone his torch on a particular part that he'd circled in biro.

'A couple of miles up the road, sir, the track splits into two, you can't cover both directions. I thought maybe me and Eric here could follow you until we get to the split. You go left, we go right. What do you think?'

Buchanan looked at the map.

'Jesus, Justin, what sort of map's this? The ones we've been looking at aren't near as detailed.'

'Satellite guides, sir, I keep a stack of them in the car,' he smiled. 'for just such an occasion.'

'Good work, son, we could've missed that.'

He turned on the vanity light and quickly glanced at his

own map.

'That road doesn't show up in our aerial one, it's obscured by trees. You and Eric draw in behind, we'll split up at the fork in the road.'

'Sounds good,' he replied as he and Eric went back to their own vehicle.

Then he stopped and walked back towards Buchanan.

'One other thing, sir ... you should maybe see if we can get hold of another chopper, it'll make things easier.'

Buchanan held up his mobile.

'Just what I'm away to do, Justin ... don't push it!'

'Sorry, sir, I wasn't trying to take over.'

Buchanan shook his head as he watched him walk away in the rear view mirror.

'Told you he was a bit full on,' said Derek.

Buchanan nodded in agreement.

'Right, Max, put your foot down.'

'If you're sure Justin can keep up, sir, it's pretty dodgy driving conditions.'

'I wouldn't let that bother you, Max,' said Derek. 'Justin does rally driving in his spare time.'

'You taking the piss, Derek?' asked Buchanan.

'No! I'm serious. He's pretty good at it from what I hear; he's won a few trophies.'

'Let's see how good he is then,' replied Max as his rear wheels spun in the thin layer of snow. He took off like a rocket as the other two carefully held on to anything within reach.

*

The going wasn't good. Once under the cover of the thick fir trees, the tracks of their quarry's car weren't so easy to see. Eventually they disappeared completely. Luckily the old stone dykes on either side would make it near impossible to veer off the track. Even in the unlikelihood that he had, the evidence would be telling. A newly broken gap in the ancient dyke would be apparent to all.

The trunks of the fir trees on either side flashing by had an almost hypnotic effect on each of the cars passengers who were all deep in their individual thoughts.

The silence between them was suddenly broken.

'We should be coming up to the split now, sir,' said Max as they flew past a wooden post pointing in two different directions.

Suddenly the radio sprang into life.

'We'll let you know if we find anything. Over,' said Justin.

'You make sure you do that…oh, and, Justin!'

'Yes, sir?'

'Don't let Eric near the old bastard, he looks extremely pissed off. I don't want him beating the shit out the guy. You got that?'

'Ten-four, sir.'

'What?'

'I'll make sure it doesn't happen, sir. Over.'

Buchanan watched him flash his headlights behind them as Max veered off to the left.

'It's fifty-fifty who's on the right track now then,' said Derek 'How long till the chopper gets here, Ronnie?'

'God knows. There's a big pile up near Westhill, they're busy coordinating things up there, could be long enough till one becomes available.'

Buchanan peered out the windscreen; he thought he saw something moving in the distance, a ghost-like apparition in the freezing fog that had suddenly appeared from nowhere.

'Shit! … Max!'

The car swerved off into the ditch at the side of the road, Max used all his skills to stop the car ploughing into the wall. He missed it by inches.

Buchanan was out the passenger seat the second the vehicle had stopped.

'Kate!'

She was visibly shaking. Probably as much from the ordeal she'd been through as due to the sub-zero temperatures. Her lips were trembling and she had a strange glazed look in her eyes.

Buchanan placed his jacket around her shoulders and led her towards the warm safety of the vehicle.

He told Derek to swap seats with him so he could climb in the back with Kate and assess her condition. Once she had warmed up a bit and had a large swig from the flask he produced from his inside pocket, she told him that she felt fine. She then relayed to Buchanan what she'd been through, and more importantly, what the old man had told her. Most of it he knew about but some of the finer details he didn't.

The strange white powder he was liberally helping himself to made sense of a few things. According to Kate, the old man didn't have a clue what the substance was only that it relieved most of his symptoms, gave him a tremendous energy and made him feel years younger. He'd found it in the pockets of one of his victims.

Derek reckoned it was PCP, rarely seen nowadays, especially in this neck of the woods. It would certainly explain the old man's strength and energy. Like he said though, there were that many new designer drugs appearing everywhere nowadays, it could be anything.

Then she hit him with it.

'Who's Melissa?'

'She's his great granddaughter, why do you ask?'

Kate was talking very fast now, probably down to the euphoria of no longer being held captive, he imagined.

He was finding it hard to understand the individual words. They all seemed to roll into each other.

'It's just that ...'

'Slow down, Kate.'

'Sorry,' she took a deep breath. 'In between telling me his story, talking to his dead wife, sniffing the white powder and breaking down over having to kill innocent victims, he kept going back to Melissa. "Poor Melissa, she didn't belong here, soon she'd be back where she should have been to begin with, if only Clara had held on a bit longer, it's a pity that … " '

'Woh! Slow down, Kate, you're speeding up again, go back a bit.

Kate's eyes looked to the roof of the car as she visibly played back the conversation in her head.

'Back to where, exactly?'

She looked confused so Buchanan prompted her.

'Back to where he said, where she should have been to begin with?'

'Yeah, back to Canada.'

Buchanan felt a chill run down his spine.

'He says he's finished with the killings. His main priority now is to get Mel … '

'Melissa,' said Buchanan, pulling out his mobile phone.

'Yes … to get Melissa back home. That bit is very clear in my mind. I can remember him slapping the dashboard with his hand, to emphasise his point.'

'Shit!'

He phoned PC Atkins.

'Jenny, get on to Melissa's foster carers. We'll need to get them and her into protective custody ASAP. I think the old guy's going after the girl.'

'You're joking!'

'It's not a joking matter.'

'Sorry, sir.'

'Just get it done, Jenny. Phone me back when you have

things organised.'

He didn't wait for a reply before he ended the call. Then he turned back to Kate.

'Anything else you can think of that might help us?'

She looked to the car roof again.

'Well … I'm not really sure. I felt sorry for him to be honest. I mean I know he's killed people. Most of them deserved it, if you ask me. As I said, he thoroughly regrets killing the officers. Collateral damage, he called that.'

'How's his mindset?' asked Buchanan.

Kate laughed.

'Haven't you been listening to a word I said? He's lost the plot. He keeps going from laughing to crying in the blink of an eye. I don't know how much of that's down to the drugs he's taking or the hallucinations.'

'Hallucinations?'

'Yeah. As I told you, he keeps talking to his dead wife. I mean talking to her like she's actually there sitting next to him. He even leaves pauses for her answers. Like I said, he's way off the deep end.'

'He could be trying to throw us off, sir?' interrupted Max.

'How do you mean?'

'Well, why would he tell Kate here about his plan to grab Melissa if he knew he was going to let her go. He must have known that whatever he told her would eventually get back to us. No?'

'I don't think he's thinking straight, Max. Remember what Lucy told us. Due to his tumour he was very likely to have such episodes. One minute he could be as sane as you or me. The next minute … '

He shrugged.

'As Kate says, he could be straight off the deep end.'

He turned once more to face Kate.

'Why did he let you go?'

She yawned. The ordeal had left her drained. All she wanted to do was go to sleep.

'He told me to listen to his story and give him an honest answer as to how I felt about it and I did.'

She yawned once more then covered her head with Buchanan's jacket.

'Anyone I can call for you, Kate? You've been through a rough ordeal.'

'My husband is away on business, call my brother Jake, his number is in my phone.'

He searched the address book.

'Is this who I think it is?'

'Yup!' she replied before falling sound asleep.

Then his mobile rang. The screen lit up. He swapped phones.

'Jenny. How are you getting on?'

There was a pause at the other end of the line.

The chill returned to his spine.

'We're too late, sir. Melissa has disappeared.'

Chapter Forty Four

'FUCK!'

Buchanan slammed his hand against the back seat. Max could feel the impact through his back from the driver's seat.

'The bastard has the kid!'

'What, physically with him?' asked Max.

'No! She was snatched sometime this evening; he must have someone working with him.'

He once again picked up his mobile. He turned on the speaker so the rest could hear.

'Jenny. Get that computer whizz kid next to you to get a list of the old guy's phone calls. I want to see who he's been in contact with. I take it he can do that, no?'

'Hold on, sir.'

He heard a muffled conversation going on in the background but couldn't make out what was being said.

'Hurry up, for fuck's sake!'

Then he heard the phone being picked up.

'Sir. He says it'll take a while; he'll have to go through the proper channels. He has to find out the guy's service provider and various other details before he can do anything.'

'Hold on,' said Buchanan.

He reached into his pocket to retrieve the SIM card he'd picked up earlier in the derelict cottage.

'He's on Virgin Mobile, or at least he was up until an hour or so ago. He must have sussed out that's how we were tracking him. His mobile was lying in bits back at the cottage, but I retrieved the SIM card.'

Another muffled conversation in the background.

'The tech guy says it'll hurry things up a bit but he will still have to go through the proper channels. He says we can't go snooping through phone records without the proper paperwork.'

'Fuck that,' said Derek, 'give the SIM card to me. I'm on Virgin, I'll swap it with mine. Tell her I'll send her the list.'

'Did you hear that, Jenny?'

'Yes, sir.'

'As soon as you receive the names, I want you to get onto it ASAP, find out who the numbers belong to. You okay with that? It's not strictly by the book but I think it's the best way to get Melissa back.'

There was a couple of minutes silence.

'Sure, you're right, we need to find the girl.'

'Good stuff! But listen, use your initiative, don't go phoning the numbers willy nilly, if the person that has the kid is on the list, and I believe there's a good chance he is, we don't want to be giving them any warning that were onto them. Be tactful, Jenny. You got that?'

'Send the numbers to my mobile; I'll get straight on it.'

The second he ended the call the radio once again came to life with a crackle.

'No sign of the perp so far. Over.'

'Shit! Justin. I was just about to contact you. He's just ahead of us. Anyway, can you get back to our route from there?'

'Roger that. We'll cut through the fields; there must be a gate through the wall somewhere. I'll be in touch when we catch you up. Over.'

Derek laughed.

'Roger that? What is all that shit? Is he feeling horny or something?'

He shook his head.

'As I've said before, he should be in an American war movie.'

*

Twenty minutes later, they found the old man's vehicle abandoned at the side of the track. Buchanan, Max and Derek left the car and carefully approached it just as Justin and his partner approached from the front.

After feeling the hood of the motor, Justin scouted the area. He wandered up and down the road, occasionally bending down near the foot of the old dykes on either side.

'What the fuck is Tonto up to?' asked Buchanan.

They all laughed.

'Looks like the old bastard's buggered off on foot,' said Derek.

He pointed over the wall towards the mass of large pine trees.

'We'll never find him in there,' said Buchanan.

'We'll get the dog team onto it but … ' He shirked his shoulders. 'The old bastard seems to disappear into the wilderness at will!'

'We could still get him,' said Justin. 'Let me show you.'

Justin unrolled his map of the area on the bonnet of his car. They all gathered around him, all except Buchanan who gestured them ahead as he answered his mobile.

Justin drew a large red X on the map.

'We're here.'

He tapped the X with the end of his pen and pointed to his right.

'At the other side of that wood lies the motorway. We have that covered.' He went back to the map. 'As you can see the motorway curves around to the left, so … '

He pointed ahead of them.

'That also cuts him off if he decides to go in that direction. So all he can really do is cut back the way. I suggest we get everyone available to start maybe two miles in front of the area where he shot the officers and sweep up towards here.'

He once again pointed at the red X.

'Excellent work, Justin. Only one problem though,' said Buchanan, who had joined the group at the map.

'What's that, sir?'

'You're assuming he went right and took off into the woods. Say he went left,' he nodded, 'into those fields over there, that would fuck up your plan wouldn't it?'

'I've covered that. Take a look over here, sir.'

They all followed Justin to the side with the fields.

'What do you see?'

'Not a fucking thing!' said Buchanan.

'Anyone else see anything untowards?'

'Same here, fuck all,' said Derek.

The rest shook their heads.

'Exactly. If he came this way there'd be footprints. There's no tree cover, plenty of fresh snow.'

Buchanan rubbed his chin.

'He could have walked back a bit before he entered the fields. There could be foot prints way back there somewhere, or further ahead come to think of it.'

'I don't think so, sir. I checked a certain distance back in both directions. No sign of anything. However … ' He raised his finger to emphasise the point, 'I did find this … follow me.'

'Make this quick, Justin, eh?'

They all looked at each other, shook their heads and then followed him over to the wooded side of the track.

He led them towards the thin layer of snow that the wind had blown on to the top of the dyke and with a flourish he showed them what he'd gotten excited about.

'Two clear hand prints and a footprint, size ten, I believe.'

'So, you reckon that's where he crossed into the woods?'

'I'd put money on it, sir.'

Buchanan clapped his hands in applause.

'Well done, Justin. You're prepared to put your theory into practice?'

'How do you mean, sir?'

'You obviously have great tracking skills.'

'You fucking well are Tonto,' said Derek's muffled voice from behind.

Buchanan ignored him.

'I also have certain skills. Delegation, that's a skill, wouldn't you agree?'

He nodded. 'Yeah, I suppose so.'

'Good, glad you agree because I'm putting you in charge of the search.'

Justin smiled broadly.

'The manhunt, you mean?'

'Call it what you will, but you're in charge. I'll get onto Jenny at control. You have everyone in the area at your disposal. The dog handlers should be here anytime now, I'd get them into that woodland over there to start with, see if your instincts are correct.'

Justin had his mobile out in a second.

'I'll get right on it, sir,' he said excitedly.

'By the way, your colleague there with the broken nose …'

'Eric? What about him, sir?'

'Is he okay, he's awful quiet.'

'He's fine, he's often like that.'

Buchanan gave him a wave as he lit up a cigarette.

Eric waved back, then he rubbed his nose with his other hand.

'He seems responsive enough.'

'As I said, he's fine, sir. I've worked with him for a while now. He often has his quiet moments.'

He nodded. 'Right, Justin, I'll leave things in your capable hands. You have my number. Keep me updated.'

'Will do, sir.'

'Max, Derek, you two come with me!'

They both joined him at their vehicle.

'Where we off to, sir?' asked Max.

'We've got a result from the old guy's phone list. Most of the calls led nowhere, but he's been in constant contact with a guy called Jerry Banks. Jenny checked him out. He's got a record as long as your arm, extortion mostly; he looks a real odious little bastard.'

He took out his mobile and showed Jerry's photo to Max and Derek.

'What an ugly bastard,' said Derek. 'He looks like a fucking ferret!'

Buchanan nodded his head.

'Let's go pay the bastard a visit! Jenny's sent a squad ahead of us. He's under surveillance, so we know he's at home.'

'Sir?'

'Yes, Max.'

'Why are you leaving Justin in charge of things? If he catches him, he'll get all the credit.'

'I don't think he will catch him, Max. I reckon he's well gone.' He suddenly stopped. 'I'll tell you how I think we will catch him though.'

'How?' asked Derek.

'He told Kate he'd now changed his plan right?'

They both nodded.

'He's no longer interested in the lawyer and the taxi driver. His focus now is on Melissa, or to be more exact, getting Melissa out the country. So … '

Max interrupted, 'If we can get to the guy who has Melissa and find out when and where he's handing her over … '

'Exactly Max, we'll make a detective of you yet. Now, let's get back to town.'

'Where exactly in town, sir?'

'We're heading for Holburn Street. He has a top floor flat across from the Malt Mill.'

'Great pub, that,' said Derek.

Chapter Forty Five

The old man was breathing heavily. He stood directly beneath a huge fir tree in the thick dark woodland. He bent over slightly and put his hands on his knees, trying his best to gain his composure.

'Old age is a bastard,' he thought.

'Comes to us all,' he heard Clara saying in his head.

He knew he was far fitter than most men of his age.

Before his recent tumour, he'd never been ill in his life. He'd always been blessed that way. He never got colds or the flu; he'd never been breathless, even when he used to smoke. Up until recently - he'd let it slip a bit since Clara's illness - he'd run four or five miles in the woods next to the farm every day. He'd done so for years.

He looked skywards.The moon had become encased in dark heavy clouds. He was in complete and utter darkness.

Looking back down, all he could see were thick tree trunks. The only light available to him was from a small head torch. He turned it on. It cast a thin beam through the low lying freezing mist, before falling on the forest floor. He focused on the small coin sized light before closing his eyes for a second. He could smell the heavy-perfumed pines all around him and it reminded him of home.

He removed a bottle of mineral water from the leg pocket of his trousers and downed it in one.

His thirst quenched he threw the empty vessel into the

darkness and had a quick glance at his map. He knew where he was heading: straight for the main road, which he knew would be heavily policed. He was stuck between a rock and a hard place. Police to the front of him and, as the ever encroaching barking in the distance constantly reminded him, he was being hunted from behind.

He'd hidden his bag of weapons in a bush earlier after first removing two hand guns and plenty of ammunition, which he'd stashed in the side pockets of his combat trousers.

It had been excess weight that he'd decided he could do without.

He took a few deep breaths and then began to slowly jog towards the motorway, being careful to keep off the thin layer of snow that lay scattered in small patches on the forest floor.

'No point in making it too easy for them,' he said to himself as he disappeared into the darkness like a thief in the night.

Chapter Forty-Six

Amidst the freezing wind and falling snow, the two police officers stood at the side of the roadblock on the hard shoulder of the motorway. Any cars containing anyone that looked remotely like the old man were filtered towards them, where, armed with their photos, they would take a good look at the driver, or passengers, before letting them continue on their journey.

'I'm fucking freezing,' said Bob. 'These new jackets are shit! The old ones were much warmer.'

The heavy set police officer stamped his huge feet and blew on his hands. His breath disappeared into the mist.

'Not the warmest of jackets, right enough,' his colleague replied. 'They probably got a job lot on the cheap. Cutbacks, they're fucking everywhere.'

Bob shook his head and sighed heavily.

He pointed across the road.

'I'm sure that bastard Larry is taking the piss. That last guy he sent our way looked fuck all like this photo. In fact … I swear the one before that wasn't even a man, it was a woman. An ugly fucking woman, mind you.'

His colleague Ian laughed.

'How long do you reckon we'll be stuck out here in the middle of nowhere?' asked Bob.

'Shouldn't be too long now I reckon, the last I heard they'd set the dogs on him. Hopefully they'll catch the old bastard soon and we can all get the fuck out of here. Mind you, the wife's sister is up at mine tonight so I'm in no rush to get home, to be honest. I'll probably nip into the pub for a couple of pints once we're finished here.'

'What's your local?'

'The Black Bull. It's a nice wee country pub: roaring log fire, great selection of beers. I wish I was sitting there now instead of standing freezing my arse off here.'

'You and me both!'

Bob sighed heavily.

'Here comes another.'

They both watched as the snow-covered BMW slowly approached them. The driver wound down his window as he'd been given instruction to do at the checkpoint.

'Is this going to take long, officer?' asked the grey haired man. 'It's just I'm on my way to an important function, my daughter's twenty first. I'm running late as it is.'

'Shouldn't take too long. A couple of minutes at the most, sir,' replied Bob.

'Do you mind opening the boot for us?'

The man did what was asked of him. Bob had a good look through the boot as his colleague shone his torch through the back windows.

After a quick look at the photo, a photo that once again looked absolutely nothing like the car's driver, he was ushered on his way.

'Looked like Bruce Forsyth, that one,' remarked Ian.

Bob hissed through his teeth.

'I'll have to take a piss.'

'Again! You ought to go and get your prostate checked out, mate.'

'Fuck that. Nobody's sticking their finger up my arse! Unless they want to lose it. I'll be back in five minutes.'

Bob clambered up the steep embankment to the sound of laughter from behind.

Once under cover of the woods, he followed the beam cast by his torch until he reached a large oak tree.

'That'll do for me,' he said to the dark of the night as he unzipped his trousers and began to relieve himself.

He'd just finished whistling the first couple of bars of some classical piece he'd heard on the radio on his way to work that morning when his legs were viciously pulled from under him.

He landed on his back with a thud, the breath knocked out of him. Then everything went dark, even darker than it had been before.

'Is there such a thing as different degrees of darkness?' he thought to himself, as he fell into unconsciousness.

*

After a short time, he regained his senses. He lay on a pile of sodden leaves looking up into the cold mist covered night sky. He could feel the cold dampness on the back of his legs. He hoped it wasn't piss. His head was fuzzy! He felt dazed and confused.

'What the fuck just happened?'

377

He shakily aimed his torch above him. His view of the night sky was suddenly interrupted. It had now been replaced by a pair of grey eyes set deep back within a balaclava.

'How do? I'd like to ask you a few questions. Answer them truthfully, then do what I ask and I might let you live.'

He tried to reach for his baton. His movement was slow. It wasn't there.

'I took the liberty of removing that,' said the old man.

*

'Ian!'

The officer turned around and looked up the embankment.

He couldn't see anyone.

'It's me. Bob.'

'Bob! What the fuck are you doing? Get your arse down here.'

'No! You come up here. I think I've found the old bastard.'

'What do you mean found him?'

'I've found a body, its lying up here, in amongst a pile of leaves. I'm sure it's him; at least it looks like him from what I can remember from the photo. Bring it up here, so we can know for sure.'

'Shouldn't we inform someone first?' asked Ian.

'No! … At least, not yet. It might just be some old tramp or something. Let's confirm it first, eh? Save ourselves looking like a couple of arseholes.'

Ian thought for a moment, then made his decision.

'Okay, I'll grab the photo from the car and meet you up there. Give me five minutes. This better not be a fucking wind up.'

'You did well,' said the man holding the gun to Bob's back. 'You stuck to the script like a pro. Now let's move back into the woods a bit until your colleague gets here.'

*

'Bob! Where the fuck are you?'

'I'm over here. Can't you see my torch?'

Ian looked to his left.

'Oh aye, I can see you now. Scary fucking place this, isn't it?'

'It's about to get a hell of a lot scarier,' said a voice from behind him.

He felt something jam hard into his backbone.

'Keep heading towards the light, officer. Don't force me to shoot you.'

Ian slowly moved towards the torch beam. There he found Bob tied to a tree, bereft of his uniform and jacket. He was wearing some strange looking attire that seemed to be made out of vegetation. The torch had been wedged under his arm pit.

'I believe you two know each other,' the old man laughed.

'Go over there and stand next to your colleague. I have a couple of questions for you both.'

Ian did as he was asked. Hands above his head, he slowly walked towards Bob.

He turned around. All he could see was the beam from the old man's head torch and a gun barrel poised a few feet below.

'How many roadblocks have been set up along the main road there?'

'Why should we tell you?'

The old man moved closer. He pointed his weapon at Ian's head.

'Because if you don't, I'll put a bullet through your skull.'

'There's six altogether. Three of those are on the main road. One further out the way, our one and there's one more between here and Aberdeen.'

'Good answer, very concise. Question two - how many miles between the one here and the one nearer Aberdeen?'

'I'm not sure exactly.'

The torch and the gun moved even closer. It was touching him. He could feel the cold steel against his head.

'Think, man, think! And make it quick. I plan to be well out of here before those dogs you hear get any closer.'

A howl came from the distance as if in answer.

'They're at three mile intervals,' shouted Bob from his tree.

'Very good, Bob.'

He pointed his weapon at Ian.

'You! Come with me. You're my passport out of here.'

Chapter Forty Seven

Buchanan, Max and Derek got out the car on a small lane just off of Holburn Street.

Max and Derek walked ahead, Buchanan a few yards behind. He was on his mobile; he'd had three calls during the drive. The last one was ongoing.

Once he'd finished with the phone, he caught up with them. They all made their way through the overgrown back garden of the block of granite flats that sat directly opposite the block containing the one that belonged to Jerry Banks. Once they got to the back door however, they found it locked.

'You going to use your lock picking skills, sir?' asked Max.

'No need for that.' Buchanan once again took out his mobile.

'Rob, we're at the back, the door's locked.'

'Hold on, I'll be right down, give me two minutes.'

He kept the conversation going as he came down to meet them.

'By the way, did Jenny tell you we have a positive sighting of the girl?'

'Aye, she phoned me a couple of minutes ago.'

He heard the lock turning a second before the frame of the muscular built Rob Byford filled the doorway.

'Hi guys, another day, another stakeout, eh?'

They all nodded.

'Follow me, we're at the top.'

They all made their way up the old antique-looking staircase.

'How many in the flat?' asked Buchanan.

'Jerry himself and two others … and the girl of course. They've shut her away somewhere while they take turns on a huge bong in the living room. They look well gone, can't see them causing too much trouble.'

'Did you get the phone jammer?'

Rob held up the small black box.

'Yep.'

'What about the land line?'

'It's already been cut.'

'Great stuff.'

They entered the flat. The place smelled of lavender and coffee. Buchanan surveyed his surroundings.

'Jesus, who the fuck owns this, Hugh Hefner?'

The walls were covered in large prints of rake-thin models in various states of undress.

'Some accountant guy,' replied Rob.

'Bet he wishes he'd hidden his stash of porn, sex toys and the wrap of coke in his bedroom before he agreed to let us use the place.'

They all laughed.

Buchanan introduced himself to the other two officers

382

in the room who were busy beavering away on a laptop attached to the small hidden camera taped to the window.

'How do you want to play this, Ronnie? It's just that we've been told to wait for armed backup before we proceed with the operation.'

'Told by whom, exactly?'

'Montgomery.'

'That useless bastard!' shouted Derek in the background. 'One of these days … I swear I'm going to shoot that prick!'

'He's planning on arriving with them himself,' said Rob. 'He says it'll take a while to get things organised though, since they're all still out in Peterculter hunting down the old guy.'

Buchanan rubbed his chin.

'We have armed backup, we have Derek here. I can't see any reason to put things off, can you?'

Rob smiled.

'Suits me, Ronnie, he'd only fuck things up anyway.'

'You got plenty of bodies?' asked Buchanan.

'We have half a dozen uniforms covering the back of his flat, between them and us, that's plenty of folk to take down these arseholes.'

Buchanan looked at Derek.

'We'll have to make you look a bit less conspicuous, mind you.'

'What do you mean?'

'Think about it, Derek. Say they just happen to look out

the window as we're crossing the street. We're all in plain clothes. You're not. I reckon a six-foot-two guy dressed the way you are and carrying an assault rifle might just give the game away.'

'Aye, right enough.'

'See if you can find anything to put on over the top of that outfit in Hef's wardrobe.'

Max laughed.

'Don't pick the gimp suit though!' shouted Rob.

This time they all laughed.

'Seriously?' asked Buchanan.

'Yep,' replied Rob. 'A full-on *Pulp Fiction* job.'

*

Rob picked up his radio.

'Meet us at the front door with the Ram-it, Jason, we're waiting outside there now.'

'On my way, sir.'

The PC let them in to the well decorated landing of the flats. He held the heavy steel battering ram in his hands. The five officers, Buchanan, Max, Derek, Rob, and Jason, slowly and carefully made their way up the stairs.

Once they reached the top, Derek unburdened himself of the oversized coat he'd found in the wardrobe, threw it over the bannister and then raised his rifle to cover the door.

The young PC moved in front, put on his safety goggles and raised his heavy lethal looking piece of equipment.

Buchanan held up a finger, then two, then three.

BANG!

The door flew open sending splinters flying in all directions.

Derek sped into the living room.

'ON THE FLOOR, THE THREE OF YOU!'

The three guys complied instantly.

One of them dropped the bong on his way down. It made a crashing sound as it smashed through the glass covered coffee table sending small burning pieces of hashish everywhere.

It looked like a mini fireworks display.

'Where's the girl?' asked Buchanan.

'What girl?' It was Jerry Banks who replied. He arched his neck to stare at the DI.

Buchanan stood on his hand. He let out a high pitched scream.

'The fucking girl we saw you with from across the road.'

He nodded towards Rob.

'These guys have been watching you for the past hour.' He increased the pressure. 'So, cut the shit, eh!'

Jerry's eyes filled with tears. He was in agony. Then it got worse. He heard a crack.

He breathed heavily. There were stars in his eyes and he was close to passing out.

'She's in the second bedroom in the hall.'

Max winced. He was thinking back to the girl in the shop.

Buchanan turned towards him.

'Max! Make sure she's okay, but first … ' he hauled out a crumpled piece of paper and handed it to him. 'Phone this woman! She's from social services, she's dealing with Melissa. You'd better get a WPC down here as well.'

'Will do, sir.'

He left the room. He was glad to get away.

'Rob, Derek. Cuff these bastards.'

He pointed down at Jerry.

'Stick that one in the chair by the window. He's going to tell us all he knows.'

Both men did as asked.

Derek wasn't exactly gentle when he threw him on the seat. Jerry's hands were cuffed behind him. He let out another scream as his injured hand hit the back of the chair.

Buchanan drew a chair directly across from him and sat down. He stared into his eyes.

'Unless you want your other hand broken, tell me everything you know.'

The man sighed.

'It was just a job like any other. He phoned me one day, out of the blue. He said he got my name from an acquaintance. We were to take possession of the girl … '

'Kidnap you mean!' interrupted Buchanan.

'We had to make sure no harm came to her. I wouldn't have agreed to it otherwise. I'm not an evil bastard. Fuck, I've got kids of my own.'

'Don't give me that shit; he could have been a paedophile for all you fucking knew.'

Jerry looked at his feet.

'Did you ever meet the guy?'

'Never, I've had a couple of phone calls, then a courier delivered an envelope full of money to the door.'

'How much?'

'Ten grand, were supposed to get another ten at the drop off tomorrow.'

Buchanan took out his notebook.

'Where's the drop?'

'The multi-story car park in Chapel Street. Third level.'

'What time?'

'Eight a.m.'

He wrote down the details. Buchanan looked at the table next to the window.

'That your mobile?'

'Yeah.'

'What name does he come under?'

Jerry looked sheepish.

'Mr Moneybags. He just changed his number earlier on today.'

Buchanan turned towards Rob.

'That jammer's still active?'

'Yeah. Do you want it off, Ronnie?'

'Please.'

Two seconds later Jerry's mobile rang.

Buchanan looked at the screen.

MR MONEYBAGS.

'Fuck!'

He looked across at Jerry.

'Tell him everything is going to plan.'

He switched it to speaker and laid it on the table next to Jerry.

*

'Jerry! I've been trying to reach you. You had your phone off?'

'No. I think there's something wrong with the network, the reception has been dodgy all night.'

'You sound different. What's up?'

'Nothing. I'm just … tired, everything's fine. We're all set up for tomorrow. I'll meet you at the agreed time and place.'

'Good. I'll see you there. I'll phone you again in the morning just before you drop her off. Make sure you have your mobile handy. I'll be out of contact till then. I'm turning my phone off. I never know who's checking up on me nowadays.'

The call ended.

'Well done,' said Buchanan.

He turned to Rob.

'Get uniform to take these three arseholes into custody.'

Just then the room was interrupted by the booming voice of DCI Montgomery.

'WHAT THE HELL IS GOING ON HERE!?'

'Fuck, what does he want?' asked Derek, 'I've seen enough of that prick this week.'

Montgomery approached them.

'Mr Byford, I thought I told you to wait till until I arrived with the armed backup?'

Buchanan stepped in.

'Blame me, sir. It was my decision. Once Rob here told me we had a positive sighting of the girl, I thought we should act on it right away.'

'But … '

Buchanan carried on.

'As for armed backup. We already had that. We had Derek here.'

Derek winked at the DCI. This just enraged him more.

'Right! That's it. I'm writing a report on this. I'm sick to the back teeth of everyone flaunting my authority. Especially you two bastards.'

He pointed to Buchanan and Derek in turn.

'Eh … that would be pretty pointless, sir,' said Buchanan.

Montgomery's eyes bulged.

'And why exactly would that be, Mr Fuckwit?'

Buchanan felt his anger rising. Time to play the trump

card he thought. He raised his height and his voice.

'Maybe because I ran all this by Superintendent Burns before I instigated it!'

He smirked. Montgomery's face turned beetroot. He stared at Buchanan for an inordinate amount of time, then silently left the flat.

The room erupted into laughter. Derek patted Buchanan on the back.

'That sorted that windbag out. I must ask though. How the fuck did you pull that off?'

Buchanan lit a cigarette.

'Believe it or not Derek, the Super owed me one.'

Derek shook his head.

'You've lost me.'

'Kate … Remember she asked me to phone her brother?'

'Aye.'

'Well by a wild coincidence, guess who her brother is.'

'You're fucking joking.'

'Nope, her brother is Superintendent Jake Burns. He was that chuffed that I'd managed to get her back in one piece that he told me, and I quote,' he put on a gruff voice. ' "Any problems you have in the future, Ronnie, just get hold of me."'

'So you did.'

Buchanan took a long draw on his cigarette.

'Yep.'

Derek laughed.

'I'm still picturing that gobsmacked look he had on his face. I thought the fucker was going to have a stroke!'

Max suddenly appeared beside them. He was flanked by a WPC and the woman from social services. He held Melissa by the hand.

'She wanted to see you, sir. She insisted.'

Buchanan bent down.

'Hi, sweetheart.' He winked at her. 'How's it going?'

She ran to him and wrapped her arms around his waist.

'I knew you'd come. You're a good guy. Those men were mean.'

'They won't trouble you any more. I've locked them up for you.'

She smiled and looked up at him.

'Thanks.'

'Now you go with this nice police lady. She'll take care of you for now.'

He made eye contact with the social worker.

'Can I have a word?'

They walked to the corner of the room. Buchanan turned to face her.

'You sent me out those forms, yet?'

'I've got them here,' she replied.

She opened up the briefcase and handed him the papers. He gave them a quick glance and then folded them up and stuck them in his inside pocket.

'What's the chance of this working out, realistically, no bullshit?'

'We take each case on its merits, but off the record … pretty good I reckon. But don't quote me on that. She obviously has a bond with you and you're both professionals. That should stand you in good stead with the board.'

Buchanan nodded.

'Thanks for taking the time on this, Liz.'

'No problem, I'll be in touch.'

He went back to join Max and Derek, Rob Byford and the other officer had already left.

'Right, guys, looks like our work is done here. I'm meeting Michelle at the pub across the road. Anyone care to join me?'

'I'm up for it,' replied Derek, 'but I'll have to get rid of the weapons and body armour first. I don't want to go scaring the shit out of the clientele.'

'Good idea.'

Buchanan laughed.

'Max?'

'Sure. I could do with a drink.'

Let's go then.

Just as they walked out the flat Max stopped.

'Shouldn't we check in with Justin, sir?'

'Can't see the point to be honest. The old guy's obviously

though, just for the moment. The two names are confusing her.'

He gave her a nod and then opened the back door.

'Hello again, sweetheart. I'd like you to meet my partner, Michelle.'

Melissa let out a broad smile, 'Pleased to meet you, Shell.'

She held out her hand.

Michelle shook it.

'Hello, Samantha, pleased to meet you. You're a gorgeous little girl.'

'People always say that!'

They both laughed.

Buchanan watched Michelle's face. He could tell she was captivated by the girl. He'd had a feeling she would be.

'We'll have to go, Ronnie,' said the voice from the front. 'We're meeting the foster carers in ten minutes. Anyway I think Samantha could do with a sleep.'

As if on cue the girl let out a huge yawn.

'No problem, I'll be in touch.'

The car took off as Buchanan and Michelle crossed the road hand in hand to the Malt Mill.

Chapter Forty-Eight

The warmth hit them both the minute they walked into the Malt Mill.

The place was rocking. There was a live band on, playing *Gimme Shelter*. The music got louder as they headed downstairs to the lounge.

An apt song to play, thought Buchanan, glad to leave the sub-zero temperatures behind him.

The staircase was decorated with tinsel and a real Christmas tree stood at the bottom. The pine smell reminded him of his cold dark trip through the woods earlier.

As they entered, Max greeted them both with a drink: a gin and tonic for Michelle and a pint of Guinness for his boss.

'I never knew this pub had waitress service,' said Buchanan as he winked at him. Buchanan downed half the glass in one gulp. 'Cheers, Max. I've been looking forward to that all day.'

He looked around the place, soaking in the festive atmosphere. The place smelled of cinnamon and cloves thanks to the huge bowls of mulled wine on the bar counter.

Michelle leaned in close towards them both so she could be heard above the band.

'Can we sit around the back?' she asked as she stirred the ice cubes in her drink with the red and white candy cane-shaped swizzle stick. 'It's a bit close to the music here.'

'Good idea,' replied Max.

'How's the head by the way?' she asked him.

He raised his fringe to show her the bruised mark.

'Not too bad. It could've been worse.'

They squeezed their way through the throng of merry makers as they carried their drinks over to a vacant table in the corner.

By the time they got there, Buchanan had about finished his but then, timely as ever, Derek arrived with another round, the four drinks sitting comfortably in his huge hands. He didn't have much manoeuvring to do, people naturally moved out of his way due to the sheer size of the man. Buchanan watched, fascinated. It reminded him of Moses parting the Red Sea.

He put the drinks down carefully then looked around for a chair. He approached a table full of business men in suits.

'You don't mind if I take this seat, do you?'

'Actually I do,' replied one of them. A portly man with a pock-marked face. 'We're waiting for a colleague of ours, as it happens, that chair is for him.'

Derek shook his head and sighed.

'So, nobody's actually using it at the moment?'

'Well, no, but … '

'That's all I need to know.'

He picked up the heavy wooden chair in one hand and carried it over to join his friends at their table.

'PRICK!' he shouted.

Buchanan laughed.

'Glad you could join us, Derek. Nice entrance by the way.'

Derek smiled, 'I aim to please.'

Buchanan nodded to his left.

'You know Michelle, don't you?'

'We've met a couple of times. The last time was at Terry Brook's retirement do, if memory serves me right.'

'Yeah,' replied Michelle. 'A guy your height is hard to forget.'

Derek laughed and took a drink of his pint. 'As is a beautiful woman.'

He winked. Michelle blushed, then she smiled.

'You bought me a couple of drinks.'

Buchanan picked up his beer.

'How did you know what to order?' he asked. 'You couldn't possibly remember what Michelle here drinks.'

'Terry Brook's do again. She's right. I did buy her a couple of drinks. The fact she drinks gin just stuck in my mind. My mum's favourite drink is gin. Come to think of it, you're the only two people I've ever seen drinking the stuff!'

'I thought you were getting changed,' interrupted Max.

'Nah. I couldn't be arsed. I left my weapons and body armour with the other armed response guys. Anyway, black combat trousers and a black T-shirt is a good look for me I reckon. I basically wear the same thing when I'm off-duty anyway.'

He shrugged.

'You look like you've just come back from a try out with the SAS,' said Buchanan.

'He looks more like that foreign guy in them expendable movies, I'd say,' added Michelle.

'Jet Li?' asked Max.

'Jet Li?' repeated Michelle. 'He's about four foot five. No! That Dolph guy.'

'Dolph Lungren,' said Derek. 'It has been remarked on before.'

Derek laughed and took another drink.

'Hey, this stuff is not bad.'

'What is it?' asked Buchanan. He was intrigued by the dark-coloured ale in Derek's glass. Derek took another drink before answering.

'Oscar Wilde!'

'Mmmmm, Mighty Oak Brewing Company. Supreme champion beer of Britain in 2011 that was. I never knew they served that in here.'

'It's a guest ale. It's only here for the week.'

'I'm going to get one,' said Buchanan, 'once I've finished this Guinness.'

He suddenly looked over towards the door.

'Atkins! Whats she doing here?'

They all followed his gaze. She walked towards their

table. The hood and shoulders of her jacket were covered in snow: a sign that the storm had started up again.

'Sir,' she said. 'I've been trying to reach you on your mobile, but I couldn't get an answer.'

'It's needing charged,' he replied. He finished the last of his pint. 'He's escaped, hasn't he?'

'Yep. He's a sneaky bastard. He … '

Buchanan held up his hand.

'Hold it right there. I could do with a refill before I hear this.' He looked at them all in turn. 'Same again, everyone?'

They all nodded.

'And you, Jenny? A Guinness?'

'Yes, sir. Make it a pint if you don't mind.'

She removed her jacket. Some of the melted snow landed on the head of the pock marked business man. He stood up and turned towards her. Then he spotted Derek glaring at him and quickly sat back down again.

'Derek! Get the lady a seat will you? I've got a date with Oscar Wilde.'

'I never knew you swung that way!' said Derek as he went off in search of another chair.

Buchanan laughed then left them to talk amongst themselves as he headed towards the bar.

Once he returned with the drinks, he asked WPC Atkins to begin her tale.

'His means of escape is still a bit sketchy, sir.'

'What do you mean?'

still on the loose. He just phoned two minutes ago. Anyway, if Justin captures him, well … a guy like that, he'd be shouting it from the roof tops. We'd find out soon enough, that's for sure.'

'Aye, he does love being in the limelight does old Double J,' said Derek.

When they got outside Buchanan noticed that the car containing Melissa was still parked in front of the flats. She was sitting in the back; Liz and the WPC were in the front.

He gave her a friendly wave.

'Sir, is that not your Michelle standing outside the pub?' asked Max pointing across the road.

Buchanan took a look.

'So it is, Max,' he smiled. 'She's always been the same. She won't walk into a pub on her own. Michelle!' he shouted.

She crossed the street and walked towards him.

'You two go ahead, I'll meet you in the pub.'

'Hi, Ronnie.'

She kissed him on the cheek.

'I got here early.'

'You always do.'

He smiled at her.

'I'd like you to meet someone.'

He knocked on the car window. It slowly came down.

'Can I have a quick word with Melissa?'

'Sure,' replied Liz. 'I'd prefer you called her Samantha

'Well, all we really know is that he managed to get hold of a uniform to impersonate one of the officers on the roadblock, and then forced his partner to drive him out of the area in a squad car.'

'How the fuck did he manage that?' asked Derek. 'The whole area was crawling with police.'

She took a sip of her drink then continued.

'The two officers were working the hard shoulder. Motorists that had a slight resemblance to the old man were filtered off the main motorway towards them. They'd take a good look at the car's occupants before ushering them on their way then ... '

'I know the procedure, Jenny,' said Buchanan, 'I just find it hard to believe that no one noticed the two officers leaving their post. Whether one of them was the old man or not ... that's immaterial.'

He sighed.

'Who was in charge of that section?'

She looked at her mobile, 'Ben Richards from traffic.'

'Ben's reliable, sir,' interrupted Max.

'He did think it strange, sir. When he saw them leaving he radioed on ahead to the next roadblock which was situated a few miles down the road. He couldn't make contact with the two officers concerned. He thought maybe they'd just got sick of freezing their arse off at their checkpoint, made themselves incommunicado and took off for the night. His words, not mine.'

'So, how did he manage to get through the second roadblock? I mean, even with a uniform on, he must have looked a bit old for the job. For fuck's sake, they all had a photo of him.'

'That's the thing, sir! He didn't get as far as the road block. He made the officer drive up a small road in between them. It led up to a farm. Once he got there … '

'You mean there was a road between the two checkpoints with no one covering it?'

Atkins shrugged her shoulders.

'What happened to the police officer?' asked Max. 'The one he took with him.'

'He's still groggy. He's gone to A&E to get himself checked out. He says once they got off the main road he felt a sharp stinging pain in his leg. He reckons the old man injected him with some drug or other. He can't remember anything after that. The officer reckons he was out for at least an hour, by the time he woke up and raised the alarm the old man was well gone.'

'What happened to the officer who he stole the uniform from?' asked Buchanan.

Atkins took a sip of her drink.

'They found him duct taped to a tree in the woods. The poor guy was freezing. He was close to suffering from hypothermia, I heard.'

'Well … at least he never shot them,' said Derek.

'That's something, I suppose,' replied Buchanan. 'Mind you, Double J won't be pleased.'

'He's still out there, sir, him and another officer, he has a bandage on his nose, his name escapes me. Everyone else has given up and gone home.'

'Poor bastard,' said Buchanan.

*

They all stood in the shelter of the doorway of the pub awaiting their taxis home.

'Remember,' said Buchanan. 'Six a.m. briefing tomorrow.'

'Why so early?' asked Derek.

'Because … I'm needing a good couple of hours to make sure this thing is set up right, unlike that fuck up earlier. In fact, I'll be in before that. I want to be there with Jerry when the old man phones. I don't trust that bastard.'

The first taxi pulled up. Max, Atkins and Derek shared it. They all stayed in the same end of town. Two minutes later, Buchanan and Michelle's car arrived. They ran from their shelter straight into the back of the vehicle.

Buchanan let out a huge yawn.

'You look knackered,' said Michelle. 'When's the last time you had a good night sleep?'

'I can't remember to be honest. I can't sleep, I've been pining for you.'

She nudged him in the ribs playfully.

'Bugger off. It's this case. You're always like this. You take things far too personally.'

He changed the conversation.

'What do you think of Melissa?'

'That's a strange question.'

'Indulge me.'

'She seems a lovely little girl. I love that cute wee birthmark she has. It looks like a heart.'

She sighed.

'What's wrong?'

'Max told me of all the shit she's been through. No one should have to deal with that sort of thing. Especially at her age.'

'Yeah, it's sad.'

'A lassie like that needs a stable environment. To help her forget all the crap she's been through.'

She turned to face him.

'Ronnie?'

'What?'

'Where exactly is this conversation going?'

He stared at her.

'How long have we been waiting to adopt?'

'More or less since we found that we couldn't have any of our own. But they said it could take a while. There's only so many babies given up and we are on such a big list ...'

'Why not adopt someone older?'

'You mean ...'

'I don't see why not.'

'You surely can't pick and choose in such situations. How do you know we'd end up with her?'

'I don't, but I've been talking to a woman who knows about this stuff. She's a social worker. She says we've got a shot. At least, as much chance as anyone else has.'

'How do we go about it?'

'I'm not sure exactly. There's some forms to fill in to start with. That's all I know for now.'

. She kissed him.

'Get the forms.'

'I hoped you'd say that.' He put his right hand in his jacket. 'I've already got them. They're here!'

He handed them to her.

Michelle laughed and then, clutching the papers in her hand, she leaned her head on his shoulder as she watched the huge snowflakes fall against the taxi windows.

Chapter Forty Nine

It was two a.m. Buchanan couldn't sleep. He'd been tossing and turning all night. He had far too much on his mind, so he decided to get up. He quietly walked into the kitchen and turned on the coffee machine. As he waited for it to do its thing, he thought back to the telephone message he'd received when he and Michelle had got home. Superintendent Burns was putting him in sole charge of the operation.

He was pleased about that, but it put him under a lot of pressure.

He laughed to himself. That must have pleased Montgomery. He'd have loved to have been a fly on the wall when he'd been told the information. He could picture him in his mind. He had a big red face with smoke coming out of his ears.

Still laughing, he poured himself a cup of the strong, hot liquid and carried it through to the sitting room.

He turned on a small lamp then picked up his cigarettes before quietly walking over to the French windows. He slid one open slightly.

'Jesus!'

He was faced by a thick blanket of white.The snow storm had been working overtime. A good four inches had fallen since he and Michelle had returned home. He lit up a cigarette and thought ahead to the morning's operation.

He'd be briefing everyone before things got underway.

Everyone, that was, except for some of the armed officers. He'd already arranged for them to be placed on a few of the buildings that surrounded the car park.

He wanted them there hours before. They'd been told to keep themselves well hidden till the designated time. He looked at the clock on the wall; they'd probably be there by now. He had a feeling that the old man might survey the area before the meet. This way they should be suitably hidden in place before that was likely to happen.

Hidden and freezing.

'They must be cursing me,' he thought.

He took a long draw on the cigarette and watched as the thick snowflakes fell on to the patio.

Then he heard the door opening. He turned around quickly. Sam ran towards him with his tail wagging.

'What are you doing up, boy?'

Sam looked at him. The Border Collie pulled his ears back and moved his head from side to side. Buchanan rubbed him on the nose. He liked that. Sam fell down and rolled onto his back.

Then Michelle came through to join them.

She yawned.

'You'll have to try and get a few hours sleep, Ronnie.'

'I'll try. Once I've smoked this.'

He held up his cigarette.

She decided not to admonish him for smoking in the house. He had enough on his plate. At least he had the window open.

She massaged his shoulders as he smoked.

'Have you got everything planned?'

'I think so ... but I don't trust this guy. He's always been one step ahead of us.'

He felt the tension ease a bit as Michelle worked on his shoulders.

'Relax, Ronnie. It'll soon be over with, then we can look forward to Christmas.'

He sighed and touched her hand.

'You're right. The sooner this is over with, the better.'

'Do you know what I can't understand?' she said.

'What?'

'Say he managed to pull this off. Got away with his granddaughter, I mean. How the hell does he expect to leave the country? I assume the airports, ferry ports, etc., will be told to be on the lookout for him no?'

'They already have been. It's standard procedure ... wait a minute, he'd surely know that!'

He threw the end of his cigarette into the snow and stared into the night.

'What are you thinking, Ronnie?'

'Just about what you just said. Listen, love. You go on through; I have a phone call to make.'

He picked up his mobile and phoned Atkins.

It rang for a good while and was eventually answered

407

with a huge yawn.

'Jenny! I want you to get on to something right away!'

Chapter Fifty

Harry Reid couldn't sleep. The bed was comfy enough, but something was bugging him. The phone call he'd had with Jerry earlier. The man sounded and acted differently than he had in their previous interactions. He'd been trained to spot such nuances. Something was definitely off. No doubt about it.

He sighed heavily. He needed to think.

'I need some coffee.'

He'd cut down on the powder for the time being. There wasn't much left and he felt he might need it later. He still felt quite focused which surprised him. He hadn't had one of his episodes for a while. He hadn't had so much as a glimpse of Clara. Not since he'd let the woman go back in the woods, he'd been completely delirious then. He had a hard time remembering much about ...

He thought for a second. He looked up trying to retrieve the information.

Kate, at least he thought that was her name.

He still heard his dead wife's voice now and again, but he could handle that.

He moved through to the kitchen and turned on the light. It was spacious and luxurious. He'd never seen so many cupboards in one room.

'Bugger this.'

He moved to the bathroom.

'Where on earth do you keep your coffee?' he asked the man tied up in the bath next to the woman. He roughly removed the tape from his mouth.

The guy let out a squeal. He stared up at him with wild eyes.

'Fourth cupboard from the left,' he answered nervously.

After replacing the duct tape he returned to the kitchen, found the coffee and filled up the kettle.

He'd let them go free in the morning.

After he'd made good his escape in the woods earlier, he'd stolen a car and driven back to town. He'd needed a place to stay so he'd parked outside some flats in George Street awaiting a likely victim.

The man and woman in the bath had come along the road just before midnight. They'd both been drinking. It was obvious in the way they walked. The man approached his flat, keys in hand. It had been so easy. He'd simply crept up behind them and bundled them into the block of flats. Once in the landing, he'd used his weapon to force them both up the stairs. Once inside, he'd simply tied them up and stuck them in the bathroom. Job done.

He heard a click. It broke the silence pulling him out of his reverie. The kettle had finished boiling. He made his cup of coffee extra strong and took it through to the sitting room. He didn't bother turning on the lights. He sat there staring out the window and watched the snow fall, as he carefully formulated his plan for later on in the morning.

Something inside told him he'd have to be wary.

Perhaps he'd arrive early. Get a feel for the area before

the drop off. He looked towards the bathroom. Perhaps …
he'd try something else.

"By failing to prepare, you are preparing to fail" came to
mind. Another saying Clara had been fond of.

Chapter Fifty One

'Everything set?'

'Pretty much, yeah.'

'I'll be arriving in a red Volvo. Park in one one of the bays and flash your lights when you see me. You got that?'

The old man sniffed.

'Sure.'

'You'll get the rest of your fee when I get Melissa.'

'Glad to hear it!'

'By the way, what are you driving?'

He stared at the hand written note in front of him.

'A black …'

The line went dead.

He turned around to face Buchanan. He was visibly shaking.

'Wh-what now?' he stuttered.

'Now you calm down and come with us.' He roughly pulled him out of his chair. 'On your feet, soldier!'

Jerry looked confused.

'Why? I did what you asked of me!'

'We're not finished with you yet, Jerry. Not by a long shot. It's like this … ' Buchanan pointed at him. 'We don't know if Mr Reid has actually seen what you look like or not.

I'm erring on the side of caution. I'm assuming he has. It's his style.'

Jerry sighed and rubbed the stubble on his chin.

'What if he notices I don't have the girl? He might fucking shoot me!'

Buchanan blanked the remark and pressed his point.

'He'll expect to see you there, Jerry.' He winked. 'So, let's not disappoint the man, eh? Cuff him and take him down to the car, Max. I'll see you down there.'

Derek walked past as they headed towards the stairs. He had a brown bag and three extra large coffees in his hands.

'Here you go, Max. Get those down you.'

He handed him one of the hot drinks and a bacon roll from the bag. The smell made Max realise how hungry he was.

'Cheers for that, Derek. I'll see you downstairs.'

'Where's mine?' asked Jerry.

'Fuck off, weasel!' came the curt reply.

Derek continued along the corridor and then, after knocking, he entered Buchanan's office.

He was busy jotting something down in his notebook.

'All set?' he asked, handing him the same things he'd given to Max.

'As much as I can be, Derek.' He walked towards him and patted him on the shoulder. 'Let's go, big fella.'

As they headed off, enjoying their breakfasts as they went, Derek suddenly stopped and looked at Buchanan.

'That's a new look for you, eh, Ronnie?'

He was referring to the well-worn leather jacket and baseball hat he was wearing.

'Needs must, Derek. I'll be sitting in the front with Jerry. The old guy's seen me before. At least with this on,' he tapped the baseball hat, 'I can hide my features a bit. I have a very distinctive face, so I'm told.'

Derek laughed.

'Aye, that's one word for it.'

On the way downstairs Buchanan took out his mobile.

'Justin! How are things running your end?' he asked in between mouthfuls of bacon.

'The men are all in position. The trouble is that we can only see so far into the car park with it being multi-story and all.'

'Yeah, I noticed that earlier. I swung by there this morning on the way in here.'

'I know, sir, we saw you! I've ensconced myself in the top floor of a strip club directly across from the East Side.'

'Private Eyes?'

'That's it, sir.'

'Good vantage point. I thought that myself earlier. We'll try and see if we can park on that side.'

'If you could, that would be perfect, sir.'

His text tone rang.

'I have a message, Justin. I'll be in touch. Check all your men's radios are working. We're just about to leave.'

'Will do, sir.'

The message was from Jenny.

Surveillance vehicles in position awaiting orders.

*

Derek stared at the vehicle.

'Wow!' he said for the third time in quick succession.

'Some motor, eh!' said Buchanan. 'Max picked it. It was impounded from some heavy duty drug dealer. It will do the job perfectly mind. Plenty of room for you and Max in the back. It even has blacked-out windows. The two of you will be practically invisible. Save drawing attention to that massive weapon of yours.'

'Is that a euphemism?'

Buchanan laughed.

Derek was still staring at the car. Then he nodded.

'I remember that motor now. It was taken off that Jamaican guy. Fast ...?'

'Fast Eddie.'

'That's the man. A real weird-looking fucker. Dripping in gold he was. Earrings, rings, necklaces, the lot. He ran his gang out of the old Golden Tree Casino off King Street. I was there when we busted his place out at Cults. He had a few fancy motors if I remember correctly. All black for some strange reason, he must like the colour.'

After having another good look around the vehicle, he turned towards Buchanan.

'Who's driving the thing?'

415

Buchanan nodded towards Jerry. He was sitting in the driver's seat. He looked nervous.

'It'll have to be him. Otherwise it'll look a bit suspicious, don't you think?'

'Aye, you're right enough.Watch the bastard though. We don't want him giving the game away.'

'Not much chance of that. I've cut a deal with him. He carries this off smoothly and I've told him I'll put a good word in for him, persuade the judge to go easy on his case.'

Derek gave him a strange look.

'Are you serious?'

Buchanan winked and took a sip of his coffee.

'Of course I am, Derek, I would never lie about such a thing.'

He placed a heavy emphasis on the word never. Derek laughed.

'Now, let's go catch this bastard!'

*

They approached the entrance to the multi-story car park just as dawn was beginning to rise. They could hardly see more than a few yards in front of them because of the freezing fog that had enveloped the area. Buchanan opened the car window slightly then lit a cigarette for himself and Derek. Their ears were assaulted by the harsh cries of sea gulls.

'Flying fucking rats!' said Derek as he eagerly took the cigarette from Buchanan. 'The bastards are everywhere nowadays.'

'Especially in the town centre. Especially at the weekend. It's all the half finished food lying around from last night's revellers that attracts them.'

'Not the best of weather for the armed response guys,' said Max as he wafted the smoke away from his side of the car.

'That's an understatement, if ever there was one,' replied Derek.

Buchanan caught the look in the huge man's eyes in the rear view mirror. He looked worried. Unusual for Derek, maybe the gloomy atmosphere was spooking him.

The huge rectangular shape of the multi-story carpark appeared like a ghost ship out of the fog. They drove straight in. The barriers had been lifted. A bright-yellow sign declared "Out Of Order". They weren't of course. It just made access easier for the duration of the police operation.

They slowly drove up to the third level. Buchanan pulled the baseball hat low down on his head.

He saw the two white surveillance vans parked diagonally across from each other on either side. Both contained armed officers. He wasn't taking any chances.

'Where do you want me to park?' asked Jerry.

Buchanan pointed ahead.

'Back the car into the left hand side there.'

Once the vehicle came to a stop Buchanan once again looked in the rear view mirror.

'That'll do nicely,' he said.

He could see the mirrored windows on the top-most floor

of the *Private Eye Gentlemen's Club* clearly. He picked up his radio.

'Radio contact only from now on, people. Justin, how's the view from there?'

'Perfect, sir.'

'That fog not obscuring your view?'

'Negative, sir. It's lying quite low.'

'Jenny, how are things your end?'

'All cars are in place. We're ready to move at your command, sir.'

'SV two?'

'Armed and ready, sir!'

'Await my orders.'

He broke radio contact and looked at his watch. Seven forty-five.

He drank the last of his coffee and then crushed the Styrofoam cup before tossing it at his feet.

They all sat there quietly, until Derek broke the silence.

'I don't trust this guy,' he said. 'He's bound to try and pull something fast.'

'I don't think so,' said Max. 'I mean as far as he's aware … ' he nodded to the front. 'Jerry there's dropping off his great granddaughter. I don't think he'd put her in danger.'

Buchanan didn't involve himself in their discussion. He just stared straight ahead.

He was watching a magpie eagerly devouring some

cold chips splattered on the concrete floor. He saluted it as Max and Derek continued their conversation. He wasn't particularly superstitious but someone had once told him that this simple act could ward off bad luck.

'I've never been involved in a case where the perpetrator was one step ahead of us so often,' said Derek. 'The guy is a fucking menace.'

Buchanan and Max both laughed.

'We have,' said Max.

'Who was that then?' asked Derek.

'A guy called Vince. I'll tell you all about him sometime,' said Buchanan, finally getting involved.

Suddenly, the radio came to life. It was Justin.

'Red Volvo heading your way, folks.'

'Everyone hold back till I say go,' answered Buchanan.

They watched as the car entered the third floor. It moved very slowly. The driver drove to the end of the car park, performed a U-turn and then stopped opposite their vehicle.

Buchanan could feel the adrenaline surge through his body. He felt like he was watching things occur in slow motion.

'Flash the headlights, Jerry.'

He picked up the radio.

'Hold on, people.'

They watched as the driver left his car. He had on a parka jacket, his features set way back deep within the hood. He looked to either side and then slowly approached their vehicle.

Buchanan screamed into the radio.

'GO, GO, GO!'

The back of both surveillance vehicles burst open. The noise was like an explosion. Heavy footsteps echoed around the interior of the car park. The man was surrounded by armed officers within seconds.

He fell to his knees. Hands on the cold concrete floor.

'Don't shoot!' he screamed.

It was the voice of a young man. Buchanan approached him and pulled back the hood.

'Who the fuck are you?'

He responded immediately.

'Danny Mackintosh.'

He was trembling, his face was flushed and his eyes were bulging.

'What are you doing here, Danny?'

He stood up and held his hands above his head.

'He's got my fiance. He told me if I did this one job for him, she'd come to no harm. The guy is a fucking psycho!'

Buchanan sighed and rubbed his eyes.

'You're here to pick up the girl?'

Danny nodded his head.

'That's right.'

'Where were you to take her?'

'I'm supposed to go to the King's Hotel. I've to wait for him there. I was supposed to phone him when I got her in the car.'

'Phone him. Tell him you have her.'

Danny took the phone out his pocket and made the call. They all watched in silence. The only sound to be heard was Danny's heavy breathing.

'There's no answer.'

'Try again. He has a habit of turning the thing off.'

He redialled. Small beads of sweat ran down his forehead. He looked on the verge of collapse.

He shrugged.

'There's no one there.'

'We should still go, sir,' said Atkins who had now joined them. 'He's not going anywhere without his granddaughter.'

He pointed to her, 'You're right. Go organise things. We'll all meet up near the King's Hotel, inconspicuous like. I don't want him scared off. Tell them to park their vehicles on the side streets and await my orders.'

'I'm on it, sir.'

She returned to the surveillance vehicle as Buchanan once again got on the Radio.

'Justin, I want you with us.'

There was no answer.

'JUSTIN!'

'I'm afraid Justin is otherwise engaged, Inspector,' answered a voice with a thick Canadian accent.

Chapter Fifty Two

'How the hell did he get hold of a radio?'

'Ah! Sergeant Maxwell, how's the head feeling, by the way? I hope it didn't cause you too much distress. I'm afraid I had no choice.'

'His head is fine, as it happens,' interrupted Buchanan. 'What have you done with Justin, you bastard?'

'Calm down, Ronnie. He's come to no harm. I simply incapacitated him and took over his vantage point so I could watch the pickup. I thought Jerry sounded a bit edgy when I phoned him last night … and again this morning, come to think of it. So, I thought I'd keep an eye on things. Imagine my surprise when I found one of your officers already on the premises.'

Buchanan turned around and stared towards Private Eyes.

'By the way, don't bother looking for me in the Gentlemen's club. I'm well gone from there, although knowing you like I do, you'll probably still check.'

'What about the guy's fiancé?'

'He'll find her safe and sound at home.'

Buchanan sighed.

'You might as well hand yourself in, Harry. You know that there's no chance in hell you're getting a hold of Melissa. However … I might be able to swing it so that you can at least get to see her before we lock you up.'

There was a couple of seconds silence.

Buchanan took advantage of it. He covered the microphone and sent Max off to see if Atkins could get a trace put out on the people locator in Justin's radio.

'Interesting proposition, Inspector, but I think I'll pass on that, if it's alright with you.'

'Please yourself. I just thought with the little time you have left you'd like to say goodbye to her.'

'Nice try. I've been in remission once. Who knows it might happen again. Beside I've found myself a magic elixir. I feel better than I have in years. Maybe it's cured me.'

The old man laughed. Buchanan changed tact.

'What does Clara think of my proposal? Maybe you should run it past her.'

More silence. Then a sniff.

'She's not with us at the moment, Mr Buchanan.'

'She could pop up at anytime though, eh? So, I've heard at least.'

The old man raised his voice.

'My relationship with my wife has got bugger all to do with you, detective.'

'Let's keep things real here, Harry. You're relationship with your dead wife. You're not thinking straight. You're having visual and auditory hallucinations. That's not normal. You're a sick man … '

'In more fucking ways than one!' came Derek's voice from behind.

Buchanan stared daggers at him.

'Harry. Hand yourself in, I'll make sure you get the treatment you need.'

'Again. I think I'll pass on your offer. I'm growing tired of this conversation.'

He yawned as if to prove his point.

'By the way, can you lot trace this radio the way you traced my mobile?'

Buchanan didn't answer.

'I thought you might be able to. Looks like I'll have to destroy the thing.'

'You have nowhere to run to, Harry.'

'I disagree, Inspector. I have my exit route planned perfectly. You'll never see me again.'

Harry laughed once more.

'Bye, Ronnie.'

'HARRY! … before you go …'

'What is it?'

'Never say never.'

The radio went dead just as Atkins appeared at his side.

'Any luck on the trace?' he asked.

She shrugged her shoulders.

'I located him to Union Street, but it's gone dead now.'

'Send a couple of cars, Jenny. Not that I've got much hope in them finding him.'

He sighed and looked to the floor.

When he looked back up Jenny was staring at him.

'Plan B, sir?' she asked.

He nodded his head.

'Plan B.'

He turned to Max and Derek.

'You two. Come with me.'

The two men looked at each other. Confusion was written all over their faces.

'Where are we heading?' asked Max.

'To the roof. Let's go, gentlemen.'

He started running towards the stairs. Max and Derek quickly followed.

'What the fuck is Plan B?' asked Derek.

'I'll tell you when we get in the helicopter!' answered Buchanan.

Chapter Fifty Three

The top floor of the car park was completely empty. Something Buchanan had made sure of earlier.

He looked up, as the navy blue and yellow Eurocopter flew towards them.

The closer it got, the colder he felt. The down draught from the rotor blades seemed to push the cold air down towards him enveloping him an icy cocoon.

Derek visibly shivered.

'I feel like I'm standing in front of an open freezer.'

'It'll be warmer inside,' replied Max.

They stood back as the helicopter landed a few yards ahead of them. They covered their eyes as the frozen slush beneath their feet was sent flying in their direction.

'Bugger this!' said Derek.

He turned around so that he faced away from the mini ice storm.

Buchanan and Max took his lead.

As the rotor blades slowed to a stop, the three men jumped in, moved to the back and strapped themselves to their seats.

Buchanan introduced Max and Derek to the crew which consisted of the pilot and two other police officers. They were observers. Each observer had a different role in the aircraft, and between them and the pilot, an effective level of support was provided to police ground units during searches, pursuits and such like. Today's mission was slightly different for them though. They simply had to get Buchanan and his colleagues to their destination as quick as possible.

The pilot turned to face them.

'Insch Airport, I believe?'

Buchanan nodded. Max and Derek looked confused as they held on tight to their seats as the helicopter took off. A strong wind had sprung up. They could feel it buffeting the vehicle from side to side as they gained height.

'You going to explain things now, Ronnie?' asked Derek.

'Hold on a sec.' He tapped the pilot on the shoulder.

'Alright if we smoke, Jock?'

'I won't tell, if you don't,' he replied. 'You'll find an ashtray in the small drawers under the No Smoking sign.'

Buchanan laughed and then reached into his pocket for his cigarettes. Derek had beaten him to it. They both lit up as the helicopter seemed to suddenly drop from the sky.

'Jesus! What the fuck was that?' asked Buchanan.

The pilot responded, 'Don't worry about it, gents. It's just the wind. You'll soon get used to it.'

After he'd calmed himself down, the DI began to explain to them why they were now flying their way through a storm towards a private airfield in Insch, a small village approximately twenty-eight miles from Aberdeen.

He took a draw from his cigarette and then blew the smoke towards the fan in the roof.

'It began with something Michelle said last night.' He

laughed. 'That woman has a distinct knack of hitting the crux of a matter.' He continued, 'Assuming he'd gotten a hold of Melissa, how was old Harry planning on getting the hell out of here with her? I mean, his face is all over the media. Transport authorities have been informed to be on the lookout for him. That leaves him very few options.'

'You think he's got a private plane lined up?' asked Max.

'I … '

Before he could answer, Derek butted in.

'That was a bit of a leap wasn't it? Or is this another one of your famous hunches?'

Buchanan pointed over at him.

'Don't be so quick to disregard hunches or gut instincts, Derek!' he said forcibly, before getting back to Max. 'I more than think that, I know it!'

'How can you be so sure?' asked Derek.

Buchanan smiled.

'I followed my hunch. I mean … it might have led to nothing, I suppose but … I phoned Atkins in the early hours of the morning. I asked her to contact all private airfields. Starting with the closer ones first, I reckoned Harry would be looking for a quick exit … '

'Sounds his style, right enough,' interrupted Derek once more.

Buchanan continued, 'After a lot of work on her part, it must be said, she found out that there was a … ' He took out his notebook, 'a Cessna Skyhawk. It arrived last week. The plane was registered in Toronto. It belongs to a guy called

Stan Fraser.'

'Who the fuck is he?' asked Derek.

'He works for a law firm. We can't get hold of him. Whether old Harry has wiped him out or not we don't know, but what I do know for certain is that Harry Reid is using his identity … when it suits him.'

'How can you be so sure?'

He flipped to the next page in his notebook.

'Two reasons,' he replied through a huge cloud of smoke. 'He used that very name when he booked into the hotel in Stonehaven and … Stan Fraser filed a flight plan last night for him and his six-year old niece for ten a.m. this morning. That's just too much of a coincidence, don't you think?'

Max whistled.

'That's the clincher, sir.'

'Eh … Ronnie,' asked Derek. 'When exactly were you planning on telling us all this?'

He looked at them both in turn.

'Listen. I'd hoped beyond hope that it wouldn't come to this. I'd have been far happier if the old bastard had just turned up for the girl. I was hoping that all this would have been over by now.'

'So, only you and Atkins know about this Plan B thing then?' asked Max.

'Pretty much … well apart from the armed officers that she sent there this morning, just in case we need them. Which reminds me … '

He took out his mobile.

'Jenny. Is everything set up?'

'Everyone's well hidden and in position. They've stashed their vehicles in an empty hanger just like you asked. The old guy shouldn't see anything when he arrives.'

'Do they have a clear view of the hanger that contains his plane?'

'Yes. There's an office building directly across from it. We have an armed officer positioned at the window.'

'Good work. I'll be in touch.'

He stuck his phone back in his jacket pocket.

'It's suddenly gone quiet,' said Max.

Derek looked across at Buchanan.

'Will I say it or are you going to?'

'The calm before the storm,' he answered.

Derek grinned.

'I have no time for superstition,' he lied, as he thought back to saluting the Magpie earlier. 'Besides I'm planning on making this short and sweet. This prick has had us running around for far too long as it is.' He winked. 'Let's show Montgomery how things should be done, eh?'

'Approaching destination,' said the pilot, interrupting their conversation.

Buchanan looked at his watch.

'He'll be a wee while yet. He'll be stuck in the rush hour traffic. It'll give us time to familiarise ourselves with the place.'

All three sat in silence as the pilot eased the helicopter to land.

Buchanan stood up first.

'Let's go, lads!'

*

The helicopter landed in the middle of the grass runway. Buchanan, Max and Derek got out. The ground was covered with a heavy frost which crunched beneath their feet. Buchanan looked towards a large orange and yellow wind sock. It hung limply from a tall white metal pole, a sign of the unnatural calm that had suddenly hit the area.

They walked across the runway towards the three aircraft hangers as the helicopter once more took to the sky.

'Turn on your radios, lads,' he said.

He spoke into his.

'Everyone hearing this?'

The other officers acknowledged.

'Atkins! You hearing this okay?'

'Loud and clear, sir. You have two men in each hanger plus the guy directly opposite on the office roof.'

'Good. Everything else in order?'

'Yep, no one will be disturbing you. To all intents and purposes the airfield is shut ... except to old Harry, of course.'

'Good job.'

He rubbed the stubble on his chin. Once again he'd given his shave a miss this morning.

'Oh! One other thing, Jenny, what hanger has the guy's plane in it again?'

'The middle one, sir.'

'We'll wait for him in there. Man on the roof, what's your name?'

'Giles, sir.'

'Well, Giles. The minute you see someone approaching, you let me know at once. You got that?'

'Will do, sir.'

As they headed towards the middle hanger, the doors opened as if by magic.

Two young officers suddenly appeared. One was armed.

Derek winked at him, 'Alright, Barry?'

'Not too bad,' he replied. He rubbed his hands together. 'I'm fucking freezing though.'

He nodded towards the other officer, 'This is Tim Flowers. He's not long passed his firearms training. Thought this would be good experience for him.'

They all made their introductions.

Buchanan thought Tim looked a bit nervy.

'You, son. I want you up on the roof with Giles.'

The young officer did as he was asked. He seemed relieved.

'I'll be needing to borrow this again,' said Buchanan as

he reached into Derek's leg pocket for his hand gun. 'Barry! Give yours to Max here.'

The officer looked shocked.

'This is highly irregular.' He looked towards Derek. He just shrugged his shoulders.

'He's the man in charge.'

Barry sighed. He put his rifle down against a wooden crate and handed the hand weapon to Max.

'Good,' said Buchanan. 'Now we're all armed. Now, we wait.'

He turned towards Derek. 'Shut the door would you, but not quite tight, leave a small gap so we can see what's going on.'

'Your wish is my command,' said Derek. He walked towards the hanger doors, stopped and looked round.

'It's your push on the smokes, I believe, Ronnie.'

He rolled the doors shut, just as the snow, once again, began to fall.

Chapter Fifty Four

'Today's weather is only going to get worse, with some predicting snowfall of up to a foot in some of the higher areas later on this evening … '

Harry Reid changed the station on the car's radio. He found BBC Radio Two. They were playing *Ring of Fire* by Johnny Cash. He tapped along to the beat with his hands on the steering wheel. He began to sing.

'I fell in to a burning ring of … '

He inadvertently hit the horn. The driver driving in the next lane gave him a strange look. Harry gave him a wave.

He had just passed Inverurie. He was now about seven miles from his destination.

'Not very good flying weather, Harry,' he said to himself.

He knew deep inside though that he had to risk it. He'd flown in worse in the past and his main mission now was to get the hell out of the UK, or at the very least Scotland. He could shelter overnight down south, assuming the weather was as bad down there, and then continue his journey in the morning. One thing he was sure of though, speed was of the essence. He had to leave as soon as possible, before the storm really kicked in and left him grounded.

He stared out the windscreen. The road was slowly beginning to turn white. Regardless, he put his foot down and took his speed up to seventy, passing the Toys R Us truck in front.

'Get in position, Giles, and keep it clean. I'm taking no chances with the old guy this time.'

'Let's make this quick, people.'

*

Harry Reid parked his stolen motor vehicle outside the hanger that contained his plane. The plane didn't actually belong to him. He'd borrowed it from an old Canadian lawyer who happened to be spending last week and this week in the Bahamas. He zipped up his jacket as far as it would go. Put up his hood and reluctantly left the warm comfort of the car.

He moved around to the boot to get his bag. That's when he felt a hot searing pain in the back of his left knee. His leg collapsed on him sending him tumbling to the cold ground beneath. Instinctively, he reached for his hand gun, but he was too late. He was surrounded by police officers. One, a particularly tall man, bent his arm behind his back when it was agonisingly close to his weapon. He then threw him on to his belly and bent the other arm around joining them together with a pair of cold steel handcuffs.

He was trussed up like a thanksgiving turkey.

He saw a black pair of boots approaching from in front of him.

He stretched his neck up as far as he could.

'Nice to see you again, Harry!' said Detective Inspector Ronnie Buchanan, as he winked at him.

He watched as the detective turned towards another officer and lit a cigarette.

'Get his leg taken care off and stick him in the back of one of the vehicles.'

'We'll take him back to Aberdeen ourselves, but I want an escort. I still don't trust this guy.'

'I'll get it organised, sir.'

Harry closed his eyes as two officers lifted him roughly to his feet.

*

The four men sat in the car, Max and Derek in the front, Buchanan and Harry in the back.

Max was doing his best to keep the thing on the road. The snow was coming down in sheets. Even with the windscreen wipers going full tilt vision was poor.

Harry sighed and looked out the window.

'I never actually accomplished much in the end, did I?'

Derek turned to face him.

'Are you fucking joking? You killed six people. Two of them were colleagues of ours! You're going to fucking rot in jail!'

'I regret killing the police officers … and Mr Whitelaw. Not the others though. They deserved it. It's just a pity I couldn't have got the other two!' He sighed and shook his head. 'I was so close to finishing off the lawyer, too.'

'There's something that's been bugging me,' said Buchanan.

'What exactly is that, Inspector?' asked Harry.

Harry turned to face him.

'The taxi driver. What the fuck did he have to do with it?'

'Ah! Mr Hastings. A real odious bastard he was. He

wasn't just a taxi driver, you know. He moonlighted as a door man in some night club in the town centre. He's well known seemingly for taking on any job going, for the right price, of course. I have it on good authority that he arranged Melissa's accident in the garden.'

'How do you mean, "arranged?" '

The old man sighed again.

'He was paid by Emily Jackson, through her lawyer, to keep tabs on Rose and Melissa and, should the opportunity arise … '

'Take full advantage of it?' finished Buchanan.

'Exactly!

'So, the bastard actually attacked the poor kid?'

'Pushed her on to the concrete path actually. Broke her arm. If that second injury hadn't occurred, my Rose would still be here today. My wife as well, probably. Clara was a fighter but since Rose died … ' He shrugged. 'She virtually gave up the battle.'

'How could you possibly know all this?' asked Derek.

The old man laughed.

'I have my sources. An acquaintance of mine went to see him under the pretence of having a job for him. He took him out for a night on the town, got him sloshed and he blurted it out. He was damned near boasting about it. No job was too dirty for him, he said.'

'I'll make sure he pays for that,' said Buchanan.

'It's impossible to prove, I imagine. There are no witnesses.' He sighed once more. 'What happens to me now,

Inspector?'

'You'll be charged with the murders. It'll be a heavy sentence, Harry that's for sure.'

'Melissa?'

'I'll do my best to make sure you can see her.'

He yawned.

'I'd rather you didn't. I don't want her to see me behind bars.'

'You might change your mind. Have a think about it.'

Harry stayed silent for a minute. Then he turned to face Buchanan.

'Maybe you could do me another favour, though.'

'What's that?'

'In my left leg pocket, you'll find my pills. I think I have a couple left. I feel one of my headaches coming on. Would you be kind enough to get them for me?'

'Sure.'

'I'll need some water as well; they're quite hard to swallow.'

Max handed Buchanan the bottle of water from the front of the car. He gave Harry the pills and then held the bottle to his lips.

'Thanks, Inspector.'

He looked towards Derek.

'You, big man! I have no intention of rotting in jail.'

He began to laugh hysterically. The laughs soon gave

way to coughing.

'What's so funny?' asked Derek.

'Potassium cyanide. That's what.'

'You're making no sense, Harry,' said Buchanan.

'Always have an exit plan. That's what I always say.'

Suddenly, he started coughing again. His eyes were bulging and white foam was forming around his mouth. Then his body went into spasms.

Buchanan watched as Harry's strange macabre dance seemed to stop as quickly as it had started.

There was a loud exhale of breath.

'The pills, sir!' screamed Max.

'Fuck!' he replied.

He shook the old man.

'Harry! … HARRY!

He felt for a pulse. It was too late. He was gone.

Buchanan sighed and shook his head.

'Looks like the old bastards escaped us again, lads.'

Then, he leaned over and he closed Harry's eyes for him.

'Say hello to Clara for me.'

Epilogue

Buchanan sipped his Guinness as he peered at the letter on the table in front of him.

He'd read it three times already. He still didn't know what to make of it.

He'd been recommended to head up a new policing initiative. The Major Crime Support Unit.

With the Scottish force becoming one, the MCSU would be tasked with providing nationwide support to anyone who needed it, especially in smaller outlying areas.

He sighed. He wasn't sure if he should accept. He didn't know if it was a step up for him or a way for the force to throw him into the back of beyond.

Michelle seemed to think it was perfect for him when she had read the letter earlier. The small contained unit would have no one to answer to but themselves. Perfect for his 'unique' way of working, she'd said. He'd also been told he could pick the team himself, to a certain extent, and draw on any Police Scotland resources he deemed necessary.

He rubbed his chin.

It looked quite a unique opportunity on paper. However, he could imagine it would put a few coppers' noses out of joint if such a unit just suddenly appeared and took over a case.

He took another drink of his Guinness.

They'd all receive special weapons training, which was

a plus. If truth be told … he'd enjoyed running around the place on his last case with the gun he'd borrowed from Derek.

He laughed to himself.

The couple at the next table gave him a strange look.

But still. He couldn't help thinking that this was all down to Montgomery bleating about how he couldn't stick to rules and procedures to anyone who would listen to him.

He'd been all for bringing Buchanan up on a charge to the disciplinary board. He'd actually gone as far as putting in a written request until Superintendent Burns had stepped in.

But his favour had come at a cost.

He had to agree to give SERIOUS thought to the MCSU recommendation.

He sighed once again.

He had some thinking to do.

As he watched the obviously drunk man sitting on the bar stool stand up and make his way to the door, Buchanan folded up the letter and stuck it back in his inside pocket. He downed the last of his pint, pulled the baseball hat over his eyes and proceeded to follow him out into the chilly Aberdeen night.

*

Scott Hastings veered off Union Street and walked around to the side of the Music Hall until he found the small alcove he was looking for. He checked his watch. Shit! He'd missed his bus. Never mind. He'd go get a taxi. He laughed to himself. He always thought it was funny. A taxi driver

It had a painting on the side of a young girl playing with a doll. His thoughts turned to Melissa.

He removed a well-worn photo of her from his inside pocket and set it in front of him on the dashboard. She was two years old. He touched the birth mark on her face as his tears began to flow.

'I will not give up on you, sweetie. I'll come back in a few months, once things die down a bit, bring you back to where you belong.'

He knew he wouldn't have a problem finding her location when he got back. He'd just contact Rupert James again. The private investigator had already provided him with good information regarding her whereabouts up to this time. If it hadn't been for him and Victor Whitelaw, he would never have managed to compile the dossier on the whole sorry affair.

He rubbed his eyes and then looked up at the rear view mirror. Clara was there once more. She was just sitting there, quietly knitting.

'I've not got time for this!'

He closed his eyes for a couple of seconds, trying desperately to block out the vision. When he opened them again, he was heading for the side of the road. He straightened the car quickly and then looked back in the mirror. She was gone.

'Sorry about that, dear, but I have to stay focused.'

He left the B9002 and headed for the air base.

*

'Vehicle approaching, sir!'

looking for a taxi ride.

After a quick glance up and down the street, he unzipped and began to relieve himself against the wall. The alcove was suddenly surrounded by steam.

'Aaaaah! That's better.'

Once finished, he looked down to zip himself back up.

Suddenly his head was yanked back then propelled full force into the cold, hard, granite wall. He felt his nose pop and what felt like an electric shock penetrating his skull. The action was repeated. His vision blurred as his attacker then forcefully twisted his arm back and put pressure on his elbow.

'Get the fuck off me!'

He felt a snap and screamed as he fell into the puddle he'd created on the ground.

'Try driving a fucking taxi with a broken arm,' said the man as he spat on his face.

He rolled onto his side and watched as his attacker walked away.

The man suddenly stopped and turned to face him.

Scott's vision was still blurry. It was made worse by the blood flowing into his eyes. All he could make out was the multicoloured glow of the Christmas lights above him and a dark figure in a baseball hat standing in the middle of the cobbled street.

'That was for Melissa,' the blurred man shouted. 'Merry fucking Christmas!'

Some other books from Ringwood Publishing

If you enjoyed this book you might want to read Steve's first novel, 'Good Deed'

Good Deed

Steve Christie

Good Deed introduces a new Scottish detective hero, DI Ronnie Buchanan.

It was described by one reviewer as *"Christopher Brookmyre on speed, with more thrills and less farce".*

The events take Buchanan on a frantic journey around Scotland as his increasingly deadly pursuit of a mysterious criminal master mind known only as Vince comes to a climax back in Aberdeen.

ISBN: 978-1-901514-06-3   £9.99

Morbid Relations
Jonathan Whitelaw

Morbid Relations is the story of Rob Argyll, an unsuccessful stand-up comedian. Following his mother's death, he returns for the first time in years to his family in their Glasgow home. Rob struggles to relate to his somewhat dysfunctional family, seeming to bounce from one mistake to another while simultaneously trying to make amends for his long absence. The narrative is a darkly comic take on modern Scottish life, family relationships, and finally trying to grow up.

ISBN: 978-1-901514-19-3   £9.99

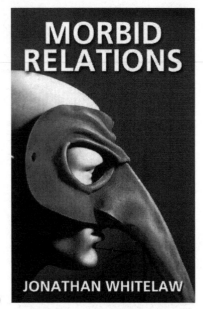

The Malta Job
Alywn James

The Malta Job follows the story of John Smith, a young Scottish journalist with literary aspirations, who is sent to Malta to complete a sequel to the very successful MacMurder, a round-up of Scotland's more infamous homicides. Once on Malta, with the dead author's notes, he gets involved in a gripping set of circumstances involving high romance, exciting adventure and a bank heist crime.

ISBN: 978-1-901514-17-9   £9.99

Calling Cards

Gordon Johnston

Calling Cards is a psychological crime thriller set in Glasgow about stress, trauma, addiction, recovery, denial and corruption.

Following an anonymous email Journalist Frank Gallen and DI Adam Ralston unravel a web of corruption within the City Council with links to campaign against a new housing development in Kelvingrove Park and the frenzied attacks of a serial killer. They then engage in a desperate chase to identify a serial killer from the clues he is sending them.

ISBN: 978-1-901514-09-4   £9.99

Cold Roses

Gordon Johnston

There is a monster walking the streets of Glasgow.

DI Adam Ralston is no stranger to the dark side of human nature, but when a young art gallery worker is discovered, brutally raped, her throat slit, and a single red rose laid upon her corpse, he is thrown into a bloody maelstrom of violence and suspicion unlike anything he has known before.

Ralston must also battle his own personal demons and hold his family together as tries to track down the killer - a killer who leaves no clues, who grows bolder and who seems to be able to strike at will.

IISBN: 978-1-901514-23-0   £9.99

A Subtle Sadness

Sandy Jamieson

A Subtle Sadness follows the life of Frank Hunter and is an exploration of Scottish Identity and the impact on it of politics, football, religion, sex and alcohol.

It covers a century of Scottish social, cultural and political highlights culminating in Glasgow's emergence in 1990 as European City of Culture.

It is not a political polemic but it puts the current social, cultural and political debates in a recent historical context.

ISBN: 978-1-901514-04-9   £9.99

Dark Loch

Charles P. Sharkey

Dark Loch is an epic tale of the effects of the First World War on the lives of the residents of a small Scottish rural community. The main characters are the tenant crofters who work the land leased to them by the Laird. The crofters live a harsh existence in harmony with the land and the changing seasons, unaware of the devastating war that is soon to engulf the continent of Europe.

The book vividly and dramatically explores the impact of that war on all the main characters and how their lives are drastically altered forever.

ISBN: 978-1-901514-14-8   £9.99

Black Rigg

Mary Easson

Black Rigg is set in a Scottish mining village in the year 1910 in a period of social and economic change. Working men and women began to challenge the status quo but landowners, the church and the justice system resisted. Issues such as class, power, injustice, poverty and community are raised by the narrative in powerful and dramatic style.

ISBN: 978-1-901514-15-5   £9.99

Torn Edges

Brian McHugh

Torn Edges is a mystery story linking modern day Glasgow with 1920's Ireland and takes a family back to the tumultuous days of the Irish Civil War.

They soon learn that many more Irishman were killed, murdered or assassinated during the very short Civil War than in the War of Independence and that gruesome atrocities were committed by both sides.

The evidence begins to suggest that their own relatives might have been involved.

ISBN: 978-1-901514-05-6   £9.99

The Gori's Daughter

Shazia Hobbs

The Gori's Daughter is the story of Aisha, a young mixed race woman, daughter of a Kashmiri father and a Glasgow mother. Her life is a struggle against rejection and hostility in Glasgow's white and Asian communities.

The book documents her fight to give her own daughter a culture and tradition that she can accept with pride. The tale is often harrowing but is ultimately a victory for decency over bigotry and discrimination.

ISBN: 978-1-901514-12-4   £9.99

Memoirs of a Feminist Mother

Carol Fox

As a committed feminist, Carol Fox has achieved success for very many women, but her greatest battle described in this book was very personal. Following serious fertility problems, Carol made the positive decision to become a single parent by choice, to have a child while she still could. Refused access to fertility treatment in Scotland she had no choice but to move to London. Through sheer determination and tenacity, Carol obtained treatment in England in the early 1990s and her daughter was born in 1992, following extensive fertility treatment and battles against judgemental attitudes which appear almost vindictive to us 25 years later. Her story has attracted media coverage, sparking debates on motherhood and the right to be a single parent in the UK.

ISBN: 978-1-901514-21-6   £9.99

Silent Thunder

Archie MacPherson

Silent Thunder is set in Glasgow and Fife and follows the progress of two young Glaswegians as they stand up for what they believe in.

They find themselves thrust headlong into a fast moving and highly dangerous adventure involving a Scots radio broadcaster, Latvian gangsters, a computer genius and secret service agencies.

Archie MacPherson is well known and loved throughout Scotland as a premier sports commentator.

"An excellent tale told with pace and wit"

Hugh Macdonald -The Herald

ISBN: 978-1-901514-11-7   £9.99

The Italian Connection

John Keeman

"My last memory was of walking down a sandy road in an Italian village along with three other soldiers..." In George Giles' mind, he is a twenty-seven year old soldier preparing to return home after Germany's surrender during World War II. But his body tells a different story; he is the serial killer Peter Hunter, who until recently was detained at Broadamoor for the criminally insane. Unlike Hunter, George has never killed, nor does he know of the 21st Century.

Faced with a London much changed from his memories, George seeks answers from the past and tries to uncover how he is connected to Hunter.

ISBN: 978-1-901514-20-9   £9.99

Scotball

Stephen O'Donnell

Scotball is a searing examination of the current state of Scottish football and the various social, political and economic forces that combine to strangle its integrity and potential.

ISBN: 978-1-901514-13-1   £9.99

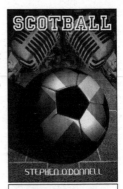

Paradise Road

Stephen O'Donnell

Paradise Road is the story of Kevin McGarry, who through a combination of injury and disillusionment is forced to abandon any thoughts of playing football professionally. Instead he settles for following his favourite team, Glasgow Celtic, whilst trying to eke out a living as a joiner. It considers the role of young working-class men in our post-industrial society.

ISBN: 978-1-901514-07-0   £9.99

Yellow Submarine

Sandy Jamieson

Yellow Submarine explains how a small football club from a town of just 50,000 inhabitants became a major force not just in Spain but in Europe.

The success of Villarreal offers supporters a model of how they too might live the dream, without having to rely on billionaire benefactors.

ISBN: 978-1-901514-02-5   £11.99

Celtic Submari

Sandy Jamieson

An invasion of Villareal by 10,000 Celtic supporters in 2004 created a set of circumstances that has led to a lasting friendship between supporters of Villarreal and Celtic. This friendship is unique in football and offers the wider football world a model of camaraderie and togetherness that shows how football can be a force for good.

ISBN: 978-1-901514-03-2   £9.99